But they were planning to end their engagement.

And being seen giving her favors to Quincy would only make the scandal when they broke things off so much worse.

The couple—for indeed it was a man and woman, talking in hushed voices—came even closer. Clara could hear their steps on the gravel path, a small giggle, a low rumble of male voice. She cast her eyes about their small space, looking for any way to disguise themselves. But save for the stone bench, hardly large enough for one person to sit upon, much less two people to hide under, they would be quite exposed when the couple passed by.

She looked up at Quincy and saw intense determination fill his face. Before she could make sense of it, he pivoted their bodies so his back was to the path. When it became apparent that even that could not completely conceal her identity, he cradled her face in his large hands and lowered his head to hers.

Praise for
Christina Britton

Someday My Duke Will Come

CHRISTINA BRITTON

FOREVER
New York Boston

Forever
Hachette Book Group
1290 Avenue of the Americas, New York, NY 10104
read-forever.com
twitter.com/readforeverpub

First Edition: January 2021

Forever is an imprint of Grand Central Publishing. The Forever name and logo are trademarks of Hachette Book Group, Inc.

The publisher is not responsible for websites (or their content) that are not owned by the publisher.

The Hachette Speakers Bureau provides a wide range of authors for speaking events. To find out more, go to www.hachettespeakersbureau.com or call (866) 376-6591.

ISBNs: 978-1-5387-1750-9 (mass market), 978-1-5387-1752-3 (ebook)

Printed in the United States of America

CW

10 9 8 7 6 5 4 3 2 1

*To my incredible son, who has grown
into a kind, sweet, caring young man.
I'm so proud to be your mom.
I love you, sweetheart.*

Acknowledgments

Quincy has to be one of my favorite heroes to date, and I want to thank all of the readers who asked for his story after *A Good Duke Is Hard to Find* released. And thank you to everyone who has embraced the Isle of Synne and its romantic misfits; your enthusiasm for this world and these characters has brought me such joy!

Thank you so much to my incredible agent, Kim Lionetti; I'm so blessed to have you in my corner.

Thank you to my amazing editor, Madeleine Colavita, who constantly amazes me with her skill and talent in turning my jumble of words into an actual book. And thank you to everyone at Grand Central and Forever for your enthusiasm, support, talent, and kindness; I cannot believe my good fortune to be part of the Forever family.

Thank you to Julie and Hannah in helping me iron out my plot. And thank you to Jayci for being my sprinting buddy. I'd be lost without you.

Heaps of love to Kathryn Kramer, whose book *Under Gypsy Skies* was the first romance I bought at thirteen years old, and who, in recent years, has become a very dear friend. I'm so thankful to have you in my life.

Most especially, thank you to my husband and children.

I will never have enough words in me to tell you how much I love you. But know I do, with everything in me. I hope I make you proud (even though there's *still* not a sword with a secret compartment in the hilt in this book...sorry hunny).

Author's Note

SOMEDAY MY DUKE WILL COME is a story of love and forgiveness, and will, I hope, give you all the happy feels with its HEA.

That being said, this book does contain content that may distress some readers. For content warnings, please visit my website:

http://christinabritton.com/bookshelf/content-warnings/

Affectionately yours,
Christina Britton

Someday My Duke Will Come

Prologue

1804

Quincy had not cried since they'd told him his father was dead.

His older brothers hadn't shed a tear. Already adults, they had stood silently by as their father's ornate casket had been interred in the family vault, their harsh faces impassive in the shadows of their umbrellas. Their mother, too, had not broken down. If anything, she had looked put out by the whole ordeal.

But then he had never expected any of the softer emotions from her.

Now, however, his father two weeks dead and Quincy back in London with his mother, he felt his grief slowly begin to break through. In this house where he had grown up, he was surrounded by memories he could no longer hold at bay.

A sob bubbled up in his throat. He pressed his fist to his lips, the metallic tinge of blood hitting his tongue as the force of his teeth split his skin. What was the point in crying, after all? Not only would it bring his mother's wrath down on his head should she hear him, but no amount of tears would bring his father back.

He dug his fingers into the worn leather spine of his father's favorite book, clutched tight to his narrow chest.

How often had they pored over the contents, folding out the maps, tracing the mountain ranges and rivers, their combined imaginings spinning adventures from the very air? So many plans for the future, dreaming of life far away from English shores, seeing together the wonders of the world they had only read about.

All gone now.

Desolation swept over him until he felt he'd drown in it. He curled into a tighter ball, doing his best to tuck his long, lanky frame into the recess under his father's desk. He used to hide here when he was young, listening as his father did business with his solicitors, resting his cheek on his father's knee and taking the biscuits he used to pass down to him with a wink and a smile. He had never once scolded Quincy for his intrusion, never told him to run off and play and leave him in peace.

Quincy was fourteen now, and it had been years since he had fit into this small space. Yet the memory was as vivid as if it were yesterday. If he closed his eyes, he could still hear the deep rumble of his father's voice, could feel his strong fingers as they mussed his hair.

Another sob threatened. How could he live without his father? He had been the only thing that had made living with his mother bearable. That woman who showed no one, not even her sons, an ounce of affection. But most especially Quincy, who she seemed to despise above all others.

As if he had conjured her from the ether, her voice trailed to where he hid; a cold, creeping mist that had him shivering.

"…Quincy must be off hiding. I've told the servants to keep a closer eye on him."

"He'll turn up for supper, no doubt." His brother

Gordon, now the head of the family, sounded utterly bored. As he ever did when speaking of, or to, Quincy. Being so far behind any of the other Nesbitt boys in age, Quincy had always been an afterthought in his elder brothers' minds. Something to be tolerated on holidays from school or outright ignored when they were feeling particularly cruel.

Their footsteps sounded in the hall, coming closer. Quincy held the book tighter, squeezing himself down as small as he was able. He remembered too late that this was no longer his father's desk, but Gordon's; his father had effectively been replaced.

But there was no time for tears. He had to escape without being seen. There would be no smile and pat on the head from Gordon once he was discovered. He peered out, his eyes hot and anxious as he scanned the room behind the desk. The windows were locked up tight against the inclement weather. Yet perhaps, if he was very quiet, he might slink to the sash and unhinge the lock...

The footsteps stopped abruptly. Quincy, preparing to creep from his hiding place, froze, holding his breath as his mother spoke again.

"I have decided what to do with the boy."

"I've already looked into other schools that might take him," his brother mumbled. "No matter his unfortunate record at Eton, our name will erase the worst of his offenses. You needn't have him underfoot for long."

"I needn't have him underfoot at all."

"I hardly think sending him to rusticate at our country estate will be a proper punishment," Gordon replied. "He will merely get into more mischief."

"Do you think I'm stupid?" she snapped. "Of course I will not send him back there. No, what I have in mind for your brother will toughen him as time in the country never could."

There was a pause. And then, "I don't understand what you mean."

"The navy is always looking for recruits. I've signed your brother up for service aboard one of His Majesty's finest ships."

Quincy's stomach dropped out from under him and he blanched. The navy? Surely he'd misheard.

Gordon seemed equally stunned. "He's but fourteen."

There was a dismissive scoff from his mother. "Boys much younger than him are made to serve."

"But our father—"

"Is dead."

His mother's voice was cold and flat, and brooked no argument. But Gordon was head of the family now. And while he had never showed Quincy even a modicum of affection, he did not hate him. Surely he would fight for him now that he had the power to.

But Gordon's voice carried to him, once more indifferent now that his initial shock had worn off. "Very well. I suppose it will save us the cost of a new school."

"Precisely. It's best he learn his place sooner rather than later. We can finalize details of the arrangement tomorrow…"

Their voices trailed off, their footsteps receding. It took Quincy some time to emerge from the stunned grief that enveloped him, to realize that he was once more alone.

Alone. That word took on an entirely new meaning. The tears came then, falling down his cheeks, soaking the soft lawn of his shirt. Life had never been ideal. But he'd at least had his father's love. Even when his pranks had gotten him sent down from school, when disappointment had been greatest, his father had always made sure Quincy understood that he was loved.

Now, however, he was simply a burden, to be gotten rid of at the earliest convenience.

The tears came faster. He let them fall unchecked until there was nothing left in him to give. When he was wrung dry of emotion, he felt his grief shift to anger. And not just anger, but a fury greater than any he had ever felt. They wished to be rid of him? Very well, they would get their wish. But it would be on *his* terms.

Running his sleeve under his streaming nose, he crept from his hiding spot and pulled open the bottom drawer of the desk. Pushing aside the ledgers that filled the space, he carefully pried open the false bottom and slid his father's book back within the shallow confines. It had been their secret from the world, their place to store dreams away from his mother's sharp eyes. Tears threatened once more. Would that he could take the book with him. But while it was compact for all the treasures it held, light travel was imperative. "I'll see them all, Papa," he vowed brokenly as he gazed down at the book, nestled in its bed of papers, before carefully closing the hidden space up tight. "For the both of us."

With one last parting look at the room he had spent so many happy afternoons in, he hurried out the door, making his way on stockinged feet through the silent house to his room. Once there he hurriedly packed what he could before slipping back to the ground floor.

Daylight was beginning to wane, the shadows deepening, and he clung to them as he made his way into the garden, letting himself out the back gate and to the alleyway that fronted the mews. And he did not look back.

Chapter 1

1818

Mr. Quincy Nesbitt had suspected his return to London would be painful—that riding down streets that were at once foreign and familiar would be like tearing open an old wound.

It brought him not an ounce of pleasure to know just how right he had been.

He took a deep breath as he headed down Brook Street from his hotel, trying to rein in the sensation of being suffocated under a wet blanket. But no matter his attempts, the feeling persisted, increasing with each clip of his horse's hooves on the cobbles. Damnation, but this had been a mistake. He had thought it the ideal plan when setting sail from Boston: he could visit with his closest friend, Peter Ashford, now Duke of Dane, before setting off on the first leg of his world travels. And with Peter in London for the season, it gave Quincy the push he needed to finally confront the ghosts of his past. It was something he should have done long ago.

Now that he was here, however...

His mount tossed its head in protest. Quincy took a deep breath, relaxing his iron grip on the reins, silently reproaching himself for his distracted ham-handedness. There was no reason for his anxiety. Though his family's townhome was two streets up in Berkeley Square, though he was closer to that place than he had been in fourteen years, he was not headed there just yet. He would see Peter first before bearding that particular lion.

The thought eased some of the tension from his shoulders. Over the past decade and a half, nearly from the moment Quincy had run from home and joined the crew of the American merchant ship *The Persistence*, he and Peter had been inseparable. And while he was thrilled for the new life his friend had made for himself since returning to England, the past year with the whole of the Atlantic Ocean between them had been a long one. With the last of their business in America sold off and his responsibilities firmly behind him, Quincy could visit with his friend and make up for lost time. He urged his mount on until, finally, he was before Peter's London home in Grosvenor Square.

Though the townhouse blended in with its surroundings in an understated way, it was an impressive specimen. Quincy gazed up at it as he dismounted, a low whistle escaping his lips. The filthy orphan he'd found hiding away in the hull of *The Persistence* had certainly come up in the world. Back then Peter had been reeling from his mother's untimely death and running from an uncertain and abhorrent future. Their fears had bound them, the friendship a lifeline for two young boys.

Now Peter was a duke. Quincy grinned, anticipation overriding his anxiety for the first time since he'd stepped foot off the ship and onto English soil. Damn, but he had missed his friend. Securing his horse, he strode up the front stairs to the imposing black door.

His knock was answered with alacrity by a stoic-faced butler. "May I help you, sir?"

"Is His Grace in?"

"Who may I ask is calling?"

Quincy grinned. "Oh, now, don't spoil the fun."

The man blinked. "Pardon me, sir?"

"I shall, and gladly," Quincy said, pushing into the front hall, "if you play along and show me to the duke."

The butler's mouth fell open. "Sir, I must insist—"

"Have no fear," he declared, holding up a hand. "His Grace will not bring down fire and brimstone on your head. Though he can be a grim fellow at times, I promise he will be happy to see me." He smiled his most charming smile. "Now do a man a favor, for I've traveled long and hard to see my friend and I cannot wait a moment longer."

The man, no doubt dazed by the barrage of charm Quincy was piling on his head, nodded and mumbled, "If you'll follow me?"

Quincy's grin of victory faded as he took in the interior of the cavernous house. Though the place had been impressive from the street, he hadn't expected such a behemoth to be hiding behind the elegant façade. They'd lived a comfortable life in Boston, yes. And he had not been a stranger to these places of wealth and excess in the past. But this put that all in the dust. Soaring ceilings painted with heavenly landscapes of cavorting cherubim basking in their divinity, black-and-white marble tiles glistening at his feet, the walls a buttery yellow and covered with all manner of paintings. He just managed to swallow down a chortle. Best to save his mirth for Peter, when it would annoy the most.

The butler stopped before a closed door. Instead of opening it, however, he looked at Quincy with a healthy

dose of uncertainty. "Sir, if you would only let me intro-
duce you—"

In answer, Quincy clapped the man on the shoulder,
winked, and threw open the door. It hit the wall with a resounding thud as he strode within. "His Grace, the Duke
of Dane, I presume," he bellowed into the silence.

Peter, seated behind the desk, jumped a foot, nearly
falling out of his chair before catching himself on the
edge of his desk. "What the ever-loving...Quincy?"

He grinned. "Surprised to see me, old man?"

When Peter only sat there, mouth hanging comically
open, eyes like saucers, Quincy laughed. "Damn, but
that expression is worth delaying my travels. Now come
and give me a proper greeting. I've missed you like
the devil."

Peter, it seemed, needed no further encouragement.
He surged from his chair, a grin breaking over his face.
Quincy barely had time to brace for impact before his
friend's bulk hit him like a veritable wave. The breath
was knocked from his body, meaty arms surrounding him
in a crushing embrace.

"You're a sight for sore eyes," Peter exclaimed.

"Air!" Quincy managed.

Peter merely chuckled, squeezing a bit tighter—how
was that even possible?—before releasing him. "When
last I heard from you, you had just sold off the remaining
business and were setting sail. What are you doing in
England, man?"

Quincy grinned, the restlessness of the past year—no,
he had been restless for much longer than that, hadn't
he?—beginning to ease. "I thought I'd visit with my
dearest friend before starting my travels in earnest."

Though Peter rolled his eyes, Quincy couldn't fail to

see the smile tugging on his lips. "I'm sure my charms pale in comparison with the wonders you'll see. You must be ecstatic to finally be setting off."

"You've no idea. If only my father had been alive to join me." A vision of his father's face swam up in his mind, that long-ago grief tempered by the distance of time, and by the knowledge that he was finally realizing their shared dream. He had worked hard over the years, surviving, building an empire to be proud of with Peter. Now, however, it was time to return to that promise he had made so long ago when leaving his family's house.

He gave Peter a considering look. "You made a pretty penny in the liquidation of our assets. I don't suppose I could ever tempt you into joining me, even for a short while?"

Peter grinned. "Not on your life. But I do plan on enjoying your company while you're in town. How long before you start off?"

Quincy smiled, satisfaction coiling within him. "I've booked passage for Spain a fortnight from now."

"You will stay here at Dane House, of course."

"Certainly not," he said in mock horror before grinning. "I'm a bachelor in London. If you think I'm going to miss out on cavorting to my heart's content, you're sorely mistaken." He laughed as Peter rolled his eyes heavenward. "But Mivart's is just a street away, so you may see me much more often than you'd like. Though"—he cast a glance about him, taking in the richly carved bookcases, the deep-blue-silk-covered walls, the towering windows looking out onto a verdant garden—"I admit to feeling more than a bit of regret now that I've seen your London residence. The place is amazing, man. Is Danesford even half as incredible?"

"Even more so." A quiet pride shone from Peter's eyes. "I thought I would forever despise the place, that I would be glad to see it fall to ruins. Yet now my feelings could not be more different."

"And I suppose having Lenora by your side has not aided in that about-face," Quincy murmured with humor.

"Laugh all you want. I don't mind telling you that she's had everything to do with it." Peter chuckled.

Quincy shook his head, grinning. "I cannot believe the change in you, man. When last I was here, you were in the throes of despair for love of Lenora. And now look at you, happily married, master of all this." He swept his arm out. "And a damn *duke*. Don't tell me I have to start calling you *Your Grace* now."

"Arse," Peter muttered. "If I hear those words from your lips, I'll gladly trounce you. Sit, while I pour us something to celebrate this visit."

As Quincy settled himself into an overstuffed chair, his friend went to the small cabinet in the corner. "Never tell me you're drinking strong spirits now."

Peter chuckled. "I've not changed that much. Though," he added, his tone turning rueful as the sound of clinking glass echoed about the room, "there are times I wish for a small dose of something stronger than lemonade or wine."

"Has it been much of an adjustment then, taking over the dukedom?" Quincy asked, stretching out his long legs.

Peter's lips twisted as he turned and made his way to his friend, a glass of whiskey in one hand and something that looked suspiciously like ratafia in the other. "Transitioning from commoner and self-made man to a duke has been…difficult," he said. "There are so many people's well-beings and livelihoods I'm responsible for. It boggles my mind. Without Lenora by my side, I don't know that I would have taken to the position with any grace."

Quincy snorted as he accepted his glass and Peter settled across from him. "Grace. That is one word I would have never associated with you. But how is our dear Lenora? I look forward to seeing her again after so long."

At the mention of his bride, Peter's face lit up. That was the only phrase to describe it. It was an expression Quincy had never witnessed before in his normally stoic friend, a softening of features typically held tight against the rest of the world.

"Lenora is wonderful. She's out with Clara and Phoebe just now."

Ah, yes, the Ladies Clara and Phoebe, Peter's cousins, daughters of the previous Duke of Dane and now under Peter's protection. Lovely girls, both of them. Or rather, Lady Phoebe was a lovely girl. Lady Clara, on the other hand, was most definitely a woman, and a stunning one at that.

Most women were pretty in some way to him, of course. He found something to admire in every female he came in contact with. But Lady Clara had captured his interest much more than he'd expected.

Not that anything could come of it. She was under Peter's protection, after all, and the man would have Quincy's head if he so much as looked at the lady wrong. And so any attraction he might possess for Lady Clara would have to be kept under strict lock and key.

But Quincy's imagination was a healthy thing, often manifesting at the most inopportune times. So it was a blessing when Peter spoke, breaking him from thoughts of a freckled, round face and dark blue eyes. Unfortunately, it was to ask about the very last thing Quincy wished to discuss.

"Doesn't your family hail from London?"

Quincy pulled a face and took a healthy swallow of his drink, his mood souring in an instant. "Yes. Not that it brings me an ounce of pleasure to realize just how close I am to them. I hope you comprehend how much you mean to me," he said with a severe look his friend's way, "that I would willingly find myself in the same city as them."

"I shall take the compliment, and gladly," Peter regarded Quincy over the rim of his glass. "Do you plan to see them while you're in town?"

"You truly know how to put a damper on a moment, did you know that?" When Peter merely arched a gold brow, Quincy let out a harsh breath and rolled his eyes. "For your information, yes, I am planning on seeing them and putting the past behind me once and for all. Are you happy now?"

"Oh, quite," Peter said with a grin. "After all, you were more than willing to feed me to the wolves, so to speak, in forcing a reconciliation I had no intention of indulging."

"I don't see you complaining now that you've got the sweetest woman in all of Christendom as a bride," Quincy drawled.

"That is true," Peter said with a happy sigh. He gave Quincy a sly look. "But you never know, you might be just as fortunate."

"If you think I'll come away from this with anything other than a headache, you're sorely mistaken. Besides, I'm not the least bit ready to settle down. A wife is not in the cards for me just yet."

A commotion in the hall blessedly interrupted whatever

sarcastic comment Peter had been about to make. In the next moment Lenora sailed through the study door.

"Peter, darling," she said, tugging off her gloves, "your aunt has bid me to tell you—Oh! Mr. Nesbitt, what a wonderful surprise!"

Quincy surged to his feet and offered a deep bow that he quickly ruined with a wink. "Your Grace."

Her laugh was like bells. "Oh, none of that. Lenora, please," she said with a warm smile.

"Lenora," he repeated with a grin. "I do hope you don't mind me dropping in unannounced."

She laughed again, accepting a kiss from her husband before taking Quincy's hand. "Why, you make it sound as if you were merely in the neighborhood and did not have to sail for weeks across an ocean to get here. But we never received word that you intended to visit."

"I admit, I had hoped to shock this fellow here." He jerked a thumb in Peter's direction.

"I do wish I had seen that. For though I try my hardest, not much surprises my husband." She sighed happily. "But this is just splendid. I'll have Mrs. Ingram prepare a room right away."

Before he could lay waste to that generous offer, a sweet voice carried from the hall. "Prepare a room for whom, Lenora?" And then Lady Clara was there, filling the doorway and his vision.

The breath caught in Quincy's chest. She was just as lovely as he remembered, if not more so. Rich brown hair in a riot of curls so soft his fingers itched to dive into their depths. Pale skin with a smattering of freckles across the bridge of her nose. A willowy figure, accentuated by the light blue of her dress.

And those eyes. Damnation, those beautiful clear blue

eyes that widened when she saw him. Her full lips parted on a soft gasp of air.

He bowed a second later than was polite. What the devil was wrong with him? "Lady Clara, it's a pleasure to see you again."

The delicate rose of a blush spread up her neck and settled, bright and warm, on her cheeks. She gave a quick, shallow curtsy. "Mr. Nesbitt. How lovely to have you back in England."

Quincy, please. He just managed to hold the words back, knowing such familiarity would be ill advised. If there was anything he didn't need right now, it was more to tempt him with this woman.

Her blush deepened as his silence crept on. She looked to Lenora. "Shall I have Mrs. Ingram make up that room then?"

Before Lenora could answer, Quincy stepped forward, his hand raised. "No need, my lady. I'm staying at Mivart's."

Was that relief in Lady Clara's eyes? Or disappointment? Before he could wonder at it, her expression shifted, taking on a pleasant if blank expression.

"Oh, but we have more than enough room," Lenora said. "And Lady Tesh will be ever so disappointed. She always speaks fondly of you."

Quite an accomplishment, that. Peter's irascible aunt, the Dowager Viscountess Tesh, was as plain-spoken and opinionated a woman as he'd ever had the pleasure to know. And he adored her.

"That is because she has wonderful taste," he teased. "But I shall be about so much, you'll no doubt grow sick of me."

"Very well, you stubborn man," Lenora grumbled.

"But you shall be the one to tell Lady Tesh." Suddenly her expression changed, her mouth falling open in dismay. "Oh! But I have quite forgotten. We're expected for tea at Lord and Lady Crabtree's and are already running behind schedule. Phoebe is recently engaged to their son, and this shall be our first informal meeting with them. They are quite the sticklers for propriety," she added ruefully.

Peter groaned. "I had forgotten." He gave his wife a pleading look. "I don't suppose I can stay behind?"

Quincy couldn't help but grin at his great beast of a friend, who looked more the part of Viking than duke, begging his wife for a respite from tea. In the next moment he was hard-pressed to keep from laughing out loud as the small and delicate—and utterly unterrifying— Lenora leveled a stern look on her husband. Especially as she had to crane her neck to do so.

"Peter, you know you must attend. This meeting is important." She turned to Quincy. "You are, of course, welcome to join us. You're family, after all."

Warmth filled Quincy at that, and he nearly relented. Especially when Peter gave him a look that fairly begged for his company.

But he knew, deep inside, that accompanying them on their outing would only be a way of delaying the inevitable. As much as he wished he could postpone forever, it was time to visit his family.

Now that the moment was at hand, he felt the beginnings of panic settling in his gut. Still, underlying the anxiety was a sense of relief. In short order it would be over and done with. And he could move forward.

Filled with a new determination, he smiled at Lenora. "Alas, I have an errand to attend to."

"You will return this evening?" Lady Clara asked. Her

cheeks bloomed with bright color. "To make certain we have enough places set for dinner," she explained. "And to mollify Lady Tesh. She'll be livid she missed you."

The anticipation Quincy had begun to feel at the thought of returning to this house suddenly increased. "Yes," he replied, unable to look away from the deep blue of her eyes, "I'll be back."

Chapter 2

*T*here should not be a single thing distracting Lady Clara Ashford from her sister Phoebe's upcoming nuptials.

Yet Clara could not focus. Seated in Lord and Lady Crabtree's drawing room, her family discussing with the groom's a possible time line for the wedding, Clara's mind wandered to inky black hair and eyes as dark as the night sky. Mr. Quincy Nesbitt. Goodness, she had not thought to see him again. Yes, Peter talked of him often, read his letters aloud when they arrived, and voiced his hope that his friend would once again grace English shores. But she had not believed the man would return.

No, that was not exactly true, was it? She peered into the milky depths of her tea, swirling the remaining liquid about with her spoon until it created a small cyclone in her cup. She had *hoped* he would not return. A selfish thing, she knew, when Peter loved him so well.

It was self-preservation, really. She had nothing against the man. He was one of the loveliest people, both in face and in spirit, she had ever had the pleasure to meet.

But from the moment she'd met him a year ago she'd found herself taken with his incredible good looks and sparkling manners. And each meeting thereafter, as few as there had been, had only increased her attraction to him, making her long for things she could never have.

Which was something she would not think about. With Phoebe marrying and beginning her new life with Oswin, the last of Clara's responsibilities was going off with her. She cast a surreptitious glance around the room. It was time to become useful elsewhere, to find her new place within the family. She refused to be a burden on these people she loved so very much.

The only question now was, where did she fit in with the new family dynamic...if she even fit in at all?

The sharp voice of Aunt Olivia—the formidable Lady Tesh—cut through Clara's morose thoughts and brought her back to the conversation at hand.

"We shall need six months at the very least, perhaps eight, to plan a wedding appropriate for a duke's daughter." She thumped her cane on the floor, spearing Lady Crabtree with a stern look. Aunt Olivia's small white dog, Freya, jumped at the sound before huffing and settling more firmly into her mistress's lap.

"Better yet," the dowager viscountess continued, "let us plan for a spring wedding. That way we may be certain that everyone who is anyone is in town for the event."

"I agree, my dear Lady Tesh, that we should take the time to plan a proper wedding," Lady Crabtree stated officiously. "However, Lord Crabtree and I insist on the wedding being held at our country estate. It is the only proper venue."

"Proper?" Aunt Olivia's nostrils flared, making it look as if she had caught a whiff of manure in the silk cushions of her chair. "To have half of society trek north for days? No, I will not allow my great-niece to be insulted by a sparse guest list."

"I hardly think the guest list will be sparse. My husband is a marquess, after all, and my Oswin is in line for the title. No one would dare turn down an invitation."

"Not to mention, of course," Aunt Olivia replied with all the silky danger of a snake about to strike, "that Phoebe is the daughter of a duke."

A triumphant gleam entered Lady Crabtree's eyes. "So we are in agreement then. The wedding shall be held at Hedley."

"Over my dead—"

"Perhaps," Clara broke in, laying a staying hand on her great-aunt's arm, "we should ask the couple what their wishes are. After all," she continued with a serene smile, "nothing matters more than their happiness. Isn't that right?"

Both women's faces settled into identical lines of rebellion. Yet they muttered their agreement, like recalcitrant children being called to the carpet. Clara let loose a small sigh of relief.

"Quite right," Mrs. Margery Kitteridge, Clara's cousin and Aunt Olivia's granddaughter, said with a bright smile. "Phoebe, have you and Oswin discussed where you would like the wedding to be held?"

Phoebe cast a nervous glance at Aunt Olivia and Lady Crabtree. Clara gave her an encouraging nod, to which Phoebe seemed completely immune. It was only when her intended laid a comforting hand on hers, giving it a squeeze, that the tension in her face eased.

The pang of sadness that rose up in Clara stunned her breathless. She had seen proof before, of course, in the past months in London that her sister did not need her as she used to. But this was the first time it had been brought so harshly into focus.

It was as it should be, she told herself stoutly. Phoebe was moving on with her life, and her first thought should be for her future husband. Yet the pain of being left behind did not abate. All the more proof that Clara's usefulness was at an end.

"Actually, Oswin and I had hoped to be married in a month's time." Her eyes drifted to her intended, her hand turning over to grip his. "And we had hoped to marry at the chapel at Danesford."

"Danesford!" Lady Crabtree sputtered. "I shall not hear of it."

"Though I take offense at Lady Crabtree's tone regarding my childhood home"—Lady Tesh speared the woman in question with a stern glare—"for once I have to agree that such a scheme is unthinkable. Why, we shall have to leave London almost immediately."

"I don't have a problem with that," Peter muttered.

"Well, I do," Aunt Olivia shot back. "After all, there are still…unfinished things to take care of here in London." Her eyes drifted to Clara.

It was the briefest of glances, but Clara felt the brand of them on her very soul. Her face flushed hot, and it took all her willpower to keep her expression serene. The hints that Clara should secure a husband were not new; they had begun years before, and at a time when Clara had not yet been considered a spinster firmly on the shelf. At the advanced age of nearly one and thirty, she should have plenty of practice ignoring her great-aunt's increasingly pointed remarks. Though no amount of time seemed to take away the sting of them.

Blessedly Peter appeared unaware of their great-aunt's machinations—quite possibly the only person on the planet who was, Clara thought wryly. He scoffed. "I do believe your visits with the fine merchants of London have done enough damage to my coffers, madam. I cannot handle many more 'unfinished things' on your behalf."

"Please," Aunt Olivia said with a roll of her eyes. "Your bank account has not even been dented by our little shopping excursions."

As Peter sputtered, no doubt ready for a fight with his favorite adversary, Lenora laid a gentle hand on his arm.

"His Grace and I would, of course, be honored to host the wedding at our home," she said, giving both Aunt Olivia and Lady Crabtree a look that proved she was every inch the duchess.

"We should, of course, defer to the bride and groom's wishes," she continued as the two older women appeared to retreat with reluctance. "Phoebe, a marriage at Danesford would be absolutely lovely. But with only four weeks to plan, and four days of that spent in travel to the Isle, it will not be very grand, I'm afraid."

"Oh, I don't care for grand," Phoebe said with a beatific smile for her intended. "If I wear a sack and carry weeds as my bouquet, I would still be the happiest bride in England."

"And you would be the most beautiful as well," Oswin murmured with a besotted smile.

Perhaps, Clara thought as she watched the young couple make calf eyes at one another, a hasty wedding was best for all involved. It was a look she saw often, when Peter and Lenora gazed at one another—right before they disappeared with some flimsy excuse, returning sometime later looking decidedly more disheveled. It indicated that time was of the essence where the passions of the newly engaged couple were concerned.

She would not look too closely at the pang in her chest.

It was not jealousy; what Phoebe and Lenora had was not something she wanted. Such desires had brought her only grief and were best left in the past with the destruction of her girlhood dreams.

"I think it's a grand idea," Clara announced firmly.

As the rest of the party erupted into excited chatter, Aunt Olivia leaned close to Clara. "You're against me, too?" she hissed. Her gnarled fingers stroked Freya's scraggly fur, making her look for all the world like a villain in a play.

Clara stifled a sigh. She should have expected the viscountess's ire; her great-aunt wasn't one to look kindly on being thwarted. Schooling her features into the pleasant expression she often adopted with the older woman—and just managing to bury the frustration that attempted to rear up—she replied with soothing tones, "There are no sides in this, Aunt Olivia."

"Of course there are sides." The older woman's eyes narrowed in suspicion. "Oh, you're a clever one, aren't you. I know why you would be more than happy to return to Synne. You think the question of you searching for a husband will be forgotten once we're away from London and the social whirl."

Well, she hadn't until just now. But if that wasn't incentive, she didn't know what was.

Rather than admit such a thing, however, she said with what she thought was an impressively innocent expression, "I don't have the faintest idea what you mean."

"Hmmm," was all Aunt Olivia would say. Though if Clara wasn't mistaken, there was a hint of respect in the woman's disconcertingly sharp eyes.

The viscountess turned back to the assembled. But any hope that she was done with the subject of Clara's marital prospects—or lack thereof—was snuffed out the moment she began to speak.

"And will your next eldest son be at Danesford in time for the wedding?" Aunt Olivia asked Lady Crabtree, her voice rising over the general din.

Lady Crabtree raised a perfectly polished brow. "I know not."

"What of Oswin's single friends? Will they be present?"

Clara's cheeks burned. "Aunt Olivia," she said, feigning a bright smile, "I'm sure we'll have more information on that soon. For now, let's keep focused on the pertinent matter at hand. Namely when we should return to Synne."

"As always, Clara dear, you are the voice of reason." Margery gave her hand a small squeeze, the compassion in her eyes a potent thing. And was it any wonder? She would have seen Aunt Olivia's attempts at matching Clara with anything that breathed during their months in London. It was embarrassing, really. Blessedly, however, everyone was oblivious to the painful fact that, even should Clara wish it, she would never know the joys of marriage. She had given up any chance of that fifteen years ago. And it had nearly killed her.

For a moment memories assaulted her, of a time when promise turned to betrayal, hope transformed into despair. When living from one second to the next had taken every ounce of effort she had possessed. She shook her head to free herself from her memories and pressed her lips tight together, annoyance rearing up. It was ridiculous, really. Half her life had passed since then; it should not still have such power over her.

Though it was different now, wasn't it? Mixed in with the familiar grief was something much sharper, much newer, a creeping regret for a life of her own, a life that had been stolen from her in one ill-conceived moment.

Why this sudden ache deep in her gut for the impossible? Was it because of these weeks in London witnessing the wide-eyed hope of young women just starting out on their futures? Or was it due to her younger sister, the last living member of her immediate family, marrying and leaving her?

Or worse, was it due to Mr. Nesbitt's return?

While the first two were natural reasons for her sudden restlessness, the last was troubling indeed. Nothing could come of it, even if she wished it. Which she did not.

At least she kept telling herself that.

"I shall concede that Phoebe and Oswin will marry at Danesford. I am not such a harridan to deny them what they wish. But"—Aunt Olivia pointed a glare at each and every person in the room—"I will not miss out on a grand London engagement ball. I will have *that* much, at least." She gave an injured sniff.

"As will I," Lady Crabtree joined in with an outraged air. "Oswin is my eldest, after all."

"Of course," Lenora soothed. "With Clara, Margery, and myself working together, we can manage it in a week, I think, and leave for Synne the following morning. Phoebe, you do not oppose such a scheme, do you?"

"Not a bit," she said with a smile.

With that the planning began in earnest. And Clara found her exhaustion returning tenfold. It had all seemed a dream, her sister leaving her. Now, however, with the dates and times pinned down, bringing that possibility into clear focus, she could see the end of their time together, the end of her usefulness. And it frightened her.

For years she had been the foundation of their family,

holding them together after her younger brother Hillram's death some four years prior, and then during their father's lengthy illness. With his passing last year she might have felt lost, for most of her time and energy had been spent caring for him. But there had been Phoebe to look after and see through the grief, and Peter to help guide in his new position as duke.

Yet now Peter was more than capable of taking on the duties that had been thrust on him, and Phoebe was setting off on a new life. And Clara was left behind.

A hand on her arm brought her back to the present. She blinked owlishly, looking into Margery's concerned face. She realized belatedly that they were quite alone.

"The others have decided a walk in the gardens is in order," she explained gently, "to get some air. And, I suspect, to provide a bit of distraction for my grandmother and the terrifying Lady Crabtree." Her full cheeks lifted in a wry smile.

"Of course," Clara said, trying with all her might to shrug off the sadness that continued to cling to her like a barnacle. She forced a smile, standing and shaking out her skirts. "Let us be off at once."

But Margery's hand landed once more on her sleeve, staying her. "I think," she said quietly, "that it might be wise for you to return to Dane House."

"Nonsense," Clara declared, though she could not meet her cousin's eyes for the understanding she knew she would find there. Margery might not know the tragedy in Clara's past, but she had an intuitive soul and had offered Clara a compassionate ear more than once in the past year of change and upheaval.

That did not mean, however, that Clara could take her up on her kind offers. Clara only knew to be strong, to help where it was needed, to prop others up when they might collapse. She didn't know how to lean on another—and feared ever finding strength again should she let her guard down.

But despite Margery's mild disposition, she could be stubborn when she put her mind to it. "I will not hear another word on it," she declared, pushing Clara toward the door. "They have gotten the important details out of the way and shall only be discussing the color of the flowers and the style of cake. Besides"—she gave Clara a sly look—"think how much help you'll be by return-ing home and giving Mrs. Ingram and Yargood advance notice of the coming move. There is no one who can start the necessary coordination of packing and preparation like you."

Clara gave her cousin a smile. "You can be a crafty thing, did you know that?"

Margery grinned. "Go," she said firmly, shooing Clara out the door.

Clara relented, giving a soft chuckle as she turned for the stairs. Just as she reached the ground floor, however, Margery called her name. Clara looked up and spied her cousin's round face peering over the banister.

"Oh, and dearest? Lenora quite forgot to tell Mrs. Ingram of Mr. Nesbitt's appearance for dinner. Can you please let her know?" Her eyes shone. "How exciting to have him back in England. I cannot wait to see our friend after so long."

Dazed, Clara could only watch numbly as Margery waved merrily and ducked out of sight. For a blessed moment she had forgotten him.

But she was not a young, impressionable girl any longer. She was a woman, with much more sense than she'd had at fifteen. Yes, Mr. Nesbitt was handsome, and kind, and she was attracted to him as she had not been to anyone in ages. But that did not mean she was foolish enough to act on her desires. With so many years of practice at keeping her head in control and in silencing the urgings of her heart, it would be an easy thing to ignore her feelings for the man.

And perhaps, she mused wryly as she accepted her outer things from the butler, she might eventually believe it herself.

* * *

Quincy took a steadying breath as he looked up at the imposing façade of his family's London townhouse. It had taken a good pounding ride, followed by several hours of walking the stately streets of Mayfair, to get him to this point. And still something deep inside urged him to turn tail and flee and not look back. When last he'd been this nervous he'd been a mere lad, leaving this place for a new life. Away from the hell that home had become and the terror of the future his mother had mapped out for him.

But no, this feeling wasn't the same. His hand tightened into a fist, his jaw clenching so hard his teeth ached. The anxiety he'd felt then had been overshadowed by youthful pride, and rage, and a certainty that the path he was about to embark on was right. And he could not regret it one bit. He had carved a new life for himself, had made himself into a man he could be proud of.

Now, however, his nervousness was accompanied by the anger of a man who knew what he'd been robbed of, who had seen that there were loving mothers in the world who did not feel obliged to ship their sons off to war in order to rid themselves of the burden of them.

Fury pounded through him, so hard and fast he could feel the pulse of it in his temples. He saw it clearly then, the reason he had delayed coming back, that thing that the anger had sprouted from like a poisonous weed. No matter he was a grown man and had spent half his life building his confidence, along with his fortune; he was still that frightened, hurt boy who could do no right.

Well, no more.

Shoulders set in determination, he strode up the front steps and rapped sharply on the grand oak door. Within moments it swung open.

Quincy had not realized what seeing the butler would do to him. For there was Byerly, still at his post, though with a decade and a half of gray hair topping his head, new lines bracketing his eyes and mouth, and extra weight about his middle.

"Good afternoon, sir," he said in his sonorous voice. "Are you expected by Her Grace?"

This man had known him since he was a babe in arms, had given him rides upon his back, and had snuck him sweets when things were at their worst. That he now had no idea who Quincy was should not have affected him as it did. Yet he felt a slight cracking in the region of his heart. He pushed the feeling aside and plastered a carefree grin on his face. "Come along, Byerly. Never say you have forgotten me."

The butler frowned at the familiarity, his mouth opening no doubt to lay Quincy low with a scathing retort. Whatever words he had been about to utter, however, stalled when recognition sparked. The man's jaw dropped. "Master Quincy?" he whispered.

Quincy smiled. "It's good to see you, old friend."

But there was no answering smile. Instead a dawning horror filled the man's features. He bowed, deeply. "Ah, but forgive me. I forget myself."

Quincy's smile faltered, his insides lurching. That sensation only worsened as Byerly's hands came together, the fingers tangling in a mass of white-gloved digits. "But you'll be wanting to see your mother. Please, allow me to show you the way. Or would you rather find the way yourself?" He shook his head sharply. "Oh, dear," he muttered. "Dear me."

Quincy, growing more alarmed by the second, stepped toward the man. He looked as if he was about to keel over on the spot. "I say, are you well?" Perhaps he was losing his faculties. Though he could not see his mother, a stickler for all that was perfect and proper, allowing Byerly to keep his post if that was so.

To Quincy's everlasting shock, a desperate laugh burst from the butler. Then, without another word, he turned and began a swift stride across the front hall and up the sweeping staircase. Utterly bewildered, Quincy nonetheless followed with alacrity. He didn't know what the devil was wrong with the man. But if the desperation in his step was any indication, he was headed to Quincy's mother to apprise her of her youngest son's sudden appearance. With that woman Quincy would finally have the answers he sought. Hopefully.

The near sprint through the house was short. Even so, Quincy was stunned by the physical reminders of his childhood, memories he had banished from his mind in an attempt to survive. Here was the railing he had slid down more times than he could count under his father's mischievous tutelage, there the bust of some long-dead ancestor he had once dressed as a woman, complete with his mother's best rouge and wig. As they made their way up another flight, turning the corner into the family apartments, he tried not to look at the long line of doors before him. But he was aware of each and every one. And in his head he recited the litany of names: Gordon, Kenneth, Sylvester, Quincy. Their bedrooms in a neat row leading to their parents' apartments. Each door was firmly closed, and it surprised him, the ache in his chest to glimpse within those rooms.

He had not been close to his brothers, being the last born long after the others. His three elder brothers had been close, in age and friendship. And forever excluding Quincy, who would have given anything to be included. Before Quincy's flight from home all three had moved out of the London house, Gordon returning only to take their father's place after his death, Kenneth and Sylvester at university preparing for their lives as younger sons. And no doubt finding relief from their mother's constant criticisms.

His boots clicked sharply on the polished wood floor of the hall, sending back echoes of his mother's sharp reprimands, something that had haunted him despite all the happiness he had managed to scrape out with his father between these walls. Would that he could go on with his life without needing this meeting to close the last of his wounds. Would that he could turn around and never think of this place again.

No matter the urges deep inside him, however, it was too late to retreat. The door to his mother's sitting room loomed. And then Byerly was pushing open the door, his agitation making him forget to knock.

"I told you I was not to be disturbed, Byerly." His

mother's voice, sharper than Quincy remembered, rang out into the hall. And suddenly he was a boy again, being called to the carpet for one of the thousand things he had done wrong. Forever a disappointment.

Drawing himself to his full height, he pushed into the room before Byerly had a chance to announce him. "Hello, Mother," he said, pasting a devilish smile to a face that felt stiff and unyielding—so quickly falling back on defenses he had always used to hide his hurt. "Have you missed me?"

His mother's face was frozen, halfway between shock and fury. As if upon seeing him her mind had simply stopped working, and she was now caught in some horrible purgatory. She was as beautiful as ever. That much was obvious to him, though he could comprehend little else. Yet that same coldness that had taken away from her beauty was still present, even in her shock. She was as flawless as a marble statue, and without an ounce of warmth. Though perhaps, now that he was returned to her after so long, she might show a modicum of happiness.

That pathetic hope died a quick and complete death as she came back to her senses. Her eyes narrowed as she took him in, from the top of his carefully mussed hair to the tips of his gleaming boots. "You're not dead."

The words were spoken without emotion. It was no different from any interaction they'd had when he was a child, and so should not surprise him in the least.

Why, then, did it hurt so damn much?

But he had never shown his pain before. He was not about to start now. He grinned and executed a flourishing bow. "Obviously. I'm glad to see your advanced age has not taken away your powers of observation."

Her lips pressed into a harsh line before she recalled

herself and her face smoothed once more. Anything to keep away the encroaching signs of aging, he thought with bitterness. Now that the initial shock was gone, he could see that the toil of time had not been held completely at bay. She was nearing six decades, after all, and her skin was beginning to show it. Fine lines radiated from the corners of her eyes, crossed the expanse of her forehead, and bracketed the corners of her mouth. Her hair, too, had not escaped the march of years. More than a few fine gray strands were worked through the deep brown.

"I see you are just as charming as ever," she said, acid leaching into her voice. Her sharp eyes took in his fine clothes with grudging interest. "Though it appears you have not been living a pauper's existence. Where have you been all this time?"

The moment the words were out of her mouth her lips twisted, as if the taste of the question offended her. Her curiosity must be great indeed for her to ignore her pride. He briefly welcomed the idea of stringing her along, refusing to answer, making her squirm.

But although he had always enjoyed baiting her, he found that he was too damn tired for such games. This reunion was taking too much out of him. All he wanted was to finish with it, to escape from this place and put it behind him once and for all.

He strode to a seat near his mother and sank down into it. She had not bid him to sit, and no doubt she never would. Well, to hell with that. He was not a youth any longer, desperate for her approval. "I have been to America," he said. "To Boston."

Her eyes flared wide. "Whyever would you go and do a thing like that?"

A sharp laugh burst from him. "England is not the center of the world, Mother."

"Yes, it is," she said, with a surety that would have done any queen proud.

But arguing would get him nowhere. He closed his eyes against a sudden pain in his head. "Where are my brothers? I would get the rest of these loving reunions out of the way so I may go back to living my life."

Instead of a sharp retort, however, there was only silence. A silence that was as heavy as it was dark. Funny that, for he had never thought a lack of sound could hold so much emotion. He opened his eyes to question his mother once again—perhaps she had grown hard of hearing as well. To his shock, however, she appeared utterly destroyed.

He bolted upright in his seat and reached for her hand. It was a foreign thing, to touch her at all. And so he did not immediately realize how cold her fingers were. "What is it? Are you unwell?"

The sound of his voice seemed to jolt her back to herself. Snapping her hand back from his touch, her lip curled ever so slightly, eyes blazing. "Of course I'm well. But what game are you playing? What do you mean, you wish to see your brothers?"

His momentary worry transformed to anger of his own. "Why else would I come back after all this time but to see my family?"

"You are cruel," she spat.

"What the devil are you talking about? How is it cruel to want to see them?"

Realization dawned in her eyes as she took him in. "But . . . you don't know then?"

"Know what, precisely?"

She shook her head, artfully arranged curls trembling in agitation. "But you have to know. It's why you came back, surely."

"I don't have the faintest idea what you're talking about." He tried to keep the words even. But unease had begun to bubble up in his gut, like a pot of water set to boil.

Her next words, said with a cruelty that stunned him, had that pot boiling right over the edge.

"You cannot see your brothers because they are, each and every one, dead in their graves." Her lips stretched into a malicious smile. "And so it is only me to welcome you home, dear boy. Or should I say, Your Grace, the Duke of Reigate?"

Chapter 3

M rs. Ingram," Clara tried for what was probably the hundredth time since returning to Dane House from Lord and Lady Crabtree's nearly an hour ago, "surely I can be of help somewhere."

"Help?" The housekeeper shook her head emphatically, even as she gently guided Clara out of the way of two maids carrying armfuls of linens. "My lady, I assure you I have everything well under control. Why, I started preparing for just such a contingency the moment Lord Oswin began courting our Lady Phoebe."

Of course she would. Clara let out a frustrated breath. The housekeeper had spent the better part of three decades making herself indispensable to the comfort of the Dukes of Dane; it should have been no surprise that she would have foreseen that such actions would be necessary, no matter that the news had completely surprised the rest of them. It also should not have surprised Clara that Mrs. Ingram would adamantly refuse her offers of help.

"Now," Mrs. Ingram continued with a distracted smile, her sharp eyes remaining fixed on the servants as they bustled about them in the upper hallway, "don't worry your head any longer about any of this. Why don't you have a nice rest in your rooms. I'm thinking you need it after the excitement of the past days."

And with that she was off, Clara already forgotten as she barked orders to two footmen carrying a chest to Phoebe's rooms.

Clara, well and truly dismissed, and knowing that any further attempts to make herself useful would only accomplish the opposite, heaved a sigh and made her way to her rooms. But instead of sitting herself down and occupying herself in pursuits deemed proper for a gentlewoman as Mrs. Ingram had no doubt intended, she strode to the windows and looked down into the verdant green that was the center of Grosvenor Square. Within the shady depths nannies held the hands of impatient toddlers, couples strolled arm in arm, young ladies giggled with heads bent together. It was a lively scene. Yet from the relative peace of her room, with only the muted sounds of work behind her closed door, she felt as if she were looking at a painting.

No, that wasn't quite right, was it? For out there was life. She was the painting, one-dimensional, lacking passion and warmth. Mere brushstrokes on canvas. And she would remain unchanging while the rest of the world moved on.

She pressed her hand flat to the glass before her and dragged in a deep breath, trying to dislodge the maudlin thoughts—as well as to tamp down on the restlessness she felt for more than what she was destined. Goodness, but this wasn't like her at all. Despite all that life had thrown at her, she had always managed to remain cheerful and useful. And she would find a way to be useful again. Her lips twisted. Somehow.

She stood there for a time, feeling as if she were

caught between two worlds, every lively interaction below or sound of busywork behind making her feel trapped until her body was nothing but a mass of tension. Unable to stand the inaction a moment longer, she pushed away from the window. Surely there was something she could do to be of benefit. A quick glance at the clock over the mantel told her the afternoon was quickly marching by. Her family was due to return soon from Lord and Lady Crabtree's. No matter that she was not needed in the packing preparations, there was still much to do. Her sister's wedding was only a month away, after all.

She faltered at that. To her, Phoebe was still that child who used to dance to imaginary music and drag her dolls everywhere she went, not a woman about to be married. But after a moment, Clara squared her shoulders, marching out her bedroom door and through the upstairs hallway. Phoebe was a woman grown, and she'd best remember it. Now was the time for joy and hope. No matter that her heart grieved that life would never be the same.

She hurried to the ground floor, her mind busy. Surely they would all appreciate a refreshing drink after being out on this overwarm day. She would go down to the kitchens, have something prepared for their return.

Just as her feet hit the last tread, she heard a pounding at the front door. With the butler in the attic directing his footmen in the removal of the trunks, Clara did not think twice about redirecting her steps. She reached the door just as another barrage of knocks sounded. In the back of her mind she recognized the desperate quality to the pounding, alerting her to the fact that this was no casual caller. Her hand, however, was late in getting the message, for it swung the door wide, to reveal—

"Mr. Nesbitt," she breathed.

Goodness, how was it that her memories from just that morning did not do him justice? She drank him in as she had not allowed herself to earlier in front of Peter and Lenora. Sun-darkened skin, so much more attractive than the pale complexions of the men of London. Inky hair that fell in thick, unruly waves over his forehead. A lean form that exuded strength and a predatory grace. And those eyes. Heavens, but they were dark, so dark she thought she might lose herself in them and never find herself again.

But what must he think of her, standing there staring at him as if he were a cream pastry. Cheeks flaming, she forced a smile. "Mr. Nesbitt. We did not expect to see you again until this evening."

"Ah, yes, my apologies, Lady Clara," he mumbled, sketching a belated bow and scanning the hall behind her with barely concealed agitation. "I seem to have lost track of the time."

Not knowing what else to do, only knowing she could not leave him standing on the front step, Clara moved back. "Please, come in."

How was it, she thought a bit wildly as he stepped inside and closed the door behind him, that the cavernous front hall could feel so intimate? The soft click of the latch, the sudden loss of bright daylight, the subsequent muffling of all outside noise made her even more aware of the tall, powerful man before her. Flustered, she looked about for something to do, and her eyes lit upon the side table nearby. Ah, yes, his outerwear. As she turned to Mr. Nesbitt, however, intending to ask him for his things, she realized he was not wearing any. His head was quite bare, his hands as well. Hands that were incredibly strong, yet appeared as if they could be gentle were the situation to call for it . . .

Desperate to tamp down on her wandering thoughts, she blurted the first thing that came to her. "You have no outerwear."

He looked utterly perplexed. His hand went to his head, and he blinked when he found nothing there. "Ah, no, I suppose I don't. Is Peter home?"

The swift change of subject took her aback. "I'm sorry, but he's not, though he should be returning shortly." When he did nothing but nod morosely, his shoulders slumping almost in defeat, she took a step forward, lowering her voice. "Mr. Nesbitt, are you quite well?"

For a moment he looked as if he might either laugh or cry. In the end he smiled. It was a wide thing, filled with his usual devilish charm. It might have made her lose her breath again had his eyes not appeared as if he were burning from the inside out.

"Never better," he proclaimed. "I don't suppose I might wait for Peter?"

Which she should have offered from the very beginning. She flushed. "Of course. Please, forgive my thoughtlessness. I'm afraid my mind is elsewhere. If you'll follow me?"

She turned and led the way up the stairs to the drawing room, stopping only to quietly direct a maid to bring a tray up. She cast a nervous glance out the window as she settled into a high-backed chair. Goodness, she hoped her family did not take much longer.

It was only as she turned her gaze back to Mr. Nesbitt

that she realized he had stopped next to a chair and was looking down at it as if he could not fathom what he was supposed to do with it.

She offered him a strained smile. "Won't you have a seat?"

He cast her a blank look before blinking and focusing on her. "Ah, no, thank you. I think I'd rather stand."

She arched a brow. "I don't know when Peter might return. It could be some time."

"That's quite all right."

Truly, the man was acting most odd. She frowned. "Are you certain you're well, Mr. Nesbitt?"

A strange noise seemed to issue from his throat, but beyond the faintest flicker of his dark eyes his face didn't show the least change.

"Quite well," he said, before, with only the slightest hesitation, he abruptly sat. He seemed to mentally shake himself, his demeanor changing in an instant to one of polite inquiry. "But how was Lord and Lady Crabtree's? Did you not attend the meeting with them?"

Again the sudden about-face. It could not have been more obvious that the man was trying his best to keep the conversation far away from his well-being. Very well, she would not press.

"I did," she said, "though I was sent home early by Margery after the pertinent information regarding the wedding was gone over."

"Were you not feeling well?"

"Oh, I'm quite fit, thank you," she said in what she hoped was not an overly bright manner. There was no way she was going to tell this man that she had been forced to leave because she had been distracted by thoughts of him.

He nodded, and she nodded. And the silence that fell was the loudest she had ever heard in her life.

Tangling her fingers together to keep from creasing her skirts, she blurted, "Peter says you are to leave England soon?"

He seemed relieved she had said anything at all, for he latched onto it with enthusiasm.

"Ah, yes. That's correct, I'm to begin my travels." In the next moment, however, his face darkened, the excitement that had overtaken his features replaced with something akin to desolation.

He cleared his throat. "And your sister, she is to marry soon?"

Which was the most painful topic he could have stumbled upon, at least after her unwelcome feelings for himself. "Er, yes. Yes she is."

Again silent nodding on both their parts. She blew out a frustrated breath. Really, one of them had to give. But she had spent a decade and a half redirecting even the most innocuous conversations away from herself. If anyone would win this, it was she.

Unfortunately he seemed to have the same idea in mind.

"Do you miss Boston?"

"I do. Do you miss Danesford?"

"Yes. Do you have plans while in London?"

"Somewhat. When does your sister marry?"

"In a month. Peter mentioned you have family here in town?"

"I do. Will you live with your sister or return to Danesford?"

"I'm not certain. When do you leave on your journeys?"

He slumped in his seat, as if the weight of the world had

fallen onto his shoulders. "I hardly know," he muttered, looking defeated.

She frowned. "You don't know when your trip will begin?"

He shook his head. "I had planned... But plans change, don't they?"

Yes," she answered cautiously when his dark eyes found hers. "Yes, they can change, quite unexpectedly at times."

He let loose a sharp laugh, making her jump. Goodness. Earlier that afternoon he'd been his usual self, cheerful and teasing. Now, however, he appeared quite altered. It was almost as if he was in the beginning stages of grief.

In an instant her own worries were forgotten. That was it. She could see it in his eyes, the slight glazed look that spoke of a recent tragedy. Her heart ached for him, for there was no doubt he was suffering.

She leaned forward. "I know you came to speak to Peter, but if you should need an ear to bend in the interim, I'm here," she murmured gently, laying her hand over his.

Too late, she remembered he was not wearing gloves. And neither was she.

A warm current snapped, searing her palm. Though the suddenness and strength of it shocked her, she was unable to pull back. Gradually, as if through a tunnel, she heard a harshly indrawn breath. She thought for a moment it was her own. But no, her breath was caught in her chest. The sound came from Mr. Nesbitt.

Before she could make heads or tails of his reaction— surely he could not feel even a modicum of what she did—he gently pulled his hand away.

She should feel relief. He at least was of a clearer

frame of mind and saw just how improper her forward manner had been. Instead a strange feeling of loss came over her.

Thankfully a maid arrived with the tea tray, giving her just the thing she needed to collect herself. She had been lady of her father's house for years; putting on the mantle of hostess was like shrugging into a comfortable coat. A coat that gave her some much needed protection against the effect that Mr. Nesbitt had on her.

"How do you take your tea?"

There was a beat of silence. She refused to look up at him. Eventually—finally—he spoke. "Sugar please."

She nodded, still not looking at him, busying herself with pouring the beverage. A job that took her far longer than normal, perhaps. She glanced up when she handed him the cup and froze. His dark eyes were intent on her, a small line between his brows. She fought the urge to look in the mirror on the far wall to make certain she wasn't sprouting feathers or something equally outrageous from her head.

"Is something amiss?"

"Not at all," he hastened to assure her. But his strange perusal did not abate.

She cleared her throat, nervous fingers flying up to pat her hair. "Are you certain?"

"Perhaps you can help answer something for me."

She blinked. "Ah, of course. What is it you wish to know?"

"If a person is set to inherit a title, and doesn't want that title, how can he go about refusing it?"

Well, that was certainly unexpected. She frowned. "But…Peter has already accepted the dukedom." There had been a time, of course, when her cousin had not wanted anything to do with her father's title. But the wounds of the past had been healed, and he had taken to the position with a drive that had surprised everyone.

"I was not referring to Peter but to...someone else I know."

"Someone from Boston?" she asked doubtfully. Truly, what were the chances of the man knowing two aristocrats in America who did not want to take up their responsibilities?

To her surprise he colored. "Er, yes. Yes, someone from Boston." A pause. "You are a duke's daughter, and so I thought you would know. I have been out of the country far too long and cannot recall the intricacies."

His tone was calm enough, yet he looked at her with an intensity that the subject should not warrant. She flushed hot, clearing her throat, and leaned forward to prepare her own cup.

"If I am correct, one may simply not claim the title, and not refer to himself as such. That does not mean, however, that the title is not his. No one else may claim the title while he's alive."

"But if he doesn't want it—" Frustration laced his voice.

"It doesn't matter, I'm afraid," she murmured, doing her best to appear disinterested as she stirred her beverage, though her insides burned with curiosity. Such an odd line of questioning, and such an intense reaction if his disheartened sigh was anything to go by. She glanced at him through her lashes as she settled back and saw that his shoulders were tense, his knuckles white as he gripped tight to the teacup. She imagined the delicate bone china shattering in his grip, so tightly did he seem to hold it.

"And so, despite his wishes, the title would just go on to his descendants after his death, should he have them," he muttered almost to himself. "Which was why Peter was so damn adamant about remaining without issue before our previous visit. Ah, but pardon me." He colored, his eyes apologetic as he glanced at her. The look quickly passed, his expression going distant again. "And to take up the title? *If* he wants it. Which I am sure he does *not*," he said with a surprising amount of heat.

She took a sip of her hot beverage, not a little confused by his swift shifts in mood. "I suppose," she said as she placed the cup carefully back on its saucer, "he must do as Peter did when he took up the title. He must apply for a Writ of Summons to the House of Lords."

He looked positively ill. Then, bringing the cup to his lips, he drank it down to the dregs on one long swallow. Surely he must have burned his tongue, yet he didn't so much as flinch.

An incredible thought came to her. Casting a quick glance at the open drawing room door, making sure no servants were within view, she leaned forward and lowered her voice. "Mr. Nesbitt, is it…are you the man in question?"

He blanched, looking at her with wide, pained eyes. Suddenly his expression shifted. He leaned toward her, his hands braced on his thighs. Tension swirled in the space between them, a space that now seemed incredibly close and intimate. She found herself swaying closer. He appeared about to speak—

A commotion in the front hall shattered the moment. She dragged in a shaking breath and sat back, putting as much distance between herself and the man before her as she could, brutally squashing the disappointment that sparked in her.

Mr. Nesbitt seemed to have forgotten her presence

completely. He stood, not noticing his shin connect with the low table and rattle the tea set, his entire focus on the door to the drawing room. As Peter's voice drifted to them he seemed to snap back into himself. "Pardon me," he murmured. Then, with nary a glance her way, he strode from the room.

* * *

There had never been a time in Quincy's life when he had needed Peter more. So much so that, as he barreled down the stairs to the ground floor, he conveniently forgot that his friend would not be alone.

He stopped in the middle of the gleaming marble floor, staring in incomprehension at the group of people before him. They were in conversation with the butler, handing over their outerwear, their voices a cacophony of cheerful sound. Not a one of them had noticed him. Thank goodness. Perhaps he could escape without being seen and return when his thoughts were not tangled like so much thread.

In the short time since leaving—no, *fleeing*—his mother's house, he had been too shocked to fully make sense of his new reality. His brothers were dead? All of them? And *he* was the new duke? His mind could not contain the enormity of that. Surely his mother had been lying. This was some nightmare he would soon wake from, the coalescing of all his worst fears. Now that his life was finally his own, the very last thing he wanted was to be saddled with the responsibilities of a dukedom.

But no, the one small sane speck of his mind whispered as he inched back, trying to remain unobtrusive, this was all too real. In all his imaginings, he could never come up with something as heinous as this reality.

The group across the hall continued to chatter on, blessedly unaware of his presence. He would locate the servants' entrance, run all the way back to Mivart's, and not return until he was in full possession of his faculties.

That plan died a swift and complete death, however, when Lady Tesh turned and spied him.

"Mr. Nesbitt," she called out in strident tones, her cane thumping like the beat of a death knell as she made her way toward him, "you are come at last. I must say, it took you long enough."

Every eye in the hall turned his way. And chaos ensued.

Lady Phoebe and Margery reached him first, their excitement at his appearance something that should have given him happiness. But he could not find joy in it. Instead, with those ladies on one side, Lady Tesh on the other demanding his attention, and Peter approaching with Lenora, he felt the last tentative hold he had managed to keep on his emotions begin to snap. They congregated about him, closing him in. Making him feel as if he would break on the spot.

"Goodness, give Mr. Nesbitt some space."

Lady Clara's voice was like a balm over the group. Immediately they settled some, stepping back a fraction. It was as if a stormy sea had suddenly calmed, as if the furious rocking of the boat he was in had been put to rights. As if the sun had arrived.

And she was sunshine. She stood poised in the middle of the staircase, all slender grace and sable curls, a serene smile lifting her full lips ever so slightly. Yet her eyes were filled with concern as she glanced at him.

Those eyes saw too much, beckoning him into her

confidence like the sirens of old. And heaven help him, just moments ago he had been prepared to gladly drown in their depths.

A dangerous thing, indeed. His future was too much in flux. He could ill afford to be tempted by anything, let alone by someone who affected him as Lady Clara did.

The momentary lull in sound, however, was short-lived. "Poppycock," Lady Tesh scoffed. "The man has been gone far too long and would have expected such a welcome, I warrant." She turned her sharp brown eyes on him. "I am quite put out with you for not taking Peter and Lenora up on their offer to stay here at Dane House. How else shall I relieve myself from boredom, I ask you?"

"Boredom?" Peter demanded. "Please. There has not been a moment of boredom since we arrived."

"So says the one person in this household who has absented himself from a good portion of our time here." She waved one heavily beringed hand in dismissal. "How often does one need to disappear into his study, I ask you?"

Quincy's head was beginning to pound. "Peter?" he tried in an effort to gain his friend's attention.

"What exactly do you think I'm doing in there, madam?" Peter questioned his great-aunt with a coolness that would have sent any full-grown man running.

Lady Tesh, however, was not one to be cowed. Quincy had every confidence that she could frighten off a bull elephant in full charge. Or rather, she would gladly flag it down to torment it, just as she was doing with Peter if the barely concealed mischief in her eyes was any indication. Such a thing would normally delight Quincy to no end, but not today.

"You are not spending time with your family, that's what you're doing," she taunted.

Which, of course, drew Peter's complete ire. As his friend straightened to his full, impressive height and stared the viscountess down with all the force of his Viking ancestors, Quincy's frustration increased. It would be no easy thing getting his friend off alone. "Peter—" he tried again.

"Do you think the books balance themselves?" Peter snapped, unable to hear Quincy in his growing outrage. "That correspondence answers itself? That the estate is managed with magic from the very air?"

"Please. All the noblemen I know have people to do those things. You needn't work yourself to the bone if you delegate."

"I am not most noblemen," he bit out.

Her answer was drier than day-old toast. "I'd gathered that."

Lenora finally stepped in. "Please, you two," she said with an exaggerated patience that told of many such fights halted in their tracks.

"I won't stand for it, Lenora," her husband growled. "As if I would hire someone to do what I can do in my sleep."

"I know," she soothed.

"Ah, I see the way of it," Lady Tesh said with an injured air. "You are taking his side."

"Once again, there are no sides," Clara interjected, moving beside her aunt to lay a calming hand on her arm.

"Like hell there aren't," Peter muttered.

"You see?" Lady Tesh said, pointing to Peter with her cane.

Margery moved into the eye of the storm then, Lady

Tesh's small pup, Freya, cradled in her arms. "Clara is right, Gran. And besides, you are oversetting yourself."

"And overstepping," Peter added under his breath.

Quincy watched it all with mounting frustration and desperation. He could see no end to the domestic battle being waged gleefully before his very eyes. As the general din increased, Lady Tesh sputtering as her nieces and granddaughter jumped in to calm her, he finally snapped.

"Damn it, Peter, I just learned I'm a duke and I need your help."

Chapter 4

*W*ell, Quincy thought dazedly as a thick silence descended on the hall, *that didn't go quite as planned.*

At least he had Peter's undivided attention. As well as that of everyone else present.

They looked at him as if he'd just opened his mouth and bayed at the wall sconce. Even the damn dog stared in some kind of canine disbelief. All save for Lady Clara, whose expression of dawning understanding nearly undid him.

As usual, Lady Tesh was the first to react. "I knew it!" she crowed, her lined face rearranging itself into triumphant glee. She turned to her granddaughter. "You recall when he first came to the Isle, and I questioned him on his last name? You all looked at me as if I were a doddering, forgetful old fool. But I was right. Our Mr. Nesbitt is the Duke of Reigate!"

Not a soul responded. Peter's eyes did not leave Quincy. "I don't understand."

As his friend looked at him in shock, Quincy remembered: Peter didn't have a clue that Quincy was aristocracy.

He blanched. Ah, God, how had he forgotten? In all

the years they had known each other, he had never once told Peter who his family was. He had told him everything else, of course, such as where he was from, about his parents and siblings, and his dreams of traveling. Yet he'd never said to Peter, his closest friend, *I'm the son of a duke.*

Why? What had prompted that glaring omission? In a flash he saw it, that uneasy night spent aboard *The Persistence* while a storm battered the merchant ship. It had been mere days after sailing from London, the first crossing for either of them. He and Peter had huddled together belowdeck, confiding in one another to keep their minds from the fear of sinking to a watery grave. It had been on the tip of Quincy's tongue to tell Peter the truth of his birth.

But Peter had begun telling his own story, of his hate for his cousin, the duke, who he blamed for his mother's death. Of his disgust for anything or anyone noble. And in Quincy's fear that he might lose his first and only friend, he had conveniently left that aspect of his past out. It wasn't imperative, he'd reasoned. Peter knew everything about him that was important, and as Quincy never intended to return to his family, he might as well cut himself off from them completely. As the years passed that omission had blended into reality until he had forgotten he was aristocracy. He was a self-made man and owner of his own destiny, and nothing else.

But the poisonous truth of what he had been born into was already erasing that life he'd built from nothing. Fourteen years of hard work undermined in a single moment.

Peter's face was still slack with stunned incomprehension. Guilt reared up in Quincy, that he had kept something so very important from this man who had shared everything with him.

"I'm sorry," he managed. As apologies went, it was the bare minimum, yet it was all he could think of to say.

If anything, Peter looked more confused. "It's true then? This is not some prank on your part?" He shook his head, his heavy brows drawing down in the middle. "But how can you be a *duke*?"

The words formed in Quincy's mind, excuses as to why he'd kept such a thing from his best friend. But they froze on his tongue. To his grief-numbed mind they sounded ridiculous. In the end he could only stare at him miserably.

A soft voice shattered the thick, cloying silence. "I do believe he was as shocked as you by the news, Peter," Lady Clara said, laying a hand on her cousin's arm, giving Lenora a meaningful look. "If you had only seen his face when he arrived here, you would know how deeply he was affected."

Lenora took the hint, snapping out of her stunned muteness. "Of course he was. Mayhap it would be best if the two of you talked in private. I'm certain he can explain everything to you then."

"Oh, no you don't," Lady Tesh interjected, waving her cane about, nearly clipping Lady Phoebe's nose in the process. "You shan't leave me in suspense."

"Gran," Margery said in an overloud manner, stepping in front of the viscountess, holding the frazzled dog before her face, "Freya is looking a bit peaked. I do think the trip to Lord and Lady Crabtree's quite did her in. We'd best see about finding her something to eat."

The diversion worked. Lady Tesh's attention was

successfully snagged, for there was little the dowager viscountess loved more than her pet. "Oh, my darling Freya," she cooed to the dog, who took the attention with all the grace of a queen. "Are you hungry? Let's see about feeding you, my love." With that she shuffled off without a word to her granddaughter, her cane thumping. Margery, with an apologetic look to Quincy, trailed after her with the dog.

"There," Lady Clara declared as her great-aunt disappeared from view. "Now there is nothing to stop you from sitting down together."

Quincy looked to his friend. "Will you hear me out?"

For a long, horrible moment Quincy thought his friend might refuse. Peter's pale blue eyes bored into him with all the intensity of a flame. Finally he gave a terse nod, turning on the ball of his foot and heading in the direction of his study.

Of their own volition, Quincy's eyes found Lady Clara in silent thanks. She gave him an encouraging smile that he felt clear to his toes. Dragging in a deep breath, he turned and followed Peter.

* * *

By the time Quincy reached the study Peter was stationed by the window. He stood staring out into the back garden, looking for all the world as if something outside interested him greatly. Yet Quincy, who had known him half his life, could plainly see the lines of tension scoring his broad back.

"Peter," he began, "I'm sorry—"

Peter held up one meaty hand and turned to face him. "I will admit, I'm having trouble wrapping my head around this." He frowned, looking more confused than Quincy had ever seen him. "Please forgive me for repeating myself, but you are the Duke of Reigate?"

Quincy swallowed hard. "Yes," he rasped.

Peter nodded and began to pace. Each movement was deliberate and slow, as if he might gain control over this insane moment by pure intent. "And who was the previous duke?"

It occurred to Quincy that he wasn't certain which of his brothers had taken the title before him. Had Gordon, his father's heir, passed first? Did Kenneth or Sylvester don the mantle before their untimely demises?

For the first time since learning of his brothers' deaths, he was filled with a cloying, bitter grief. He and his siblings had not gotten along. Yet they had been of his blood. They had been family.

"I don't know," he managed.

Peter must have heard something in his voice, for in a moment he was at Quincy's side, steering him to a chair. And then a glass was being pressed into his hands.

Quincy could only stare at it in incomprehension. With a gentle nudge Peter lifted it to his lips.

The first sip seared him from the inside, finally jarring him back to the present. He blinked, looking to Peter, who had seated himself across from him and was looking at him in worried expectation.

"I don't know where to start," Quincy said haltingly.

Peter shrugged. "Start at the beginning."

It was so simple, wasn't it? He nodded, fighting the urge to drop his gaze, forcing himself to look in Peter's eyes as he finally revealed a truth that should have been spoken long ago.

"I'm not who you think I am," he began slowly. "Or

rather, I'm more than what I led you to believe. And while I never explicitly stated that I was a commoner, I never once admitted otherwise. It was a lie by omission."

That pronouncement was met with a careful nod. "And so you are an aristocrat?"

"Yes." Quincy hesitated before, with a quick, desperate motion, he threw back the remainder of his drink in a bid for courage. "In fact," he continued in a rush, pressing the empty glass to his chest as if he could dig out the guilt that filled him, "I am not Mr. Quincy Nesbitt at all, but rather Lord Quincy Nesbitt. Youngest son of the Duke of Reigate. Or, rather"—his lips twisted painfully—"I was."

"Now you are Duke of Reigate." It was no longer a question, but still plain as day that Peter was trying his hardest to comprehend this new turn of events.

Regardless, Quincy answered him. "Yes." As Peter remained quiet, Quincy continued. "Peter, I am more sorry than I can ever say. I should have told you on that very first day—"

Again his friend stayed him with a hand. Quincy's mouth closed with a snap of teeth, and he sat in misery.

"Yes, you should have told me," Peter finally said, his voice low. "But you are still the same man I've known this past decade and a half. I know who you are, Quincy. Or at least, I know everything that matters."

Quincy swallowed hard, his throat suddenly burning, his eyes hot. It took him a long moment to realize he was damn close to crying. It was the closest he had come since the day he'd left home. He looked down to the glass in his hands, at the remnants of whiskey within. "Thank you, Peter," he managed thickly.

Peter scoffed. "You've nothing to thank me for. And

I know you did not keep the truth from me to spite me. I can well understand the need to distance yourself from the past, to forge a new life on your own terms."

Quincy shook his head, more in wonder that his friend could be so generous with him than anything else. "You make it out to be much more noble than it is. The only reason I kept it a secret was so you would not hate me."

"Hate you?"

The disbelief in his friend's voice brought Quincy's gaze up. "You despised the nobility and all it stood for. I was fourteen, alone in the world for the first time, frightened. And you were my only friend." He shrugged helplessly. "I could not chance losing you."

"You could never lose my friendship," Peter said fiercely, before he flushed and cleared his throat. "Arse."

Quincy felt something deep in his chest lighten. Meaningless insults he could handle. They meant that things had not completely changed, that at least in this he was still the same person.

With that Peter rose and fetched Quincy's glass from him, striding to the sideboard. Once again came the sound of clinking glass and splashing liquid. A moment later he was pressing Quincy's glass back into his hand, this time fuller than before. And this time there was a matching glass in Peter's hand, a testament to just how much Quincy's revelation affected him.

"I expect the whole truth from you now that the proverbial cat is out of the bag, of course. But first," he said, holding his own glass aloft. "To reluctant heirs."

Quincy stood, letting loose a relieved laugh. "To reluctant heirs," he replied, clinking his own glass against Peter's, his chilled heart warming with the knowledge that, in this, he was not alone.

* * *

Peter and Mr. Nesbitt—er, the duke—closeted themselves up for the remainder of the afternoon and into the
early evening. In that time Clara learned one new thing
about herself: her curiosity, while not as blatant as Aunt
Olivia's, was just as potent. Her mind swirled with questions, each one spinning round and round Mr. Nesbitt's
new dukedom like dancers around a maypole. The man
had been pale as a sheet when he'd first arrived at Dane
House, and in shock. That, combined with the strange
questions he had put to her regarding the refusal of a title,
made it plain as day the man had not expected or wanted
his sudden dukedom.

She would never forget the haunted look in his eyes
when he had first told Peter. Her heart ached even now,
just recalling it. She rubbed at her chest absentmindedly,
as if to ease the small pain there. Beside her, Aunt Olivia
tapped her gnarled fingers with impatience on the arm of
her chair. The rest of the women were grouped tightly
together, their seats facing the wide-open door of the
smaller downstairs sitting room, the better to catch sight
of Peter and Mr. Nesbitt—*the duke*! Goodness, this was
going to be difficult—when they finally emerged from
the study.

"What is taking so blasted long?" Aunt Olivia muttered.
She craned her neck, peering with a scowl to the hall
beyond the door, as if she could magic the two men into
being by sheer will.

"I'm sure they have much to discuss," Clara said in
as cheerful a voice as she could manage. Which was not
very cheerful at all, as the same phrase had been repeated
in myriad ways over the past hours.

"I just wish I could recall the particulars of the Duke of Reigate's family," the viscountess grumbled. "Truly, it is beyond ridiculous that no one in this house remembers."

As Dane House had kept a skeleton staff over the past several decades of sitting empty, and the rest of the staff had either come with them from the Isle or been hired on for the season, there was no one to glean information from—much to Aunt Olivia's disgust. And she had tried to wheedle information from any staff she could. Which explained the obvious lack of footmen in the hall, seeing as they were now keeping as far from Aunt Olivia as was possible.

"I'm certain Peter and Quincy shall be able to answer your questions in short order," Lenora soothed.

Her calming words were met with a glare by the older woman.

Phoebe, who had been diligently sketching beside Lenora to the duchess's quiet instruction, laid her pencil aside and stretched her arms over her head, sighing. "It is frustrating, I admit. Perhaps, Aunt Olivia, you might go over the details you do remember once more. Revisiting it might jar some forgotten memory."

Clara, Lenora, and Margery let loose low groans. There was little they wanted less than to be forced to listen to the dowager's musings on the "Reigate Conundrum," as she had begun to call it.

Aunt Olivia, however, either did not hear their collective—albeit quiet—protests or chose not to heed them. Knowing her great-aunt, Clara rather thought it was the latter. "It is tragic, to be sure," she said with a frown. "The elder duke passed away a decade and a half or so ago of apoplexy or ague or something similar."

The two diseases were not at all alike. But just as she had done when Aunt Olivia had last recited her limited knowledge of the Duke of Reigate's tragic family history, Clara refrained from pointing that out.

"He had four sons. The eldest inherited the dukedom, very quickly becoming the greatest wastrel the world has ever seen, and was dead within a few years at the hands of a jealous husband. Lord Kenneth took on the title and gambled away most of what was left of a once expansive fortune before he, too, died, this time in a drunken carriage race. Lord Sylvester did attempt to recoup his brothers' losses by aligning himself with the daughter of some neighbor of theirs. But he was not the brightest, and while picking wildflowers for his prospective bride he stepped off a cliff."

As it had before, the simple retelling of that long list of lives cut short made a chill sweep over Clara. She wrapped her shawl more firmly about her shoulders as if to ward off the remnants of the tragedy that surrounded the family.

"But for the life of me," Aunt Olivia continued, her tone turned sharp in her frustration, "I cannot recall a single thing about the fourth son. It was like he disappeared into thin air after his father's death. Neither the duchess nor his brothers ever mentioned him."

Again that ache in Clara's chest for Mr. Nesbitt—er, the duke. She blew out a frustrated breath, her fingers playing over the calfskin cover of the book she had picked up to read yet had left unopened. If she were at all brave, she would just call the man Quincy and be done with it.

But the thought of speaking his name made her shiver once more, this time with a disconcerting heat. She moved the shawl away from her neck, suddenly overwarm as she thought of her lips and tongue caressing his name. Such an intimate thing she could not think of doing. Not with him.

To distract herself, she focused on the cold facts of the perplexing case. She did not doubt her great-aunt's memory of the Duke of Reigate's family. The woman had the sharpest mind Clara knew, and could recall the smallest, most unimportant details with frightening ease.

And the timing of it all matched perfectly with the history she recalled hearing from Peter. He had first met his friend upon his own escape from England fourteen years before. Both men, mere boys at the time, had found places with an American sea captain, had sailed for Boston, and had quickly grown close. What had followed was years of friendship, with the two not only growing up together, but later becoming business partners in a lucrative real estate endeavor.

It was entirely possible His Grace was indeed the missing fourth son. If so, why had he left? And why did it appear as if his family had erased him from their minds as easily as the tide erases writing in the sand?

All of a sudden Freya, who had been napping beside her mistress, stirred. She lifted her head, her over-large ears swiveling toward the hall. The women stilled, even Aunt Olivia going quiet. In the silence they could hear the faint sound of boots on the polished floor.

"Finally," Aunt Olivia muttered.

Before Clara could think to quiet her great-aunt, the two men filled the doorway.

That they appeared tired was an understatement. Both were slightly disheveled, dark smudges beneath their eyes. But there were smiles about their mouths, proof that their talk had done some good.

Too late, however, Clara registered that Peter's was decidedly lopsided and almost—silly?

"Lenora," Peter said with a husky intimacy that had Clara's cheeks flaring with heat. "Damnation, you're beautiful. Quincy, look at my beautiful wife."

"I see her," his friend murmured with amusement. He grinned as Peter went to Lenora on slightly uneven feet.

"I would ask you to forgive Peter," he said as he took the chair indicated by Aunt Olivia—one much closer to Clara than she was comfortable with. "But I am the one who needs your forgiveness. I'm well aware of his disinclination for strong drink, yet I did not dissuade him from imbibing with me."

Peter scoffed. "I'm not *that* drunk."

Lenora, who was busy fending off her husband's amorous affection, rolled her eyes. "As I can only assume your inebriated state has to do with Quincy's news, you are forgiven. *If* you can behave."

At once Peter straightened, though the sage nod he gave her nearly had him tipping right back into her. "Anything you say, my love. And as you are all no doubt waiting on the story behind Quincy's news—and my head is spinning at a frightening speed—I'll leave the floor to my friend here."

But Aunt Olivia was through with waiting. She rounded on the duke. "Are you or are you not the missing fourth son of the Duke of Reigate?"

There was a flicker of pain in the man's eyes. "I see you recall the history with impressive clarity," he replied. Then he flashed her a devilish grin that did not fool Clara one bit. "Not that I'm at all surprised. I would never underestimate you, my lady."

"Don't pour that charm on me, m'boy," she said with

an arch of her brow. "You've kept me waiting long enough while you got my nephew here drunk out of his mind."

"I am *not* drunk," Peter repeated before looking to his wife with a frown. "Am I talking too loud?"

"Hush," the viscountess said before turning back to the duke. "Out with it. And no more of your prevaricating."

His attempts at levity were gone in an instant. "I suppose there is no sense in delaying it. I am the missing son," he replied quietly.

Aunt Olivia fairly puffed up at that. "And you all thought I was losing my mind," she said to the room at large. "I am not so old that I do not recall such an important detail as the old duke having four sons and not three."

Again the pain in his face. Clara realized in a horrified instant that, having been separated from his family by an entire ocean for so long, he would not have learned of his siblings' deaths until today. His shock at his new status confirmed that he had not believed it possible. How devastating must it be to lose nearly your entire family in an instant?

Without thinking Clara leaned toward him. "I am so very sorry for the loss of your brothers."

He blinked, and she thought she detected a sheen of moisture in his eyes. But his expression was warm as he murmured in his deep voice, "Thank you."

His dark gaze bored into her, and she felt for one brief, shining moment a link between them that stole her breath. In the next instant his expression changed, his eyes going flat as he seemed to close himself off from her. He stood with a suddenness that had her jerking back.

"But I'm exhausted and still have much to do. My tipsy friend here has insisted I stay at Dane House for the time being. He claims it's because he will be able to assist me more easily as I transition into this new position of mine. I do believe, however, that he cannot stand to be out of my charming company." He gave a small laugh.

The rest of the women laughed along with him, declaring their joy that he would be staying with them, bidding him cheerful farewells as he said his goodbyes in order to fetch his things from Mivart's.

Clara, however, could only look on the scene with a frown. How was it that no one seemed to see the strain the man was under? How were they oblivious to the turmoil brewing just beneath the surface?

He strode out into the hall and out of view. Clara was on her feet before she knew what she was doing.

"Your Grace," she called, hurrying after him. He froze halfway to the front door, his broad shoulders tensing under the snug fit of his dark coat at her use of his new title, and she winced.

Turning, he gifted her with a strained smile. "Lady Clara, I'm glad you've come after me, for I must ask your forgiveness."

She stumbled to a halt before him and blinked. Of all the things she had expected him to say, that was not it.

"You must have thought me a candidate for Bedlam when I arrived. Yet you have been all that is kind and helpful. You eased my discomfort, helped facilitate a conversation between Peter and myself." He grinned. "Reined in Lady Tesh."

She gave a small, startled laugh, even as embarrassment filled her at his praise. And a disconcerting regret that he saw her merely as a friend who had come to his aid.

Which was ridiculous. That's all she was to him, and all she ever should be. She would gladly help him as she would anyone else who was in distress. And determinedly ignore the small part of her that wanted more.

"Thank you," he finished, with an intensity that sent her brain momentarily scrambling for purchase. "Thank you so very much for your help."

She nodded, flustered. "Of course."

He cocked his head to one side. "But I have not let you have your say. You were coming after me for something?"

Was I? She blinked, thoughts whirling, trying to latch onto something coherent. The only thing that filled her mind was the image of his devastatingly handsome face peering down into hers.

Finally—*finally!*—she lit upon one thing that would make perfect sense. That it was far from the comfort she had initially hoped to provide could only be seen as a positive.

"You came on foot."

One of his dark eyebrows arched. "Yes."

"You are going to fetch your things. I assume you don't have a carriage to assist you in that endeavor."

"I assure you, I don't mind walking back to the hotel. And I can hire an equipage when I'm ready to return."

"Which is truly silly, when Peter has plenty on hand to help. I'll have one sent on to meet you there. Would an hour suffice?"

A small, bemused smile lifted his sculpted lips. "It would. Thank you, Lady Clara. As I've said, you are most kind."

A small, rebellious voice suddenly whispered inside her, urging her to show him that she was not all unselfish goodness and helpfulness. It surprised her, that voice. She had become quite expert at ignoring it in the decade and a half since her ruination, so much so that it had not made an appearance in a good long while.

Why, then, did it reappear now? And why was it so hard to quiet? But she would not allow that passionate side of herself to gain the upper hand. She had vowed long ago never to let it rule her again; she was not about to lose that battle now.

She dipped into a proper curtsy, keeping her expression serene. "Until later, Your Grace."

As she turned to go, his voice stopped her.

"Please, call me Quincy."

She nearly lost her balance. His voice, so deep and soft, was like temptation in the garden. She shivered against the pull of it. "Oh, no. I couldn't possibly."

"Please." When she opened her mouth to refuse once again—hadn't she already had this fight within herself just moments ago?—he spoke. "You all are like family to me. It would mean the world if I remain simply *Quincy* with you." His lips quirked, a sad imitation of a smile.

Her heart plummeted—how could she possibly refuse such a request, though she knew it was the most foolhardy thing she could do?—even as she saw this development for the positive thing it was. Family. They could treat one another as family, and surely her strange infatuation for him would disappear. Especially with him staying at Dane House, being around her at all hours. He would be like a brother to her. Or a cousin. A very, very distant cousin.

Who was much too handsome for her sanity.

She plastered a bracing smile on her face. "Of course...Quincy." Heavens, her tongue tingled from the very sound of his name leaving her lips. "And please call me Clara."

"Clara," he repeated. The smile he gifted her with had

all the brightness of a new penny in the sun. It was nothing she hadn't seen from him before; he was as talented in charm and good cheer as Lenora was in watercolors. Yet coupled with her name on his lips, the husky sound of it burying itself deep under her skin, a frightening realization hit as she watched him bow and leave: no matter that he saw them as family, she would never see him as such.

Chapter 5

*A*re you certain we haven't missed something? Some far-flung property, an overlooked investment?"

It had been three days since Quincy had been hit with the unwelcome news that he was duke. Three days spent sitting in his solicitor's offices, slowly realizing that becoming the Duke of Reigate was the least of his problems.

"I'm quite certain, Your Grace." The solicitor, Mr. Richmond, seated behind his massive desk, clasped his hands on the cluttered surface. His dark brown face was lined with worry, but there was compassion there, too. A compassion that Quincy did not deserve one bit, not after the hell he'd made the man's life for the past seventy-two hours.

And yet Mr. Richmond was just as patient as he'd been all those years ago when, as a young man just starting out on his career, he'd visited Quincy's father to conduct business. He'd never minded the presence of a small child beneath the duke's desk, often bringing Quincy sweets, allowing him to sit on his knee, telling him fantastic stories of his travels as a boy aboard his father's merchant ship.

Those stories had inspired Quincy, making his dreams

to see the world much more concrete and attainable. And now that same man, through no fault of his own, was the one forced to snuff that dream out.

Quincy cast a despondent eye over the piles of papers and documents and ledgers before him. Each one alone was a simple stone to be stepped over. But together they were an unscalable mountain. Or rather, a wall, each stone laid with devastating precision, one on top of the other. Like some macabre mausoleum, closing him off from his childhood dreams.

How had his brothers done it? How had they destroyed the entire dukedom in fourteen short years?

Anger flared in his gut, hot and bitter. He knew, of course. They had been too much like the duchess, self-centered and privileged, believing a chance of birth gave their lives more value. Not realizing—or caring—about the many lives they'd trampled to get there.

Maybe that was why his father had taken Quincy so firmly under his wing, why he had been so determined to instill in him a sense of honor.

"I will, of course, keep looking, Your Grace," Mr. Richmond said. "Though your cousin was blessedly quick to hand over the reins now that he has been informed he is not the duke, we've still to receive everything from the steward at Reigate Manor. There may be something there." He gave Quincy a bracing smile. "Don't give up hope just yet."

Hope? No, he hadn't given up hope, though it was in danger of being snuffed out for him.

But he couldn't keep the man from the rest of his work indefinitely. Standing, he held out his hand. "Thank you, Mr. Richmond. For everything. You have always been a great support to my family. And please do tell Mrs.

Richmond she has my eternal devotion for allowing me to steal you away for a time."

Mr. Richmond chuckled and took Quincy's hand in a firm grip. "I rather think my wife was happy to have me out from under her feet for a few evenings." Suddenly he sobered. "I only wish there was something I could have done to prevent this from happening."

Quincy gave him a halfhearted grin, shrugging. "What could you have done? No, the fault is on my brothers for ignoring your advice. But you will let me know the moment you receive word from Reigate Manor?"

"Certainly, Your Grace."

Quincy took his leave, striding through the bustling offices. But with each person he passed, for each *Your Grace* and deep bow, he felt the walls closing in on him, the hallway lengthening, until he had to fight the urge to yank off his cravat and sprint for the door.

Finally he stepped out onto the street. Gulping in air, he hardly registered the warmth and faintly putrid smell of it, so grateful was he to be outside.

And yet, now that his head was clearing, he could not stop the litany of words that spun about it like manic dancers, bouncing against one another but never slowing their mad twirling: *Ruined, Bankrupt, Insolvent, Impoverished.*

Every property, every parcel of land not entailed had been sold off on the altar of his brothers' greed. But they had not stopped there. No, they had ransacked every bit of the dukedom not nailed down. Furniture and antiquities, statuary and paintings—some priceless to their family, portraits of long-dead ancestors—so much history, gone.

He should not complain, of course, he thought as

he strode blindly down the bustling street, sidestepping merchants and bankers and men of business. The sale of his portion of the business back in Boston had left him with just enough funds to keep the dukedom afloat. More important, he could provide much-needed relief for the people who worked Reigate land; they had suffered horribly under his brothers' mismanagement, and he'd be damned if they endured a moment's more heartache.

But his dreams of travel...

His lips twisted. Unless some miracle fell from the sky, those dreams would never be realized.

Exhaustion overwhelmed him. He'd been so close, had had it in his grasp. And now, by some quirk of fate, it had been yanked from his fingers. He stumbled to a halt on the walkway. Several men jostled him, letting loose obscenities at having their paths impeded. But a few angry businessmen were the least of his worries. He ran a hand over his face. What the hell was he going to do?

He thought of his mother with her damnable pride. She kept control over everything in her orbit with a fanaticism that bordered on obsession, most especially her older sons. Surely she would not have allowed them to squander everything.

But the very idea of seeing her again made him physically ill. If only he had a way to prepare for the necessary meeting. Or had support.

Peter's face flashed in his mind. Of course. There was no one Quincy trusted more. He would keep a clear head when Quincy could not. And maybe Quincy might come out of it with his sanity intact.

That faint spark of hope flared back to life. Filled with a new energy, he turned about, eager to collect his horse and return to Dane House and, hopefully, salvation.

* * *

Clara sifted through the immense pile of responses before her, diligently adding small checks down the long column of invitees to Phoebe's engagement ball. Just as she was finishing up Phoebe entered the drawing room, busily adjusting the brim of her bonnet. Clara set aside the last of the responses and smiled at her sister. "Aunt Olivia and Lady Crabtree can only be pleased that their combined importance has ensured your engagement ball will be the height of the season," she said. "Not that they'll admit any such thing, of course."

Phoebe laughed, moving closer to look over the list. "Goodness! How can they fail to be content with such a guest list? I had no idea it would turn out to be such a crush. You're an angel for keeping track of the responses. Though," she continued with a worried frown, looking over the invitations and handwritten notes and half-formed plans that were laid out in neat piles on the desk's surface, "you've taken on entirely too much of the planning. You should let us take some of the burden from your shoulders."

"Nonsense," Clara declared. "I'm happy to do it. Now you'd best be on your way. I'm certain that our great-aunt is impatiently awaiting you in the front hall with Margery and a fleet of footmen even as we speak, ready to lay siege on the fine merchants of Bond Street."

Phoebe, laughing, allowed herself to be shooed from the room. Alone once more, Clara turned to the pile of invitations she had yet to address for the wedding itself. Keeping the two events separate, ensuring that every detail was gone over meticulously, was proving to take up much of the household's time, and Clara's more than anyone's. As she had intended. Being useful filled the time while she figured out her place once the wedding was over and done with.

Not to mention, it also kept her from spending more time than necessary in the presence of a certain handsome male.

At the unwelcome thought, Clara's pen went skidding off, leaving an unsightly scrawl across Lady Pennyweather's invitation. She scowled down at it before, with a huff of exasperation, she tossed it aside and picked up another to begin again. Yet now that Quincy had infiltrated her thoughts, he would not be kept out of them.

Not that she had seen much of him in the past three days. Between the engagement ball and wedding taking up her every waking moment, and Quincy preoccupied with his newly realized dukedom, she seldom saw him. Why, it was almost as if he were not staying at Dane House at all—which had proved to be equally a relief and a disappointment, much to her consternation.

That was not to say there had not been attempts by a certain someone at getting them together.

She frowned as she dipped her quill once more in the inkstand. Aunt Olivia had appeared to see the presence of an eligible duke under her roof as an invitation to play matchmaker. Not that Clara should have been surprised. The woman had made it no secret that, with Phoebe happily engaged, she was not going to rest until Clara was matched as well. It was a relief that Quincy had appeared to be completely unaware of the viscountess's meddling the few times they had been together. It was as if the idea of Clara being an eligible female had not even entered his brain. Yes, it was a relief. And she would continue to tell herself that.

She let out a breath, pressing her lips tight in annoyance. One of the reasons she had come to the drawing room to work on Phoebe's wedding preparations was to ensure she did *not* think of Quincy.

Which she was failing at spectacularly.

Letting out a low growl, she refocused her attentions on the pile of invitations before her. No easy thing, especially when Aunt Olivia's voice carried to her from the front hall.

She feared for a moment that her great-aunt might once more attempt to convince her to join them on their outing. Not counting her growing list of things to accomplish before the ball, Clara had no wish to be paraded in front of the eligible men of London again, especially as Aunt Olivia seemed to be growing more desperate in her attempts at matchmaking, not only with Quincy but with every other unmarried male she came across. And so she waited, hardly breathing, her ear cocked for the faintest sound of that telltale cane on the stairs.

Instead she heard the welcoming echo of the front door closing. She slumped in relief. It seemed she had managed to escape any such scenarios today. With Peter and Lenora away from home for the time being, and Quincy still off at his family solicitor's office, she could return to the job at hand.

Tightening her fingers on her quill, she put her head down and was in the process of rewriting Lady Pennyweather's address when a deep voice sounded behind her.

"Clara, good afternoon."

She jumped with a gasp, just managing to keep her pen from damaging the carefully penned directions. That did not stop the large drop of ink from shivering from the tip and splattering the creamy vellum, however.

"Blast," she muttered, the frustration of ruining yet another invitation combined with Quincy's appearance making the word come out in a hiss.

"What was that?"

"Oh! Nothing at all." Clara turned and offered him a feeble smile. "What are you doing here?"

Which sounded horribly like she did not want him here. Only too true, of course, seeing as how her body was already reacting to his presence, her heart galloping about in her chest and her breath coming faster. Yet she could not in good conscience be so rude to the man.

"That is," she managed, her cheeks flushing hot, "you've been busy these past days. How nice that you are able to step away from it."

It was a weak excuse at best, yet seemed to suffice. "It's been unconscionable of me to spend so much time on my own matters when I have such wonderful hosts. Would that I could put them off indefinitely." He grinned, moving into the room.

This was the most time they'd spent in one another's presence in three days—and the first in all that time that she'd allowed herself to truly look at him. The sparkling smile was the same as it ever was, of course. But there was something brittle to it today. She was shocked by the pale cast to his skin and the dark circles smudged beneath his eyes. As he came closer those circles became more pronounced. And if she was not mistaken, there was a new slump to his broad shoulders, proof of the toll his increased responsibilities were taking on him.

Biting her lip, she saw her productive afternoon vanishing before her very eyes. She had no wish to be in the man's presence any longer than she had to, but she could not very well turn her back on him. Heaving an internal sigh—truly, she was the biggest fool in England—she placed her quill down and stood. "You look as if you're dead on your feet. Sit, and I'll order us up a tray. I'll assume you haven't eaten a thing since your early breakfast."

He smiled as she gave directions to a maid in the hall before ordering him into a chair. "Clara, you are, as ever, the voice of reason and kindness personified."

She accepted his praise with a nod. Yet bitter regret weighed heavy on her. Confused by her reaction, she turned it over as she sat, and was shocked to realize she did not want him to see her as prim and proper. She wanted to let loose her inhibitions, to follow her heart. To show him she was not all rules and lists.

A sentiment that she was swift to nip in the bud. What the devil was wrong with her? Following her heart had given her nothing but ruin and shame, and a secret heartache that haunted her to this day.

"Do you know where Peter is?" he asked as the silence stretched between them. "Before she left, Lady Tesh said I might find him here."

And any generous thoughts Clara might have been harboring for her great-aunt went right out the window. The woman had known well and good that Peter was out, and that Clara had planned to spend the day working on the wedding preparations. Her polite smile turned to a grimace. "I'm afraid my aunt was mistaken. Peter left this morning to accompany Lenora on a painting expedition."

A gleam of understanding lit his eyes, and Clara thought she might melt from embarrassment. Of course he would have seen Aunt Olivia's ill-concealed attempts at pairing them up. She had been a fool to think otherwise.

"Do you know when they might return?" he asked.

"I'm sorry to say I don't."

For a moment the cheerful mask slipped, and he appeared absolutely disheartened. Her humiliation disappeared, compassion and a burning curiosity taking its place. *Don't ask him the reason, don't ask him the reason.* The litany repeated in her mind, stern and unyielding, yet she found she was helpless against the words bubbling up in her when faced with his downcast expression. "Was there a particular reason you needed Peter?"

The man flushed—actually flushed. "It's silly, really."

Well, now she was truly curious.

She bit her lip and scooted forward in her seat. "Perhaps I might help in Peter's stead, if you're comfortable sharing."

He let loose a chuckle, though there was an undercurrent of strain to it. "Truly, it's so ridiculous as to be laughable. I'd hoped to meet with my mother this afternoon. There's only so much I can glean from papers, and there are certain aspects of the dukedom I find...unsettling." His lips twisted in a pained smile. "I admit, I'm dreading it. We've never had the healthiest relationship."

"And you had hoped to bring Peter with you as support?" Clara asked quietly.

The warmth in his eyes sent her heart right up into her throat. "You're uncommonly perceptive. Yes, that is exactly what I'd hoped. I should perhaps have planned more in advance for this. But once the idea took hold I only wanted to get it over and done with." He let out a breath. "You must think me a veritable coward, that I would need my friend to accompany me."

"Oh, certainly not cowardly," Clara was quick to declare. She leaned forward and laid a hand on his sleeve, heart aching from the self-disgust barely concealed in his dark gaze. "This situation cannot be easy on you. We all need support from time to time; there's no shame in it."

He looked down at her hand as if trying to make sense of it, making her realize just how forward she had been. Just as she was about to pull it away, however, he laid his hand over hers.

Every one of her senses centered on her fingers, trapped between the hard muscles of his forearm and the strength of his hand. A longing in her belly reared up, swift and potent. How starved she must be for physical touch to react in such a way to something so innocent. A feeling that only intensified as his eyes darkened and dropped to her lips. She found herself swaying closer to him—

The butler's voice tore through the moment like an arrow through the heart of a target. "The Duchess of Reigate."

* * *

It took Quincy several long seconds to comprehend what was happening. One minute he was transfixed by the deep blue of Clara's eyes, the rosy fullness of her lips.

The next she'd pulled away with a gasp as the butler announced...his mother?

Well, hell.

"Reigate."

The title, spoken in that hard, bitter voice, latched onto the base of his skull like talons. And any peace he might have found in Clara's presence went right out the proverbial window. He lurched to his feet, spinning to face his mother, his breath leaving him in a low hiss. She'd purposely come here with no warning, knowing how much he would hate being caught unawares. It was a wonder she hadn't stormed the solicitor's offices.

Quick to recover, he sketched a shallow bow that would be certain to infuriate the woman, rearranging his features into an unconcern he didn't feel. "Your Grace. To what do I owe this pleasure?"

Her hard eyes traveled to Clara before settling on him again. "You have remained absent since your abrupt departure from Reigate House. It was only after some effort that I learned you were staying with the Duke of Dane. I'm glad to see you're at least not bringing your uneducated American ways back with you, and are embracing your status by consorting with your own kind." She arched one perfectly manicured eyebrow. "Though I certainly did not expect to find you entertaining a lightskirt in His Grace's home."

Fury pounded, swift and fierce, through his blood. He was not one to anger quickly, and it hit him all the harder for it, a crashing wave that drowned out his intention to remain aloof. He took a step forward, unable to control the trembling in his clenched hands. "You will not insult Lady Clara. Apologize to her. Now."

His mother's eyes narrowed. "*Lady* Clara?"

Her tone dripped with disbelief. Before he could demand she leave, however, Clara moved to his side, her hand light on his back, grounding him as nothing else could have.

"Your Grace," she said, dipping into a graceful curtsy. "In my cousin the Duke of Dane's absence, I welcome you to Dane House. I am Lady Clara Ashford."

It was prettily said, with not a hint of censure in it. Yet the undercurrent of steel beneath the words, the emphasis on her status, did not go unnoticed by him. Or his mother, if the considering look she gave Clara was any indication.

The duchess inclined her head in a regal tilt.

And that was all. No apology, no remorse for the great slight to Clara. But Clara's brief feather-light touch to his back had reminded him to rein in his raging temper. He perhaps should have been concerned by the strength of his reaction to a mere touch from her. In that moment, however, he could only be grateful. If there was anything he needed just then, it was to remain in tight control of his emotions. His mother had ever looked for weaknesses in others, and exploited them wherever she could.

"Yargood," Clara said into the silence, "if you would be so kind as to add two extra cups for Her Grace and her guest to the tray being prepared?"

As the butler turned to go, Clara's words brought Quincy's notice to the slight woman half hidden behind the duchess. She was a colorless little thing, her blue eyes wide in her pale face. Her blond hair, so light as to be nearly white, was pulled back into a tight bun at the nape of her neck. Even her gown was without color, the pale gray dress only enhancing the waxen look of her.

A choked sound escaped her thin lips when his eyes fell on her. She dipped into a deep curtsy and held it so long, he nearly rushed forward to assist her back upright.

The duchess considered him with sharp eyes as the girl straightened. "May I present Lady Mary Durant."

No other explanation as to who the girl was, or why she had accompanied the duchess to so private a meeting. No doubt, from the way his mother gazed at him like the proverbial cat that licked the cream, she wanted nothing more than to see him squirm in curiosity.

But though the name Durant snagged at something

just out of reach in his memories, he would not give his mother the pleasure. He schooled his features into his typical rakish devilry and dipped into a bow. "Lady Mary, how absolutely enchanting to make your acquaintance. May I present Lady Clara Ashford?"

As Clara greeted her, deftly guiding the two women to a circle of comfortable seats, he cast a sideways glance at his mother. The smug smile had not left her face, instead only increasing into a kind of cold satisfaction.

Trepidation wormed under his skin, a chill shiver that had his hair standing on end. What the devil was the woman up to?

Though there were plenty of seats to choose from, he found himself gravitating toward Clara, sinking down beside her on the settee. His mother could be cruel and had already insulted Clara beyond bearing. He would protect her as well as he could.

Yet he knew, deep down, it was Clara doing the saving. He needed her calming presence, as the effect of her touch on his back had proven. This meeting was unsettling him much more than he would ever admit.

"Lady Mary," Clara said with a small smile for the girl, "have you been in London long?"

The sudden infusion of color to the girl's cheeks did nothing to help her complexion, leaving mottled splotches across her face and down her neck. "I have arrived just this morning," she choked out.

"Goodness, how tired you must be! I hope you did not have a long journey." When the girl only gave a jerky shake of her head, Clara continued. "And what brings you to the capital?"

Lady Mary's eyes swiveled to the duchess for a moment, wild with uncertainty, before skidding off in his general direction. The unease that had begun to creep up on him intensified.

"To meet with His Grace," she replied, her voice barely discernible for the trembling in it.

"You have come to meet with the duke?" Clara looked to him, a question in her eyes, before turning back to Lady Mary with a kind smile that should have put the girl at ease.

Yet her agitation seemed only to grow. With another choked sound, she looked in desperation to the duchess.

That woman did not so much as acknowledge Lady Mary, instead keeping her focus on Quincy and Quincy alone. "Mayhap," she said in silky tones, "Lady Clara might give us a moment to discuss family matters."

Over my dead body. If there was anyone sane in this scenario, it was Clara. He needed her there. A fact that he would not look too closely at until this infernal meeting was behind him.

Clara inclined her head and made to rise. Of course she would, he thought in a panic. She was far too accommodating. Which was something he was apparently only too happy to exploit. Before he quite knew what he was doing his hand shot out, catching at Clara's. She let out a soft gasp and tensed. In the next moment, however, her fingers curled around his, a bold attempt at comfort.

"I assure you," he drawled, "Lady Clara is more family to me than my own ever was. Whatever you have to say to me can be said in her presence."

Clara sank once again beside him, her fingers tightening about his own. He ignored the warmth that spread in his chest at the show of solidarity, needing his wits about him. "And besides," he continued, "I hardly think it can be at all sensitive, if Lady Mary's presence is any indication. No offense to you, my lady," he said to the girl. She was an innocent in this, after all.

The duchess's soft laugh turned his blood to ice. "I was certain, Reigate, that you would understand Lady Mary's presence here and what it meant. You have been quite busy, from what I hear, poring over the documents from our solicitor. Surely you've come across Lady Mary's name in one or two of those papers."

Her taunting words finally jarred loose the elusive bit of information. Of course, Lady Mary Durant. Orphaned daughter of the Marquess of Eccleston, heiress to a vast dowry, including a lucrative property next to the Reigate country home in Lancashire.

And briefly engaged to his brother Sylvester before his untimely—and idiotic—passing.

He looked at the girl with new eyes. Sylvester had been dead a mere six months. His mother's stark black wardrobe reflected that. Lady Mary wore the gray of half-mourning. Had she loved Sylvester?

He inclined his head. "Of course. Forgive me, my lady. My condolences on your loss."

"Yours as well, Your Grace," she stammered, her cheeks mottling once again with bright color.

He nodded, uncomfortable, as yet unused to accepting condolences over a brother he had hardly known. It was a situation he had found himself in during his interviews with the solicitors and men of business associated with the Reigate title over the past days. Each mention of his loss was a new cut to him, a reminder that he had not known Sylvester as he ought to have. The sting of it was made worse by the realization that he never would know him now, or any of his brothers.

Even as he struggled with this, however, his question

regarding the girl's presence during such a volatile meeting remained unanswered. Surely his mother didn't care for Lady Mary. The duchess had never been one for softer emotions, after all. Yet the passing of so many years and the loss of so many children might change a person. Perhaps she loved this girl who would have married her son and taken her place.

The idea of viewing his mother in such a pitying light was as foreign to him as breathing underwater. He shifted in his seat, looking to her, trying to attach this new, more tender idea of a mothering person to the duchess. Her hard eyes and stiff posture, however, made that a near impossibility.

"You must see what has to be done then," she said, her sharp voice obliterating the remnants of his generous attempts to dust. "It will be the mere matter of editing the contract, supplanting one name for another."

Clara made a small sound in her throat at that. When he glanced over, her eyes were wide on his face, her fingers, still tucked in his, tightening. He frowned and turned back to his mother. "I don't understand."

The duchess rolled her eyes, making no effort to hide her disgust. "You always were slow. Surely you must see, after viewing the evidence of your brothers' wastefulness, what has to be done. Sylvester's marriage to Lady Mary was an important lifeline for our family's solvency. That has not changed. And Lady Mary is eager to take her place as Duchess of Reigate, something that she has been groomed for since infancy."

He shook his head, his eyes flying to Lady Mary and back to his mother. Surely she could not be saying what he believed her to be saying.

That pitiful hope was dashed in a moment.

"You shall wed Lady Mary."

"No."

There was no hesitation in the word. It broke through his lips, all the revulsion of the idea present in it. On the ride from the solicitor's he'd prayed as he hadn't before, begging for a solution to save the dukedom. But not this. Not marriage to a stranger, who looked as if she might faint if he breathed wrong.

"No?" His mother's sharp voice pierced the haze of shock that enveloped him.

He turned to Lady Mary. "I am so very sorry. I mean no disrespect. But I cannot marry you."

The girl's eyes were huge in her face, though what emotions filled them he could not guess. She inclined her head in a jerking sort of nod, looking down to her lap.

"You will marry her," his mother bit out, forcing his attention back to her. "I demand it."

Beside her, Lady Mary made a strangled noise deep in her throat. Pity joined the horror swirling in him.

"Mother, stop it," he rasped. "Can't you see you're upsetting the girl?"

"*I* am upsetting her?" The duchess's eyes snapped furious fire at him. "You refuse the girl and *I* am upsetting her?"

"Enough. Let us continue this another time."

His words fell on deaf ears. "I have already begun the process of having the documents redrawn. They will be ready for your signature by this evening."

"Mr. Richmond agreed to such a scheme?" Surely not. The man would have said something.

"Richmond? Of course not; the man was always loyal to your father, even after his death. Do you take me for a fool?"

Relief filled him, and with it a bit of the devil as well. "Do you really wish me to answer that, Mother?"

She glared at him but for once didn't rise to the bait. "You will sign those papers, and you will wed Lady Mary. The future of our family depends on it. Would you refuse to offer the girl a place in our family? Would you refuse to save the dukedom?"

"The dukedom will be fine."

"With what, the pittance you brought back from America?"

"It is not a pittance, madam," he gritted.

"It may regrow our coffers, but Lady Mary brings the promise of property, and the status to bring us back to the glory we once were. You would not be so selfish as to refuse such a thing."

Dear God, she talked of the girl as if she were cattle. As she spoke, Lady Mary only seemed to shrink more into herself.

He saw it then, the power his mother had over the girl. And what she hoped to gain from this union. Here was a young woman, alone in the world, owner of a vast fortune. The duchess had coerced her way into the girl's life, seeing the weaknesses in her and exploiting them. She had managed to connect her to Sylvester before he went and fell off a cliff. Now she hoped to wed her to Quincy, no matter her dislike of him, so that she might continue that control over the dukedom. She would stop at nothing to force him into marriage with this girl.

A ringing started up in his ears. As he struggled to come up with a reason, any reason, to lay waste to this mad scheme of his mother's, Clara's fingers squeezed his.

He had forgotten for a moment she was there. He looked to her, hoping to glean some of the calm and wisdom she exuded. Her dark blue eyes peered back into his, myriad emotions crowding their depths. And then her expression changed, a grim determination settling over her features.

Before he quite knew what was happening, she pulled his hand—until then hidden by the soft folds of her gown—into her lap and clasped it tight. In full view of the duchess and Lady Mary.

As his mother looked down in outrage at their clasped fingers, Clara spoke, her voice trembling but strong in the thick silence of the room.

"Your son cannot wed Lady Mary. He is engaged to me."

Chapter 6

Oh, dear God. What have I done?
If the ground had opened up to swallow Clara whole, she would have gladly dove in headfirst. Engaged to Quincy? What madness had prompted her to say such a thing? Yes, she had been stunned by what the duchess would do to that poor girl and to her own son, but Quincy was a man grown. Surely he could extricate himself from such a fate. Just as she had determined to leave the room and let Quincy handle things without an audience, however, he'd turned and looked at her with such desperation, as if he were pleading with her. She had acted on instinct.

But what instinct had her falsely claiming engagement to a man? Most especially one with whom, had she been able, she would have gladly considered marriage in truth.

That devastating thought was still reverberating in her mind when the maid entered, deposited the heavily laden tea tray on the low table, then hurried out. Not a person acknowledged it. The duchess gaped at her, her face held slack in an expression Clara would have bet had never crossed it before. Lady Mary, too, was staring at her in shock, her pale eyebrows high up her wide forehead.

But it was Quincy's reaction that her whole being was focused on. His fingers had gone slack in hers, his body jolting as if struck by a bolt of lightning. Any second now he would declare her mad. She held her breath, waiting for the inevitable axe to fall.

"Is this true?" the duchess breathed, the shock in her eyes turning to outrage as they shifted to Quincy. "Are you engaged to be married to this person?"

The change in Quincy was immediate. He moved a fraction closer to Clara, his fingers tightening on hers as he dragged her hand into his own lap and covered it with his free one. "I am," he said, his voice firm and strong.

Clara just stopped herself from gaping at that blatant lie. Calling on her years of practice, she schooled her features into tranquility and met the duchess's furious gaze head-on, though in reality her mind was whirling with the implications of what she'd done. Had she only made things worse? Had she merely trapped him in another type of cage?

But she would not think on that now. It was done, and there was nothing she could do to change it; she would get through this disaster and deal with the ramifications when she had the time and privacy to do so properly.

"How is this possible?" the duchess demanded, her eyes narrowing as suspicion took hold. "You have only been in the country for four days. There is no possibility you could have formed an alliance with the Duke of Dane's cousin in that time."

"On the contrary," Quincy said with an ease that impressed even Clara, "I met Lady Clara on the Isle of Synne a year ago, and we struck up a friendship. Over the past months of communicating through letters, that friendship transformed into something more." He looked to Clara with warmth, a small smile lifting his deliciously full lips. "She has only just accepted my hand, and I could not be happier."

Goodness. Clara swallowed hard, doing her damnedest to retain control over mind, body, and heart even as she felt herself sinking into the liquid depths of his eyes. *It's all an act*, she told herself sternly. Even so, the response in her was immediate and complete. And utterly devastating.

But she would maintain the façade she had begun. Especially as it meant freeing Quincy from the sly machinations of his mother, who had already proven herself to be the devil incarnate in the short time Clara had known her. No matter the danger to her emotions.

She smiled as if there was no greater joy on earth. Doing her best to pretend it wasn't true.

"This is an outrage," the duchess sputtered.

Quincy looked to his mother, finally releasing Clara from the spell of his gaze. For a moment she felt adrift, as if she had lost something precious. It took incredible effort to keep the smile plastered to her face.

"Won't you wish me joy?" Quincy drawled with a cheerfulness that did nothing to hide the steel beneath. "Not only is Lady Clara the daughter of a duke—a connection even you cannot balk at—but we also care for each other. Surely my happiness is important to you, Mother."

The woman's face suffused with color, her hands clenching into fists in the black silk of her gown. For one horrifying moment Clara was certain she would reach across the space between them and strike Quincy.

Suddenly her demeanor changed. Her gaze, which had been welded to Quincy in a furious fire, cooled and shifted to Clara. Clara shivered. Beside her, she felt Quincy lean toward her, as if he, too, sensed danger.

The duchess lifted a perfectly manicured brow. "How old are you, my dear?" she asked in a silky smooth tone that did not fool Clara one bit.

A low growl issued from Quincy. "I hardly think that signifies—"

"It's all right, Quincy," Clara said, desperate to deescalate the storm brewing between the two, wanting nothing more than to end this debacle. Lifting her head high, she met the duchess's cold gaze with her own, making sure not a hint of fear or uncertainty showed. "I am nearly one and thirty, Your Grace."

"Older than Reigate, then. Hmm. And unwed?"

"She's spent her time caring for her ill father," Quincy said, his voice tight. "He passed just last year."

"I don't think the late duke was ill these fourteen years," the duchess replied, her tone thoughtful as she considered Clara with narrowed eyes. "Rather, I recall it being a fairly recent illness, some two years or so before his death at the most." She paused, letting the silence punctuate her suspicions, before a chilling smile slipped across her face. "One wonders why Lady Clara did not marry before his illness, that's all. When one's only remaining son is about to be wed, one must look out for his best interest."

Clara felt the blood leave her face. The duchess's implication was clear.

The woman could not know just how right she was.

"You have never looked out for my best interest," Quincy bit out.

The duchess's cool control transformed to hot fury in an instant. "Oh, haven't I?" she snapped.

In a move that stunned Clara with its suddenness, Quincy surged to his feet.

He bowed to Lady Mary. "I thank you for your visit," he said, extending a hand to the girl. "And to my mother as well, of course. Shall I see you both to your carriage?"

What could the girl do but take his hand and allow him to assist her to her feet? The duchess, too, had no other recourse. Though, Clara thought as she rose and dipped into a curtsy, the calculating look the woman gave her before turning for the door was proof that she was not quite done with the matter of who Quincy should marry.

Once the trio was out of sight Clara, unable to hold herself up a moment longer on the jellied limbs her legs had become, sank back down to the settee in a miserable lump. What had she been thinking? Yes, she had wanted to help Quincy. Yet in her efforts to ease the situation from the hell it had become, she had only catapulted him into another unwelcome one. Her fingers tangled, as if in an attempt to strangle one another. Surely he must despise her.

Each second that Quincy was gone from the drawing room seemed to drag into the next. All the while she listened, ears straining, as Quincy saw the duchess and Lady Mary away. And then—nothing. Silence stretched on as her misery grew. It would serve her right if he never spoke to her again. He had played along with her announcement, but he was a gentleman. Of course he had not outed her for the fraud she was.

Finally steps approached. Clara tensed, closing her eyes tight. Which, while saving her from seeing the anger that surely filled his features, made her other senses that much more acute. So she was more aware as his steps traversed from polished wood to plush carpet, as the settee dipped when he sat beside her. And still the silence stretched.

Unable to take it a moment longer, she spoke into the void. "Quincy I am more sorry than I can ever say."

He began to tremble beside her. "Truly, I cannot apologize enough," she said. "I will do anything I can to fix this."

The trembling only increased, until the whole settee seemed to shake with the force of it. Keeping her eyes tightly shut, bowing her head, she hardly breathed as she waited for him to break free of his anger-induced muteness and rain recriminations down on her. She deserved whatever he meted out.

But no angry words filled the air. Instead a choking sound erupted from him.

It was then she heard it: a laugh.

It was quickly muffled. But she heard it nonetheless. Her eyes flew open, her shocked gaze swinging to Quincy. Surely she had not sinned so horribly that she had reduced the man to madness.

Though it was certainly a possibility. As soon as he caught her eye, he threw back his head and let loose his mirth.

Her jaw dropped nearly to her chest. "You're *laughing*?"

In response he laughed harder. Tears tracked down his cheeks.

She blinked several times, trying to make sense of his reaction. As his chortling dragged on, annoyance began to rear up. "There is nothing remotely funny about this."

"Yes there is," he gasped. He collapsed against the back of the settee, his hand going to his midriff. "Her face—did you see her face?—she was furious—"

She shook her head. "Don't you understand the repercussions of what I've done?" she demanded. "I've declared we're engaged. Not only did you not denounce it, but you verified it. In front of your mother, a duchess. In front of the daughter of a marquess." She let out a frustrated breath as his chuckles continued. "If we don't continue on with this farce, there will be a terrible scandal. For all intents and purposes, Quincy, we are now engaged."

That finally seemed to reach something sane in him. His laughter died as suddenly as it had started and he was left staring up at the ceiling, a look of grim understanding dawning on his face. "You're right," he said.

"Yes," she replied in a whisper, her outrage of a moment ago gone, in its place the crippling remorse that had preceded it.

"Ah, God, of course you're right." He straightened, and she flinched as those dark eyes landed on her; surely now he would rain hellfire down on her head.

Instead he reached for her hand, pressing her numb fingers between his own. "I am so sorry."

Once more she gaped at him. "*You* are sorry?"

His expression was earnest. "I forced you to remain. And now you're embroiled in my mess."

She shook her head, still not comprehending. "You should be furious with me. I launched you from one horrible situation into another."

Again a laugh escaped him. This time, however, there was little mirth in it. "What did you do but attempt to help me when I was floundering? It was a selfless thing you did, putting your reputation on the line to help me."

As she grappled with his far-too-generous view of the situation, he blew out a breath and released her hand, rising to his feet. "What I cannot figure, though," he mumbled as he paced the perimeter of the room, "is how I shall get you out of it."

Clara watched his agitated steps with a self-punishing kind of fascination. "Your mother didn't seem pleased by the idea of us marrying. If we keep quiet, perhaps our false engagement will just disappear," she said with more optimism than she felt. "You can continue on with your life and I can retire back to Synne. No one need be the wiser."

He halted mid-step, looking at her. And she nearly stopped breathing at the intensity in his eyes. "As if I would leave you to that," he said quietly. He made his way back to the settee and sat beside her once more. "My mother won't forget her plans being thwarted so completely. Once she finds out it was a ruse, your reputation will be in tatters. Truthfully, I doubt she would stop until your entire family is ruined."

Clara felt the blood leave her face as a ringing started up in her ears. She had never been particularly frightened of ruination for herself. But Phoebe . . . All of Clara's actions of the past fifteen years had been to ensure her sister would be protected from heartache. The very thought that it might all be destroyed in a moment's unthinking response made Clara physically ill.

Quincy must have noticed her reaction, for he was soon preparing a cup of tea from the untouched tray and pressing it into her hands.

"I'm not so Americanized that I don't acknowledge the good a cup of bracing tea can do. Drink," he demanded, gently pushing the fine bone china to her mouth.

She drank mechanically, letting the warmth seep into her. In the back of her mind she recognized the taste of milk, just as she preferred it. He had noticed how she prepared her tea?

The feel of moisture in her eyes snapped her back

to her senses. She prided herself on her tightly leashed emotions, but she was dangerously close to letting them overwhelm her.

Now is not the time to lose control, she told herself firmly. She downed the rest of the beverage, feeling the burn of it sink into her chest before putting the cup aside with a determined clink.

A small smile lifted his lips. "Better?"

A warmth that had nothing to do with the tea and everything to do with that devastating smile spread through her. Ignoring it as best she could, she nodded. "Quite. Now let us put our heads together and figure a way out of this mess."

* * *

An hour later and they were no closer to a solution.

Clara picked at the crumbled biscuit on her plate. She and Quincy had decimated every bit of food and drink on the tea tray as they pored over option after option to end their accidental engagement. Yet they seemed even more mired in their dilemma than ever.

"If only Phoebe were not marrying the son of such a harridan," she repeated for what felt the hundredth time. "Any hint of scandal and Lady Crabtree will force Oswin to separate from Phoebe. I have never known a woman to place such importance on status."

"And you would not think twice about inviting a scandal on yourself if Phoebe's future happiness was not at stake?"

His words were faintly teasing, but Clara couldn't bring herself to smile. She placed her plate down on the low table with more force than necessary.

"There must be something we're missing," she said.

"There's nothing. We've covered every possibility, from every angle. If we tell my mother immediately that we're not engaged, she will be furious and ruin you, and by extension your sister and her chances with her fiancé. If we pretend the entire thing never occurred, my mother will eventually find out and ruin you. In every scenario, she will wreak vengeance on you. And I refuse to let that happen."

It was not the first time Quincy had stated such a thing. And it never failed to warm her from the inside out.

Even as she struggled to dampen her reaction to his fierce protectiveness of her, he stilled, his gaze suddenly razor-sharp as he looked at her with renewed interest. "We've thought of every scenario possible to extricate ourselves from this. Except one."

His visible excitement sizzled in the air, awakening something deep in her. She had thought herself too frustrated and tired to respond to anything, but she'd been wrong. Nerves strumming, she straightened. "What is it?"

He grinned. "We remain engaged."

Hurt crashed through her, that he might think this a joke, that he might laugh at her. Standing, she turned to leave. "If you aren't going to be serious, we have nothing more to say."

He caught at her hand. "I am serious. Don't you see? It's perfect."

She gave him a dubious look.

His grin widened as he tugged at her. With reluctance she allowed him to pull her back down to the settee.

"We both have certain problems to deal with. I have a horrid mother who would see me married off to a stranger, and who will no doubt stop at nothing to see it happen. You have Lady Tesh, who has made no secret that she will see you wed come hell or high water."

Heat suffused her cheeks. He had the decency to look abashed.

"I'm sorry to be so blunt. She doesn't exactly hide her attempts."

"You're right, of course," she managed. "Please continue."

He nodded, once again warming to his subject. "We continue with our fake engagement, simultaneously blocking my mother's plans, giving me time to concoct a different plan to save the dukedom, freeing you from your great-aunt's machinations, and making certain a scandal does not break before your sister's wedding. Then, when Lady Phoebe is safely wed, you can break off our engagement. I, heartbroken, will—hopefully—begin my travels. You can live your life as you wish, with everyone heaping praise on you for escaping a union with such a rake."

Finally a laugh sputtered from her. "You, a rake? You are quite the most gentlemanly man I know."

Which perhaps she should not have said, as it spoke too much of what was in her heart. But being the man he was, Quincy did not acknowledge her effusions beyond a grateful nod of the head and a slight darkening of his cheeks.

"I assure you," he quipped, a teasing light in his eyes, "that I can be quite rakish and scandalous should I put my mind to it."

At her dubious expression the kind, easygoing man she had come to know vanished. His eyelids lowered, transforming his previously amused expression to one filled with heat and promise. Even his body changed, his relaxed, loose-limbed posture taking on a hypnotic, predatory grace as he turned to face her, each movement charged with intent. As she watched, stunned, he took hold of one errant curl that had escaped her coiffure and hung down the side of her neck. His knuckles skimmed over the sensitive skin there, making her shiver, and a strange warmth settled between her legs.

"Oh," she breathed, unable to look away from the inky depths of his gaze.

Then his eyes changed again, the practiced seduction replaced by vulnerability, as if curtains had been ripped aside to reveal what was hidden within. The longing in his gaze called to that place inside her that she kept locked up, where all her dreams and desires and passions had been sent to languish.

Mouth suddenly dry as dust, she licked her lips. His gaze snagged on the small movement, settled there. A look of intense hunger filled his face. She found herself swaying in her seat, her body seeming to react of its own accord, wanting his touch more than air to breathe...

In the space between one breath and the next he straightened away from her, a grin lifting his lips. "There, you see?"

She blinked, at once confused and relieved and hurt beyond bearing. Goodness, it had all been an act? She would have to be careful. Very careful indeed.

Forcing a smile to her lips, she surreptitiously shifted toward the far side of the settee, the better to put distance between them.

"Yes, I do see," she said in a bright tone. "That was very convincing."

He held out his hand. "Are we in agreement then? Shall we continue with this false engagement?"

It was the height of folly. The past seconds had proven

that much, and no doubt his pull on her emotions, and on her body, would only worsen as time went on.

Yet she would be a fool to not see how it would directly benefit her. Not counting the fact that it would prevent a scandal, and thereby protect Phoebe's future security and happiness—which was incentive enough— as well as prevent Aunt Olivia playing matchmaker for the duration of the wedding, but it would prevent all future matchmaking.

Why had she not seen it before? Either from the small scandal that would certainly come with a broken engagement, or from impassioned declarations that she'd suffered a broken heart and could never think of another, this would provide her with the excuse she needed to end her great-aunt's attempts once and for all.

There was, of course, the danger to her heart to think about. But she had kept the dam up around it this long; surely she could withstand another month.

Dragging in a deep breath, excitement buzzing through her, she grasped his hand with her own. "Yes, we're in agreement."

His grin widened, and that damnable warmth started up in her chest again at the mere sight of it.

Just then a commotion could be heard from the front hall. Peter and Lenora were home.

His expression fell. "Ah, I've forgotten Peter. He'll be furious."

Clara bit her lip. Quincy was right; Peter would not be happy in the least. Though perhaps there was a way to lessen his anger? "Mayhap we should tell him the truth," she said. "It might help to have an ally." Especially after the entire thing ended and she was left to deal with Lady Tesh's disappointment.

"Yes, that's brilliant." The troubled look eased some from his face, but the worry in his eyes did not abate.

Peter's voice was louder now. Any moment he would enter the drawing room. Quincy dragged in a deep breath. "It's time to face the dragon, I suppose."

A small smile lifted her lips. "Shall I play squire and fetch your armor?"

He chuckled. "I rather think you're the knight in this scenario, Clara."

Chapter 7

*P*eter reacted to their news as expected. Which was to say, not well at all.

"What do you mean, a fake engagement?"

For the first time since knowing him, a frisson of unease worked through Quincy at the sight of his friend's anger.

"It came about quite by accident," he said.

"Accident!"

Lenora, seated beside her husband, laid a gentle hand on his arm. "I'm sure Quincy and Clara have a perfectly reasonable explanation for this," she said brightly. The crease between her brows, however, was proof of her disquiet.

"Of course." Quincy hastened to reassure her. He opened his mouth to continue, to tell them the details of the debacle Clara and he had found themselves embroiled in.

The words, however, wouldn't come. How ridiculous it sounded. Were it his cousin being taken advantage of, he would be furious.

Clara, as ever, came to his rescue. "It was my doing, Peter. I couldn't sit by and say nothing."

"But why in hell would you say you were engaged? You had to have known the repercussions."

"I admit, I didn't think beyond the moment." Clara held her head high, though a faint blush stained her cheeks.

"Of all the idiotic, thoughtless…" Peter muttered, yanking mercilessly at his cravat until it lay in limp disarray about his neck.

But Quincy had heard enough abuse leveled on Clara's head. He pinned his friend with a stern glare. "It was not thoughtless or idiotic. She did it to protect me. And I continued the subterfuge to save her."

That stopped Peter cold. He leveled narrowed eyes on Quincy. "How so?"

"I may not have told you *who* my mother is, Peter. But you've heard enough stories of *what* she is. And she hasn't changed. She is just as cruel, just as vindictive. She would have shredded Clara for daring to thwart her. And if we come out now with the truth, it will be not only Clara who suffers, but Phoebe as well. What do you think will happen to her upcoming nuptials should Lady Crabtree get wind of this?"

Lenora made a worried sound in her throat. Peter, too, appeared slightly shaken, though he jutted out that stubborn, whiskered jaw of his in defiance. "Your mother would not dare."

"She would. You forget, she's a duchess, and despite the setback in our family's finances, she holds much power. She'll make us rue the day we crossed her."

"Damnation." Peter scrubbed at his beard with agitated fingers. "And so we're to just go on as if this is an engagement in truth?"

"Yes."

Peter shook his head. "It's madness." He speared Clara with a look that would have frightened a stronger person. "You cannot mean to tell me you think this is a good idea."

Clara lifted her chin, not at all daunted by her brute of a cousin glowering at her. "I think it's a brilliant idea. And if the repercussions for Phoebe's future happiness are not enough to make you see the wisdom of this scheme, perhaps you might take my own situation into account."

In a heartbeat Quincy knew she meant to throw her pride out the window to see this happen. "Clara, no—" he tried.

She held up one slender hand, though her eyes did not leave Peter's. "Do you think it's been easy these past months, having Aunt Olivia throw me at man after man as if I were some pitiful worm on a hook? She refuses to accept that I don't wish to marry, nor shall I ever."

When Peter, looking decidedly abashed, opened his mouth to speak, she continued, louder this time. "Quincy's suggestion that we remain engaged gives me a certain amount of freedom. If I'm single, do you think Aunt Olivia will stop her attempts at matchmaking once we're back on Synne for the wedding? No, she'll only grow more desperate to sacrifice the last of the fatted nobles on the altar of my spinsterhood. And I'm tired of it, Peter."

Her voice broke at the very end, proof of a vulnerability barely held in check, wrenching at Quincy's heart.

Then she paused, closing her eyes, breathing slow and deep. When she opened them again the vulnerability was gone, replaced by determination.

"So you see," she continued, her voice quieter now that the storm in her had been leashed, "this false engagement is a godsend. It will give me a month of peace, so I might enjoy my sister's fortune, before settling back down to life as I like it, on Synne with my family."

Peter, looking decidedly chastised, nodded solemnly. "I'm sorry, Clara."

"You have nothing to apologize for, dear cousin," she said, smiling in that calm way of hers. "We only need your word that you shall both keep our secret safe."

Quincy studied her with a troubled heart. He felt he was watching a master actress. She had turned off her emotions so quickly, so easily. He wondered if she always lived thus, keeping her more volatile self under lock and key.

Peter nodded. "Of course we will," he said in a gruff voice.

"Certainly," Lenora said with a smile.

Clara leveled her cousin with a firm look. "And you shall not blame Quincy for this. It was entirely my doing."

Although a low growl issued from Peter, he gave a reluctant nod. "Very well."

Lenora rose, her green eyes sparkling with suppressed mirth. "Perhaps it's best to end this on a positive note."

Quincy was of the same opinion. Not due to his friend's possibly reawakening anger—though he was certain that, had they been alone, Peter would have gladly punched him in the eye.

No, it had everything to do with how Clara was beginning to change in his mind. There was a depth to her he hadn't expected. And to his consternation, it intrigued him.

A dangerous thing, indeed. Physical attraction he could handle. But this was something more.

Peter speared Quincy with a glare as he rose to stand beside his wife. "Don't think this gives you leave to be alone with her. With women, I still don't trust you as far as I can throw you." He extended an arm toward his cousin. "Clara?"

A rather brilliant opinion, Quincy thought. Clara rose and gave him a small smile that made his heart lurch.

As Clara linked arms with Lenora and the trio made their way out into the hallway, Peter, not finished punishing Quincy, threw out over his shoulder, "And you're the one telling Lady Tesh."

* * *

Clara had never been so tired in her life.

Once the rest of the family had been told, she realized that she had not properly prepared herself for their abundant enthusiasm. Between squeals of glee and tears of happiness and loud—and constant—declarations of joy, Clara had been hard-pressed to keep the mask of the blushing bride in place.

Finally, however, it was time to retire. As Aunt Olivia approached her, a beatific smile on her face, Clara inwardly winced, maintaining her own smile by sheer will alone. Truly, her cheeks couldn't take much more of this.

"Oh, my dear," her great-aunt said, reaching up with a gnarled hand to pat her face, "I cannot begin to tell you how happy you've made me."

Which was not remotely true, as it was the only thing the woman had talked about all the night long. As Clara watched Aunt Olivia join Lenora and Margery, she reached deep down for the sweet relief she should be feeling at finally being free of her great-aunt's matchmaking. There at the center, though, was a surprising bitterness. Like biting into a decadent dessert, only to find it rotted within.

She could not regret what she and Quincy had planned. It was the only way she could retain her sanity. But she had not realized how much it would hurt knowing that this was how life should have been. How many times had she dreamed of just this when she was a girl, finding a man she could love, starting a life with him?

Yet this was all an act. Some cruel pantomime of the future she should have had, when instead she had been so impatient to start a life of her own that she had latched onto the first man to show her a promise of that dream. And in the process of soaring for the stars, her wings had been clipped forever.

Phoebe sidled up to her, wrapping a slender arm about her waist.

"My goodness, Clara," she said in her ear, the delight in her voice apparent. "The way that man looks at you."

Without meaning to, Clara looked to Quincy. He was talking quietly with Peter in the corner—or rather, Peter was talking and Quincy listening. But his eyes were on Clara. When their gazes met he smiled, that sensual curve of lips turning her insides molten.

That expression shouldn't affect her so. She knew it was an act. They had to pretend to an affection neither of them felt to make this engagement at all believable.

Her body, however, had yet to get that particular message.

Face flaming, she busied herself with smoothing her shawl.

Phoebe chuckled low. "Truly, I had no idea you had formed a tendre for one another last year; you never let on. I might be angry at you for keeping it from me if I wasn't so very happy for you." Phoebe gave a happy sigh, her arm tightening about Clara's waist, her eyes glowing with emotion. "I worried how my engagement would affect you. You've given so much of yourself to all of us, and to me especially." She frowned, shaking her head almost mournfully. "No, that isn't true. You have given your whole self. Your entire life has been in service to us. I didn't want you to feel you had been left behind."

She smiled again, her eyes shining bright with unshed tears. "Now I can rest easy knowing you'll be taken care of. And by a man you love so very much."

Phoebe embraced her, which was a blessing. Clara didn't think she could hide her dismay just then.

She was not upset at her sister's concern, however, though Clara was certain that would come when she had the peace and quiet to think of it again. No, it was Phoebe's certainty that Clara was in love that weighed on her.

Wasn't this what they had hoped to convince everyone of? But even though it had worked in their favor, she couldn't help but wonder why there had been no doubt of her affection for Quincy. Had she revealed her attraction to the man before this, making the quick jump to love so believable? Or had she spent so long concealing her true self that her family didn't even know who she was? How could they believe she would so quickly fall in love with Quincy?

She might have been able to, long ago—young Clara, who had been so full of hope and life and passion. But she was no longer capable of opening herself up to something that would make her vulnerable.

As if to give lie to that, her heart lurched as Quincy approached. She ruthlessly ignored it, smiling widely instead. They had parts to perform.

"Phoebe," he said, though his eyes didn't leave Clara,

"would you mind terribly if I escort my fiancée to her room?"

Giggling, Phoebe kissed both their cheeks. "Oh, this is just wonderful," she said before joining Peter and Lenora.

Clara, placing her hand on Quincy's arm and following behind the rest of the party, slid him a sidelong glance. "You're very good at this," she murmured. Too good, perhaps. If she wasn't careful, he would have even her convinced.

He grinned down at her. "Who would have thought? I knew I had a multitude of talents, but I never guessed that *faux-fiancé* would be one of them."

Despite herself, she laughed. But her humor was short-lived, the strain of the day quickly overshadowing it. She remained quiet as they made their way upstairs and to her bedroom door—with Peter keeping careful watch, of course—every bit of her remaining strength centered on keeping up the act. *Just a few seconds more.* Finally, bidding them good night, she closed the door and was alone.

And almost immediately realized that this solitary quiet was the very last thing she needed. With nothing to distract her she began to replay the whole disaster of a day in her head. And *what if*s began to take shape in her mind. What if she had refused to stay for Quincy's meeting with his mother? What if she had kept her mouth shut when the duchess had pushed Lady Mary on her son? What if...?

Well, then, she thought, heading determinedly out the door and hurrying through the house on silent feet, she'd be damned if she was going to sit around and fall prey to her thoughts. In short order she reached the ground floor, found the door that led to the back gardens, and let herself out into the cool night.

The London air was sour with refuse and coal, and so different from the fresh ocean breezes she was used to back on the Isle. But she welcomed it all the same. For there beneath the faint stink was what she needed: the rich earth, the vibrant plant life, the heady perfume of flowers. They were scents that had been there for her through every happiness and heartache, through every joy and tragedy. They reminded her of her mother surrounded by roses, of the soaring glass walls of a greenhouse, of being surrounded by vibrant life even as she mourned a life gone.

The moon was out, bathing the garden in a silvery light, and she used it to find her way to the small fountain at its center. This place had been a refuge during her first tumultuous weeks in London. And though she had been too busy to make use of it these past days, it welcomed her back just the same, the soft sigh of rustling leaves and the faint splash of water like old friends.

She sank down on the stone bench with a sigh and rubbed at the ache that had taken root in the base of her skull. This false engagement was merely playacting, something she was quite used to. And wouldn't the reward be worth it? Once the ruse was complete and her "engagement" at an end, she would be free to stay with her family for the rest of her life.

Which was what she wanted. Truly.

And if she could not find joy in it just now, it would come soon enough. She was sure of it.

"Clara."

Her skin pimpled at the familiar deep baritone. She looked up to see Quincy smiling down at her.

"What are you doing out here?" she asked as she pulled her shawl more firmly about her shoulders, trying and failing to ignore just how alive her body suddenly felt.

"I saw you from my window and was concerned. May I?" He motioned to the empty seat beside her. Face heating, she nodded.

"I assure you," she said as he sat, "I'm absolutely fine. There was no need for you to come all the way out here."

"My dear Clara," he drawled, raising an inky brow, "I have sailed the width of the Atlantic numerous times. I assure *you*, taking a short walk in a garden is hardly my idea of lengthy travel."

"Nevertheless, it was unnecessary. I only needed some fresh air"—she smiled wryly and waved one hand to the night sky—"such as it is. The evening was not easy. But it's over now, and it will only get better from here. If we can keep Aunt Olivia from posting the banns and procuring a special license, that is."

He didn't acknowledge her pathetic attempt at humor, his dark eyes instead boring into hers with a disturbing understanding. "I never thanked you for what you did for me," he murmured.

She flapped her hand in dismissal. "Nonsense. We're both benefiting from this."

"Perhaps for now. But what of after? The scandal—"

She gave a small, strained laugh. "What scandal? I'm a nobody."

"You are not a nobody."

The fierce certainty in his voice startled her, but more so for the warmth that bloomed in her chest. It was almost as if he cared for her as more than Peter's cousin. She swallowed hard. A dangerous thought indeed.

She laughed lightly, needing to bring normalcy back to the situation. "Ah, yes, there is me being a duke's daughter."

"That's not what I meant."

Her breath stalled. There was something infinitely tender in his eyes. For a single, shining moment she could almost believe this engagement was real.

Then she blinked and his expression shifted to the easy friendliness she was used to. "Do you think Lady Tesh will be able to keep from shouting it to the rooftops until we're on Synne?"

It took Clara's brain a second to latch onto the question. She had made the request in a moment of desperation, at Aunt Olivia's suggestion that the engagement ball be a combined affair. Though they needed this to appear, for all intents and purposes, an engagement in truth, Clara refused to take a moment of attention from her sister.

That, and she knew that if it were made public she would have a harder time convincing herself it wasn't real.

Aunt Olivia had not been happy at the delay, nor that she was thwarted in her wish for a double wedding, a glorious coup to end all coups in the history of the London season.

It had taken the combined efforts of Quincy, Clara, Peter, and Lenora to make Aunt Olivia see reason. Or, if not to actually agree with them, to at least decamp, though with a decided lack of grace.

"I'm certain she'll heed our wishes," she said now, though with much more conviction than she felt. Aunt Olivia was never one to let others dictate her actions. Not for the first time Clara sent up a prayer of thanks that Peter and Lenora were in on their deception. She would not be able to rein in the viscountess alone.

"You're an optimist, I see," he teased.

It should have been a comment easily laughed off. But just then, with this debacle of an engagement hanging over her head, the very last thing she would consider herself was an optimist. "Hardly that," she mumbled.

Curiosity flared in his eyes. Realizing that she had let too much of herself show and needing a change in subject, she blurted, "But I worry about you."

He let loose a surprised laugh. "Me?"

She nodded, worrying at her lip with her teeth as she studied him. "You've mentioned vaguely that the dukedom needs saving. If it's truly as dire as that, perhaps marriage for money would be the best thing."

He cocked one black eyebrow in disbelief. "Are you suggesting I cave into my mother's demands?"

She shrugged. "Mayhap?" When he continued to look at her slack-jawed, she hurried to explain. "As duke you're responsible for a great many families. Marrying Lady Mary might be the only option open to you in such a short time." She ignored the bad taste that left in her mouth.

"It's not unheard of," she continued. "Men in your position marry for money all the time."

"Not I."

There was such conviction in his voice she couldn't help but ask, "Do you believe in marrying only for love then?" An idea that should not interest her as much as it did.

His lips twisted. "I've never really given it much thought. Peter and Lenora perhaps might sway me in this, I suppose, being so in love themselves." His voice was quiet and intimate in the night air. "But at this point in my life I'm nowhere near ready. I've no wish to saddle myself with a wife, or to saddle that wife with a husband who has no intention of acting like an adult for the foreseeable future." He gave a soft chuckle, then sobered, eyeing her with a strange, tense curiosity. "And you? Do you believe in marrying for love?"

How she didn't outright flinch from the pain that soft question gave her she would never know. "That's something I gave up long ago."

The bright curiosity in his eyes made her realize that, once again, she had said far too much. Clearing her throat, she pasted a bright smile on her face. "If you won't marry to save the dukedom, I assume you have other options?"

His slight pause told her he was fully aware that she was attempting to distract him. She waited with bated breath for him to press her.

Thankfully, he let it pass. "Not as yet," he admitted. "My brothers were uncommonly thorough with their destruction, I'm afraid. But I'm hopeful something will turn up."

"And if it does not?"

He smiled faintly. "I'm not without funds myself. I'll just have to use the money I've brought back with me from Boston. No rich wife required."

Though he did his best to keep his expression easy, the undercurrent of pain in his voice told a different story. "And you shall have to give up your travels," she said slowly, understanding dawning. "Your travels are very important to you. Why?"

He looked away, letting his long fingers trail over the glossy leaf of a nearby bush. "As horrible as my mother is, my father was the opposite. We were incredibly close and shared a dream of seeing the world and all its wonders. We pored over maps and globes and books, planning the trips we would take when I got older." The air of gentle reminiscence faded from his voice, replaced by a muted kind of grief. "But he died when I was a boy. And then I ran away."

"Why?"

He cast her a wry glance. "I think you can guess after today. My mother was determined to ship me off to the navy. I, however, had other ideas."

"And so you wound up on that ship with Peter, headed for America."

"Yes. And though I still wound up on a ship, it was at least on my own terms."

She shook her head in wonder. "You're very brave."

He gave a startled laugh. "Hardly brave."

"Oh, please," she said with a roll of her eyes. "You left behind the comfort of your status, secured a position aboard a ship, and set sail for an unknown and far-off land, all when you were just a boy. You're quite brave."

He was outright laughing now, that maddening dimple flashing in his cheek. "Very well," he said, waving his arms in surrender, "You win. I shall admit to my exceeding bravery. But," he continued, "only if you admit to a fair bit of bravery yourself."

It was her turn to laugh. "Me, brave? You're delusional."

He rolled his eyes in a blatant pantomime of her. "Shall I list the reasons off as you did for me? You took care of your father when he was ill, helped Peter settle into his new position, came to London—a place you appear to despise—for your sister while having to deal with a stubbornly interfering viscountess, and stood up not only to a horrid duchess who would love nothing more than to eat you for breakfast, but also to that surly brute of a duke you call cousin. If that isn't brave, I don't know what is."

"Ridiculous," she declared dismissively, busying herself with smoothing her skirts, at once pleased and embarrassed and confused. He saw all that in her?

He took hold of her hand, and she gasped at the electric touch of his fingers cradling hers. She looked into his eyes and was shocked to see a fierce certainty there.

"I am ridiculous in a good many things, but not in this. You think because you've led a quiet life at home that you're not brave. It's easy to leave everything behind when times are hard. Often it's the person dealing with the difficulties of day-to-day living that turns out to be the bravest there is."

"Oh," she managed on a soft exhale, melting under his regard. She tried to remember why she should keep her heart barricaded against the pull of him as, with a smile, he wished her a good night and headed back for the house. But goodness, he was making it difficult.

Chapter 8

*T*he day of Phoebe's engagement ball came with a swiftness that would have stunned Clara breathless had she time to breathe at all. As it was, her days had been packed to the gills with planning and organizing the myriad tasks necessary to pull off such a momentous occasion in such a short time. Not to mention the added necessity of taking on the persona of bride-to-be, taking walks on Quincy's arm, sitting with him after dinner, blushing and smiling and appearing incandescently happy.

All of which had been much too pleasurable for her peace of mind. And taking up entirely too much of her thoughts and energies.

She could only be grateful that Quincy had been called to his solicitor's offices and would not be present for the beginning of the ball. Though she was grateful for Aunt Olivia's retreat on the matchmaking front, Quincy was proving to be a troubling distraction. And so, peering once more at her reflection in her full-length cheval mirror, studying with a critical eye the beautifully made pale green silk gown and the small seed pearls threaded through her hair—and trying her hardest not to wonder what Quincy might think of her when he saw her—she set her jaw and strode out the door.

Phoebe was already dressed, her maid putting the final touches to her hair when Clara entered her room. Margery was there, trying her best to rein in Aunt Olivia, who was loudly directing the maid on the placement of the creamy white roses being threaded into Phoebe's golden curls.

It was a scene she had witnessed numerous times since the beginning of the season. She had not realized until that moment just how dear such things were becoming to her. Swallowing back the sudden burn of tears, she smiled and moved forward. "Goodness, Phoebe darling, you look like an angel."

And she did, in the faintest pink silk, embellished with small roses and ivory ribbons twined into fanciful rosettes, ivory lace overlaying the bell-shaped skirt. When Phoebe's eyes met hers in the glass, her sister's entire face was shining with her happiness.

"Do you think Oswin will like it?" she asked, her voice breathless, cheeks blooming.

"I think he'll love it," Clara said with utmost honesty. The maid smiled at her, handing her a rose. "Thank you, Justine," Clara murmured, and as had become custom over the last months she carefully tucked the last bloom into Phoebe's soft curls.

"Oh, my dear, you are a vision," Margery murmured with a wide smile.

"Yes, yes, a vision," Aunt Olivia said with no attempt to conceal her impatience. "And as your intended is below as we speak, awaiting your appearance—along with his overbearing mother—it's past time we were off."

She wielded her cane, shooing them toward the door. As Clara made to walk alongside her sister, however, Aunt Olivia's voice held her back.

"Come and help an old woman, Clara."

Phoebe gave her an apologetic smile before, linking her arm with Margery's, she sailed from the room, her eagerness to get to Oswin palpable.

Clara heaved a barely perceptible sigh, forcing a smile and offering her aunt her arm. "Well, Aunt Olivia," she said, patting the woman's hand as they made their way down the hall, "it's finally here. We managed it. You must be so very happy."

"I'll be happy when I see that this event is the crush I wanted it to be," the woman muttered. "Otherwise that harridan Lady Crabtree will never let me hear the end of it."

"Oh, I'm certain she would not be so petty," Clara said, impressed with the even confidence in her voice. She didn't believe what she said one bit.

Aunt Olivia cast her a severe look. "Don't think you can fool me, girl. The woman is worse than me for holding things against a person. And I've had more practice than she has. Besides, even should this event prove successful, there's still the matter of the wedding itself to worry about. What if no one makes the ungodly trek to the Isle for it? What if it's a disastrous failure?"

"Then you shall be content that Phoebe will still be the happiest bride in creation," Clara said firmly, guiding her great-aunt down the stairs. "Truly, none of that matters to her."

"Hmph," Aunt Olivia grumbled.

They reached the ground floor, and Clara's eyes were immediately drawn to Phoebe and Oswin. They stood just off to the side of the hall, their hands clasped tight, their faces alight with love. A small ache started up in Clara's chest. She was so very glad for her sister's good fortune. There was nothing more she wanted than Phoebe's happiness.

And she would determinedly ignore her grief for all she'd be losing.

"I don't see that fiancé of yours, girl."

"Didn't I tell you?" Clara said in an offhand manner, knowing full well she hadn't, as she'd been studiously avoiding her great-aunt for the better part of four days. "Quincy received a missive from his solicitor earlier this afternoon. Something about documents from his Lanca-shire estate. He said to expect him later this evening."

Which, as she'd expected, did nothing at all to assuage Aunt Olivia's ire.

"His place is beside you. Why I ever agreed to keep quiet on such a momentous bit of news I'll never know."

"Aunt Olivia," Clara hissed as Lady Crabtree eyed them with more than a fair bit of interest. She gave the woman a sick smile, dipping into a curtsy before doing her best to guide Aunt Olivia away.

But the woman would not budge. "Don't *Aunt Olivia* me, girl. My great-niece, at the advanced age of nearly one and thirty, finally lands herself a husband, a *duke* no less, and you expect me to stay quiet? It's ridiculous."

"But Phoebe—" she tried helplessly.

"Will not know a moment's less joy from having her dear sister announce her own good fortune. If anything, it will increase it exponentially."

A valid point. Hadn't Phoebe told her that very thing more than once over the past days? When Clara consid-ered her decision to delay the announcement, she found there were only two possible reasons. The first, that she feared for the widespread damage to her reputation once she ended the engagement—laughable, really; with

Phoebe wed she had no use for such a thing. And the second, that her feelings for Quincy ran deeper than she had first surmised.

She blanched. No, that could not possibly be true. She could not be so stupid as to fall for the man. Physical attraction she could understand. And control. But if she were falling in love with him—

No, she would not even consider such a thing. To prove that her heart was in no way in danger, she purposely turned to her great aunt and declared, "You're right, Aunt Olivia. It's ridiculous to delay. We'll announce it tonight."

Her great-aunt blinked at the abrupt about-face before she grinned. "Splendid, my girl. You are, once more, my favorite niece."

Before Clara could think what to say to that, Peter approached.

"Aunt Olivia, Lenora has set up a chair for you here in the receiving line so you don't have to miss a minute of gloating."

The viscountess's eyes narrowed as she took his proffered arm. "I think I've a right to gloat, don't you? Especially now that Clara has agreed to let us announce her engagement as well."

Peter glanced at Clara, his shock palpable. "Has she?"

"Yes," Aunt Olivia said with a fond smile for Clara. "And so my happiness is complete. All save, of course, for Freya." Her voice turned stern once more. "Why you won't allow her to come down is beyond me."

"She's a dog, Aunt," he gritted as he guided her away, shooting Clara a troubled look that warned of a later conversation about her unexpected reversal. "She has no place at a London ball."

"She is not just a dog to me, my boy," she said in ringing tones. "And besides, she'd be a good deal better behaved than many of our guests, I'd wager."

Lenora joined Clara as they moved out of earshot. "You truly wish to have the announcement tonight?" she whispered in her ear.

"There's no sense in putting it off," she said with a bright smile. "It will make everyone happy. Especially Phoebe, whose joy is paramount to me."

"And what of your happiness, dear?"

Anger flared deep in her, a spark to dry tinder; when had her happiness ever been a consideration? Since her tragic youthful mistake she had always put her own wants and desires last. And everyone had seemed more than content for her to do so. If her happiness had ever been part of the equation, she would—

What? She blinked, her anger draining from her as quickly as it had come. What would truly make her happy? And it hit her: she had no idea.

She shook her head, nearly blanching. Of course she knew what would make her happy. Making this blasted engagement seem real enough that, when the time came to end it, she would be free of ever having to deal with her great-aunt's matchmaking again. And finding her new place in her family so she might feel like she wasn't a burden to them.

"This will make me happy," she said firmly.

Lenora gave her a cautious look. "Should we wait to talk to Quincy?"

"No. I'm certain he would agree. We'll do it tonight," Clara said, with much more conviction than she felt. And prayed that she wasn't making an enormous mistake.

* * *

If Quincy hadn't promised he would make an appearance at the ball, he would have gladly crawled into bed and pulled the covers over his head.

He put the finishing touches to his cravat, trying and failing to rein in the hopelessness that threatened to engulf him. Mr. Richmond's letter informing him that the papers from the Lancashire house had arrived had seemed a beacon of hope. But in the last hours Quincy had come to the realization that he'd been fooling himself. If anything, the documents had only made his situation more dire. Reigate Manor was fairly rotting from negligence, the grounds in no better shape. Added to that the repairs demanded in the village, a decade and a half of inattention leaving the people desperate, and a need for expediency had been added to the whole mess. He could not let the tenants hurt any longer than necessary. And so it seemed there was no more hope to be had.

But now wasn't the time. He had a ball to attend, and people to charm. And a fiancée to see to. He did not have time for self-pity.

Clara's face swam in his thoughts, and for a moment he forgot his troubles. These past days, as he'd waited with increasing anxiety for word from Lancashire, she had been the brightest spot. And his suspicions that there was more to her than he'd first assumed were proven right with each stroll, each conversation.

He peered at himself in the glass, making one final adjustment to his cravat before hurrying from the room, suddenly anxious to get to her. How was she handling this evening? Was she enjoying herself? Was she so fixated on her sister that she forgot to eat?

Then and there he determined to focus on Clara tonight. Not only would she have someone looking out for her—not a common occurrence, as he'd seen firsthand—but it would take his mind from his own troubles as well. And if there was anything he needed, it was to pretend for a few blissful hours that he was still the same carefree fellow he had always been, before the noose that was the dukedom had been placed around his neck.

The sounds of revelry grew in volume as he reached the stairs, proof that Lady Tesh's wishes on this being the crush of the season had come to fruition. He hurried around a group of stragglers loitering in the front hall, hardly noticing as they fell silent and stared as he passed, his focus on the hall clock.

Damnation, was he truly that tardy? Not a one of Peter and his family would reprimand him for the lateness of the hour—well, save for Lady Tesh, who would be only too happy to rake him over the coals. No, his guilt was self-inflicted. These people were more family to him than his own had ever been. He should have been here for them, to celebrate Phoebe and her good fortune, to raise a glass with the others on this momentous occasion.

To lend an arm for Clara to lean on.

It did not matter that they were not engaged in truth. He cared for her. *As friends*, he reminded himself sternly. But all the more reason to help her where he could.

The noise grew louder, conversation and laughter and music all coalescing into a nearly unintelligible roar. It should have perhaps warned him of what he was to find at the end of his journey. Just then, however, he ducked around a group of ladies conversing near the doors to the ballroom. They fell silent as well, their eyes widening when they saw him before they began a mad whispering.

A sliver of unease dug its way under his skin as he entered the ballroom. That unease transformed into shock as he caught sight of the sea of humanity before him.

Which made it that much worse when the butler, having spied him, announced in sonorous tones, "His Grace, the Duke of Reigate."

Well, hell.

The hush that momentarily fell over the room suddenly exploded in a din of voices even louder than before. So much for making a quiet, unobtrusive entrance. How had he forgotten just how title-hungry the *ton* was? That the appearance of a new duke in London was like waving a red cape before a bull?

And he couldn't blame them one bit. A long-lost heir, returning from America to find himself a duke? It was a story straight from a novel, too sensational to be real. His lips twisted. This was his life now. As much as he wished it otherwise.

Plastering a carefree smile on his face, he sauntered down the stairs and into the throng.

And was immediately set upon by a veritable tidal wave of well-wishers.

Though *well-wishers* was a generous term. They smiled and shook his hand heartily, claiming whatever tenuous connection to his father or his brothers or, worse, his mother that they could manage to concoct as an excuse for ignoring the rules of polite society in not waiting for a proper introduction, the calculation in their eyes unnerving.

But Quincy, while completely unprepared for such a barrage—though why he had been foolish enough to think his first entrance into London society might go unremarked upon was beyond him—was not without talents. He grinned and shook hands heartily and winked at the ladies, charming his way across the ballroom.

Even so, he could only be grateful when Clara came charging through the crowd, his knight in shining silk, wielding a fan instead of a sword.

"Your Grace, my cousin requires your assistance," she said, tucking her hand in the crook of his arm. She smiled at Lady Fulton and her two eager daughters, gave pretty excuses to Lord Kendrick and Lord Greeveson, complimented Lady Bulville on her turban, and deftly extricated Quincy from the small crowd that had closed in around him.

He exhaled for the first time in what felt hours, letting loose a small chuckle. "Well, you've gone and saved me again, Clara. Truly, I have a running debt with you that I'll be hard-pressed to pay off."

"You may not be thanking me in a moment," she muttered, sidestepping a group of elderly ladies that would try to intercept them. "But we have to do this before I lose my nerve completely."

He blinked, taking in for the first time the seriousness of her face. Before he could question her on it, however, Lady Tesh called to them, her strident voice carrying through the crowd, seeming to push a clear path through sheer intent alone. She waved her cane, and the few people who had not heeded her unspoken wishes to get out of the way scuttled aside with alacrity. Quincy, bemused and not a little apprehensive, rather thought that if she donned a long white beard she would make a fine Moses.

"It's about time, my boy," she snapped as Quincy and Clara approached.

If he hadn't already adored her, that short, clipped sentence would have earned her his eternal devotion. After the past minutes of fawning flattery, all of which had made him feel akin to a damp rag wrung out to dry, her insistence in seeing him as nothing more than *Quincy* was like a balm to his soul.

"Missed me, did you?" he murmured, kissing her lined cheek. "Well, I have missed you, too."

"Flatterer," she said, though the faint flush of pleasure on her face softened the arch tone considerably. "But we've delayed long enough." And with that she peered up toward the orchestra gallery, giving a regal nod.

"You didn't have to wait on announcing Phoebe and Oswin for me," he said.

"Oh, we didn't."

Quincy, more confused than ever, waited for her to elaborate. But the dowager viscountess was apparently done with him, for she turned to Lenora and Margery and fell into heated conversation. "Clara," he said, his apprehension returning, "what is going on?"

But she was prevented from answering him as Phoebe, her face alight, approached and linked her arm through Clara's free one.

"I thought my joy could not be greater," she said through a throat that sounded suspiciously thick with tears. "But this has increased my happiness tenfold."

What the devil was going on? He looked once more to Clara, but the worry in her eyes only confused him more. The rest of her family was not a bit of help, either. Margery smiled while dabbing at her eyes with a handkerchief, Lenora chewed on her lip in a blatant sign of anxiety, and Lady Tesh looked as sly as a fox about to raid a chicken coop.

Just then the orchestra, which had been playing a lively cotillion, fell silent. And suddenly Peter was on the balcony, calling for everyone's attention.

"As you know," he said, his voice strong, silencing the few guests still talking, "we are here to celebrate the good fortune of my cousin Lady Phoebe Ashford and her intended, Lord Oswin. What you may not know is that our family has been doubly blessed, in the engagement of Lady Phoebe's sister, Lady Clara Ashford, to my friend the Duke of Reigate."

The room, already quiet for Peter's announcement, went silent as a tomb. One young woman stomped her dainty slippered foot and gave a frustrated growl.

"Oh," Quincy managed. Clara's hand, still tucked in his, tightened.

Peter looked down at Quincy and Clara, his features fierce, belying his cheerful announcement. "And so," he said, his displeasure palpable, "please raise your glass in toasting the happy couple. May they know years of joy."

A glass was pressed into his hand as the room erupted in cheers. He looked down at Clara. But the worry was gone from her face, a beaming smile in its place.

"Clara?"

She looked up at him, and the breath was knocked from his body. Damnation she was beautiful. For a shining moment he believed this was real, that she was his. The yearning that reared up in him at the very idea had him nearly staggering back in shock.

"Smile," she whispered. "You have to look happy."

He started. Of course this was all a ploy. A necessary subterfuge. He shook off the longing that she might care for him as more than her cousin's friend. What the devil was wrong with him?

Gifting the room with a dazzling smile, he raised his glass to Clara before downing the lot, hardly registering the light, sweet tickle of the champagne. The cheers grew louder as the orchestra started up a lively waltz. Without a word, he handed off his glass and offered Clara his arm.

"I'm assuming you have a perfectly logical explanation for this," he said under his breath as he guided her to the floor.

"Aunt Olivia," was all she said.

"Of course."

Chapter 9

I take it," he said, swinging her into a turn, blessedly distracting Clara from how lovely it felt to be held in his arms, "that your great-aunt used her considerable powers of persuasion to finally get her way?"

"Partly." At his raised brow her cheeks heated. There was no way she would tell him it had also been a way to prove to herself she wasn't falling for him. "And I thought it would hold more weight if our engagement went public."

"You're right, of course. However," he continued, the only indication that he was annoyed being the charged tone of his voice, "perhaps next time tell me what you're planning ahead of time? Or leave a note for me so I don't stumble in unawares?"

"I would have," she gritted, the sting of his censure added to the strain of the past hours finally snapping her patience, "if you had been here for me to tell."

The floor was beginning to fill. He maneuvered them past a young couple staring at them with avid interest, sidestepped another that seemed intent on catching Quincy's eye. "It was not by choice," he growled through a smile that was quickly transforming into a mere baring of teeth. "Though the next time I'm in the process of learning the dukedom is entirely bankrupt I'll keep that in mind."

Clara nearly stumbled, her annoyance gone in an instant. It was only his steady hand that kept her on her feet. "Bankrupt? Was the news from your solicitor so dire as that?"

"I shouldn't have mentioned it," he muttered, regret replacing the simmering anger in his eyes, "especially now. You have your own concerns; you've no need to worry about mine as well."

"As if I would let you get away with such a flimsy excuse," she declared, and was rewarded with his strained chuckle.

But the dance floor was no place for a serious conversation. She caught sight of the garden doors over his shoulder, left ajar to let in the cool night air. *Well*, she thought with a mental shrug, *in for a penny, in for a pound*.

"Guide us to that side of the room, will you?"

Quincy gave her a curious look but did as he was bid, expertly weaving them through the thickening crowd of dancers. Once they reached the edge of the dance floor she broke from his embrace, taking hold of his hand and pulling him out the doors into the night beyond.

The balcony was blessedly empty, any guests who had taken advantage of the cool night air having been lured back to the ballroom by Peter's announcement. There was not a single person to act as witness as she dragged Quincy down the stone steps to the garden beyond.

Between the bright moon and the lantern light it was a simple thing to locate the small alcove nestled between towering box hedges. Secluded and quiet as it was, with its small stone seat, it was yet another place in the garden she had escaped to in her early days in London. She gave a small sigh of relief when they were safely inside.

"Now we may talk freely," she said as she spun to face Quincy.

Only she hadn't realized how close he was to her. Or how intimate the darkness would be. The sounds from the ballroom were hushed behind the dense hedge, cool blue moonlight barely reaching to where they stood. Everything was leached of color, shadows surrounding them, closing them in. Yet the night had never been more alive. Her heart pounded out a desperate rhythm in her chest, the sound of it drowned out only by the harsh rasp of their combined breaths. Her overly sensitive skin reacted to every brush of the faint breeze, to every wave of heat emanating from him. The soap-and-sandalwood scent of him enveloped her, combining with the rich earth and foliage, and the faint scent of roses. It was a heady perfume that had her mind swimming. She swayed.

His hands were suddenly at her waist. She gasped softly, planting her palms on the broad expanse of his chest, an attempt to steady her wildly spinning head. But nothing would help with that; she was quite lost in that regard.

The heat of his skin seeped into her gloved fingers through his tailored coat and waistcoat and fine linen shirt, the pounding of his heart making her palms tingle. Her gaze, which had been centered on the strong column of his throat, tripped up over his square chin, over the generous curve of his lips and his aquiline nose to find his eyes. They glittered down at her, seeming to hold all the brightness of the stars, all the brilliance of the moon.

"Oh," she breathed.

He cleared his throat, tried to speak, cleared his

throat again. "Why are we out here?" he asked, his voice hoarse. His breath, warm and still sweet from the champagne he had drunk, further scrambled her already addled thoughts.

"I...I don't recall," she managed.

He let loose a small, breathless laugh. "Me neither."

She swallowed hard. "Mayhap we'd best return."

"Mayhap," he whispered. Yet his fingers tightened on her waist, drawing her closer until her breasts brushed his chest.

Desire, stronger than any she had ever felt, shot through her, pooling between her thighs. It left her shaken. She sucked in a sharp breath, hoping the cool night air would help to free her from the spell of him. But it only managed to make the scent of him more potent. Her fingers curled around his lapels, tethering her to him as surely as any chain.

Suddenly his eyes, which had grown heavy-lidded and hot in the shadows, cleared, his gaze sharpening. A low curse escaped his lips. She blinked, cheeks heating, and made to pull away.

When she heard the voices, coming closer, her eyes widened and her grip on him tightened again. She looked up into his face, saw the same panic there that was coursing through her. Being found together would be understood; their engagement had just been announced, after all. The rules were relaxed for betrothed couples, allowing them much more freedom to enjoy one another's company.

But they were planning to end their engagement. And being seen giving her favors to Quincy would only make the scandal when they broke things off so much worse.

The couple—for indeed it was a man and woman, talking in hushed voices—came even closer. Clara could hear their steps on the gravel path, a small giggle, a low rumble of male voice. She cast her eyes about their small space, looking for any way to disguise themselves. But save for the stone bench, hardly large enough for one person to sit upon, much less two people to hide under, they would be quite exposed when the couple passed by.

She looked up at Quincy and saw intense determination fill his face. Before she could make sense of it, he pivoted their bodies so his back was to the path. When it became apparent that even that could not completely conceal her identity, he cradled her face in his large hands and lowered his head to hers.

The moment his lips touched hers the world exploded in color and sensation. Molten fire seared her from the inside out, burning her defenses to ash, releasing the passions and desires she had so carefully hidden away. She gasped, her fingers finding his broad shoulders, and she held on tight, as if he could save her from the flames that licked at her. When all along he had been the one lighting the spark.

He stilled, his shock palpable. Embarrassment, immediate and staggering in its intensity, tore through her. Of course he would be taken aback by her reaction. This was an attempt to escape from detection, camouflaging them as just another amorous couple hiding in the bushes. It was in no way due to any desire he felt for her. She made to pull away, desperate to escape.

His low groan stopped her. And then his mouth opened over hers, the kiss deepening, and she was lost.

Ah, God, how good it felt to be held. Even as the thought flitted through her mind, she knew it was not just a need to be held that had her reacting thus. No, it was because Quincy was the one holding her. His arms stole around her, dragging her flush to the hard planes of his body. She arched up into him, the need in her so great she thought she'd weep from it. Gone was the fear and pain and heartache of the past decade and a half. She felt reborn, a phoenix rising from the destruction.

His tongue pressed against the barrier of her lips, a plea that was incredibly gentle for all the strength and barely leashed power apparent in every inch of his body. She opened to him readily, shuddering as his tongue touched her own. He growled into her mouth, the vibration of it rippling through every nerve in her body. Their tongues clashed, his hands splaying across her back, moving down to cup her bottom, pressing her up into his hardness.

"Oops! Someone has beaten us to this alcove, my sweet."

The strange voice, jarring and much too close, was like a bucket of ice water, cooling Clara's raging passions in a moment. She stilled, every muscle in her body going rigid as the sounds of giggling and footsteps receded.

Quincy, too, stilled beneath her hands. Yet neither of them pulled away. She wasn't certain what kept Quincy's arm tight about her. For Clara, it was mortification, plain and simple. She could not bear to look up into his face, to see the pity that surely must be filling it. What else would he be thinking, after her little performance? The passion-starved spinster, clinging to him like a limpet, so eager for any bit of physical affection that she had lost all control.

He was the first to move. No wonder; if she could have buried her face in his chest for the rest of eternity to keep him from seeing her embarrassment, she would have done so, and gladly. Clearing his throat, he said, "Well, that worked beautifully, didn't it?"

She couldn't even manage a nod in response, closing her eyes tight. How sad he must think her.

Again he cleared his throat. "I suppose we should get back to the ball."

She latched onto his suggestion; that's what she needed now, to surround herself with people, where it would be easier to don her calm mask again. Where she could pretend, at least for a few hours, that she hadn't forgotten everything she had worked toward since that youthful indiscretion that had cost her everything. "Yes, let's," she said with a false brightness that sounded brittle even to her own ears. Wincing, she pushed past him and marched from the alcove, walking as quickly as she was able to back to the house.

A bit of normalcy was needed. He could not see how he had affected her. Which shouldn't be difficult to accomplish, considering her particular talent for acting as if nothing was amiss. "Goodness, that was close," she said in a cheerful tone, as if they had just experienced some small mishap.

His steps, which sounded behind her, faltered for a moment before starting up again. "Yes, it was."

"I do hope my family hasn't missed us. Of course, now that our engagement has been announced it will be expected that you dance with Phoebe. As a show of solidarity with the family. I do hope her dance card is not yet filled. She has always been popular, but tonight she is more so." She gave a small laugh as she hurried up the steps to the balcony. "Though that should not be a surprise, seeing as it is her engagement ball."

Quincy grabbed her hand, stopping her. "Clara," he said, his voice achingly gentle.

She turned to face him, keeping her eyes on his cravat.

The small emerald nestled in its snowy depths winked in the light from the chandeliers that spilled across the stone balcony, and she focused on it with all her remaining willpower.

His thumb, moving in comforting circles over her knuckles, firmly dismantled what little pride she had left. Exhaustion filled her. She had remained strong for so long, pretending everything was well. Strange, then, that this gentle, caring gesture should be the thing that finally tore free the mask of a decade and a half.

But no, it was more than just this tenderness that had done it. She had been destroyed the moment his lips had touched hers. Forgotten were those reasons she had denied her passionate heart in the first place—all the kisses she had welcomed, the caresses that had made her body come alive, only to leave betrayal and heartache and loss in their wake.

Had she been fooling herself all this time? She'd thought she'd become strong over the years, that she could withstand any temptation. But one kiss from Quincy and she was lost.

"Clara," he said again, "I'm sorry—"

She closed her eyes. "Don't," she managed, all bravado gone. She had been a fool to think she could escape the embarrassment of such a scene. "Can we please not talk about it?"

A horrible silence. And then, "Very well."

She nodded. "Thank you."

"For now," he said when she would have turned away, his hold tightening on her hand, keeping her in place.

She finally met his eyes, frustration at his stubbornness beginning to rear its head. "For now?" she repeated, incredulous.

He shrugged. "I won't pretend it didn't happen, Clara."

"Why?" The word came out as an agonized cry that startled her for its intensity. Flushing, she looked around the balcony. It was not empty now, a few couples having abandoned the revelry within for a moment's respite. Yet even across the stone flags Clara could see their surreptitious glances, their interest palpable.

She stepped closer to Quincy to better keep their conversation quiet. A mistake. His cologne washed over her once more, and she was overcome by memories of being in his arms, of his mouth on hers.

She shook her head, forcibly dispelling the potent reminder, and glared at him. "It was a mistake. Why can't we just forget it?"

"Because I don't wish to."

Clara sucked in a breath at that simple, devastating statement. He met her gaze unflinchingly, his dark eyes glittering.

Before she could demand that he explain himself, he added, "We should get back to the ball. I had other plans for later this evening, but now...Anyway, we'd best see about securing your sister's hand for a set."

The change in subject was so swift it took Clara some seconds to understand that, at least for the moment, they were done discussing their kiss. She would have to be content with that.

Schooling her features into politeness, she meant to nod and head for the ballroom with all haste. Anything to escape from the disturbing intimacy of the balcony.

But her mouth had other ideas. "Where had you planned to go off to?"

The question hung in the air, stalling their reentrance into the crowded ballroom. Proof that, though she knew better, she was not quite ready to relinquish him to the mass of people within.

Thankfully he saw nothing odd in it. "There's a memento of my father's I had wanted—no, needed—to fetch from my mother's house. Though now that I won't require use of it, I suppose there's little sense in it." He let loose a bitter laugh.

Clara, disturbed by the sudden hopelessness that seemed to come over him, drew even closer to him despite knowing better. Much better. "What is it you wanted to retrieve?"

He shifted his gaze back to her. And she was struck mute by the quiet despair there.

"My father's map book. I was forced to leave it behind when I left England as a boy. I'd hoped to retrieve it before beginning my travels. But as it seems I'll be remaining in England for a good long while it's silly to go hying off in the middle of what is essentially our engagement ball to get it."

She recalled then the conversation they'd begun on the dance floor, his admission that the dukedom was bankrupt.

Which, if true, would make it doubly important that he lay claim to something so very dear to him. She laid a comforting hand on his sleeve. "You must get your father's book."

"I will. Eventually."

"No, now," she pressed. "You cannot allow something so important to you to remain under your mother's roof any longer. And besides," she continued when he gave her a dubious look that nevertheless revealed the pain her statement caused, "you don't know that you'll never see those places. You mustn't give up hope."

He gave her a small smile full of longing that quickly disappeared as the sound of laughter from within the ballroom reached them. "No, I couldn't. It would be unforgivably selfish of me to leave you to that crowd. Especially with the announcement of our engagement turning them positively manic."

"I assure you," she said with an arch look, "I can handle myself, sir."

"Oh, I've no doubt you can."

The admiring glimmer in his eyes, the intimate murmur of his voice, turned her bones to liquid. And her brain as well, if the next words that came out of her mouth were any indication.

"Take me with you."

His eyes flared wide. "What was that?"

It was the perfect opening to recall the words. It was a mad scheme; she knew it the moment the words left her mouth. To sneak off from the ball, to travel alone with him in a carriage after dark? Especially after the kiss they'd shared...

Absolute insanity.

And yet the very idea of him leaving without her had every fiber of her being crying out in protest.

Surely it was not the thought of being without his company that had her reacting so. It must be the realization that, after the announcement, she would quickly be set upon by everyone present. Those people would no doubt have questions regarding her speedy engagement, how it had come about, when they would marry. And in that moment she could not stomach it in the least.

Yes, that was most assuredly the reason.

Having convinced herself, she said, her voice firm, "Take me with you."

For a split second his eyelids grew heavy, a spark of something lighting the depths of his gaze. All too soon, however, it was gone, and he shook his head, a denial forming on his lips.

Determined to head off his refusal, she added, "You would not want to leave me to deal with the fallout from our engagement alone, would you?"

It was manipulation at its very core. Instead of growing annoyed with her, however, he laughed. "Clara, I didn't know you had it in you to be quite so openly devious."

He was going to let her accompany him. He did not say it, of course, but it was there in every amused line of his face.

Relief washed over her. Which was silly, really; it was not as if she had anything riding on this trip to his mother's home. Yet she couldn't help the grin that spread over her face. Casting a glance around the balcony, finding that the other couples had left and they were blessedly alone, she grabbed Quincy's hand. "Come along then," she said, pulling him back down the stone steps and into the dark garden toward the mews. And as his quiet laughter trailed them like the wake behind a ship she tried—and failed—not to focus on how happy that sound made her.

Chapter 10

$\mathcal{H}$e shouldn't have brought Clara with him, Quincy thought some time later as he stared up at the grand façade of his family's Berkeley Square townhouse. He'd had the thought several times during the quick drive here. The carriage interior had been too dark, too close, the tension between them a palpable thing despite the laughter that had started them off on this adventure. Yet how could he leave her behind when she had turned those beautiful eyes on him and smiled?

Even now the remembrance of her lips lifted in that sly smile as she turned his decision on its head took his breath away. *It will be easier to capitulate*, he'd thought as they'd hurried to the mews, her fingers wrapped tight around his, no doubt to keep him from making a run for it. As if he would have been able to.

He knew deep down this was not easier, not one bit. Had he been alone he could have walked with greater speed than it had taken to secure a carriage, have the horses harnessed, and be driven through the congested streets around Dane House. No, the truth of the matter was, now that he'd held her in his arms, he was loath to let her out of his sight.

It was a mad notion. This was a fake engagement,

not the beginning of a new life together. They would be parting soon enough.

Yet the thought of walking away from her had every inch of his body rebelling.

"Are you all right?"

Her soft voice echoed in the close confines of the carriage, bringing him back to the problem at hand. He would focus on this most pressing issue now and revisit his concerns over his feelings for his faux-fiancée later. When he was not in danger of dragging her back in his arms and finishing what he'd accidentally begun in the gardens.

"Never better," he declared with much more confidence than he felt. "Let's go."

He threw open the carriage door, vaulting to the pavement before turning to hand Clara down. Soon they were before the grand doors.

Byerly answered their knock. His eyes widened as he bowed deeply. "Your Grace, we did not expect you."

"Is my mother at home?" he asked as he strode into the front hall, fighting for a tone of confidence when in reality he wanted to vomit.

"No, Your Grace. She is out for the evening."

The surge of relief he felt at that bit of news infuriated him. He should not still be so affected by her. But he would count his blessings where he could. Goodness knew there were too few of them.

"I would appreciate it if Lady Clara and myself could have access to the study," he said.

The butler's eyes widened. "But of course, Your Grace. It is your house, after all."

His breath left him in a rush. Yes, it was. As he'd known from poring over the papers relating to every bit of property the Dukes of Reigate had bought and sold over the past several generations.

Yet it had not sunk in until now, standing in the front hall of this house he had grown up in. He had always seen the house as his father's, but through a horrible quirk of fate it now belonged to him.

Clara touched him lightly on the arm. "Quincy?"

He blinked, looking down at her. Her face was drawn into tense lines, her gloved hand in a tight fist where it held the rough shawl she had borrowed from a groom close about her shoulders. "Sorry," he muttered. With a curt nod for Byerly, he strode off in the direction of the study.

Their footsteps echoed back to them as they hurried through the house. It was only then he saw what he hadn't during his last visit here: the house was too empty. It wasn't the lack of people he found disconcerting, it was the lack of *things*. As if each room they passed contained great gaping voids. In one room, the thick wool rug that had graced the floor was conspicuously absent. In another, most of the heavily carved Tudor-era furniture that had held a place of pride was missing. There were pale spots on walls where landscapes had hung, empty stands where vases had been displayed.

Fury rose up, nearly choking him. Damn his brothers. Nothing had been sacred to them, it seemed. No doubt they would have sold the house from under their mother had it not been entailed.

A sudden realization hit him, making his steps falter on the bare wood floor: if all of this was gone, wasn't it possible that his father's heavy wooden desk, beautifully carved, a work of art, was gone, too?

He broke off at a run, his steps echoing through the

hall, his pumps skidding on the floor as he reached the study door.

It was cold here, only pale moonlight reaching into the musty, unused space. Yet the great hulking desk was there, just as it had always been.

The relief in Quincy was so great he collapsed back against the wall. "Thank God," he whispered.

Clara came hurrying up. "Quincy?" she asked breathlessly. "Are you all right?"

"Yes," he croaked. Clearing his throat, he tried again. "Yes, I'm well. Sorry about that."

"You have nothing to apologize for," she said, her voice soft. "This cannot be easy."

"No," he agreed, looking down into her concerned eyes. Gratitude surged in him. "I'm glad you're here." It surprised him just how much he meant it.

A small smile lit her shadowed face. "As am I."

Just as in the gardens when he'd made the colossal mistake of embracing her in order to protect her identity, he longed desperately to kiss her. Damnation, but she had felt like heaven. He wanted nothing more than to claim her lips again, to feel once more her surprisingly passionate response.

But now was not the time or place. Not that there would ever be a time or place for such a thing. Squaring his shoulders, he walked with purpose to the desk. Memories assailed him the closer he got, and he saw in a brilliant flash his father's smiling face as he beckoned Quincy forward. Then he blinked and it was gone, replaced with the sad reality of this cold room devoid of all heart.

Tears burned the backs of his eyes. Rounding the desk, he quickly lit the lamp on the desk's cluttered surface.

The warm light illuminated what had only been hinted at in the shadows.

A thick coat of dust covered the once gleaming surface of the grand desk, all manner of papers strewn across its top. One glared up at him from the pile, the date scrawled across the foolscap proving it had been several years since this desk had been made use of. The globe that used to sit in the corner that Quincy and his father had pored over during many happy afternoons was gone, as were the majority of the books that had graced the shelves, ones that he and his father had made use of so frequently, they had kept them in the study for easy reach.

Bile rose up in him at this further proof of his brothers' perfidy. But he would not mourn those losses; what was the point? They were just things, and their absence could not take away the memories.

The map book, on the other hand . . .

Grabbing the lamp, suddenly desperate to get his hands on the thing, he pushed the chair back and dropped to his knees. He paused only a moment, his hand on the handle of the deep bottom drawer, before yanking it open. A clutter of papers filled it to the brim. He dug them out and tossed them aside. Finally his fingers reached the bottom, found the small latch that released the hidden door.

It popped up with a faint creak. Holding his breath, Quincy lifted the lamp and peered inside.

The years fell away in an instant. Just as it had been that day fourteen years before, the small calf-bound map book was lying within, undisturbed in its nest of papers.

With shaking fingers he took it up. The surface was smooth and worn, the pages dog-eared, stained, and torn in places.

It was beautiful.

"Is that it?"

Clara had dropped down to the floor across from him, the delicate silk folds of her ball gown billowing about her like a cloud, the dark wool cloak a stark contrast where it lay against the finer fabric. But it was her face he could not tear his gaze from. Her eyes glowed in the candlelight and were glued to the book, as if there were something sacred about it.

His heart warmed that she could so fully understand the importance of such a simple, worn thing to him.

"Yes."

"I'm glad." She smiled, her relief for him palpable. It shone brighter than the candle's flame, that smile, until he found an answering one spreading across his own face. It was something he never thought to do in this house again.

"We should go," he murmured, rising to his feet, helping her up. "With luck we will not have been missed yet. And Peter won't have cause to call me out on the morrow."

Her laugh, light and low, trailed across his skin. As he bent to secure the door back in the bottom of the drawer, Clara took up the candle, and the flickering candlelight washed over the hidden space, bathing it in a golden glow.

Frowning, he froze. His father had always kept childhood drawings and small notes and mementos in the compartment—things the man had held precious. They were all still there, as they'd always been.

But an odd bundle lay within as well, snagging at his attention.

Without a word he reached inside, taking it up. Then, sweeping an arm out, he scattered the teetering piles of correspondence and merchant notes from the desk in a billow of dust and laid his father's bundle on the dull surface. There was no doubt in Quincy's mind that it had been put there by his father before his death; the secret chamber had appeared just as it had the day Quincy left for America, undisturbed and undiscovered all this time.

Why, then, could he not remember just what this packet was?

"Quincy, what is it?"

"I'm not certain," he muttered. He worked the twine loose, unwrapped the brown paper packaging, and began rifling through the items within: a dance card, a lock of jet-black hair encased in a brooch, a small collection of letters tied up tight with string. And…

"A deed," he breathed.

He raised the expensive vellum with shaking hands, bringing it closer to his face in an attempt to read the formal words. As if heeding his call Clara moved closer, positioning the flame so it illuminated the document. He could not even muster a smile for her in thanks, so desperate was he to read the contents.

Some minutes later, the air thick with tension and dawning excitement, he raised his head and looked to Clara. Her lovely face was drawn, worry in every line.

"What is it, Quincy?"

He grinned, his entire body thrumming with excitement. "This might be the thing I need to save the dukedom."

Chapter 11

My dearest Clara (for that is how a man should address his fiancée),

I hope you've arrived safe on the Isle. London is frightfully dull without you lot here. How I managed the last year without Peter's glowers and Lady Tesh's haranguing I'll never know. Speaking of Lady Tesh, has she forgiven me for remaining behind? I'll make it up to her and am prepared to unleash my full arsenal of charm to do it. Anything to prevent that deadly cane of hers from finding my nose... or any other part of my person, for that matter.

Mr. Richmond is quite certain after a cursory examination of the deed that it is genuine. And I have learned something incredible about the property that will stun you speechless. But as I'm bursting to write it down, and have determined I would rather see your face when you learn of it, I had better sign off now.

Yrs,
Quincy

My dear husband-to-be (for two can play at that game),

Why you have insisted on keeping the identity of the property a secret I don't understand. I, of course, was willing to overlook such a thing when you feared that the document might be false. But now I do think it prudent that you tell me everything you can. It's what a proper fiancé would do, after all.

The trip to Synne was long and tedious but uneventful. I had thought to perhaps rest, seeing as the engagement ball was firmly behind us and I could not very well run to the milliner's to discuss fabrics. Aunt Olivia, of course, had other plans. As I ruined my best traveling gown with ink while trying to copy down her lengthy lists in a moving carriage, I'm not inclined to look favorably on the experience.

~~I miss you.~~ Lady Tesh misses you terribly; we're not amusing enough for her, it seems. And so you have earned your forgiveness already.

Until later,
Clara

My heart's desire (goodness, I should hire myself out for these things),

If you think to guilt me into revealing details of the property you are quite deluded; guilt washes off

my back like the proverbial water off a duck. Ask
Peter if you don't believe me; goodness knows I
let him take the blame for many a boyhood prank,
and with absolute glee. You must wait along with
everyone else.

With luck I won't be long in London. ~~I cannot~~
~~wait to see you.~~ *I was of the opinion that Dane*
House was a monstrous place but did not fully
realize it until you left. The remaining staff, I fear,
grow tired of my constant need to drag them into
conversation. I've even taken to talking to the stat-
uary. And so I give you fair warning that your ears
will all suffer once I reach Danesford and can talk
to my heart's content.

Faithfully Yrs (goodness, even my closing is a thing
of beauty),
Quincy

"Oh, isn't this lovely?" Phoebe lifted a hair comb from
the interior of the delicate wood inlay box before her.
"This color will complement the peach in my wedding
gown beautifully."

Clara lowered Quincy's latest letter, received just that
morning—and already dog-eared—and focused on her
sister. It had been a week since they'd left London for
Synne. A week filled to the brim with travel and wedding
preparations.

A week since Clara had seen Quincy.

In an instant she was awash in memory: his strong
arms about her, his mouth hot and open over hers, the
sweet taste of champagne on his tongue, his hardness
pressing into her belly...

She blinked. Such flashes had not abated over the past sennight. Though she was getting more adept at pushing them aside—at least during her waking hours.

This time apart was what had been needed, she told herself stoutly. Their physical distance from one another, alongside the playful banter of their letters, had surely succeeded in putting their indiscretion in the gardens behind them. She had every hope that, when they met again, they might do so with no more emotion than two good friends. After all, it had been just a kiss. A heated, passionate, all-consuming kiss...She cleared her throat, using the letter as a makeshift fan on her suddenly overheated face. It had been just a kiss all the same. A momentary lapse that would not be repeated.

"I remember Mother wearing this piece," she said, running her fingers over the carved coral cabochons set in delicate gold. "Father gave it to her their very first Christmas. She used to bring it out every Christmas Eve to wear to church."

Phoebe gave a sigh. "I wish I'd known her."

The small hitch in her voice tugged at Clara's heart. Though Clara had done her best to fill the void the loss of their mother had left, she had never been able to patch it completely.

Not that Phoebe was one to complain. Still, during moments like these that emptiness was brought into harsh focus.

Clara placed an arm about her sister's shoulders. "She would have been very proud of you."

Phoebe's eyes shone with unshed tears. "Do you think so?"

"I know so," Clara replied firmly. "And I think you're

quite right on this hair comb. It will go beautifully with your gown." She lowered the lid on their mother's box.

"Which do you think you'll wear for your wedding?"

Clara's breath hitched in her chest. "Oh, I hardly know," she said brightly. "Quincy and I won't marry for some time. He has so much to settle with the dukedom." She paused, tension threading through her though she tried to keep her tone flippant. "As a matter of fact, I thought I might join you after your wedding trip. You'll be in a new place, surrounded by strangers. It might prove helpful to have an ally against Lord and Lady Crabtree."

Phoebe laughed. "Oh, I'm not worried a bit about them. Besides, you'll be preparing for your own life. You won't have time for such things."

"But mayhap—"

"Clara," Phoebe cut in softly, placing a gentle hand on her arm, "I know you still worry about me. But I'm looking forward to the challenge of it, truly. And I could not be happier that you'll be able to finally focus on yourself. Now then," she continued, the subject obviously at an end, "I insist you pick a piece. I'll be with Oswin at Hedley by the time you begin planning and will miss much of it."

Stifling a sigh, Clara smiled as if she could think of nothing she would like more and reopened the box.

Thus far every one of her attempts to discover where she might be needed after Phoebe's wedding had been firmly rebuffed. And no wonder, seeing as everyone believed she would be happily married soon. Though her fake engagement was proving to be a stumbling block in this particular venture, she could only be happy it had proven successful in other matters, namely in keeping Aunt Olivia content enough to leave her be . . . for the most part.

She would take her great-aunt's grumbling about double weddings over men being thrown at her head any day.

She moved aside a brooch and froze. Nestled in the velvet interior was a ring painfully beloved to her. The turquoise forget-me-not was as vibrant as ever, the small diamond at its center sparkling brilliantly, the two gold hands lovingly holding the gem flower rubbed to a sheen for all her mother had worn the piece. Until the swelling in her hands from her last illness had forced her to remove it forever.

She had slipped it on Clara's finger once, her eyes shining bright with happiness. "I wore this the night of my come out, the night your father fell in love with me," she'd said with a soft smile. "My dream, my darling Clara, is for you to wear this to your own debut, and to find a love as wonderful as the one I've been blessed to share with your father."

Blinking back tears—that dream had never come to pass, and never would—she pulled the ring from its bed.

"Oh, Clara, how lovely. Try it on."

Before Clara could react, her sister plucked the ring from her palm and slipped it on her finger. It fit perfectly, as if it had been patiently waiting for her to grow into it all these years. Tears burned her eyes, though happy memories had supplanted much of the sadness she expected to feel.

"Oh, Clara, it's like it was made for you." Phoebe sighed, resting her head on Clara's shoulder as she admired the ring. "It's hard to believe we'll soon both leave this place. I'll miss Danesford."

"As will I," Clara murmured, trying and failing to banish the feeling of hopelessness that coursed through her as she removed the ring and placed it back in the box. She loved Danesford so very much. Yet she also knew she would never leave this house. She would grow old here while Peter and Lenora raised their family. And later, when their children were grown, she would watch them go off to live their own lives.

She started at the unexpected grief. Wasn't that exactly what she had wished for, to stay here with her family, to remain useful to them?

Why, then, did that dream suddenly sit heavy on her?

Blessedly Lenora arrived, breaking her from her melancholy. "Clara dear," she said with a smile, "this came for you from London."

Her heart leapt in her chest as she spied the now-familiar handwriting. In an instant everything else was forgotten as, a smile breaking over her face, she rushed to take the letter from Lenora.

"Thank you so much." She turned to Phoebe to excuse herself, but already her sister was laughing and shooing her out.

"I'll put Mother's box away," she said with a grin. "Go and enjoy your letter."

A quick glance at Lenora's face, still smiling but strained with underlying worry, nearly had Clara halting her exit. But the call of the letter in her hands was too great. She didn't stop until she was safely ensconced in her room. Leaning back against the closed door, she eagerly cracked the seal.

Quincy's handwriting, as bold and exuberant as the man himself, jumped out at her from the page.

My sweet turtledove (and once again my brilliance shows),

Mr. Richmond must be tired of my company, the poor chap, for he has suggested I travel to Synne posthaste, as there's nothing further to be done here in London. In fact, I'm so anxious to get to the Isle that I won't be long past the arrival of this letter. Though this correspondence is scandalously short, and in order to hasten my departure, I wish you a temporary adieu…

Your besotted beau,
Quincy

Her heart pounded in excitement that, by tomorrow, he should be at Danesford. The very thought left her dizzy.

Suddenly she froze, crushing the letter in her grip. What was wrong with her? This was no mere excitement for an acquaintance's arrival. This anticipation was much more potent, affecting her entire being. Especially those secret parts of her that had reawakened with their kiss.

She had been fooling herself in believing she and Quincy could ever be mere friends. Though she had been certain they could put their kiss behind them and act as if it had never occurred, it had, in fact, changed everything.

Was this the reason, then, that the idea of staying on at Danesford felt so wrong now? She knew it was the only path available to her, but the drive to make the best of it was gone. And as anticipation, not concern, continued to sizzle along her veins, she knew: she was in trouble.

* * *

He was in trouble.

Quincy urged on his mount as he left the ferry dock.

His heart beat in rhythm to the horse's hooves on the road, excitement building in him. It wasn't due to the promise of sleeping in a soft bed or seeing his closest friend, though. No, it was the thought of seeing Clara again.

It surprised and troubled him how much he had missed her. How had she gotten under his skin with one kiss? Even as he wondered it, however, he knew it had started before then, with every dinner spent beside her, each walk with her on his arm. She was kind and humorous, smart and quick-witted. There was a depth and passion to her that fascinated him, making him want to uncover what she was hiding from the world. Their kiss had only brought into sharper focus how affected he was. And it hadn't waned in her absence. When he wasn't at his solicitor's office, his days had been spent searching the townhouse for things she might have left behind and waiting impatiently for her letters to arrive.

He wouldn't even think about his nights...

He frowned, shaking his head sharply to dislodge the thought. Was there something more at work here than desire? Was it possible he was beginning to fall for her?

He blanched. He was about to see everything he'd ever wanted realized. The devastating mountain of inheriting a bankrupt dukedom was about to be scaled; with a bit of effort he would see the deeded property quickly sold off, the money used to patch up the dukedom and help the tenants, and he could be on his merry way again. He had no time for falling in love.

Which he most certainly wasn't. He was a passionate fellow, after all. And flighty, and a hopeless romantic as well. He'd been infatuated over the years more times than he could count. And perhaps, in feigning love for Clara, he'd begun to fool himself as well. Were his acting abilities that impressive? Had their playacting gone to his head?

He let loose a strained chuckle, though only the horse was there to hear it. Of course that was it. There was nothing in his relationship with Clara to endanger his plans. No matter that he was attracted to her, that he had kissed her—that he would gladly kiss her again—he was certainly not falling in love with her. He breathed in deep of the warm sea air, welcoming the promise of summer into his lungs, relief filling him—until another equally disturbing question took shape in his mind: while he was certain his heart was safe, had she formed a tendre for him?

No, surely not, he told himself fiercely. Clara was much too smart to fall for a frivolous fellow like him. Yet there was still a hint of unease in his chest when he topped the rise and spied the great manor house down below.

Danesford was like a slumbering giant cradled in the rolling hills of Synne, all red brick and gables and mullioned windows glistening in the sun. He pulled his mount up, taking it in. Peter had told him of the place in his letters, Lenora adding small, fanciful sketches to go along with her husband's sparse prose. Yet nothing had prepared him for the majesty of it all. It was not an ostentatious beast, taking over the countryside. Rather, it had been built with the landscape of the Isle in mind, using the grandeur of the surrounding vistas to enhance its already impressive beauty.

For a blissful moment excitement overrode his worries. Just a few minutes more.

His horse seemed to sense his mood. It tossed its head

in impatience, pawing at the ground. Quincy chuckled, patting its neck. "Looking forward to a stall and a great quantity of oats, are you? Very well, have your head then." And with that he kicked the horse on.

It responded with eagerness, bolting forward, tearing down the grassy hill. They careened down the front drive, stopping before the great double doors. At once a footman rushed out, taking the horse's reins as Quincy dismounted.

"Make sure he's spoiled rotten," he said with a grin. "Goodness knows he deserves it for getting me here so speedily."

As the man led the gelding away, Quincy turned to bound up the front steps—

—and stopped short. Clara stood in the doorway, her eyes wide, her cheeks stained a becoming rose.

"Quincy," she said.

Her soft voice caressing his name sent fire to every inch of his body. "Clara," he said.

And that was all he seemed capable of saying. For a long moment they stood staring at one another. He felt as if he were parched, and the sweetest, most delectable wine was before him.

An imperceptible male voice sounded behind her. She started, her flush deepening and spreading down her neck to the high cobalt bodice of her gown. "Yes, Yargood," she said over her shoulder, "please make certain His Grace's room is ready. And please inform my family that we'll be joining them shortly."

And then her eyes were back on him, sending his thoughts spinning off again. She smiled. "Quincy, please come in."

He took the wide stone stairs two at a time, not

bothering to hide his eagerness. They had parts to play, he told himself. Time to act the besotted fiancé.

He would not worry himself by looking into why it was so damn easy to do.

"Hello, my dear," he said with a grin. "You're looking lovely this afternoon."

And she did, all fresh and blushing, the dark blue of her gown enhancing the rich sable of her hair.

"It's the sea air," she replied with a smile.

"It does do wonders."

"That it does. Why anyone would prefer London is beyond me. But tell me about your journey," she continued as she divested him of his outerwear, placing it on a table by the front door. "You made good time."

It was innocuous conversation, friendly and easy, with no hint of nervousness or shyness. It seemed his concerns were unfounded. Thank goodness. Her reaction to his kiss had been one thing; physical passion did not necessarily indicate a strong regard. But he would not want her hurt by this for anything.

He breathed a silent sigh of relief, purposely ignoring the twinge of regret in his chest.

"I'm sure tomorrow I'll be feeling the effects of being so long in the saddle," he replied with a grin. "But pushing through was worth it. I had forgotten how much I love the Isle. Oh, and to see all of you, of course."

She laughed, leading him through the front hall. "The Isle holds a unique power over the people who visit her. But we were excited yesterday to learn of your arrival. Peter was certain you would wish to visit your property before coming here and would be another fortnight at least. Which, I must say, we're all waiting anxiously to learn of. I'm not the only one who's perturbed by your need for secrecy."

"All in good time," he said with impressive gravity. Inside, however, he was rubbing his hands with glee. He could not wait to see their reaction when he told them.

"Hello, Ashford clan," he announced when they reached the drawing room, speaking over the hum of conversation. The response was immediate and satisfying, the air filled with exclamations and greetings and the thump of Lady Tesh's ever-present—and often dangerous—cane as she demanded his attention.

"I must say, it took you long enough," she bit out as he bent to kiss her cheek. "I'm still put out with you for staying behind in the first place."

"No you're not," he said with a wink and a grin before taking a seat close to Clara. "So tell me, how have the preparations been going for our dear Phoebe's nuptials?"

"Oh, no you don't," the woman in question declared. "You won't distract us so easily."

Margery leaned forward in her seat. "Tell us about the property," she demanded with uncharacteristic forcefulness.

Quincy gave a startled laugh and looked to Peter, who raised a golden eyebrow. "Don't look to me for help. I'm just as curious as they are."

Quincy schooled his features into an innocent expression. "But wouldn't you rather—"

"No!"

He didn't know who had spoken, for their voices all rose up in outrage, blending together in an impatient cacophony. Chuckling, he held his hands up in defense. "Very well. Quiet down and I'll tell you."

At once they fell silent, like obedient schoolchildren. He grinned, his anticipation rising. "Would it surprise you," he asked his captive audience, "to learn that the property in question is...on Synne?"

There was a moment of stunned silence. And then Lady Tesh, the aggravation in her voice plain to hear, said, "Don't fun with us, my boy."

"I swear I'm not. The property my father left for me is on Synne."

"Goodness, what are the chances?" Lenora exclaimed.

"What property?"

Clara's voice held a strange undertone of tension to it. When he looked at her, however, her expression was only mildly curious.

He frowned. Something was off in her eyes. Before he could question her on it, however, Lady Tesh spoke up. "Well, my boy, answer your fiancée. What property?"

Excitement threaded through him once more. "Brace yourselves, for you are looking at the owner of Swallowhill."

Chapter 12

*S*wallowhill.

Clara felt the blood leave her face. No, it couldn't be. Surely she'd misheard.

Deep in her heart, however, she knew she hadn't. Quincy owned Swallowhill.

A memory surfaced, of sharply peaked gables, stone walls reaching for the sky, a dark gray slate roof. All surrounded by a garden that had provided her relief from seemingly unending pain.

But her history with the place went back so much further than that, starting when she was still small, joining her mother on her visits to the young woman who had lived there. Clara couldn't recall much about her, except that she'd been kind, and beautiful, and very, very sad. And in those gardens, most especially in the greenhouse that graced the far end of the property, the two women distracted a rambunctious Clara by letting her run wild and teaching her to find joy in nature.

Those had been happy days. But then the woman had died, and her mother soon after. Clara had forgotten about the house until she'd come across it again during the darkest time of her life. In the overgrown confines of that abandoned place she had found the piece of herself she'd lost with her mother's death, could almost feel her mother's presence in walking the paths and sitting under the soaring glass dome. And for a time, she'd been able to forget her heartbreak. There was no cramped, isolated cottage that hid her away from the rest of the world while everyone believed her to be visiting her old nurse, no memories of promises broken.

No tiny grave without a headstone, looking out over an unforgiving sea.

She hugged her arms to her middle, as if she could hold herself together by will alone. Desperate to distract herself, she forced her attention back to the others.

"Goodness, that's a pretty property," Aunt Olivia said. "And how fortuitous that you should find yourself the owner. Why, it's as if your marriage to Clara had been destined."

The snort that exploded from Peter quickly transformed into a coughing fit at one stern look from his wife. "Sorry," he muttered. "Choked on my tea."

"I had a feeling you'd know of it," Quincy drawled. "Your mind is as sharp as anyone I know."

"It's sharper," she rejoined with a haughtily raised brow.

Margery stirred her tea, frowning. "I know of Swallowhill but have never visited. It's been abandoned since I was a girl, if I recall."

"I can't remember anyone living in it," Phoebe mused. "At least, not as long as I've been alive. Do you recall the history, Aunt Olivia?"

"Certainly," their great-aunt pronounced, as if highly offended anyone had doubted it of her. "There was nothing there but farmland for centuries until a Lord Harris bought the property and had the house built to please his bride. But the man was rubbish with money. Not a decade had passed before he was forced to sell it off. It was quite a scandal at the time, of course, and garnered much attention. Not that I ever engage in gossip," she finished in lofty tones.

This time Peter's snort was much more pronounced, and not at all excused as other than what it was. Lady Tesh glared daggers at him, of which he seemed unaware. All save for the slight quirk of his lips.

"I recall Lord Harris's name on the deed," Quincy mused. "And it's sat empty all this time."

"No, not entirely."

Quincy paused, his hand suspended as he reached for a strawberry. "Not entirely what?"

"Not entirely empty."

"But who could possibly have been living there?"

"There was a young woman who took up residence after the property changed hands," Lady Tesh said, her focus on her biscuit, which she was feeding crumb by crumb to Freya. "She kept to herself—an easy thing, Swallowhill being quite secluded from most of the Isle. Though as I recall, Clara and Phoebe's mother befriended her. Unfortunately, the woman died quite young." She frowned, a bit of biscuit suspended in the air, which Freya was trying valiantly to reach. "What was that girl's name? Wanda? Wisteria?"

"Willa," Clara whispered.

Her face heated as all eyes turned her way. She hadn't meant to say a thing, hoping the subject would eventually drop. But her great-aunt's attempts to remember the woman's name had dislodged the memory, and it had escaped unbidden from her lips.

"What was that?" Aunt Olivia demanded.

Clara cleared her throat. "Willa. Miss Willa Brandon."

Her great-aunt blinked. "Why yes, I do believe you're right. But how in the world did you know that?"

"My mother used to bring me along with her on her visits."

"But I don't understand," Quincy said. "If my father owned the property, what was a Miss Brandon doing there?"

"I'm sure I don't know," Aunt Olivia answered primly.

"Oh, I'm sure you have a theory," Peter drawled.

She gave both Clara and Phoebe pointed looks before glaring at her nephew. "Regardless, it's not for mixed company."

Which meant it was scandalous. Which meant she believed Miss Willa Brandon had been the duke's mistress.

No, that didn't seem right at all. Clara remembered the young woman's stark black wardrobe and constant air of muted grief. She had looked more like a widow than anything else.

"I see," Quincy said, his voice flat.

Without thinking, Clara slipped her hand in his and squeezed. It seemed to snap him out of whatever dark thoughts had taken hold of him. He looked at her with a bright smile.

"But regardless of its history, I'm glad to have it now." He turned to Peter. "I assume you know of a good house agent?" At Peter's scoff he grinned. "Of course you do. Whatever was I thinking?"

"Shall I take you there tomorrow?"

"That would be brilliant. The sooner I can unload the place the sooner I can save the dukedom with the proceeds. Though perhaps I'd best take a look at the property first."

Clara bit her lip as he laughed. There was something

too bright in it. She knew that he had the greatest regard for his father. No doubt the idea of the man possibly having a mistress pained him. She knew if she ever learned the same thing of her own beloved father, it would destroy her.

"Clara, will you join us?"

Quincy's voice in her ear startled her. "Join you?"

He gave her a small, amused smile, making her wonder how long he'd been trying to get her attention. "On our trip to Swallowhill tomorrow. It's been decided that we'll leave immediately after breakfast."

She nearly recoiled. Plastering a smile on her face, she gently extricated her fingers from his and reached for her teacup, praying her hand didn't tremble. "Oh, I don't think so. The wedding preparations—"

"Can wait a few hours while you take some much-needed air," Aunt Olivia cut in, spearing her with a stern glare. "You've done little else over the past sennight. I'm beginning to think there will be nothing within your head at the end of this month other than bits of lace and a few crumbs of cake."

Much of the fault in that lay with Aunt Olivia and her constant nagging, of course. But Clara would never say such a thing aloud.

"You need an outing," her great-aunt continued, a note of finality in her voice. "And this is just the thing."

What else could she do? Heart dropping—she hadn't returned since that dark time—she smiled nonetheless. "Very well."

Relief flashed in Quincy's eyes. Before she could wonder at it, however, Yargood entered.

"His Grace's room is ready."

"Splendid. Thank you, Yargood." Lenora, smiling,

looked at Quincy. "If you're done with your tea, I'll show you the way."

"Nonsense," Aunt Olivia said. "You're needed here. Clara will bring him."

Barring any further discussion, she deftly wielded her cane, and before Clara knew what had happened she found herself with Quincy out in the hall.

He gave her a bemused smile. "Well, that was impressively done."

"She has her talents," Clara replied with a grin that quickly faded as they made their way through the house. She glanced up at Quincy, noting the new lines of strain about his eyes, and her heart ached for him. "I'm certain Miss Brandon couldn't have been his mistress," she murmured low.

He shot her a rueful look. "And here I thought I had hidden my disquiet."

She flushed. "I'm sorry."

"You've no need to apologize. Besides, whatever the truth, it doesn't change who my father was to me. And so it doesn't matter who Miss Brandon was."

Clara bit her lip. No matter his words, there was an undercurrent of strain in his voice that told her it did matter. Quite a bit.

"If you've a wish to know who she was," she ventured quietly, "I'm certain there's someone on the Isle who can answer that for you. There must have been someone working at the house while she was there."

There was a moment of tense silence. She feared she'd overstepped.

When he spoke, his voice was low and threaded through with emotion. "I'll consider it. Thank you."

They reached his room then. But when she might have

brought him inside, she stopped cold. Or rather, hot, for at the sight of the large four-poster bed that dominated the space she couldn't help but think of him amid the sheets. Which led to her body warming as she imagined herself amid those sheets with him . . .

Drawing upon every ounce of willpower she possessed—similar to when he'd arrived and she'd wanted to throw herself into his arms—she smiled brightly. "Here you are then. We'll be sure to have a maid show you the way to the dining room when dinner is ready."

"Thank you, Clara."

She nodded and turned, making her way down the hall. And she did not let down her guard until she had turned the corner and was well out of sight. As she leaned heavily against the wall, exhausted, she wondered how she would be able to get through the next weeks without falling in love with him.

* * *

Clara had not visited Swallowhill in nearly fifteen years, not since those days of heartbreak and pain, when all hope had seemed gone. The property had returned a modicum of that hope to her, showing her that, even in ruin, something could still hold grace and beauty. That though something might be cast aside, it still had worth.

She had not imagined how altered the house would be.

The gray stone exterior was chalky from the salt air, pockmarks dotting its surface. Ivy grew wild up its façade, lacing over windows, latching onto downspouts and tearing them from their moorings. Several windowpanes were cracked or broken, the paint peeling from their casements to show the bleached gray wood beneath.

The gardens, however, had received the brunt of time's heavy hand. The plants grew wild and unkempt, seeming to have swallowed everything in their path. Clara shivered. If the state of the front garden was this grim, what must the back gardens look like? Images of the paths she had walked and found so much solace in rose up in her mind, the overgrown rosebushes and hedges only the more beautiful for their determination to thrive with no one to care for them. Her heart ached at the thought of it all going to ruin.

She should have perhaps visited before now. This place had given her just what she'd needed when she'd been at her lowest, and a horrible guilt filled her that she'd allowed it to be reduced to this.

No, she reminded herself firmly. Swallowhill was not hers to care for.

"Goodness," Margery said, peering up at the façade. "It's in worse shape than I expected. Though after it was abandoned for so long, this shouldn't come as a surprise."

Phoebe came up beside Clara, linking arms with her. The simple act grounded Clara, and she drew in a shaky breath.

"Is it as you remember, Clara?" her sister asked.

"A bit," she said vaguely. "Though it's been some time since I've been here."

"It's heartbreaking to see what must have been such a beautiful house gone to ruin." Lenora tucked her hand into the crook of her husband's arm. "Do you think it will be difficult to renovate?"

"No doubt," Peter said, his cool blue eyes skimming over the exterior.

Quincy shrugged. "We've seen worse."

"We've not seen the interior," Peter said. "There are

broken panes there. It could be in worse shape than the exterior. Especially in this sea air. The moisture and salt will do more damage than any climbing vine could."

"Then let's get to it," Quincy replied with a grin, apparently undaunted by the sad state of the outside and the grim possibilities within. He took the stairs two at a time, sidestepping broken urns, and made his way to the front door. They all followed, crowding close. From this distance the cracked and flaking varnish on the once beautiful door was painfully clear. But the fan-shaped window that topped it was intact. Perhaps it was a harbinger of positivity. At least, Clara hoped it was.

Quincy reached into his coat pocket, pulling a tarnished key from its depths. "I found this tucked deep in my father's desk," he explained. "I'm hoping it fits. If not, I suppose one more broken window won't matter." And with that he slid the key into the lock.

It fit easily enough. Yet the first few tries to turn it didn't provide much hope that their attempt to enter the house through the front door would prove successful. "Once more," Quincy muttered before, with a deeply indrawn breath, he put both hands on the key.

It turned with a grating that fairly rent the air. Quincy turned back to them, a victorious smile on his face. Clara's heart flipped over as his eyes met hers. He was doing a fine job of remaining jolly and positive, and seemed to have fooled everyone into believing this was nothing more than an adventure. They didn't see the tightness about his eyes, the stiffness to his smile that was louder than words to her.

Quincy pushed the door inward, the hinges, unused for so long, protesting mightily. With a deep breath, Clara followed the rest within.

The musty, unused air was the first thing to assault her senses. It sat heavy and stale, and she wrinkled her nose against it as she stepped cautiously across the bare floorboards, the sound echoing back to her. After the bright late-morning light, it took her some minutes to adjust to the dim interior. Gradually, however, her surroundings became clear.

She hadn't seen the interior since she was a child. Even then it had been rare, with most of her time here spent in the gardens and greenhouse. But suddenly it came rushing back to her, though the simple beauty of her memory vied with what it had become. The once carefully polished staircase that swept up the back wall, with its gracefully arched handrail and intricately carved balusters, was dull now, coated in decades of dust. The walls, too, had been given no quarter, the fine hand-painted wallpaper stained and falling off in tatters, showing the bare walls beneath. A glance up high saw the once elegant plaster ceiling cracked, chunks missing.

She looked to the floor, remembering the intricate wood inlay, now covered in a thick coating of dust and fallen plaster. As she watched, Peter nudged a chunk aside with his boot.

"It's not pretty, that's certain. But it appears to be sound. The floor doesn't seem to be warped in any way. It's a miracle, really."

"Do you think it can be salvaged, then?" Lenora asked.

Quincy, in the process of studying the stair treads, smiled over his shoulder. "Most certainly."

Peter gave him a severe look. "You cannot make such a claim on this one portion of the house."

Quincy rolled his eyes, rising to his feet. "Why must you be so pessimistic?"

"Why must you insist on ignoring cold facts?"

"It's part of my charm," Quincy quipped with a grin. "Why focus on the negative? We've only this one life to live. I prefer to look at the best possible outcome, and to enjoy myself while I'm at it."

"With no regard for caution or safety," Peter rejoined. But there was no heat in it, only a weary kind of echo, as if it was a frequent argument between the two.

Lenora stepped between them. "Neither of your hypotheses will be proven if you insist on standing about and arguing. Let's find out for ourselves the extent of the damage, then I will happily leave you to finish your debate."

The party began a lively discussion regarding the merits of staying together as a group versus breaking off into pairs. Clara watched them for a moment. It was a scene she would normally be in the midst of, taking control, making sure no one was slighted. But she could not take the steps forward to join in. She sighed, a sudden exhaustion overcoming her. Would that she could break off from the group and explore alone. She needed solitude now more than anything.

The idea was so tempting, she started up the curving stairs before she quite knew what she was doing. Soon she was on the upper floor, heading off down the hall, the sounds of happy bickering falling away behind her.

She had never been to this part of the house before. The unfamiliar feel of it calmed her, and she took a deep breath for what felt like the first time since she'd arrived. The shadows were thick here, the tightly closed doors of the rooms that spread out on either side keeping away the sunlight, shrouding the space as surely as the dust that settled thick over every surface. Going to the closest door, she turned the knob and pushed inward.

The door swung open with a creak, revealing a large square room with wide windows looking out over the sea far below. Cloth-covered furniture rose up like specters, crowding the space. She went to the first, pulling a corner back. A side table, still beautiful, its glossy finish dull but protected for the most part by its covering. The next revealed a low settee, the rose damask brittle. More seating and a low table followed, proving this room had been used as a sitting room. The last piece, a delicate white desk, had a place of honor against the large windows. She looked down on the painted top, running her fingers over the surface. Had this been Miss Brandon's desk? Had she sat here, looking out over the sea, penning letters?

But she was growing maudlin. Flipping the dusty cover back over the desk, she left the room and went to the next. Here was a larger space, the square cloth-covered piece dominating the floor proclaiming it to be a bedroom. Her eyes scanned the other pieces. Surely that tall one there was an armoire, that long one a dressing table. There were chairs before the cold hearth, small side tables bookending the bed.

She noticed a small, low shape that stood out awkwardly from the rest. Frowning, she walked to it and pulled back the cover.

A baby's cradle. Pain exploded in her chest. Without pausing she threw the cover back over it. Dust rose up as she spun away, desperate to leave the room. Quite another cradle rising up in her mind, for a child who would never have reason to use it.

So intent was she on escaping, she didn't realize anyone had followed her until she was upon him. Strong hands came up to grasp her arms, halting her before she barreled into his chest.

"Clara, are you well?"

Quincy. The sudden urge to lay her head on his broad chest nearly overwhelmed her. How wonderful it would be to stop fighting against those painful memories. She was so very tired of that never-ending battle.

But she couldn't. Not ever. If she did allow it to escape, she might never rein it back in again.

She stepped away from him, gifting him with a bright smile that felt brittle on her lips even as her heart ached at the loss of his hands on her. "Of course I'm well. The dust affected me, that's all. I was trying to escape before it caused me to sneeze." She peered over his shoulder. "Where have the others gone?"

An expression much like frustration passed through his eyes before they cleared. "Phoebe dragged Margery off to the kitchens, and Peter and Lenora have taken to exploring the drawing room."

"I'll find them, then," she said, trying to move past him.

His hand caught hers. "Clara—"

"I'm fine," she said hastily.

"No, you're not."

She heaved a sigh, closing her eyes against the urge to confide in him. "I'm fine," she repeated, rearranging her features into pleasant calm.

He peered down at her, that same frustration rearing again. "If you're certain."

"I am. Now," she said, "I think I've had enough of this part of the house to know it's all bedrooms and sitting rooms and such. I'll leave the rest to you to explore. My favorite part was the greenhouse; I'll go there."

"I'll go with you."

She wanted to scream at him to leave her in peace. Instead she smiled, tilting her head in acquiescence, taking his arm when he offered it.

The back garden, when they finally reached it, was just as bad as she'd feared. The meandering paths had been swallowed up by vegetation, the beautiful rosebushes choked by weeds and vines. She paused at her first sight of it, swallowing back her gasp of dismay.

But it would be restored, she told herself bracingly. Quincy would sell it to someone who would bring it back from the purgatory it was in. It was her one solace in all this, that the house and gardens would find a new life.

"This will take some work," Quincy muttered beside her. "But there's a good base to it, I'm thinking." He pointed off to the side. "There's a sunken garden there, rosebushes with some life in them hidden in this bramble, a nice tree line ahead. I'm betting, with some care and love, this garden will find itself again."

His words were calm and certain, helping to quiet her despair. And suddenly she saw it, too; that under the ruin was still a thing of beauty. That if only someone would take the time, it would blossom. She tightened her fingers in his wool sleeve, grateful now that he'd come with her. "Yes," she replied quietly. "I do think you're right."

He smiled down at her, and it was like the sun emerging from behind a heavy cloud. "Let's find that greenhouse, shall we?"

Chapter 13

*H*e should be focusing on the outer condition of the house, he thought as he and Clara tramped through the overgrown garden. The price he managed to get from it would be determined in no small part by the state of the building, after all. And the more funds that were brought in from the sale, the more it would benefit him.

But all he could seem to think about was how relieved he was to be out of it. There was something unnerving about the house that he couldn't quite put his finger on. It wasn't an unease so much as a...recognition?

It was ridiculous that there could be a familiarity about the place. He hadn't even known about it, much less ever stepped foot in it. But there was the constant feeling in his belly that there was something missing, a kind of ache.

He breathed deep, hoping to clear his head. No doubt it was merely his disquiet over Miss Willa Brandon. What had she been to his father, that he had bought a house on the Isle and allowed her to live out her days? Had she truly been his mistress as Lady Tesh had implied? Why did that idea hurt so much?

And how would it change his memories of his father when he finally learned the truth?

To him his father had always been all that was good,

never capable of hurting a soul. And the thought of him hiding a woman away to use at his pleasure, no matter how ill suited he'd been with the duchess, sat wrong on him. Surely it couldn't be true.

"Quincy, are you well?"

Clara. He let the calming effect of her quiet voice wash over him. Time enough to think of Miss Brandon later. Or perhaps not at all. Mayhap it was best if he never learned who she had been to his father.

He smiled. "I'm well. Sorry, my mind must have wandered."

She nodded, turning her attention back to the blanket of leaves under their feet. Yet he didn't miss the tense lines at the corners of her eyes, proof that she was not as tranquil as she'd have him believe.

That faint air of sadness had hung about her all morning. He frowned. No, it had started last night, when he'd first mentioned Swallowhill. Was it the house then? What upset her about it? She'd mentioned coming here with her mother; could that be what pained her?

Would that she would confide in him. He would give her a shoulder to cry on, if she would allow it. But he had a feeling that she did not confide in anyone, even those closest to her. No one else, even her sister, seemed aware of her troubled mind.

He helped her over a low branch, stomping down a patch of thigh-high grass as they trudged through the shadowed confines of the garden. She moved through the tangle, certainty guiding her feet. Yet still there was no sign of her greenhouse. "Mayhap it's fallen down," he ventured.

"No," she replied, her gaze focused ahead. "It will be there. I'm sure of it."

The words had barely left her lips before a glint in the trees caught his eye. And then it was there, an oasis in a jungle.

The wrought iron was rusted, the glass grimy. Yet it was beautiful for all that. The fanciful metalwork, as delicate as it was, stood strong in the afternoon sun, the great glass dome with all its panes of glass seeming intact.

She exhaled beside him, her grip on his arm tightening. When she looked up at him, her eyes were glowing.

"I told you it would still be here."

He grinned. "Yes, you did. I'll never doubt you again."

She smiled. It was a small thing, but it made his heart soar that he could bring it about.

"Let's go in, shall we?" he asked.

In answer, she moved forward, tugging on his arm. He went willingly, aware of a desire to go wherever she might lead him.

Where the air within the house was stale with disuse, the air within the greenhouse teemed with life. It was rich and warm, filling his lungs with a humid heat. He breathed in deeply, stopping just inside the doors to stare.

Whatever had been planted within had thrived. It had grown wild, yes, but in a glorious kind of way, a celebration of life instead of a slave to its destruction. Twining vines had attached themselves to the iron, creating a glorious living dome, letting filtered sun in. Small trees spread their branches like yawning children just waking. Flowers bloomed in a riot of vibrant color amid the greenery. The ground beneath their feet was thick with years of dead leaves, covering whatever path might have been laid, creating a rich base for it all to spring from.

Clara dropped his arm, moving forward as if in a trance. She peeled off a glove, letting her slender fingers trail over the glossy dark leaves of the closest plant. He watched her, unable to look away from the straight line of her back, the ungiving angle of her chin. He thought he saw a muscle tic in her jaw, and that small tell made his heart ache. He should leave and give her some privacy.

Yet he couldn't. He wanted to be here should she need him. Not that Clara appeared to have ever needed anyone before. But he couldn't shake the thought that she was close to breaking.

Just then her hand came up to her cheek, wiping hastily.

Damn her pride. He couldn't stand there and not at least try to help her.

In several long strides he was at her side, his hand on her arm, pulling her about until she was in his arms.

"Quincy—" she tried, planting her hands on his chest. He didn't fail to notice that she didn't push him away.

He pressed his lips to the crown of her head, her soft curls tickling his nose. "For once, just let someone give *you* comfort."

She gave a startled laugh, which transformed into a sob. It was quickly stifled, and she pressed her face into his chest, her shoulders tight beneath his hands.

"Clara," he whispered, "you can let go, you know."

She shook her head, her hair rasping against his cravat. "I can't."

The words were broken, as if dredged up from some deep place within her. "You can," he replied, his hands rubbing over her back. "Clara, you don't have to be strong all the time."

She shuddered beneath his touch, and he sensed the urge in her to let go. But stubborn thing that she was, she held on tight to her control. He imagined her face was scrunched up in determined concentration.

He sighed into her hair. "Though I can't understand why, this place seems to bring you pain. I shouldn't have asked you to come."

She stayed quiet. Then, her voice so small he hardly heard it, "Some of the sweetest memories of my mother are here, and it's dear to me because of it. And when I was at a very low point in my life I rediscovered this place and—"

Her hastily cut-off confession only brought about more questions: She'd returned later in life? What low point? But he sensed that she would retreat for good should he press her. Instead he stayed quiet, his hands moving in gentle circles over her back.

The shaking in her grew. Was his touch bringing her distress? He was about to step back when her shoulders dropped, a long sigh escaping her. And he felt her tears soaking his shirt.

She cried as if years of pent-up grief were being released, an undulating wave that appeared to have no end. He remained silent, giving what comfort he could. Finally, after what seemed an age, the faint shaking stilled. She sniffled loudly.

Reaching into his waistcoat pocket, he extracted a fine linen handkerchief and handed it to her.

"This is ridiculous," she muttered into his chest as she took it, her voice hoarse. "I never cry."

"I daresay that's because you're much too busy doing the consoling, and not allowing others to do the same for you," he said.

She gave a small, watery laugh. "You're more stubborn than I am, that's certain."

He grinned. "Quite certain. And you'd best remember that."

In answer she hiccuped. Then, with a sigh, she relaxed further into his embrace. Her arms stole about his middle, holding on tight. As if he were her port in the storm.

They stood that way for a time, quiet, merely holding one another. Finally she stirred and raised her head.

His breath caught in his chest. Her lashes were darkened from her tears, and incredibly long, framing the brilliant sapphire of her eyes. Eyes that seemed clear now, and miraculously free of the tight control she'd kept over herself. Then she smiled.

It was as natural as breathing to lower his head to hers. Her lips gave beneath his, soft and welcoming. This was no frantic kiss, made desperate with hot want. Though desire for her stirred in his blood, just as before when they'd kissed in London, it was the spreading warmth in his chest that overwhelmed his senses this time. It made his hands gentle where they splayed across her back, holding her close as if she were a treasure beyond worth.

And she was, so much more than he'd first assumed. There was heartache in her, and passion, the part of her that she kept hidden from the world as vast and unfathomable as the sea itself.

He cupped her cheek, deepening the kiss. As before, in the garden at Dane House, she responded with an enthusiasm that stunned him. Desire pounded swift through him. He wanted more, so much more from her.

But he couldn't take it. Not only did he refuse to disrespect her by starting something physical with her that they could never finish, but she was emotionally vulnerable. To take advantage of that would be the grossest betrayal.

He pulled back, nearly regretting his chivalry when he caught sight of her sweetly flushed face, her kiss-bruised lips.

Her eyelids fluttered open. "We shouldn't have done that, I'm thinking," she whispered.

"No," he replied softly, his thumb caressing her cheek, "we shouldn't have."

She smiled, then with a sigh she stepped back, untangling herself from his arms. He felt the loss down to his bones.

"I'm sorry for that," she murmured, her eyes falling to the ground. "I truly don't know what came over me."

"Please don't apologize. I don't regret it." He paused. "Do you?"

Her gaze met his again. "No," she said on a breath, as if she could not quite understand it. "At least"—her lips quirked—"not yet."

He offered his arm, and as one they left the greenhouse. "Have no fear," he quipped. "I shan't kiss you again. Unless you ask prettily."

His attempt at humor was meant to lighten the mood, and he was rewarded with her small smile. "You shall have a long wait, then. For I'm not planning on asking, ever."

I'm counting on that, he thought grimly. For if it was up to him, he would take her in his arms again. And this time he would never let her go.

* * *

"Can I refresh your drink, Clara?"

Clara smiled, passing her glass to Quincy. "Thank you."

He gave her a wink, walking off across Danesford's drawing room with a fluid grace that she was hard-pressed to look away from.

Aunt Olivia leaned in close, a sly look in her eyes. "That boy is utterly smitten, it seems."

"Yes," Clara murmured with a blush that was not feigned in the least.

It had been a week since the trip to Swallowhill. A week since their second kiss, one that had been tender and beautiful and had effectively undermined whatever defenses she'd managed to hold on to after that first devastating kiss in London. A week since she'd cried herself out in his arms...

Of the two, the latter had been the more intimate. She had held so tightly to her emotions for so long it had been the sweetest release, made all the more beautiful because she had been comforted by Quincy. If she had acted in such a way with anyone else, they would have pressured her to reveal what had upset her. Quincy, however, had merely held her, letting her cry without judgment or questions.

Since then he had been all that was proper, of course— at least as proper as a besotted fiancé was supposed to act. Just as he'd promised, he had not kissed her again; nor had he so much as touched her in a scandalous manner.

That didn't seem to matter. After the intimacy of their time in the greenhouse, blurring the line between friendship and something more, each day Clara found herself more in danger of falling completely and irrevocably in love with him.

Which made her need to find a new and useful place in her family more important than ever. Up until now her attempts had been blocked from every direction—really no surprise, as everyone believed she would soon be happily married. More troubling, however, had been the lack of drive in her. The prospect of living out her days in such a way didn't hold the same draw it had when she'd first realized it needed to be done.

But ignoring it was not an option, so she turned to the viscountess. "Once Phoebe's wedding is behind us, I'm afraid things will become quiet around here. I worry about you being alone at Seacliff. Would that someone could stay on with you."

It was meant to plant a seed, making Aunt Olivia realize she would need a companion when all was said and done. Unfortunately, it backfired spectacularly.

"Oh, you've no need to worry about that," the viscountess said. "I've a girl in mind to take on as a companion. As a matter of fact, it's already been decided, and Miss Katrina Denby shall be here just after the new year." She speared Clara with a stern look. "But if you don't pin down when your own wedding will be, you'll be able to meet her yourself. Goodness, child, but I cannot believe you've yet to set a date. Truly, you must be mad. Why, if it was me, I would be angling for a special license. One can't feign an early delivery if the infant is born mere weeks after the wedding."

"Aunt Olivia!"

The viscountess shrugged, sitting back with a knowing air. "There's a reason my eldest was born in November, when I was married in May."

Quincy chose that moment to return. Clara snatched her glass from him, draining the wine in a long swallow, praying the alcohol would dull her senses after that mortifying exchange.

He eyed her askance a moment before turning a melting grin on Aunt Olivia. "And what were my two favorite ladies talking of so intently while I was away?"

Aunt Olivia opened her mouth, no doubt to regale him with the exact truth of the matter. Desperate to stop her, Clara blurted, "I do hope Lord and Lady Crabtree arrive soon. I don't think Phoebe can take the suspense much longer. She's grown increasingly impatient waiting for Oswin's arrival."

Quincy gave her a sly look that said he knew she was lying and was only letting it pass due to his generosity. "It isn't any wonder, I suppose," he said. "Goodness knows the week I spent away from you had me going mad." He took up her hand, bestowing a kiss on her knuckles.

There was simultaneously a dreamy sigh from Aunt Olivia and a low growl from Peter half the room away. Clara hardly heard either. Her entire attention was focused on the feel of Quincy's lips on her skin. A flush of molten desire traveled from her fingers, up her arm, across her breasts, and down to the very depths of her belly. She squirmed in her seat, swallowing hard.

"But what of the meeting with your house agent?" Aunt Olivia asked, apparently done with romantic musings. "He sent you a note this afternoon requesting an audience, did he not?"

"He did, indeed," Quincy replied, as ever unperturbed by her brusqueness. "It seems Mr. Dennison has a possible buyer for Swallowhill, a Lord Fletcher. I'm told he's a longtime resident of the Isle and has been leasing a place in Knighthead Crescent. Perhaps you know him, Lady Tesh?"

"Lord Fletcher, yes," Aunt Olivia murmured, a thoughtful look in her eyes. "Jovial fellow. A bit soft about the middle, and balding. But then we can't all be Adonises like you."

Quincy grinned. "Why, Lady Tesh, you shall turn my head."

"Scamp," she scoffed. "Though you're probably wanting to know if he's solvent. Well, I can assure you, he's got enough money to buy Swallowhill several times over. And he's generous to a fault. You'll get no argument from him on price, as long as it's fair. He's wanted to purchase a sizable property on the Isle for some time. If Dennison says he's interested, then you've got this sale made."

Lord Fletcher. Clara looked down to her empty glass. She'd crossed paths with him on several occasions. He was just as Aunt Olivia said, jovial and generous. A widower, his sons were all grown now, one daughter left at home to keep house for him. An ideal buyer.

Why, then, did it feel like a pebble had lodged in her throat?

"Clara, what do you think of Lord Fletcher purchasing the property?"

She started, smiling brightly to cover up her momentary melancholy, and answered with utter honesty, "I think Lord Fletcher is the perfect person to purchase Swallowhill."

"If you're certain. I know the house means much to you."

There was a hint of worry in his eyes. She forced her smile even brighter. "Of course. It will be wonderful to see Swallowhill brought back to its former splendor."

Margery approached then, blessedly preventing him from asking her anything more on the subject. "Clara, dear, we've all decided to visit the Elven Pools tomorrow. Oswin has never been to Synne, and Phoebe is excited to show him the sights. Do say you and Quincy will join us."

"I'm so sorry, Margery dear, I still have ever so much to do for the wedding," she said, genuinely disappointed. The pools were quite possibly her favorite place on the Isle, and she hadn't been in years. But she had set out to make this wedding something special for Phoebe to look back on with joy, and she wasn't about to fail now that it was a mere week away.

Aunt Olivia made a disgusted sound. "Quincy," she said, her eyes fixed on Clara in an uncomfortably intense manner, "I do believe your intended has been working too hard these last weeks."

Clara rolled her eyes. "Quincy, please tell my aunt I cannot take the afternoon off."

She expected him to comply. He'd been amazingly supportive over the past sennight. So it was that much more of a surprise when he said, "I think Lady Tesh is right."

She gaped at him. "You must be joking."

He raised one inky brow at her. "Not in the least. You deserve to enjoy this time with your sister. In a week she shall be married and off on her new life."

She had been ignoring that fact as best she could. But coming from Quincy in such a simple way, it cut her to the quick. And the problem was, she could not even be angry that he had brought it up. He was right; after the wedding it would be some time before she saw Phoebe. It was devastating, when they had been inseparable since their mother's death.

All but for that year, when she had hidden away to birth a child that would not live to take its first breath.

The memory crashed over her, taking her off guard. She quickly tucked it back into the darkest region of her heart, but the flavor of it stayed with her, making her stomach churn.

She schooled her features into a mild outrage, praying Quincy's sharp eyes didn't catch the moment of shocked grief. "I cannot abandon the wedding plans. It's in a *week*."

Lady Tesh eyed her with pursed lips before she turned to Margery. "Can Lenora and Mrs. Ingram take over the remainder of the planning?"

Margery, eyes gleaming in understanding, nodded emphatically. "Oh, certainly. Why, Clara has done such a wonderful job that there's hardly anything left to do at all."

Clara gaped at her. "*You* are against me, too?"

"Not against you, dearest," her cousin answered. "Merely wanting to make certain you don't regret anything. In the coming years, when you look back at this time, I guarantee you it will not matter a whit that the flowers were just so, or that the dress was hemmed just right. The thing you'll remember most, the thing that will live on in your heart, is the time spent with Phoebe."

There really was no fighting that. Clara slouched in her seat. "Very well," she grumbled.

Margery beamed, clapping her hands. "Oh, wonderful. Phoebe will be so happy."

"You won't regret it, my girl," Aunt Olivia said, giving Clara a small smile that was entirely too smug. Before Clara could make sense of it, Freya, seated in her mistress's lap, gave a soft yip. Lady Tesh's attention was immediately diverted. "Do you wish for a little something to eat, my darling?" she crooned.

Margery moved forward. "Shall I take her to the kitchens?"

"Nonsense," Aunt Olivia snapped. She cradled Freya with one arm, holding her other hand out imperiously. "Help me up. I'll find her a bit of something myself."

Margery, looking thoroughly confused—for when had Aunt Olivia ever turned down a chance to have someone else do her bidding?—nonetheless helped the viscountess up and, giving Clara and Quincy an apologetic look, guided her grandmother away.

Quincy chuckled quietly. Clara shot him a dark look. "And just what is so humorous in this?"

"You act as if you're about to ascend the gallows." He grabbed at her hand, giving it a squeeze. "It will be enjoyable. You'll see. And the wedding won't collapse without you. I promise."

If his words hadn't been enough to soothe her, his touch certainly was. A delicious warmth crept through her, making her fairly melt in her seat. Without meaning to, her thumb drifted over his knuckles.

Immediately his expression shifted. The smile fell from his lips, his lids lowering over eyes that burned with a mesmerizing fire. He leaned closer to her, and she found herself swaying, like a puppet on a string, toward him. The space between them on the settee disappeared in an instant. Her gaze pulled away from his, settling on his firm lips. She drew in a shaking breath, wanting more than anything to taste him again...

A commotion sounded at the drawing room doors. And then the butler's voice, ringing through the air.

"Lord and Lady Crabtree, Lord Oswin. And the Duchess of Reigate."

* * *

Quincy's first thought upon hearing his mother announced was that the woman had the damnedest timing, for wasn't this the second occasion she'd disrupted such a moment between him and Clara?

The second thought was much more violent in nature. What in hell was his mother doing here?

He released Clara's hand, lurching to his feet. Surely this was some lurid nightmare. That was it, he was dreaming. Why else would he have come so damn close to kissing Clara again? He had spent the better part of the past week burning for her, made worse by the necessary subterfuge of him playing the part of besotted fiancé. The more time he spent in her presence, the more the line between fact and fiction was blurred. There were times, he found to his dismay, that it wasn't so much an act as it was the deepest desire of his heart.

Even so, he never allowed himself to forget that this was all for show, and would be over once Phoebe was safely wed. And he had never once attempted to kiss her again. Until now.

Yes, this was surely a dream. With his mother's presence quickly turning it into a nightmare.

He surreptitiously took the skin of his wrist between two fingers and pinched, hard. But he did not wake tangled in sheets from a night of restless tossing as had become his custom. His heart dropped. No, this was most assuredly not a dream. Damn it.

His mother stood with all the regality of a queen beside Lord and Lady Crabtree and their son. Her eyes landed on him, and her lips lifted in a cool smile. "Reigate."

He stiffened. "Mother." He cast a glance around the room. Every eye was on him in varying degrees of dismay and confusion. He should smile and feign politeness, then guide her into the hall to rain fire and brimstone down upon her in private for daring to come here. She was up to something. He was sure of it. Her self-satisfied smirk was proof enough of that.

But despite knowing better, he found he couldn't move his feet. He swallowed down the angry words that fought to break free, the bitterness of them leaving him sick to his stomach. "What are you doing here?" he asked instead, the words forced out through gritted teeth.

"Lady Crabtree and I have become quite close recently, as both our sons are to wed the daughters of the previous Duke of Dane. They've kindly invited me to attend their son's wedding, to get to know my future daughter-in-law better." Here she turned a syrupy sweet smile on Clara.

A violent protectiveness surged through Quincy, and he nearly stepped in front of Clara to hide her from the cunning in his mother's eyes.

Instead he managed a smile that was so stiff and brittle he thought his lips would crack from it. "How serendipitous that you have become such good friends."

Her eyes narrowed in recognition of the subtle jab, but her smile only widened, as if it pleased her to see him squirm. And no doubt it did. The woman always did enjoy the discomfort of others.

She turned to the room at large. "I do hope it's not an imposition. My dear Lady Crabtree pressed me so, I could not possibly refuse. Especially as she has become so very dear to me." Here she gave the woman in question a doting smile before turning an apologetic gaze to the rest of the inhabitants.

"Oh! Of course." Lenora jumped up, hurrying to them. "It's our pleasure to have you here at Danesford, Your Grace. Isn't it, my dear?"

Peter glanced at Quincy, concern clouding the clear blue of his eyes, before he stepped up beside his wife. "Certainly. Welcome to Danesford."

The palpable tension in the air eased as introductions were made. Phoebe, who had been watching the whole affair with wide eyes, jumped from her seat, hurrying to Oswin. They clasped hands, their eyes glowing, and quickly tucked themselves into a private corner. Once niceties were seen to, the small party broke up. Peter guided Lord Crabtree out, muttering something about guns, and Lenora quickly took Lady Crabtree and the duchess in hand, her bright voice regaling them on the details of their rooms as she led the way out into the hall.

Leaving Quincy and Clara quite alone. Well, as alone as two people could be with a pair of whispering love-birds hidden away in a corner.

Still Quincy stood there, as if rooted to the spot. He'd hoped never to see his mother again. Yet here he was about to be stuck in the same house as her for the next week. Once again, he wondered what she hoped to accomplish by coming here. Dread settled heavy on him.

Suddenly a small hand tucked itself into his. "Quincy, are you well?"

Clara. He closed his eyes, dragging in a deep breath, letting her calmness wash over him. "No," he answered with utter truthfulness, casting her a wry look. "But I think you've guessed that much."

"Yes." Her eyes were sober as she peered up at him. "I'm so sorry."

He shrugged. "I suppose I should have expected this. She always was one to throw a stick in the wheels when-ever things were going too smoothly." He gave her a stern look. "But don't think this gives you leave to get out of your agreement to join us all tomorrow."

She frowned. "Surely plans have changed after this new development."

"Surely not," he declared officiously, even as the idea of leaving her alone in his mother's vicinity left him physically ill. "I find I need the distraction of a good, fun outing now more than ever."

She must have seen the desperation in his eyes, though he strove to hide it under his teasing. Concern shone tight on her face. But she was as adept as he at burying emotions, wasn't she? "I suppose you do," she murmured with a small smile. "Though I warn you, I don't know the first thing about having fun."

He grinned, relief flooding him at this bit of normalcy. "You may not know, my dear Clara," he said. "But I do. And the next week I will dedicate myself to teaching you."

Chapter 14

*T*he mood of the household had definitely shifted since the duchess's arrival the day before. Phoebe had remained blessedly oblivious, wrapped up as she was in Oswin. Clara could only be grateful for that.

But the rest of them were strung as tight as nocked bows.

Clara had not thought she could possibly relax during the outing to the Elven Pools. There was too much to do for the wedding, no matter how Margery claimed the contrary. That, and she still hadn't found where she would belong when the commotion of the wedding was over; it seemed everyone was excited for her to go off on a life of her own, and her absence would not make a whit of difference in anyone's life. A lowering thought indeed.

Yet the minute she'd stepped foot from the house she had felt a wonderful relief that she was leaving everything behind, no matter how briefly. Now, the delicious picnic lunch consumed, seated as she was on a blanket in the warm sunlight, the band that had constricted her chest since yesterday began to loosen. As the rest of the party, consisting of not only the younger people from Danesford but several of Phoebe's closest friends as well, cavorted about the flat valley just beyond the pools, she raised her face to catch the warm sun and breathed in deeply. This trip, one based on pure pleasure, was something she had fought tooth and nail against. Now, though, she was grateful she had been coerced into joining. Not that she would ever let Quincy know that. She smiled to herself.

As if he had heard her thoughts—something that made her mildly panicked after the improper daydreams she'd had of him recently—Quincy spoke in her ear. "Happy you came?"

She cast him an arch look where he lounged beside her, trying and failing to rein in the shiver of desire that whispered over her nerves when her gaze met his heavy-lidded one. "You needn't look so smug."

The grin he sent her had butterflies taking flight in her stomach. "Come on then, admit it. I was right."

"If you think to ever hear those words from me, you are delusional."

He chuckled. "You can be stubborn when you've a mind to be."

"As can you," she quipped. "The only question is, who will win in the end?"

"Oh, I've no doubt you will," he murmured. The heat in his eyes called to something in her that made her feel at once powerful and confused.

Flustered, needing to redirect her quickly spiraling thoughts—in which she imagined what she could claim from him for being victor in this little battle of wills—she latched onto the first thing that came to mind. "I overheard you tell Peter this morning that you'll be meeting with Lord Fletcher soon?"

He started. "What? Oh! Er, yes, I will." He cleared his throat, shifting on the blanket as if physically uncomfortable. "Lady Tesh, it seems, was right; the man is eager to talk over terms and Mr. Dennison is quite confident we can get the price we want, despite the house being in such poor shape."

At the mention of that place, her heart ached. But it was a good ache, that the house would finally return to what it had been.

It was not the first time they'd talked of Swallowhill since their visit. Yet Quincy had been glaringly quiet regarding one very important part of it all: Miss Willa Brandon. She might have thought he'd forgotten all about her, if it weren't for the melancholy in his eyes when he thought no one was looking. She knew what it was to carry a silent heartache around with you, like a manacle about your foot, never allowing you to escape from the oppression of it.

Leaning toward him, she said in a low voice, "Did you think about my offer?"

Instant understanding flashed in his eyes. "You are referring to finding out more about Miss Brandon?" At her nod he shook his head. "I'm afraid I'm no closer to a decision. I just—I don't know—"

She laid a hand over his. "I understand," she said. "I'm in no way pressuring you. I can only imagine how hard this must be for you, loving your father as you did. Just know, whatever you may learn, should you choose to learn it, it will not change who he was to you."

"I know you're right," he murmured, giving her a sad smile. "That doesn't make it any easier, though, does it?"

"No," she agreed softly.

They shared a quiet moment, each lost in their thoughts. Suddenly a shout went up from the rest of the group. Mr. Ronald Tunley was on the ground, a shuttlecock at his feet, laughter shaking his body. The rest of them were equally overcome, their laughs mingling with his in a joyful cacophony.

Clara smiled at the sight, her gaze lingering on Phoebe. She could not remember the last time she had seen her sister so utterly happy.

"Do you want to join them?"

She blinked and looked to Quincy beside her. Then lost her breath entirely. He had stretched out on the blanket, propped up on one elbow, his strong thighs outlined by his buff breeches, looking for all the world like a feast laid out for her to devour at her leisure.

Taken aback by her suddenly lascivious thoughts, she cleared her throat and tried to hide her flaming face by busily smoothing her muslin skirts. "Join in their game? No, thank you."

"Don't you enjoy battledore and shuttlecock?"

"I'm not certain. Truthfully, I cannot remember when last I played."

"Certainly you indulged in sport as a child."

"Oh, I did. But—"

He tilted his head when she abruptly broke off, a frown marring the strong line of his brow. "But?"

She gave a small sigh. "But I put all that aside when my mother died."

"Ah," he murmured. "And how old were you when she passed?"

"Nine." She went silent a moment, remembering. Needing to say something more on that devastating time in her life—the first of many to come—she added, "Phoebe was just an infant at the time. And my brother, Hillram, not much older than her. They needed someone to care for them, to watch over them."

"And so you gave up your childhood for theirs."

She shrugged. "They needed a mother."

"So did you."

"Yes, well." She looked into his eyes. Eyes that were full of compassion. Suddenly it was imperative that he understand. "But I had been the lucky one," she continued, leaning toward him. "I'd had her for nine entire years. She was kind, and thoughtful, and brave. And they never had a chance to know her. I wanted them to experience some of what she gave me."

He cocked his head, looking at her as if seeing her anew. A small smile lifted his chiseled lips. "You're an amazing woman, Clara."

"Nonsense," she said on a breath, face suddenly burning. She looked to her lap.

He hooked a finger under her chin, lifting her gaze to his. "You are," he insisted quietly. "You decided at nine years old to be everything to everyone, to sacrifice your childhood for those you love. And it appears you have not stopped since. Even"—he grinned—"giving up playing battledore and shuttlecock."

She laughed. "You are ridiculous. It's not anything anyone else wouldn't have done."

"That's not true in the least. You're a rarity, Clara."

Again her face flushed hot. Needing to steer the conversation into safer waters—waters that did not have her aching to lean into his hand, to press her lips to his, to stretch her body alongside his until she didn't know where she ended and he began—she pulled away from his touch and looked to the others. Phoebe, with a look of concentration, brought her battledore back and swung it up in an arc. It hit the shuttlecock with a whack, sending it back up into the blue sky as Oswin cheered her on.

"I expect shuttlecock is not typically something played

much past childhood, anyway," she said bracingly. "Current company excluded, of course. But then, one can expect playfulness during such a joyous occasion."

"Perhaps," he conceded. "But surely there are other things you've had cause to join in on. Maybe croquet? Archery? Tennis?" At her blank look he rolled his eyes. "Very well, you're not an outdoor person. Perhaps something indoors, such as theatrics, or billiards? Fencing?"

She was tempted to wave him off. He was being ridiculous.

But the realization that she had not indulged in most, if not all, of those things became mortifyingly clear. She was much more likely to take on the role of chaperone, looking on from the side, taking her joy in watching.

But had it truly been a joy? As a young girl she'd been high-spirited. But she'd conformed herself into what she thought others needed from her after her mother died. Mayhap that was why she had rebelled as a young woman. Not even sixteen, and so desperate to find her place in the world she had blindly believed the false words of a young man who had wanted nothing more from her than a distraction while his family vacationed on the Isle.

But she would not let *him* in. He had no place in her thoughts.

As her silence stretched on, Quincy sat up. "Do you mean to tell me," he said, slowly and distinctly, disbelief ripe in his voice, "that you have not tried a single one of those things?" At her nod he let loose a startled laugh. "Well, what do you do for fun?"

She rolled her eyes at that, grateful that he had turned the conversation back to innocuous things. "I've no room for fun."

He reared back as if poked with a sharp stick. "No room for—what?—" He looked at her as if she had committed a mortal sin. "You cannot be serious."

"When do I have time for fun?" she countered.

His expression altered so quickly she didn't have time to process it. "You do now." In one smooth move he stood and tugged her to her feet.

She was so startled she lost her balance, falling into his chest. "Oh," she managed.

His eyes flared with heat, zeroing in on her mouth for a tense moment. But once again his features transformed. A wicked grin spread over his face as he started off toward the others, her hand still grasped tight in his.

It took her some seconds to realize what he was up to. When she finally did, she gaped at his back. "Oh, no."

"Oh, yes," he said over his shoulder. "You are not some elderly matron who must watch life go by, Clara. You are young, and vibrant, and deserve to have a bit of fun."

They reached the flat meadow. "Ho, there. Do you have a couple extra racquets? Lady Clara and I have a mind to join you."

A cheer went up from the assembled before Clara had time to refuse. In a moment the wooden handle of a battledore was being pressed into her hands and Phoebe was pulling her into the fray.

"Oh, this is brilliant," she exclaimed, her face glowing. "I cannot recall you ever joining in, no matter how I begged."

That took Clara aback. Phoebe had begged her to play with her? Just as she was about to laughingly denounce such a thing, however, she suddenly remembered her sister, small and delicate with braids flying behind her, running up to Clara, asking her to join in fishing, or races, or any number of activities she was currently interested in.

Each time Clara had refused. Before she could ask herself why, however, she knew with distressing certainty: she had believed her worth had lain in what she could do *for* her sister. And all along she had missed out on what she could have done *with* her.

But she could not think of that devastating fact just now, not in front of so many others.

"Just keep the shuttlecocks from hitting the ground, Lady Clara," Miss Coralie Gadfeld, the vicar's niece, called out, her dark skin flushed from her efforts, onyx eyes sparkling. "It's not difficult."

"Not a bit," Mr. Ronald Tunley, the sheepherder's son, said with a grin. "And besides, no one can possibly be worse than Horace here." He punched the arm of the man in question good-naturedly.

Mr. Horace Juniper, son of the local innkeeper, flushed a mottled red and sent a horrified glance Miss Coralie's way, longing and embarrassment clear in his eyes. "At least I didn't fall on my . . . behind," he shot back, to which Mr. Tunley guffawed.

"Shall we start then?" Oswin called out cheerfully, the shuttlecock held aloft.

An enthusiastic chorus started up, and the feathered cork was dropped to connect with Oswin's racquet. And chaos ensued.

Clara held back, watching the rest of them lunge and swing with abandon. She held the battledore before her chest like a shield, at once excited and nervous for the shuttlecock to come sailing her way. She searched for Quincy. He was in the midst of them all, laughing and calling encouragement. He'd laid his jacket aside, rolling up his sleeves, and the sight of his strong forearms made her knees weak.

Suddenly he caught her eye. Then, with a devilish twinkle, he caught the shuttlecock with his racquet and sent it flying purposely her way.

Time seemed to freeze. She stared at the oncoming cork-and-feather creation as if it were a rabid animal about to attack and tear out her throat. What if she missed? What if she fell? Every horrifying possibility flashed through her mind in the split second it took for the shuttlecock to reach her. Closing her eyes tight, she pulled the battledore back with both hands and let it swing.

A resounding thwack sounded, the feel of the cork hitting the strings reverberating up her arms. A cheer went up. She opened her eyes to see the shuttlecock sail in an impressive arc before it fell at the feet of a gaping Mr. Tunley.

"Well done, Lady Clara," he called out.

And then Quincy was there, his face beaming with pride. And she was caught up in his arms in a celebratory embrace. And she wished the moment might never end.

* * *

Later that evening Clara was still basking in the happy glow the afternoon had given her. Truly, she could not remember a time she had so enjoyed herself.

She smiled, taking a sip of her wine, letting her gaze linger on Quincy where he stood across Danesford's vast drawing room. And he had been the center of it all. She felt as if she were a different person when she was with him, someone who was more than just a caretaker or a spinster. Not that her family had ever indicated they ever saw her that way. No, she had been the one to don those cloaks.

Now, however…Quincy looked at her then, and a shiver ran through her body. No, not *however*, she told herself sternly as her thoughts veered to a possibility of something more with him. No matter what her heart might want, this was temporary. Her future did not include Quincy. Nor any man.

He murmured something to Peter, then made his way toward her. She smiled as he approached, her determination to remember that this was not permanent flying right out of her head.

"I do hate to say *I told you so*," he quipped as he sank down onto the settee beside her. "But not so much that I won't."

She quirked one eyebrow at him, trying and failing to rein in the happiness that surged at his nearness. "You really needn't look so smug," she said. "It isn't becoming at all."

"Oh, I sincerely doubt that," he said with a grin. "I think it looks quite well on me."

"No one ever accused you of modesty, I'm guessing," she drawled.

He let loose a laugh. "But you have to admit, I was right when I told you that things would not fall apart if you were to take an afternoon off."

"Very well," she conceded, rolling her eyes. "I'll admit that one afternoon did no harm in the wedding preparations."

"And you enjoyed yourself," he pushed, a teasing gleam in his dark eyes.

She could continue to tease him, she supposed. But her

heart was so full of happiness, she could say nothing but the truth. "I did." She smiled. "Thank you, Quincy."

Something infinitely tender passed through his eyes. "It was my pleasure," he murmured.

Her cheeks heated under the regard in his gaze, unable to remember a time when she had been so happy.

"You seem inordinately pleased with yourself, Lady Clara."

The Duchess of Reigate's voice, sharp and accusatory, was like a bucket of ice water dumped over her head. Clara's spine snapped straight, her smile falling away, the spark lit from that afternoon blowing out as quickly as a candle in a hurricane.

Quincy, too, seemed deeply affected by his mother's presence. Gone was the easy, happy gentleman, and in his place was a stern, forbidding man.

"Mother," he said. "You've decided to finally join the rest of us, have you?"

She shrugged, somehow making the common action elegant, and sank down into the seat facing them. "No one can blame me for resting, surely."

"No doubt. Especially after such a lengthy journey. And at your advanced age."

Her eyes narrowed. Clara, watching the exchange with wide eyes, decided it was time to step in.

"I do hope you like your rooms, Your Grace. Lenora wanted you to have the very best accommodations. The gold bedroom has the most striking views of any room at Danesford."

"They are adequate," was all she said.

While Clara was still reeling from her rudeness, the duchess spoke again.

"Reigate," she said, keeping her eyes on Clara in a

disconcerting manner that had her feeling disturbingly exposed, "why don't you leave Lady Clara and I to chat? I would get to know my future daughter-in-law better."

Quincy let loose a rude noise. "I think," he said, his tone clipped and tense, "that you must be mad to think I'll leave you alone with her."

"Now, now, Reigate," the duchess cooed. "You really must learn to be more civil. It would be a shame if Lord and Lady Crabtree overheard. I've gotten to know them quite well in the past week. And I can say with certainty that they will not be happy should even a whiff of unpleasantness or scandal touch their precious son and his upcoming nuptials."

Clara felt all the blood leave her face. A horrible ringing started up in her ears, for it was a threat, plain and simple.

As she and Quincy stared at her in stunned silence, the woman's smile widened, a cruel kind of victory lighting her cold eyes. "Now, be a good son and leave us to a cozy chat."

Quincy fairly trembled with outrage beside her, heralding an explosion of volcanic proportions. Needing to keep the peace between them, she placed a hand on his arm. "It's fine, Quincy," she murmured low. "I can handle her."

The duchess laughed. "You hear that, Reigate? She can handle me," she said in a mocking voice.

Clara shot her a warning look before, fighting to hide the dread that was quickly rising up like a floodwater, she rearranged her stiff features into a bright smile and turned back to Quincy. "Truly, I'll be fine," she said. Then, in a whisper, "Don't let her win."

Her words seemed to penetrate his mounting fury.

Dragging in a deep breath, he smiled at her. "Of course, my dear," he said. "I shall be close by if you need me." Taking up her hand, he kissed her knuckles before rising and striding off, not once looking at his mother.

"Well done, Lady Clara," the duchess drawled. "I thank you for your handling of Reigate. Goodness knows he won't listen to me."

"It was not done for your benefit, I assure you," Clara managed.

"Ah, of course not. You would do anything to save your sister heartache, wouldn't you?"

Clara just managed to hide her shudder as the slimy slink of revulsion worked its way over her skin. "Let's make this quick, shall we?" she said. "Dinner will be called soon, and I'd rather not have my appetite threatened with thoughts of having to continue this conversation."

A grudging respect flared in the older woman's eyes. "You've got spirit, haven't you?" she murmured. "I don't know whether to be impressed or annoyed."

Clara ignored the attempt to bait her, keeping her eyes steady, her head high.

The duchess inclined her head. "Very well. I shall not take up too much of your precious time. I only wished to get to know you better. Surely you cannot fault me for that, Reigate being my last remaining son."

"What would you know?"

"You have lived on the Isle of Synne all your life, have you not?"

"I have," she answered, mind spinning as to where this could be going. She wasn't fooled one bit that this line of questioning was pursued out of mere curiosity.

The duchess raised a hand imperiously. At once a

footman approached with a tray. She took a glass of wine from it, keeping her eyes fixed on Clara as she took a sip. The considering gleam in that hard gaze had the hairs on the back of Clara's neck standing on end.

"You and your sister seem to love it here," the older woman mused. "Else why would Lady Phoebe be so insistent that everyone trek to this far-flung part of the country for her wedding?"

Once again the woman fell silent. She was trying to unnerve her. But Clara refused to let that happen. She inclined her head, drawing upon years of practice to keep her expression bland.

"And you've never had a London season?" the woman continued, seemingly undaunted by Clara's silence. "Never had a lengthy holiday anywhere?"

"No, Your Grace," Clara said.

"Really?" the duchess purred, her smile widening in a feral manner. For a moment Clara thought she saw the flash of knife-sharp teeth.

Shaking off the vision, she was about to state emphatically that, no, she had never stepped foot from Synne's shores.

Until she recalled the one time she was thought to have taken a trip, to visit her old nurse. When in reality she had been hidden away on the remote northern tip of Synne.

Her fingers tightened about the glass in her hands, and she felt she might cast up her accounts all over the duchess's skirts.

The expression of satisfaction on the woman's face gave her the appearance of a predatory snake about to strike.

Too late, Clara realized she had shown her hand. She quickly rearranged her features into unconcerned boredom. But her stomach sank, knowing the duchess's sharp eyes had missed nothing.

"Pardon me," she managed, "I had quite forgotten a trip I took to visit my old nurse some fifteen or so years back. You can understand, surely, it being so long ago."

"Oh, certainly. And where was it you went?"

She froze. There was too much knowledge in the woman's gaze for Clara to ignore. In desperation, she searched her mind for something, anything to say. But in her horror she came up blank.

The duchess's smile widened further.

Blessedly Yargood announced dinner, interrupting their standoff. Her salvation.

Quincy was at her side in an instant. "Clara," he murmured, holding out a hand for her, "are you ready?"

"Yes," she managed. Taking his hand, she allowed him to pull her to her feet, thankful for his arm to lean on when her legs trembled.

"We can finish this conversation later, Lady Clara," the duchess murmured.

"Your Grace," Clara said, dipping into a shaky curtsy, not meeting the woman's eyes.

Quincy led her out the drawing room door, leaning toward her when they were out of earshot of the rest of the party.

"What did she say to you, Clara?"

His voice was vibrating with tension. "Nothing," she said, trying for a calm she didn't feel.

"Clara."

"Truly, it was nothing at all."

Without warning, he ducked into a small room off the side of the hall, pulling Clara with him. Darkness shrouded them, the sounds of the rest of the party fading.

"Quincy," she gasped, "someone will notice."

"I don't give a damn," he shot back.

She gaped at him. Even the deep shadows weren't enough to hide the frustration on his face.

Her heart twisted, that he worried so for her. She stepped close, laying a hand on his cheek. "I'm well. Please don't give it another thought."

"She upset you, Clara. I can't let that go."

"You have to."

He growled low. "No."

She smiled. "Stubborn man."

His lips twitched, his voice turning gruff when he spoke again. "Stubborn woman." Then his expression resumed its serious mien. "Tell me, Clara. What did she say that upset you?"

In that moment, in the dark, with this man she was growing to love, she wanted to. With everything in her she wanted to tell him of that great tragedy, and the weight on her soul that would never leave her in peace. How easy it would be to speak the words, to transfer some of that burden, to have someone she could lean on and share it with.

But she couldn't. He would look at her differently, and she couldn't bear the thought of that. He would pity her, or think her ruined, or a hundred other horrible possibilities.

She put her mask firmly back in place, though it was more difficult to do now than it had ever been.

"Truly it was nothing," she said with a smile though she wanted to cry. "She merely asked if I've lived on Synne all my life."

"Clara—"

"Truly."

He looked as if he didn't believe her one bit. She concentrated with all her might to keep her smile in place.

Finally he nodded, though he didn't look the least bit happy.

"Very well," he said. "If you're certain."

"I am."

He studied her for a moment more before, with a sigh, he nodded and led her from the room. "But you will be joining the rest of the party on outings for the remainder of the week," he said in a tone that brooked no argument. "I won't allow her to get you off alone if I can help it."

And for once, Clara didn't fight it.

Chapter 15

Quincy should have been glad that Clara agreed to join the planned outing the following day. But the sight of her eyes, haunted with specters of some secret devastation, could not be forgotten.

He leaned back in his chair in the Beakhead Tea Room and watched her with a mixture of frustration and worry. To the casual eye she would appear to be utterly content, happy even. But to Quincy, who felt more attuned to her than he had to anyone since his father passed, the strain underlying it all was only too clear.

She laughed at something Miss Coralie said before turning to the girl's older sister, Miss Felicity Gadfeld, to impart some amusing anecdote. Then she was thanking the young tearoom proprietress, Miss Peacham, for the additional pitcher of lemonade, and offering to fill her sister's empty glass.

He was exhausted just watching her. She always kept herself busy, making sure everyone was taken care of, gently guiding conversations, making certain no one felt left out. Yet there was something different in her today, an almost manic busyness. Her laugh was grating to his ears, the dark circles under her eyes confessing to a sleepless night. It was as if she were trying with all her might to keep something at bay.

Immediately an image of his mother rose up, her eyes sharp and full of a smug glee as she'd talked to Clara the night before. Fast on the heels of that was Clara's attempts to deflect his questions about their conversation. Whatever his mother had said, it had upset Clara immensely.

And its effect on Clara had not disappeared. Just as it had last night, rage nearly blinded him. He would not allow his mother to give Clara even a moment more of pain.

The rest of their party began to gather their things and stand, Clara with them. Without thinking he grabbed her wrist, stopping her. She cast a mildly curious look at him that did nothing to detract from the faint trembling he felt in her hand.

"Stay a moment, my dear," he murmured.

Already the others were departing. She gave him a smile that didn't reach her eyes. "But the rest of the party—"

"Can go on ahead while you rest a moment."

Phoebe popped her head back in the door of the tea-room. "Are you coming, Clara? Quincy?"

Clara searched his face for a moment before letting loose a small sigh. "We'll meet up with you shortly, dear," she said to her sister.

Phoebe gave a happy nod and departed.

"Now," Quincy said, gently tugging on Clara's hand, "why don't we talk a bit?"

The look she gave him was cautious, but she nevertheless sat as he bid her. "I don't know what we have to talk about," she said, not meeting his eyes, her tapered fingers taking an uneaten biscuit from the plate in the center of the table. She didn't eat it, instead worrying it into a pile of crumbs on the pristine tablecloth.

"Last night—"

"We talked about everything worth mentioning."

The finality of her tone had his mouth closing with a snap. He studied her with narrowed eyes, trying to figure out how to get her to open up without putting her back up. She resembled nothing so much as a small cornered kitten, ready with sharp teeth and bared claws to fight back any threat.

Not knowing what else to do, he leaned toward her, lowering his voice. "I won't let her hurt you, Clara."

Her gaze swung up to meet his, and for a moment he could see straight to her soul. "You can't promise that," she whispered.

His heart twisted. He had the mad urge to pull her into his arms and fend off every threat to her sanity and happiness, to keep her safe from all the world's hurts and evils.

But that was not something he could do. Not only were they not betrothed in truth, but even were they set to be married he could not protect her from everything.

"I know she did something yesterday to upset you," he said. When she opened her mouth to argue, he held up his free hand. "I'm not trying to coerce you to confide in me. But know, if you need an ear to bend, I'm more than willing." He grinned, hoping to ease the look of pain in her eyes. "And I stay silent as a tomb when a confidence is given."

She attempted a smile back, though it was clear from the way her gaze suddenly shuttered that she was not the least bit convinced.

"Now," he said, reaching for the lemonade pitcher and refilling her glass, "I need your opinion on something of the utmost import."

She blinked several times, no doubt confused as to his lightning-fast change of subject. But she let out a relieved breath and tilted her head. "Of course."

"Now that I have the means to save the dukedom and I can plan my travels in earnest again," he said, sitting back in his seat, "I find myself not at all content with starting in Spain, as I had originally intended. I've a mind to go a bit farther afield. If you were to sail the world, where would you start your journey?"

"Goodness." She gave a startled laugh. "I'm not sure I've ever considered it."

He raised a brow. "Surely you learned geography from your governess."

"Of course," she scoffed.

"Well then?" he prompted, clasping his hands on his stomach and waiting expectantly.

She pursed her lips, taking a considering draught of her lemonade. "I suppose," she ventured slowly, "that I would love to go to Italy. Though," she finished hastily, her cheeks coloring, "you might think that too expected."

"Not at all," he murmured. "I would love to see it as well. But why Italy?"

She shrugged, picking up another biscuit on the table and crumbling it with her fingers. "My father often told us tales of his Grand Tour. My brother, Hillram, was fascinated by the idea, and begged Papa to tell him of his travels there so often we had them memorized. He dreamed of going one day. But of course, with the war raging, he was never able to."

"Hillram," Quincy repeated quietly. "He was the one engaged to Lenora some years ago, was he not?"

"Yes." Her smile turned sad. "He was a good man. It was devastating when he died. He was too young."

He studied her a moment. The expression in her eyes was one he'd never seen in her before. Wanting to know more about this side of her, he said quietly, "Tell me about him."

She gave a small laugh. "You don't wish to hear me wax poetic about my late brother."

"I assure you," he said, "there is nothing I would like better than to hear about your brother." And in the process, to learn of something that had made Clara *Clara*.

The realization hit him hard. It was not only this part of her past he wished to know, but all of it. Every triumph, every heartache. To know what had shaped her into this amazing, giving, complex woman.

This was so much more than the physical draw he had for her, and well past the close friendship they'd developed in recent weeks. Such a realization couldn't fail to open a door he had not considered before: that he was growing to care for Clara much, much more than he had thought possible.

"He was younger than you, was he not?" he prompted, as much to get her talking as it was to distract himself from his unexpected thoughts of her.

"By five years," she replied, the doubt leaving her, a fond remembrance taking its place. She smiled. "He was a vibrant thing from the start, always so happy, with a boundless energy and an optimism that could not be stifled, even when the odds were stacked against him."

The look in her eyes was so unguarded, his heart stalled in his chest. "You helped raise him?" he asked, his voice a touch hoarser than it had been. She nodded. "Tell me what he was like as a child."

And she did. Tales emerged from her, like a dam that had been breached, of Hillram's childhood antics, the pranks he pulled on his tutors, the time he had been sent down from school for some infraction or other. She told it all with a pride in her eyes, and a fondness that was made bittersweet by the muted grief in it.

He was struck that he had never met anyone so perfect for motherhood. And he wondered again why she had never married and set up a house of her own. She was beautiful, kind, loving. She came from a good family. What had happened that had kept her from having children of her own?

His mother's voice came back to him then from that fateful day in Dane House's drawing room when Clara had jumped in to save him by claiming they were engaged.

I do not think the late duke was ill these past fourteen years… One wonders why Lady Clara did not marry before his illness.

He nearly recoiled at the invasive memory. But now that it had taken hold it would not let him go. From all accounts her father had doted on her. Why had he not given her a season? Why had he allowed her to remain a spinster, toiling away in his home, watching over his younger children? Quincy had learned through letters from Peter that the previous duke had made them promise to give Phoebe a season. Why, then, had Clara been allowed to languish?

But what was this? Was he going to allow his mother to poison his thoughts, to pollute his opinion of Clara? He damn well wouldn't.

Blessedly she was so engrossed in memories of her brother, she didn't notice his inattention. Nor would she have reason to, he vowed. For the next half hour he made sure his focus did not waver from her. Their table was cleared, their drinks refreshed, and all the while she talked of Hillram, and Phoebe, and her life on the Isle with gentle prodding from him. And the image he had of her became clearer, more in focus, the colors more vibrant than he'd thought possible.

Eventually her attention was snagged by something out the tearoom window. She started, her cheeks turning red. "Goodness, how long have we been sitting here?" She gave a strained laugh, pushing her seat back, lurching to her feet. "What you must think of me, prattling on."

He rose beside her, grabbing her hand when she would have hurried away. "I'm glad you told me all of that," he murmured. "I like knowing more about you."

Her gaze rose to his, the vulnerability and longing in her eyes touching something deep in him. He ached to lower his head, to take her lips in a kiss...

Miss Peacham approached just then. "Lady Clara, if you have the time I have some questions about the cake for Lady Phoebe's wedding?"

Clara gasped, breaking their locked gazes. He felt the loss down to the very depths of his soul.

"Of course," she said to the young proprietress. "We can go to your office, can't we?"

Oh, no. She wouldn't bury herself in work again, not if he could help it.

"Actually," Quincy said, smiling his most charming smile at Miss Peacham, "Lady Clara is taking time off from wedding preparations to spend these last days enjoying her sister's company. Any questions can be relayed to the Duchess of Dane or Mrs. Kitteridge."

"Of course, Your Grace!" Miss Peacham exclaimed. "How wonderful to be able to enjoy time with your sister, Lady Clara. I'll send a note to the other ladies posthaste." She smiled brightly and hurried off.

Clara gaped at Miss Peacham's retreating back before turning to glare at him. "You had no right."

"It is my duty to make certain you enjoy yourself to the fullest," he declared. "No work for you, not as long as I'm around. Now," he added, holding out his arm, "shall we find your sister and the rest of the party? I do believe there was talk of ribbons and frippery."

She grumbled but nevertheless took his proffered arm. "You cannot force me to put aside all my duties."

"I can certainly try."

She gave him an exasperated look as he guided her from the tearoom. "You are a horrible influence," she said, squinting as they stepped into the bright afternoon sun. "But despite your efforts, I will never be the laze-about you want me to be."

"Perhaps," he acknowledged, then grinned wickedly. "But you have to admit, it will be fun trying."

She laughed, and the happiness lighting her face nearly had him stumbling on the walkway.

He knew in that moment he would do everything in his power to keep that light in her eyes. And part of that, he acknowledged grimly, keeping his features pleasant though his insides churned, would be making certain his mother stayed as far from Clara as possible.

* * *

Later that evening, as the rest of Danesford dressed for dinner, Quincy strode to his mother's room. Guests would begin arriving tomorrow from all over England; he'd best get this out of the way, and quickly. He didn't think he would be able to stomach being in her presence for long.

His sharp rap on her door was answered with alacrity by her maid. "Her Grace is not yet ready," she said in reply to his query.

"Is she decent, at least?"

The maid blinked. "Yes—"

"That's all I need then," he said, pushing into the room.

"But, Your Grace—"

"You may go," he said over his shoulder, his gaze already on his mother.

The duchess, seated at the dressing table, a box of jewels open before her, narrowed her eyes when she saw him. She studied him for a moment in the looking glass, as if weighing her chances of banishing him from her presence, before she said, "Leave us. I will ring for you when we're done."

"Yes, Your Grace," the maid said, dipping into a deep curtsy and hurrying out.

One side of the duchess's mouth lifted in a condescending smile as she turned back to her jewels. "I suppose your future bride ran to you crying."

Fury sliced through him. She was as good as admitting she had attacked Clara. He was tempted to lash out, to put his mother in her place.

At the last moment, however, he remembered Clara's whispered *Don't let her win*. Immediately he subdued the fire in his belly. The duchess would do everything in her power to bait him, as surely as the monsters who set rabid dogs on manacled bears did. He would have to work hard to keep the power in this confrontation.

He moved forward, sinking into a chair close by the duchess, hooking one leg over the arm in a blatant show of disrespect. Her lips pressed together for a moment before her features smoothed into her typical disdain. He grinned. So it was to be a war of wills, was it? Well, she would soon learn he had no intention of losing this particular battle. His thoughts returned to Clara, her eyes haunted. He had too much riding on it.

The seconds passed, the ticking of the clock on the mantel seeming to grow louder with each jerk of its hand. Quincy remained silent, waiting, knowing how it would unsettle his mother and taking a disturbing amount of pleasure at the thought. She ignored him and continued to dig through her box, the grating scrape of jewels and gold dragging against one another rending the air. Brilliant rubies and sapphires winked at him as she rummaged. He had seen enough of his brothers' papers to know that they had replaced most of the family jewels with paste copies in their quest to bleed the dukedom dry. He wondered how many of his mother's pieces had been sacrificed in their attempts. And if she even knew.

His lips twisted. No doubt she did. The woman might be cold and cruel, but she was also frighteningly cunning, with a need to have her talons in every aspect of the dukedom. And after her elder sons' stealth in selling out everything they could manage right from under her, there was no doubt in Quincy's mind that the sting of nearly losing everything had transformed that need for control into an obsession.

Nothing mattered to her more than appearing capable, in control. In power. She would hold her head high and pretend those jewels were the real thing with her dying breath if it meant she would not lose her status.

Still he remained silent. Finally, when the air in the room was so thick he imagined he would be able to quite literally cut it, she snapped.

"Not going to answer my question then?"

"About Clara?" He shrugged, studying his nails inso-
lently, even as he weighed his answer. He could admit the
truth, that Clara had refused to reveal the subject of their
troubling conversation. But would it be like offering up
the tender underbelly, inviting attack?

Or would pretending to know what had been said
give him the greatest advantage? Mayhap showing a solid
front with Clara would work in his favor.

In the end he went for vagueness. His mother would
latch onto the negative, he knew, and her defense would
guide his offense.

"I think you must know the answer to that," he said.
"Else why ask at all?"

She let loose a sound of disgust. "The girl is weak."

Yet another attempt to bait him. It was with effort
this time, however, that he kept his emotions in check.
Breathing slowly and deeply, forcing a relaxed pose he
didn't feel in the least, he said, "Actually, she is the farthest thing from weak. But you would not know anything
about that, would you?"

"If you are implying I'm weak—"

"Oh, now, don't put words in my mouth, Mother," he
drawled.

She closed the lid of the jewelry box with a snap
that reverberated through the air and turned to face him.
"Enough of this. I'm assuming you've come to warn me
away from upsetting the girl. Well, you'll be waiting a
good long while before I do such a thing. If you think I'll
let her become the next Duchess of Reigate, you are very
much mistaken."

"Worried you'll no longer have a puppet in place?"
She stilled, a small tell, and he grinned, more a baring of
teeth than anything. "You don't actually think I missed

your little play with Lady Mary, do you? Come now, Mother, it's not wise to underestimate an opponent."

That finally seemed to break her tightly held control. "You'd do best not to underestimate that fiancée of yours," she snapped. "She's hiding something; I know it in my bones."

"I don't give a damn if she is," he shot back, surprised to realize just how much he meant it. No matter his curiosity regarding what gave her such intense pain, it didn't matter to him in the slightest what was in her past. He wanted, above all, to be her future.

What was this? No, he had no intention of having a future with Clara. He had no intention of having a future with *anyone*; at least not yet, not until he was much older, with most of his life behind him. He had too many places he wanted to see, too many adventures he wanted to experience. With the sale of Swallowhill to Lord Fletcher, he had every intention of enjoying his life with no obligations except to himself and his own pleasure.

But now that the idea of Clara as his wife had taken hold, it would not be easily shaken.

Blessedly, his mother was wholly unaware of the chaos reigning in his mind. "I do," she said, her voice dripping ice. "Do you think I want some strumpet as the next Duchess of Reigate, for some scandal in her past to one day come to light and tarnish our entire heritage?"

"Enough!" Quincy roared, surging to his feet, forgetting his determination to keep his emotions in check in the face of her abuse of Clara. "You will listen to me, *Your Grace*," he snarled. "I want you gone from here at dawn. I don't want you speaking one word more to Clara, much less breathing in the same air as her."

She gaped at him, a stunned understanding shadowing

her cold eyes until they appeared to be filled with the icy shards of a deep winter. "She has gotten her claws in you, hasn't she?"

He slashed a hand through the air. "Clara doesn't have it in her to manipulate me in such a way. You, on the other hand," he bit out, "have no other reason to oppose my marriage to her than your own need to have someone easily controlled at the helm."

Her expression didn't change, but he saw the flicker of something in her eyes. Not guilt; she would never feel guilty for even something as heinous as this. No, it was more of a recognition, and a regret that he had seen so quickly to the heart of the matter.

He drew himself up to his full height. "I want you gone at daybreak. You can stay at the London house for as long as you like. But beyond that I want no further contact with you. You can reach me through my solicitor." He bowed, a shallow, mocking thing. "Good day, madam."

He turned to go, expecting to feel relief at finally cutting her from his life completely. Instead he was only aware of a hollowness deep in his chest, and a simmering anger that she had stolen his right to a loving mother.

Her voice, however, stopped him when he would have opened the door.

"I'm surprised you haven't asked me about her," she drawled.

He gripped the knob, refusing to look at her again. Yet he couldn't help asking, "Ask you about who?"

"Why, Miss Willa Brandon, of course."

Chapter 16

Quincy might have kept his countenance if his mother had spoken of anyone else. That name, however, spoken with such smug condescension, nearly floored him. He spun to face her, the demand that she explain herself sticking in his throat, choking him.

Triumph lit her eyes. "Did you think I did not know of her? Of course I was aware of your father's sidepiece. And that he hid her away on this godforsaken island."

He thought he might be sick. Yes, he knew men of his station took mistresses. Yes, he knew it was an accepted fact in society that a man would betray his marriage vows. That did not mean Quincy had ever seen it as anything other than reprehensible. Even for someone who had been in such an unhappy union as his father had been.

And there was the true crux of the problem. He had looked up to his father as what all men should be: a good, kind, giving man who had been dealt a bad hand in life with his wife, but who nevertheless always did the right thing.

Now, however, that exalted image was tumbling down about his head.

As if she read his thoughts, her smile widened,

transforming her beautiful face into a terrible mask. "How it must gall you, to know your father was not perfect."

Her words, said with such cruel glee, finally snapped him from his shocked silence. He glared at her. "This changes nothing," he lied. "And if you think this little ploy of yours, baiting me with knowledge I'm fully aware of, will keep me from throwing you off the Isle, you are sadly mistaken."

"Mayhap not," she conceded, though she didn't look the least bit convinced. "But there is still the matter of Lady Phoebe and Lord Oswin's marriage."

Damnation. And with her recent friendship with Lady Crabtree, the duchess's influence over that woman would be that much stronger.

"If you do anything to threaten their marriage—" he growled.

"I wouldn't dream of it," she drawled. Suddenly her gaze sharpened. "As long as you don't cause any trouble."

Furious, impotent, he pulled open the door and stormed out into the hall. Damn cruel woman. She was Satan in a gown, the very devil in his midst. And she held all the cards.

At least for the next few days, until Phoebe and Oswin were safely wed. After which there would be nothing holding him back from telling her exactly where she could go.

And in the interim, he would not allow her to harm even a single hair on Clara's head.

* * *

Clara adjusted her skirts over the rock she was perched on and breathed in deeply of the fresh sea air. Trying and failing to rein in her anxiety from doing absolutely nothing.

Farther out on the beach Phoebe and her friends—the group swelled to double its previous number with the arrival of several wedding guests just that morning—packed away their picnic lunch. Their happy chattering carried on the breeze, laughter threaded through it, like busy seabirds making merry along the shore. And here she sat, watching as they cheerfully worked at clearing up, forbidden by Quincy to lift a finger. Clara let loose a frustrated sigh.

"You make it seem as if sitting back and letting others take control is torture."

Quincy's voice rumbled with suppressed laughter. She cast him a disgruntled glare where he perched beside her, looking more relaxed than she probably ever had in her entire life. "That's because it *is* torture."

He chuckled, leaning back on his elbows, giving her a wicked grin. "I'm glad I'm here to guide you in the ways of the lazy, then."

Clara rolled her eyes, even as she longed to drink in the sight of him stretched out beside her in the cheerful afternoon sun. "I hardly think you're lazy, Quincy," she couldn't help saying. Truly, the man was all long, lean muscles. Something she could attest to due to that kiss they'd shared in London. A form like that did not come without hard work and effort.

She shivered despite the warmth of the day. And not because she was in any way chilled. Oh, no, quite the opposite.

"I've been known to shirk my duties for a day of fun,"

he quipped. When she did nothing more than blow out an irritated breath, he surged to his feet.

Startled by the abrupt movement, she stared up at him. The suddenly intense look in his eyes didn't bode well for her.

"That's it," he declared, holding out his hand. "Allowing you to sit and watch the work being done is not helping you one bit. You need to be removed from the scene. Come along then."

"I don't see how that will change anything," she scoffed. Nevertheless, she placed her fingers in his and stood before him. "And where are you proposing to take me off to?"

A hot look flashed in his dark eyes, his fingers tightening on hers. It was gone in an instant, the devil-may-care grin back in place. But that was all it took to send her thoughts spiraling to wholly improper places. Made so much worse by his murmured, "You'll see." When he tugged on her hand she followed readily, even eagerly, her heart pounding in anticipation as her steps shadowed his.

Warning bells pealed in her head, a frantic indication that if he were to take her in his arms she would be utterly lost. But they were distant, muffled, and losing their power by the instant. She was hardly aware of the sand slowing her half boots, of the breeze tugging at her bonnet, or of the fading sounds of gaiety. Her entire focus was on the feel of his fingers gripping hers and the sight of his strong back as he guided her along the cliff face that butted up to the small beach.

"I am going to assume," he said, turning to help her over some rocks, "that you have not been exploring since you were a young girl."

She dropped her gaze to the ground beneath her feet, praying he would attribute it to her need for balance and not to a need to avoid his gaze. She was already aching for him; goodness knew what it would do to her if she looked into those mesmerizing obsidian eyes of his.

"You have the right of it," she said, lifting her skirts and placing her foot down with care on a flat rock rubbed smooth by sand and wind and sea. "That's not to say I didn't visit the Isle's beaches when my siblings were young. But I never joined in on the exploration portion of those trips." No matter how much she might have wanted to.

"What a veritable waste of a childhood," he said.

"I wouldn't call it a waste," she said, frowning at his back. He turned, flashing that maddening grin of his. "Ah, I see." She gave him a wry smile. "You're teasing me."

"Of course I am. Did you actually think I have anything but the utmost respect for what you've done for your family?"

A warmth filled her that had nothing whatsoever to do with her desire for him. And she knew this newest predicament was the biggest danger to her by far, for it heralded something far more powerful.

"But that does not mean it isn't an absolute shame that you had to miss out on something so purely childlike, so free and innocent and *fun*." He grinned at her over his shoulder. "How lucky that you should have me to teach you the lost art of foolery."

"Foolery?" she queried, praying he would not hear the sudden breathlessness in her voice that his wicked look prompted.

"Absurdity?" he tried. "Hmm, yes. I quite like that word. Very well, we shall call this Reclaiming Your

Absurdity. Or in your case, Claiming Your Absurdity, as you never utilized that talent to begin with. I may even write a book."

She laughed, his ridiculous little speech awakening a joy and freedom in her she had never thought to possess again. As well as a recklessness she suddenly had no wish to control.

"I'm not completely without skills, you know," she quipped. "Despite your low opinion of me."

The doubtful look he threw over his shoulder told her exactly what he thought of her assertion.

"You don't believe me."

"No."

"Well," she said, fighting a grin, "I'll just have to prove you wrong."

With that she released his hand, picked up her skirts, and darted in front of him.

"I was born on this Isle, Quincy," she called over her shoulder as he stumbled to a stunned halt. "If you think you know it better than me, you're quite mistaken."

He was silent as she raced ahead, his shock palpable. Then, letting loose a surprised laugh, he was off like a shot after her. She squealed, hurrying her steps over the uneven ground. Her heart pounded, a heady excitement racing through her veins as his steps, muffled by the sand, came closer. She kept her eyes on the cliff line. Just a few feet more.

Just as he growled a low, "I've almost got you," she saw the opening in the rock. With a triumphant cry she deftly stepped to the side. His fingers brushed her skirts as she ducked into the small cave hidden in the cliff wall.

She turned just in time to see his stunned features as he barreled past the opening. The expression was so comical she doubled over laughing. Arms wrapped about her middle, she laughed as she hadn't since she was a small child, letting it take over her until tears were running down her face, until she could hardly breathe.

And then she couldn't breathe at all. For she was suddenly in his arms, his laughter joining her own, his gaze warm with wonder as he looked down at her in the shadows of the cave.

"You minx," he murmured, his fingers stroking rebellious curls from her cheeks. "You knew this was here all along."

She grinned unrepentantly. "Surprised you, have I?"

"Oh, yes."

His voice had dipped, turning husky. Molten heat filled her. Her hands, which had been braced on his arms, slid up to his broad shoulders.

She swallowed hard, fighting for composure. "You shouldn't underestimate me, you know," she managed.

"You're right," he whispered. His gaze fell to her mouth with a ragged exhale. "And yet I continue to do so."

His breath washed over her face, sweet with the berries he'd eaten at lunch. She waited, hardly breathing. The recklessness he'd reawakened in her was making her want things she'd denied herself for too long.

But he held back, his mouth hovering a hairsbreadth from her own. She remembered vaguely his promise to her, that he would not kiss her again unless she asked.

There was every reason to pull away from him, to walk away and not look back. There were good reasons. Strong reasons.

But for the life of her, she couldn't think of a single one.

Her fingers threaded through the inky curls at his nape. He shuddered under her touch. And with that small tell, proof that he was as affected as she was, a daring swept through her, burning down the woman she had been into someone new, someone bold and assertive.

Someone who was brave enough to grasp joy and hold on tight.

She raised her chin, looking him full in the eye. "Kiss me."

His eyes flared wide, shock and desire and something deep and earth-shattering filling his features. "Are you certain?"

"Yes." There was no hesitation in her answer; she had never been more sure of anything in her life.

Still he waited, this honorable man who would protect her even from herself. So she did the only thing she could: she rose up on her toes, pulled his head down, and captured his lips with her own.

An inferno. That was the only way to describe the sensations that incinerated her in their brilliance. Her heart pounded out a fierce beat, and she let her defenses topple. No hard thing; he'd been slowly eroding their foundation for weeks now. But running over the sand, the wind tugging strands of her hair free, her skirts snapping about her legs—and Quincy, close behind her, their laughter joining in the air—made her realize she didn't want to go back to who she had been. She wanted this. She wanted him.

He groaned, his hands crushing the delicate muslin of her gown, the muscles in his arm bunching as he pulled her flush to him. When his mouth opened, hot and urgent over her own, she was ready, welcoming his tongue as it twined with hers, reveling in the taste of him.

Her hands moved frantically over him, each play of muscle under the soft wool of his jacket driving her nearly insensible. He pressed her against the smooth cave wall, his lean body hard against her soft curves, his arousal pressing into her belly. And still it wasn't enough. She wanted more of this, more of *him*, until she didn't know where one of them began and the other ended.

As if she had spoken the need aloud, his hand slid to her leg, hiking it up over his hip as he pressed into the core of her. Bright lights burst behind her tightly closed lids. She tore her mouth free, her head falling back against the stone wall, a low moan escaping her lips.

"My God, you're glorious," he rasped as his mouth moved to her jaw, down the length of her neck. His lips were firm yet achingly soft, the faint stubble of his beard a heady contrast. Nothing could feel better than this, surely.

That foolish thought was decimated the moment he gently cupped her breast.

She gasped, arching up, offering more. Begging for more. He growled, the sound vibrating across the sensitive skin where her neck met her shoulder. When his thumb dragged over her straining nipple, the layers of her clothing no barrier to the exquisite torture, she thought she might scream. He cradled her in his palm, the warmth and intimacy making her mindless with want.

Suddenly his hand was gone. She nearly cried out her frustration, until he shifted her in his embrace, hiking her other leg over his hip, his arms strong under her as he held her away from the stone wall. For a single moment she was suspended in the air, unmoored, drifting. And then she settled against him, her port in the storm. "Quincy."

His name on her lips, hoarse and breathless, rebounded against the close walls of the cave, mingling with their ragged breaths, the gentle hush of the sea, the faint cry of seabirds. His kisses grew more frantic, teeth and tongue coming into play, trailing over her shoulder, her collarbone, brushing against the bodice of her gown.

Tightening her legs around his hips, she rocked against him, the bulk of her skirts and chemise doing nothing to hide the power and strength of him straining against her. His groan mingled with her gasp, his fingers tightening on her bottom, pressing her more firmly against the hard length of him.

"Please," she whispered, every inch of her aching for more. "Please, Quincy. I want—" Her throat closed off, unable to give voice to the clamoring inside her.

"What do you want, Clara," he rasped, rocking against her, making her gasp. "Tell me."

She shuddered. "I—I want—"

But her mind went blank. She struggled to give voice to the overwhelming chaos within her. What did she want, exactly? To feel his bare skin against hers, to have him inside her?

Oh, yes. All that and more. But a small, quiet question infiltrated those passion-glazed fantasies: *What then?*

She froze. What then, indeed. Hadn't she already been down this road and suffered the consequences?

But Quincy is not like him, her desperate heart tried to reason. Which only made her head, which had been in control for more than half her life, dig in its heels more. *That's what you thought before*, it chided. *And look where it got you.*

Ah, God, what had she done?

Dragging in an unsteady breath, she managed in a small voice, "I'd like to be let down now, please."

A shock seemed to go through him, seizing his muscles. But he quickly recovered, lowering her with infinite care to the cave floor. He stayed close to her, his strong hands rubbing her arms. She kept her gaze on his rumpled cravat, unable to look him in the eye.

"I'm sorry," he murmured. "I shouldn't have taken advantage as I did."

"There's no reason to apologize," she whispered. "I was the one who asked for the kiss."

"Yet it became so much more than a kiss." He sighed, cupping her cheek, his thumb rubbing across her temple. She just kept herself from closing her eyes and leaning into his touch. If she did, she would be gone. There was nothing she wanted more than to lose herself in his arms again.

His deep voice rumbled through her. "I've never felt this way about anyone before."

"Nor I," she admitted before she could think better of it. Realizing how vulnerable such a statement made her appear, she gently extricated herself from his arms, righting her clothes with trembling fingers as she did so.

"But that's only to be expected, I suppose," she said, tucking a stray curl back into her chignon. She let loose a strained laugh, praying it didn't betray just how hard it was to feign that nothing was amiss. "We've been play-acting all this time, pretending to a stronger affection than is truly there. Perhaps we've begun to believe a bit of the lie ourselves. Now then," she said brightly even as panic began to rear, her control, always so easy to call upon, stubbornly eluding her, "shall we join the others?"

And with that she marched out of the cave, trying and failing to leave her heart back in that dim place. For she knew, with devastating certainty, she had done the one thing she'd vowed never to do: she'd fallen in love with him.

* * *

Quincy watched her leave with equal parts frustration and dismay. Her mask was back, more firmly in place than it had ever been. Questions bounced about in his head, keeping him from stopping her: What would he say? Would he apologize? Perhaps he'd spout something trite and lighthearted to ease the strain that had cropped up between them? Or maybe he'd choose the most ridiculous option of all and suggest they make their fake engagement a real one?

He blanched and stumbled to a halt in the cave entrance. Marriage? No, he was most assuredly not ready to marry. And even if he was, which he was *not*—something that required repeating, apparently—she wasn't, either. It was why they had entered this farce in the first place, a situation that benefited them both in that it kept them from marrying.

Yet the idea settled in his soul, burrowing deep just as Clara had. And to his shock, it felt right.

He shook his head sharply, trying to dislodge the thought by force. But it stayed where it was, nice and snug. Frowning, he watched Clara walk with purpose across the sand. What the hell had changed in him so suddenly, so completely?

But he knew in a flash it had not been sudden. Every day that he was in her company, witnessing firsthand her deep love and unselfish devotion to her family, she had settled deeper into his heart. Even more powerful, however, had been those glimpses of the woman she hid from the world. Her passion, her vulnerability, the deep joys and sorrows that she tried so valiantly to lock away. They made him want to know more about her, to discover every hidden cove of her heart. He wanted to give her a life where she could express those emotions freely, where she didn't feel the need to be someone else. He wanted to be able to love her.

He started. Love? No, he didn't love Clara. That was ridiculous.

As his gaze caressed the stiff line of her back, however, he felt the truth of it down to his bones: He loved her. He loved her and wanted to give the world to her.

No, he wanted more than that. He wanted to *share* the world with her. Every adventure, every new horizon, even the heartbreaks that were bound to come. He wanted her by his side—not just anyone, but *her*—to teach her to embrace a joy in life she was only beginning to uncover, and to learn from her that calm strength that had made her who she was. Suddenly he knew that marriage, which had seemed like something that would anchor him in place, would be what filled his sails and propelled him toward a brighter future.

The next moment found him sprinting across the sand after her. In seconds he reached her, planting himself in her path. She skidded to a stunned halt. "What if we marry in truth?" he blurted.

Not the most elegant proposal, he realized belatedly. Her eyes flared wide. Though it wasn't only shock from his asinine question that clouded them; no, betrayal and disappointment were there in spades.

"You needn't promise marriage to coerce me into your bed, Quincy."

She may as well have slapped him. He gaped at her, hurt smothering the hope in an instant. "Do you truly think me capable of such a thing?" he managed. "Haven't you come to know me at all in the last weeks?"

She hugged her arms about her middle, looking as brittle as anyone could. "I don't know that anyone can truly know a person after so short a time."

The stark vulnerability in her posture and voice finally broke through his wounded ego. Her reaction had been too violent to be anything but the effects of some past emotional injury.

He had a flash of her face after her conversation with his mother, an expression that was hauntingly like the one lurking in her eyes now. Added to that the duchess's insistence that Clara had some great scandal in her past, and it didn't take him long to conclude what was upsetting her.

Someone had hurt her, had destroyed her trust. He wanted nothing more than to find the bastard, whoever he might be, and make him pay.

But what was important wasn't the past. It was their future, hopefully together.

But how to convince her? "I know you said you would never marry—" he started.

"Correct," she said. "I daresay I would not make a good wife. I'm nearly one and thirty and quite set in my ways, not some young debutante easily molded at her husband's whim. Besides," she continued, her words tumbling from her as if she was afraid he would speak and break her resolve, "you said yourself you've no intention of marrying, either. With both of us so set against it, it would be foolish to discount our initial reservations because of a simple kiss."

She smiled, so wide he feared her cheeks might crack, and turned to go. He caught her hand, holding her back. She drew in a sharp breath.

"Just consider it, Clara," he said.

She shook her head, refusing to meet his eyes. Her fingers remained slack in his grip, but they trembled. "No, I don't think—"

"I'm not asking you to answer me this moment. Just do me the honor of considering the possibility." Then, when it seemed she would definitively refuse, "Please."

He filled the one word with the emotions of his heart, waiting as she stood silent, her head bowed. Finally, after what seemed an eternity, she nodded. It was sharp, and barely perceptible for the tension in her. But it was a nod nevertheless.

He let out a breath, cautious joy spreading through him. It was on the tip of his tongue to declare his love for her; he should have done it from the start, and in his excitement he had blundered and left that pertinent information out. He winced. It was beginning to dawn on him just how unromantic his blasted proposal had been.

But one look at her face and he sensed instinctively it wasn't the time. No doubt whoever had hurt her before had declared the same. He would just have to show her how he felt. In the meantime, she needed normalcy.

"Wonderful. Now," he said in a cheerful tone, releasing her hand, "I heard Oswin mentioning a plan to gather everyone for footraces after lunch was concluded, and I've a mind to show these young whelps how it's done."

She blinked in confusion but nodded, starting off again across the sand. As he fell into step beside her, he let his relaxed expression slip. Phoebe and Oswin's wedding was less than a week away, after which they had agreed to part ways. How the hell would he get past the hurt in her to convince her to give them a chance?

For he could not contemplate sailing away from England without her by his side.

Chapter 17

What if we marry in truth?

Hours later, Quincy's words were still swirling in Clara's mind as she lay in her bed, staring up at the dark ceiling. Tempting her as nothing had in too many lonely years.

She flinched at the thought, guilt sitting heavy on her. No, not lonely. She'd been surrounded by loved ones, had never been without companionship.

Yet hadn't she still been alone? Her father had been the only one who'd known of her past shame and heart-ache. And though she had fairly broken his heart with her reckless, thoughtless behavior, he had never wavered in his love and support of her. Something he had let her know day in and day out, through words and actions.

She'd made certain he never knew how deep her wounds cut, and that they would never heal. It was a promise she'd made to herself when she had finally emerged from the darkest days of her life, when she was able to comprehend what her mistake had cost, not only to herself, but to him as well.

With her father's death she had not only a beloved parent, but her last connection to her child as well. The only proof that her son had even been here was a secret grave overlooking the sea and the small bundle hidden away in her room, containing a lock of palest blond hair and a threadbare blanket she had cried into for years after.

She had spent half her life keeping the memory of that child safe in her heart, at once her most treasured and her most agonizing secret. It was necessary, she'd told herself over and over. If the truth got out, she would be ruined, and by extension her entire family. Most especially Phoebe.

Now, however, as she thought of marrying Quincy, as she considered revealing everything to him, she realized that the fear of ruination, while always her greatest deterrent, was also accompanied by a need to keep the memory of her child protected. If she shared him with others, they would think him a curse, or something to be reviled. And she couldn't stand his memory to be altered, not when he'd been so perfect in her eyes, that child she would always love and never forget.

Mayhap if Quincy were a mere *mister* she might have disappeared with him and had a happy life. But he was a duke. If she married him, she would be a duchess. She would be under constant scrutiny, her every move and action combed over. Her past looked at under a microscope. And eventually the truth would come out. Mayhap not that secret child. But the seduction, the ruination, would eventually come to light. She could not do that to Quincy, could not visit that upon him.

But how beautiful life would be if she could marry him and spend the rest of her days loving him.

She did not realize she was crying until her tears began to cool in the night air. She scrubbed at them, wishing she could as easily wipe away her heartache. She would have to watch him leave. With nothing to remember him by but the few kisses they'd shared, nothing to keep her warm as the years passed but a handful of passionate embraces.

Anger flared bright. Rolling on her side, she punched her pillow before pulling it tight against her chest, as if it could extinguish the fury building in her. She'd been foolish and naïve, allowing herself to be manipulated by that man when she'd been a girl. Her future had been stolen from her before she'd been able to claim it.

She shook her head sharply, her hair grating against her sheets. She wasn't foolish or naïve now. And she decided, then and there, she did not want to spend the rest of her life with that long-ago act as her only remembrance of physical love. She would not take to her grave the hasty groping she'd endured with a man who had thought only of himself. No, she wanted something passionate and loving to remember as she grew old. With a man who had shown her nothing but respect from the first.

She was throwing off her covers before she knew what she was doing. She didn't falter when she reached his room, raising her hand and knocking lightly at the door. In a moment it was thrown open.

Quincy's chest was bare, his feet as well, his snug-fitting breeches leaving little to her imagination. His hair was damp from a recent bath and falling over his forehead in inky waves. His eyes flared wide when he saw her.

"Clara. What are you doing here?"

In answer she pushed into the room, closing the door firmly behind her, giving the key a twist in the lock for good measure. Then she turned to face him.

The cautious hope that flared in his eyes nearly undid her. She held up a hand to stop the words that were forming on his lips, knowing if he renewed his question to her, the one she had promised to think over in a moment of madness, she would not be able to do what she had come here for.

"I'm not here to accept your proposal," she said, aware of a trembling in her voice but unable to control it. "I still have no plans to marry. I need you to understand that."

She looked closely at him. His lips pressed tight, disappointment clear in his face. But he nodded.

She cleared her throat, suddenly unsure how to continue. How did one go about asking for a night of lovemaking? She suddenly had a new respect for the widows in society who had the confidence to carry on affairs. This was no easy feat.

Finally, deciding that transparency was the only way to broach this delicate situation, she straightened her shoulders and looked him square in the eye.

"I want you to take me to your bed."

He drew in a sharp breath, longing and desire and shock and worry all coalescing in his face. "Clara—"

"I know this is highly unconventional," she continued, cutting him off for fear he would refuse her outright. "And I know that unmarried women don't often participate in...these things." She cleared her throat, feeling the heat of a blush staining her cheeks but refusing to back down. "But I am not an innocent you need worry about marrying. I am a grown woman who has decided to take control of her desires. And the truth of the matter is, I want you."

His dark eyes, glowing in the faint light from the fire in the hearth, flared with heat. She took it as encouragement to continue.

Nevertheless, it was no easy thing to get to the business side of such an arrangement. She cleared her throat and, laying her hands flat on the door behind her to keep from keeling over, said in a voice that shook only a small bit, "I want you, and I would very much like to spend a night with you. I, of course, have requirements."

He blinked. "Requirements?"

"Yes. You need to understand that this is in no way a promise of a future relationship between us. It is merely physical, two people enjoying one another, one night of passion." She took strength from his nod to soldier on. "I also need to know that there will be every effort made to prevent a child. You are a man of the world; I assume you know of such things." Again a nod, this time hesitant but firm nonetheless. "Good," she said on a relieved breath.

But with that all gone over, her bravado left her. She pushed away from the door, clasping her hands before her, her gaze falling to his bare feet on the polished wood floor. How did one move to the next step in these things? Did she simply kiss him? Did she wait for him to remove her clothes? Did she climb under the covers and wait for him to come to her?

The seconds ticked past. Still he remained silent. Her nerves began to fray. Perhaps she had misread him. It was possible; hadn't her history proved she was not the best judge of character? She shifted, pressing her bare toes into the floor. Wishing she could sink into it and disappear.

Instead she said, her voice small, "Unless, that is, you have no wish to."

Immediately he was there, pulling her into his arms. She went gladly, burying her face against his chest as he stroked strong hands over her back.

"Of course I want to, you silly woman," he whispered into the crown of her hair. "I have wanted to from the moment I met you. You are beautiful, and desirable.

But more than that, you are loving, and passionate, and strong. How could I fail to care for you? How could I help but—"

She tensed, her entire body going rigid in his arms. Surely he wouldn't declare himself in love with her. It would be the cruelest joke life could play on her, to have this amazing man, who she had grown to love so very much, equally in love with her. One broken heart when this ended would be bad enough.

"How could I help but want you," he finished. He kissed the top of her head before putting her away from him. "I want you so much I can hardly see straight when I'm with you. Even when we're not together I think about you, dream about you…"

She laid a hand on his bare chest. His muscles bunched under her fingers, his ragged breath giving proof to his words. She ached to admit she felt the same. Instead she whispered, "I would have some beautiful memories to hold on to after you leave."

"Clara," he rasped, "you deserve more."

She couldn't help the bitter laugh that escaped her. "Mayhap long ago."

Something intense lit his eyes. Not wanting to see what her small, unintentional confession might have stirred up in him—whether that be questions, or pity, or disgust— she dropped her gaze. A muscle ticced in his jaw, a day's growth of beard shadowing it, the tight press of his lips proof of his disquiet. But at least it was not his eyes, so open and revealing, telling her things she didn't want to know. She swallowed hard and continued.

"I want this, Quincy. I want *you*." And then, "Please."

The word had barely left her lips before she was once more in his arms. Her hands gripped tight to the smooth expanse of his shoulders, a tremor going through her as he pressed his lips to the side of her neck.

"You're certain?" he rasped. "You'll tell me if you want me to stop?"

She drew in a shuddering breath, his scent filling her, the clean smell of his sandalwood soap making her dizzy with longing. "I won't want you to stop."

"Promise me you'll tell me if you wish for me to stop," he pushed.

Her heart lurched, tears burning her eyes at his insistence that, no matter what, he would not allow her to regret this. Yes, she had given her heart to the right man. Though he could never know just how desperately she loved him.

"I promise," she whispered.

Those two words unleashed a raw desperation she had not known he'd kept hidden. He pressed his mouth, open and hot, against the side of her neck. His teeth scraped the tender skin, his low groan vibrating through her until she thought she'd shatter. Suddenly his arms swept beneath her, lifting her, cradling her to his chest. He strode across the room and lowered her to the bed as if she were a priceless treasure.

"I'll make certain you won't regret a minute of this," he vowed, his hot gaze finding hers in the dim light.

She reached for him, pulling his head down to hers, pressing her forehead to his. "I could never regret being with you, Quincy."

Questions swam in his eyes, and a tenderness that touched her down to her soul. Frightened of the feelings he was dredging up, she took his mouth in a kiss, hoping to bury the bone-deep need to confess her past sins, to accept his proposal and spend the rest of her days with him. She would forget the past, forget the future. Her entire world was here and now in his arms.

He needed no further urgings. He kissed her with a desperation matched only by the one deep inside her, a need to lose themselves in one another, to make this coming together as beautiful as possible so it might remain with them long after their parting.

His eager fingers grasped the hem of her nightgown, pulling it up and working it over her head. His mouth found hers again when she was free of the garment, and he pressed her down into the soft mattress, his bare chest meeting the straining tips of her breasts, making her gasp into his mouth.

He lifted his head, his dark eyes searing into her own, the tenderness in them going straight to her heart. "So beautiful," he whispered as he stroked a loose curl back from her cheek. "So passionate." He shook his head in wonder. "You are amazing."

Tears burned. She blinked them back, wanting nothing to mar this perfect moment. "Love me, Quincy," she breathed.

"I do."

Not *I will*, but *I do*. Before the ramifications of those two simple words could destroy her, he dipped his head, letting his lips trail along the length of her neck. And she was lost.

He worshipped her skin. That was the only possible description for the kisses he trailed over her, each one full of the tenderness that had been present in his voice, hinting at so much more. When his lips found her breast she arched up, eager for what was to come. And he didn't hold back, his mouth opening over the straining tip. Fire pooled between her legs and she let out a low moan, her fingers diving into the soft, still-damp waves of his hair.

His hands, too, were driving her wild, and everywhere at once, plumping her breast for his kisses, trailing down her side, gripping her hip. When they trailed over her belly, she held her breath. And then he was dipping his fingers between her legs, and she had to bite her lip to keep her eagerness from rending the air.

"So ready for me," he gasped, caressing her folds, the slickness there creating a dizzying sensation. She opened her legs, pressing up against his hand, silently begging for more.

In answer he trailed kisses lower. Before she could react to the unexpectedness of it, he came to the core of her, pressing his mouth against the thatch of curls there. And everything was forgotten.

With tongue and teeth and lips he loved her, and that part of her quickly became the very center of her universe. He drew her into his mouth, stroking his tongue over her folds, starting up a rhythm that had her rocking her hips against him. She gripped tight to his head in silent encouragement. He let loose a growl of approval, his fingers digging into her hips, and she threw her head back as the pleasure brought by his clever mouth sent her higher and higher. When he slipped a finger into her, she came undone.

Bright white light exploded behind her lids, as if she had soared up past constricting storm clouds to find herself in brilliant sunlight. She hung there, suspended, for one incredible moment, before drifting back to earth. She opened her eyes to find Quincy beside her. He brushed back hair from her temple and smiled.

She returned the smile, her chest light, her body

deliciously relaxed. In all her imaginings she'd never dreamed such pleasure existed. And yet she wasn't tired; not in the least. Rather, Quincy had awakened her to a joy she hadn't thought possible. She tugged on his shoulders, letting him know this was in no way over.

He understood immediately. Rolling from her, he removed his breeches. And then he was over her again, and sliding between the welcoming cradle of her legs, the low hiss of pleasure telling her more than words that he was as affected as she by the feel of their bare skin coming together, of his hard muscles pressing into her softer curves with nothing between them. The desire that had been sated in her burst into glorious life.

"I want you inside me," she whispered, her lips trailing hungrily over the side of his neck.

He shuddered, her name escaping his lips, a benediction in the quiet night air. He pushed forward, the blunt tip of him poised at her entrance before, with a low groan, he slid inside her.

There was not a single moment of discomfort or pain. She held him tightly as he slowly buried himself, each inch exquisite torture.

"Are you well?"

His anxious words rasped against her shoulder, his muscles straining under her hands, his back slick with the sweat of the effort of holding himself still. There would be no words, she knew, that would ease his mind. His every concern was centered on her well-being, and would not be easily waylaid.

To calm his worries the only way she knew how, she wrapped her legs about his lean hips and guided him farther into her.

He gasped, raising his head, looking down into her

face. She smiled, stroking a lock of hair from his fore-head. "Quincy."

He groaned, taking her lips in a kiss, the desperation and longing in it matched by the thrust of his hips as he began to move inside her. Her fingers scored his back, her hips moving in time with his, the pleasure building higher than before until she felt she might never come back down.

He ripped his mouth free, pressing it to the side of her neck. "Come for me, Clara," he whispered, the words searing her from the inside out. "I want to feel you come around me."

And she did, breaking apart into jagged pieces before realigning into someone completely new. As the last quivers of pleasure shimmied through her trembling body he pulled himself free and, his breath harsh in her ear, spent himself in the rumpled sheets at her side.

Sated, near exhaustion, she was hardly aware as he whisked the sheet from the bed, dragging a warm blanket up over her limp body before sliding in beside her and pulling her into his arms.

They lay there for a time, saying nothing, as the fire in the hearth burned down and the night air cooled. She had never felt so safe as she was right now, held tight in his arms, her head on his chest and his heart beating steadily under her ear. His fingers trailed languidly over her arm, his breath blowing soft in her hair. Her eyelids grew heavy, contentment filling her. How easy it would be to drift off to sleep.

But she would not allow it. This moment was fleeting as it was; she would not waste a second of it in sleep. Instead she would focus on every detail to better remember it, from the curling of dark hair sprinkled over his broad chest, to the strength of his thigh between her own, to the soft kiss he placed on the crown of her head.

But her eyelids were growing heavier. Just as slumber was about to take over, however, he spoke.

"Clara, we need to talk."

His voice rumbled under her ear, the familiar sound of it soothing her. So much so that, for a brief moment, she couldn't understand the implications of his words.

When she did, however, she tensed. "Quincy—"

"Please, Clara, hear me out."

She lurched upright, breaking his hold on her, and looked down into his face. Her heart beat out a frantic rhythm, the sight of the grim determination in his dark eyes stealing her breath.

"I told you my requirements, Quincy," she said low. "This was not a promise of a future for us."

"I understand," he soothed. "But can you at least consider—"

"I have considered it," she broke in, longing and frustration and anger and grief all fighting for dominance. "And I will not marry you."

"Will not, or cannot?"

"What's the difference?"

"There is every difference." He reached up, tucking a stray hair behind her ear, his face infinitely tender. "Clara, you must know I lo—"

"Don't," she rasped, turning away from him and pulling the covers up over her breasts. "Please, don't say it. It will only make things worse."

He was silent for a moment, the ticking of the mantel clock and the faint crack and pop of the dying hearth fire the only sounds in the room. When he spoke again his voice was careful, cautious, as if he was afraid she would shatter. "Clara, I don't care what may have happened in your past. I want you as my wife."

She pressed her burning eyes to her knees. "No—"

"Clara." He sat up, his arms going around her, his lips fervent on the nape of her neck. "I know something or someone has hurt you. And I swear I won't press you to tell me. Whatever it is, it's yours to reveal when you're ready. But it won't affect my feelings for you. I want to marry you, Clara; that won't change."

She shuddered. "You don't know that," she rasped into her knees, fighting the desire to lean back into his embrace, joy and despair warring in her.

"I do." When she only shook her head he let out a frustrated breath. "Just don't say no yet. Please. Let me prove my sincerity to you."

Temptation swirled in her. How easy it would be to take that leap, to entrust Quincy with this thing that ate at her from the inside. She was certain he believed his own words. The earnestness in his voice was clear even to one as untrusting as her.

But once that Pandora's box was opened it could never be closed again. She needed to protect her son's memory with everything in her. And she needed to protect Quincy from himself. Even were his feelings to somehow remain unchanged, he could not know the weight that such a truth had on one's soul, what the constant fear of discovery did to a person's spirit. If it were ever made public—and there was every reason to believe that his mother would be only too happy to see her humiliated—he would hate her for it.

But his arms were wrapped about her like a blanket, his lips doing tender things to the nape of her neck, his scent filling her up, and those logical arguments were losing their strength by the second. Instead they were being taken over by imaginings of what could be, small vignettes of waking beside him in the mornings, sharing quiet conversation beside a fire, laughing as they dressed for an evening out.

Ah, God, she wanted that life with him.

"I need time," she rasped.

"I can give you that," he vowed. "I can stay beyond Phoebe's wedding; we can work things out. You can take all the time you need."

"No," she said, her voice overloud in the quiet of the room, knowing that the longer he stayed the more he would work under her skin, tempting her, when she needed this decision made on clear facts. "I'll decide before then."

"Very well," he murmured, his hands rubbing with infinite care over the tense curve of her back.

She nodded, then made to throw off the covers and rise from his bed. His hand stayed her.

"Please don't go," he whispered.

She closed her eyes. "Quincy—"

"I swear I won't attempt to sway you. I only want to hold you, Clara."

Her body responded to the raw need in his voice before her mind could. She turned back to him, stretching out alongside his hard body, wrapping herself around him even as his arms drew her flush to him. She would focus on the here and now, and not on the impossible decision she had to make in the coming days. And certainly not on the bitter irony that, lying beside him here in the dark, her heart had finally found where it belonged.

Chapter 18

*H*e knew before opening his eyes that she was gone. There was an absence in the air around him. The great gaping loss hit him like a blow. Glancing at the pillow beside him, he could just make out the impression her head had left on it. Proof she had been here, and not just a figment of his imagination.

Taking the pillow, he pressed it to his chest and rolled to his side. Her scent was still there, something akin to sun-warmed linens and fragrant meadows and fresh breezes, filling him with longing. In a rush the memories of the night before came flooding in, every kiss and sigh, every embrace. She had curled against him when he'd begged her to stay, her head resting on his chest, her arm tight around his waist, holding on as if she would never let go. And simultaneously as if she were memorizing him, for there had been a goodbye in it that was unmistakable.

He'd wanted to howl and curse into the cool night air. This miracle that had fallen into his lap, the possibility of a life with this woman he loved, was slipping through his fingers, and he felt there was nothing he could do to stop it. Every instinct in him screamed to bombard her with affection and charm and persuasive words until she couldn't help but accept him.

Instead he'd held her tighter, and prayed as he hadn't since he was a child.

Now he stared at the strengthening light streaming in through his window, feeling the fracture in his heart grow. Whatever horrible thing had happened in her past, she would not easily let it go. It had rotted her self-worth for so very long, he feared she would never be able to break free of it. He suspected what that tragedy might be; she had not been an innocent. And his heart broke, thinking of what she might have suffered, and was still suffering. He had been tempted to tell her, in no uncertain words, that he knew and didn't care, that he loved her regardless. But that was her secret to tell, and forcing it from her would only cause her to withdraw further.

He let loose a frustrated breath, hopelessness washing over him. Phoebe's wedding was less than a week away. Scaling the years of hurt and pain and grief that rose up about Clara would take time. And time was one thing he didn't have.

But lying here thinking of her would not help one bit. Rolling from the bed, he strode to the adjoining dressing room. He longed to bare his heart to her as she hadn't allowed him to last night, but he knew in his state of mind he would only muck things up further. And so he dressed quickly, hurried out to the stables, and was soon on his way.

The fresh air was a balm to his soul as he let his horse have its head. The faint scent of salt and sea filled his lungs, the coolness of it on his face and the tug of it in his hair helping to clear some of the turmoil in his breast. He would take the morning to think. And, with luck, he would return to Danesford knowing just what to do in regard to Clara. Though he doubted it would be so easy.

The small town that butted up against the beach, the center of all social activities for residents and visitors alike, was just waking as he rode down the main thoroughfare. The grocers were opening their shutters, the baker already hard at work, the scent of it making Quincy's mouth water. On impulse he stopped, dismounting and tying up his horse before heading inside.

His purchase was quickly made, and soon he was stepping back out into the bright early-morning sunlight. Removing a warm bun from its wrapper, he bit into the soft, fragrant bread before starting off down Admiralty Row. Synne's main avenue, leading down to the beach and the endless sea beyond, was wide and clean, and already beginning to bustle. The Isle was at its height of popularity in the summer months, and its season was just beginning. No doubt in a week or so these streets would be teeming with humanity. It was just the type of location he gravitated toward, a bustling town that never seemed to sleep. It was why he'd been more than happy to settle in Boston all those years.

But for the first time in perhaps his entire life Quincy didn't want company. Which might be a dangerous thing, for it gave him too much time to think. The more he pondered what to do about Clara, the more mired in doubts and frustrations and fears he became. He knew she cared for him. She would not have lain with him last night if she didn't. But she was so adamant that there could be nothing more between them. Even the idea that he might declare himself to her had sent her into a panic. As it stood, he could not see a way past that, did not know how to breech the walls she had put up about her.

So caught up in his tumultuous thoughts, he didn't immediately hear his name being called. It was only when the person doing the calling stepped in his path that he was aware of anyone around him at all.

"Your Grace," the man said. "I say, you're in your own world, aren't you?"

Quincy blinked, looking into not one but two familiar faces. "Mr. Dennison, Lord Fletcher. My apologies. I'm afraid you've caught me eating my breakfast. I was quite entranced by the deliciousness of these rolls."

"I don't blame you one bit," the house agent replied. "Mrs. Lambe is a wizard with flour and yeast. As I can attest to." He chuckled, patting his generous girth.

Quincy forced a smile, wanting nothing less than to be pulled into small talk. But he couldn't very well snub the men. "What were you gentlemen doing up and about at such an early hour?"

Lord Fletcher, exuding his typical energetic air, spoke up. "We were discussing when we might visit Swallowhill. I'm quite anxious to finalize the sale." He chuckled. "Although this proof of my eagerness can only work to my detriment. There's no way I shall haggle a good price now." He faltered, a concerned look passing over his face. "Are you well, Your Grace?"

"What? Oh! Yes, I'm quite well." Quincy forced a smile. "I didn't sleep last night, I'm afraid."

"Strange, that, with such healthful sea air to lull you to sleep," the man quipped. "But were you off to anywhere in particular this fine morning?"

"Not at all."

"Splendid. I don't suppose you have time for us after your meal? I'd love to see Swallowhill as soon as possible."

It was on the tip of Quincy's tongue to refuse. He had no wish to accompany these men today to visit the property. He hadn't set foot there since his mother's cruel confirmation of what Miss Willa Brandon had been to his father. The idea of going there now, when his heart was so troubled over Clara, and knowing he would see the place with new eyes, made his skin crawl.

But mayhap it was for the best. After last night, and the decision he was waiting for Clara to make regarding their future, he was more determined than ever to move forward with the sale. If she accepted him, he was eager to whisk her off and show her the world. And if she refused, he wanted to leave England as quickly as possible.

In the end he nodded. "Nothing would please me better. But why don't we head over now, and you can both share my breakfast with me?"

And perhaps, he thought as Lord Fletcher and Mr. Dennison took the rolls he offered with heartfelt thanks and they headed back up the street in search of their mounts, he might know how to persuade Clara by the time he returned to Danesford.

* * *

As Quincy had predicted, all the wedding preparations that Clara had agonized over had been taken care of beautifully by Lenora and Margery and Mrs. Ingram. Every hem was altered, every delicacy planned, every flower and ribbon and ingredient for the decadent food delivered. The house had been cleaned top-to-bottom, the guest rooms aired and readied for their myriad guests. There truly wasn't much for Clara to do. She should have, perhaps, been concerned at this proof that she was superfluous. Wasn't that her great fear, after all, that she had no place any longer? That her family didn't need her?

But she was too busy trying to hide the turmoil inside her.

She had known, of course, that the aftermath of following her heart would be painful, that it would take an incredible amount of mental and emotional effort to fall back into her old ways.

She had not expected it to affect her physically, making her entire body ache and her head pound. How the faint soreness in her thighs would remind her of what she and Quincy had shared. Exhaustion pulled at her, and she wanted nothing more than to be left in peace, to climb back under her covers and hide away from the world.

To remember every beautiful moment with Quincy.

That was something, however, she could not indulge. She had known what she was about last night, and that today would be difficult. It was why she had stayed curled in his arms as long as possible, why she had feigned sleep when all along she had been memorizing the steady pounding of his heart against her ear, each beat one second closer to leaving him. Now, however, it was time she accepted that whatever they'd had was over.

But that didn't make focusing on the necessary duties of the day any easier. Especially as the guests were now arriving in droves, carriages pulling up Danesford's long drive by the hour. This was the more tedious portion of the wedding, that of helping Lenora play hostess. It should have been a blessing that she was able to make herself useful again. But there was nothing Clara wanted to do less than smile and see to everyone's comfort.

She sighed, stretching her neck from side to side to relieve the stiffness in her muscles as she saw some distant relation of Lady Crabtree's off with the butler. She looked out over the front hall, making certain there was no one left wanting attention. And perhaps, secretly looking for Quincy...

No. She shook her head sharply, forcing her focus on Lenora and Phoebe by the front door, greeting an ancient matron with a towering bright green turban. She had promised herself she would not look for him. Peter had informed her earlier after receiving a letter by messenger that Quincy had gone to Swallowhill with Mr. Dennison and Lord Fletcher. It was a relief he was gone, really. After last night she had no wish to see him, to look into his eyes and recognize the awareness that would no doubt light their depths.

Yet she could not seem to keep from searching for him. Even now, moments after berating herself for breaking her silent promise, she felt her gaze drifting, looking for his lean form, his piercing eyes, the soft waves of his inky hair. Hair she had run her fingers through just last night.

In a flash it washed over her, the remembrance of his body moving over and in hers. Of his soul-searing kisses, of his strong hands, equally eager and gentle on her heated skin.

Of his near declaration of love, something that should have brought her joy and instead had broken her heart.

Flooded with memories, she ducked out a side door and hurried into the garden. There, among her mother's roses, a place she typically found peace and strength, she tried to corral her emotions back into submission. But now that they had broken free, they would not easily let her go.

For the past weeks, without her realizing it, Quincy had effectively demolished her defenses. No, not demolished. He'd peeled them back with aching gentleness, layer by layer, until, last night, in his arms, she'd found a part of herself she had thought lost forever. The joyful, impulsive girl that she had subdued for responsibility's sake after the death of her mother, that had rebelled in a quest for a life of her own when she was nearing womanhood. And that had thrown her into the deepest despair because she had been fool enough to follow her heart.

She had thought that part of her was the enemy, and had viciously subdued it in the years that followed. But Quincy had awakened it in her again. And she saw now she wasn't whole without it. She wasn't confined to what others needed from her. She had her own desires and joys, things she wanted above all others.

And she wanted to explore that part of her with Quincy. Not as a caregiver, but as an equal partner in life, walking at his side and shouldering the worries of the world with him.

Quincy cared for her and wanted to marry her. The man she had come to love with her whole heart, who could make her happier than she had ever dreamed possible, wanted to make a life with her.

For a single moment of weakness she imagined that life: falling asleep in his arms as a ship rocked them to sleep, reveling in the tug of sea air in her hair as they stood side by side peering out at the horizon, stepping foot in countries she had not even dared to dream of seeing with her own eyes. They would have days full of adventure and excitement; nights brimming with endless passion.

And after that, when a quiet life called to them, they would grow old together. Looking back on the adventures they'd shared and finding comfort in one another in their old age.

Her heart ached with the need for that life. She closed her eyes against the pull of it. But it beckoned, a temptation that was quickly undermining every excuse she had for refusing Quincy.

"Clara."

She sucked in a sharp breath at that familiar voice, so close to her. Surely her imaginings had created him out of the ether. She squeezed her eyes closed even more tightly, longing washing over her in a wave, not wanting to break the magic of that moment.

And then a hand, gentle on her cheek. Her eyes flew open to find Quincy's face hovering over hers.

He smiled and lowered his head. And she forgot why she should refuse.

His lips touched hers, gentle, hesitant. He was giving her the choice on allowing it to continue. Tears sprang to her eyes, his deep respect for her decisions clear. She longed to throw caution to the wind and melt into his embrace.

Instead she drew in a shuddering breath and gently pulled away.

With a sad smile he clasped his hands behind his back. "I suppose you've been keeping yourself busy and at the center of the chaos," he said, his tone light.

The utter normalcy in his voice took her aback until she realized what he was doing. He was giving her time and allowing her to breathe. To make her decision on their future without pressure.

And here she had not thought it possible to love him more.

"Er, yes," she stuttered. Clearing her throat, she tried again. "That is, it's been a constant stream of guests arriving. Lenora and Phoebe cannot be expected to handle it all on their own."

He gave an easy chuckle as they started down the gravel

path and came into view of the front drive. Guests were descending from carriages and bags were being unloaded in a controlled kind of chaos. "I'm thinking Danesford will be bursting at the seams by nightfall. Lady Tesh will be so pleased. Well, one can hope at least."

She laughed along with him, though inside her heart ached. Their masks were firmly in place, the lie trotted out for all to see.

Yet she couldn't help but be aware of the wish deep inside that it was real.

Chapter 19

Dinner that night and the gathering in the drawing room after were lively times, the myriad guests providing the last necessary ingredient for the festive spirit that a wedding often brought. Especially one where the couple were so very much in love.

Clara smiled fondly at Phoebe, who was sitting beside one of Oswin's shy cousins, gently drawing her into a quiet discussion. It was clear that Oswin's family adored her. Even the irascible Lady Crabtree seemed to have a soft spot for her. And no wonder, for Phoebe was a veritable fairy of light and laughter, flitting from person to person, her natural enthusiasm and sweetness putting everyone at ease. She would do well in her new life.

"She got that from you, you know."

Clara looked up at Aunt Olivia. She had been so focused on her sister she hadn't heard the woman approach.

"What was that?"

"That kindness, the ability to bring joy to people." She pointed her cane in Phoebe's direction before jabbing it toward Clara. "You gave her that gift."

"Oh." Clara blushed, rearing back from the cane as it nearly clipped her nose. "I'm sure that's all Phoebe. No one can teach that."

"Poppycock," Aunt Olivia said before shooing Clara to the side.

Clara slid over on the settee so the viscountess could sit. "How are you enjoying the wedding festivities thus far, Aunt Olivia?" she asked. "You must be so pleased; I don't believe anyone expected such a turnout."

The older woman didn't answer. Instead she peered closely at Clara as if searching for something. Finally, when Clara had begun to think she wouldn't answer, she said, "I'm as pleased as you expect me to be. Which is not very, for there is still room for improvement. I shall not be satisfied until Lady Crabtree admits she was wrong. And I suspect that will only be gotten when hell turns to ice. But what's different about you? Something has altered since yesterday that I can't quite put my finger on."

Clara, in the process of taking a sip from her wineglass, promptly choked. "I don't know what you mean," she croaked. "Mayhap Anne did my hair differently tonight. And this dress is new."

"No," Aunt Olivia said, her eyes narrowing. "It's not something so simple and obvious."

Flustered, desperate to distract the woman—for there was one thing, and one thing only, that Aunt Olivia could have sensed different in her—Clara said, "I'm sorry you were unable to bring Freya down. I know she would have been well behaved, though others feared otherwise."

As expected, the change of subject worked beautifully. "Oh, that Lady Crabtree," the viscountess grumbled, shooting the woman in question a dark look. "I know she was behind it. She's as sour a woman as I've ever met. And she still isn't over me bringing Freya to her house when we visited her in London. As if my darling pet acted as anything but the angel she is." Aunt Olivia sniffed, her offense at such a snub palpable.

Clara's relief that she had successfully redirected her great-aunt's attentions was short-lived.

The viscountess swung back to pin Clara with a piercing look. "But don't think you shall get out of answering me. I know there's something different about you. And I'd be willing to bet you're aware of it, too, or you wouldn't have taken such pains to bring up something that infuriates me so." Her look turned smug as Clara gaped at her. "I'm not as senile as you all think I am; I know when I'm being manipulated, young lady."

"Oh, do you?" Quincy drawled, sauntering up to their corner of the drawing room.

Clara's entire body responded to his approach, her heart picking up speed and heat blooming low in her belly. She had always wanted him, of course. But it was so much stronger now.

More than that, however, was the happiness that bloomed in her chest from his presence. Just being near him brought her joy that had nothing whatsoever to do with physical desire and everything to do with his effect on her heart.

"Don't think to charm me, my boy," Aunt Olivia said. "I've dealt with your kind before."

"Now, that's highly doubtful," he said with a wink and a grin. "I'm certain there are no others quite like me."

"Well, that's true enough," the viscountess grumbled. "But don't just stand there. Sit; my neck aches from looking up at you."

As he sat, Aunt Olivia speared him with a sharp glare. "I hear you spent much of the morning with Mr. Dennison and Lord Fletcher at Swallowhill."

"You are, as always, impressively well informed. I met up with them quite by accident after an early ride into town, and Lord Fletcher was eager to see the place. Though the house is in bad repair, he was so taken with the view I don't see a problem in getting the highest price possible."

They droned on, discussing the merits of its position, the fertile soil, the bones of the house. But Clara couldn't focus on any of it. She was too aware of Quincy's nearness. His hand rested on the arm of his chair, mere inches from her own. She couldn't help but remember those strong fingers on her skin, bringing her to such pleasure.

What would he do if she reached across that small space and laced her fingers with his?

She tightened her hand around her wineglass to keep it in place. Such an act would be as good as a declaration to Quincy, considering what was between them and what had yet to be resolved. He would see it as a sign that her decision had been made.

When in reality she was even more mired in doubt.

That morning she had been so certain she should refuse him. But now…

Now, after spending the evening in his company, pretending what they had was real, she couldn't imagine ending it. What they had wasn't just a physical connection, nor merely a shared association of secrecy. No, it was much deeper, built up over the past weeks into something abiding and true, bringing a light and joy to her life she never thought to have.

And she wanted a future with him so much she ached.

It was stupid to even consider it when just hours ago she had been so certain it could never be. It was the maddest of mads.

And yet nothing had ever made more sense.

"And there's a small property with a tidy little cottage on it that butts up against Swallowhill. Lord Fletcher's of a mind to purchase it as well."

Quincy's voice was like a bucket of cold water over her head. Her insides turned frigid with shock, her mind going numb. "A cottage?"

"Yes," he said, blissfully unaware of her turmoil. "It sits right between Swallowhill and the path to the beach. It's not part of my holdings. We're determined to find out who owns it. Dennison believes he can secure a larger price if Fletcher can get his hands on both."

Clara's ears started to ring, and her vision blurred. She recalled with agonizing vividness a pain unlike any other, her body torn apart. And then a much worse pain as heartbreak quickly followed.

"Clara."

Quincy's voice came to her as if in a tunnel, far off and distant, growing closer as reality intruded. She blinked, looking in incomprehension at him. His face was close to hers, alarm clear in his eyes. His fingers were wrapped around her arm, as if holding her in place.

"Clara," he said, his voice low, "are you well? You nearly fainted."

It was then she realized where she was. Not back in that small cottage, hidden away from the world. No, she was in Danesford's drawing room, preparing for her sister's wedding. With Quincy at her side.

She thought she might be sick.

Drawing herself up—she had slouched down in her seat in an alarming way—she composed herself as best she could. "I'm fine," she managed.

But Quincy didn't look the least bit convinced by her efforts. If anything, he appeared even more worried. "I think it would be best if I see you to your room," he said. "You've pushed yourself today."

"No," Clara said, embarrassment—and the far more troubling desire to have him comfort her—rushing through her. "I'd rather stay here. Truly, I'm fine now."

"Nonsense," Aunt Olivia declared, thumping her cane to draw Clara's attention to her. As if her strident tone hadn't been able to do that just fine. "Pushing yourself will not help one bit. You wouldn't wish to be ill for Phoebe's wedding, would you?"

To Clara's consternation there really was no arguing with that. Before she quite knew what was happening, Quincy had risen and was helping her up. "I don't need assistance," she protested. Unfortunately her body decided to betray her, her legs nearly giving out under her.

"No more arguing," Quincy declared, slipping an arm about her waist to steady her. And then she was being whisked from the room.

"I'm merely tired," she protested as he guided her up the stairs. The noise and chaos of the drawing room faded behind them, the quiet giving them a false sense of privacy. She ached to cry her heart out in his arms. But she could never allow herself to be that vulnerable again, not after the stark reminder of the cottage.

She had been ruined, had birthed a child out of wedlock. And that small cottage nestled on Synne's farthest northern corner had been witness to it. All too soon it would come out that the property had been her father's, that the deed had been transferred to her. And that she had sold it off when the pain of owning it finally grew too great. No one in her family knew of its existence. Once it was unearthed that it had been hers, questions would arise. And the truth would out.

Again she felt her stomach lurch. And she knew it was not so much that she feared tainting her family with a scandal. It had been them finding out at all.

There was a chance they might react with the same loving understanding her father had, of course. But even if they, by some miracle, did not despise her for her actions, they would view her differently, would pity her or see her as broken. After dedicating her life to them all these years, and loving them as she did, she couldn't bear it.

"Quincy," she tried again as they rounded the hallway to the family apartments. "Please leave me. I'm fine now, truly."

Still he guided her on, his hand under her arm and his arm about her waist gentle, yet his profile stern and unyielding. Finally, they reached her room. She thought he might leave her then, and the idea filled her with equal parts relief and pain.

Instead he pushed her through the door, following her before closing it firmly behind him. Before she could protest he spun to face her. The wild worry in his eyes stole her breath.

"What happened?"

Her gaze fell from his, her arms wrapping about her waist as she stepped back from him. "Nothing."

He let loose a frustrated breath, his hand combing through his hair. Tension rolled off him in waves. "Clara, please don't lie to me. I saw the change that came over you when the cottage was mentioned. You appeared utterly devastated."

"Don't mention it to me," she choked, trying and failing to forget her son's tiny, pale face. Her heart shuddered, all the unhealed cracks she'd tried so hard to hold together coming undone.

"Clara—"

She reared back as he reached for her. "Don't!"

He froze, his shock a palpable thing. "I'm sorry," he said, his voice slow and careful as he backed away.

She stared at him, impotent grief filling her. Tears burned her eyes. She'd been a fool to think she could escape her past, or that she would eventually forget her heartache and all she'd lost.

"I need you to leave," she mumbled.

"Damn it, Clara—"

"Leave."

The single word was quiet and stark, as broken as she felt. And more powerful than any shout could have been if his reaction was anything to go by. He sucked in a sharp breath, dropping his hands to his sides, his strong shoulders drooping as if all the fight had drained out of him.

"I told you I had no intention of marrying," she continued, purposely slicing through her pain, needing the wound to stay open and bleeding in order to find the strength to break from him. He was stubborn, perhaps even more stubborn than she. It would be no easy thing to convince him that what they'd had was over.

She rearranged her features into cool disdain and forced herself to lie.

"Mayhap you thought my coming to you last night was a confession of deeper feelings than are truly there. But it was just physical, Quincy. If you believed that our proximity today was an indication that I had changed my mind about marrying you, you're wrong. How else were we to continue making the others believe our engagement was real if not to continue pretending we were in love? I intend to see this agreement of ours through, and then we may both go our separate ways after Phoebe's wedding without any expectations. Just as we determined we would from the start."

He stared at her a long moment, the only sound their harsh breathing mingling in the gaping abyss between them. Then, with a silent nod, he turned and walked out, closing the door quietly behind him. Leaving her alone with her heartbreak.

* * *

Quincy didn't know how long he sat on the stairs with his head in his hands. The sounds of merriment drifted down the hall to him, the muted laughter and conversation making him feel more alone than he ever had in his life. Even after his father died, when he had huddled under his desk crying, he'd not felt such desolation. Then, he'd used that grief to fuel his anger enough to leave that place and forge a new life. Now, however, there seemed no option where he would win. A life without Clara was no life at all; no matter that he'd told himself he would leave if she refused him, he saw now he'd been fooling himself. And he could not see a way past whatever was holding her back.

After what seemed an eternity, he felt a hand on his shoulder. But though the weight of it was too heavy to be Clara's, it was still one he knew well.

"Peter," he said without looking up. "Shouldn't you be helping your wife?"

His friend grunted then sank, with a sigh, to the step beside Quincy. "I do believe this is a more pressing problem."

"I'm perfectly fine," Quincy muttered. Even so, he could not dredge the strength to raise his head.

There was a beat of silence. And then his friend's gruff voice softer than Quincy had ever heard it: "You've fallen in love with Clara, haven't you?"

That finally was the prodding Quincy needed to rally some energy. He straightened, casting a disgruntled look at Peter. "Don't you have somewhere to be?"

"Right now, there is no place more important. And I've two good ears to hear whatever you might need to get off your chest."

Just then a burst of laughter rose up from the drawing room. "But not here," Peter muttered, casting a glare in the general direction of the sound. He rose, nudging Quincy's shoulder. "Come along then. We'll hide away in my study and you can tell me everything."

"And if I don't wish to tell you everything?" Quincy grumbled as he rose and fell into step beside Peter, torn between frustration that his feelings had been seen so clearly and relief that his friend wanted to help him.

"Then you can stay sullen and silent and listen to me prattle on about what a horse's arse you are."

The normalcy of the insult drew a reluctant laugh from Quincy. Soon they entered the study and Peter closed the door firmly behind them.

"I swear," Peter muttered as he strode to the sideboard, "I was a damn fool for agreeing to this mad scheme of Phoebe's. Whole house overrun with spoiled aristocrats. This is my worst nightmare come to life."

"Except you are now one of those despised aristocrats," Quincy said with as much levity as he could muster. Which was not very much. With a groan he lowered himself into a chair before the hearth. The fire blazing merrily away could not warm the chill that had taken root inside him.

"Don't remind me." There was the faint clink of glass. And then Peter was at his side, pressing a drink into his hand. "Besides, you're one of those aristocrats, too," he said as he lowered himself into a chair. "Though after getting to know your mother's character these past days, I understand why you wanted to leave it all behind. Just let me know if you want me to throw the woman out on her ear. I shall do it, and gladly."

Quincy snorted. "Do you truly want the wrath of the Duchess of Reigate on your head, man?"

"She may be a duchess," Peter said with a wicked smile, "but I'm a bloody duke now. And if I can't utilize it for something good, what the hell is the purpose of it?"

The laugh that burst from Quincy's lips was freeing. "Damn, but I've missed your company."

Peter grinned. "And I you. Though," he continued with a stern look, "don't think this gets you out of discussing Clara."

In a moment Quincy's mood, which had begun to lighten, fell back into its hopeless gloom again. "What is there to talk about?" he muttered, taking a drink of his whiskey. "She won't have me, and I see no way to get past the defenses she's put up around her."

"You've proposed then?"

"I did ask her if she would marry me in truth, yes."

"And you told her your feelings?"

"I tried."

Peter snorted. "Tried? There is no trying, man. Only doing."

Quincy gave a humorless laugh. "She wouldn't let me."

There was a beat of silence. Peter stared at him, uncomprehendingly. "I don't understand."

Quincy exhaled in frustration. "I started to say the

words. *I love you* was literally coming out of my mouth. She stopped me; refused to hear it."

"Refused?" Peter's jaw dropped. "How the hell does a person refuse to hear a declaration?"

"I don't know," Quincy replied with a grim smile. "But she did it, I assure you. Said she didn't want to hear it. Claimed it would make things worse." He drained his glass, needing the burn of the whiskey in his gut to drown out the desolation that was beginning to take over him again. "I know something happened to her, something that damaged her ability to trust. But she won't tell me." He slammed the empty glass down on the small table beside him, the agitated action doing nothing to ease his frustration.

Peter remained quiet. Too quiet. Quincy looked at him and was shocked at the guilt that filled his features. His senses sharpened, and he sat forward. "What is it, man?"

Peter studied him for a long moment, his clear blue eyes clouded with whatever troubled thoughts were swirling about in his head. Finally, he spoke.

"You're right that there's something in her past that nearly destroyed her."

The breath left Quincy in a rush. Before he could ask what that thing was, however, Peter held up a meaty hand.

"But I cannot tell you the particulars. She told me in confidence last year when I reconciled with her father. It took an incredible amount of strength to reveal it to me; I cannot break her trust. Not even for you."

Whatever excitement and hope had been building in Quincy was doused in a heartbeat. "You're right," he said, slumping back against his seat. "And I wouldn't want you to tell me. I need her to trust me, or this won't work between us."

Peter nodded morosely. "I wish with all my heart I could tell you, to help you in any way I can. Though—"

"Though?"

Peter frowned. "I do get the feeling she didn't tell me the whole of it." He shook his head, as if clearing a troubling image from his brain with force. "Truthfully, I'm not certain she's ever told anyone the whole of it. Though everyone around her adores her, I don't think I have ever seen anyone so lonely."

The words chilled Quincy. It was too true; he'd sensed it himself. Whatever happened to Clara, she'd made a life out of distancing herself from everyone around her. And it seemed years in the making.

"I've seen a change in her since you arrived," Peter added quietly, his gaze considering as he regarded Quincy. "There's something different about her, a joy in life that wasn't present before." When Quincy could only stare at him, Peter leaned forward, clapping a comforting hand on his shoulder. "I pray she confides in you, my friend. For both your sakes."

"I do, as well," Quincy said quietly.

Chapter 20

No matter the heartbreak of the night before, no matter the sleepless hours Clara had spent staring up at the ceiling in a futile attempt to forget Quincy and what they might have had, the world kept turning. It seemed impossible that it could do so. And yet there was the proof of it, the sunlight streaming in through Clara's window as the following day dawned bright.

Rising from her bed was the very last thing she wanted to do. So she pulled the covers up over her head and curled into a ball on her side instead. Mayhap if she pretended the day hadn't begun, it might hold off indefinitely. And she need not face Quincy again.

That hope was dashed minutes later when her maid entered.

"Lady Clara, the sun is shining on this wonderful day," Anne chirped. "Let's get you up and dressed; I'm sure there's much to do."

Clara only closed her eyes tighter. Beyond her cocoon of blankets the maid moved about the room, her cheerful whistle accompanying the closing of doors and the rustle of clothing as she set out Clara's gown and things for the day. The pathetic hope that Anne might leave when Clara stayed stubbornly tucked under her fabric mound died a swift death when the maid yanked the covers back. The sunlight assaulted her senses and she recoiled from it with a low moan, pressing her face into her pillow.

"Come now, Lady Clara," Anne said with a bright smile. "It's a beautiful day, and you've only so many hours in it to enjoy."

Normally Clara appreciated Anne's optimism. Now, however, it grated on her. It seemed nothing should be happy again, not while her heart was in tatters.

But she couldn't put off the day indefinitely. Heaving a sigh, she rose from her bed, wincing as her muscles protested. She had not realized just how tense she had been throughout the night, how stiffly she'd held herself in an attempt to contain her heartache.

Anne quickly went to work, and in no time Clara was nearly ready for the day. As the maid put the finishing touches to her hair, however, Clara's mind began to wander. And what should it wander to, but Quincy.

She would never forget the stark hurt on his face last night. Or how badly she had wanted to call him back and retract every cold, untruthful thing she had said.

But this was for the best, she told herself firmly. They needed a clean break. Surely he would leave her in peace now.

She nearly let loose a bitter laugh. *Peace.* As if she would ever find peace with this.

"My lady? Excuse me, Lady Clara?"

Clara blinked, focusing on her maid in the looking glass. "I am so sorry, Anne. I'm afraid my mind has wandered."

The other woman smiled in understanding, patting Clara's shoulder. "What with Lady Phoebe's marriage quickly approaching, and your own upcoming nuptials, there must be much preying on your mind. But which of the hair adornments did you want today? The silk flowers or the ribbons?"

Upcoming nuptials. Clara gave Anne a weak smile, not wanting her to see how affected she was by those innocent words. "The silk flowers I think, thank you," she managed.

The woman prattled on as she worked, tucking small white blooms into Clara's curls. Only now that her attention had been diverted from Quincy, Clara could not help but hear what Anne had been talking about minutes ago. And its subject was far from welcome.

"And that Duchess of Reigate's maid is a maddening piece of work. Always questioning, sticking her nose where it doesn't belong. I ask you, what business is it of hers where you might have gone off to when you were a girl? Or why you were so ill for so long when I first came on?"

Clara's heart stalled in her chest. There was only one reason for the maid's questions: the duchess was still after the truth of Clara's past, and like a dog on the scent of blood she had sent her maid to infiltrate the people who knew the most in a household—the servants.

Forcing herself to breathe, Clara asked as casually as she could, "And what did you tell her?"

"That it was none of her business," Anne scoffed, tucking a particularly unruly curl in place. "But she's a persistent thing, kept badgering me and anyone else who would pay her the least mind. Finally I said to her, 'I came on when Lady Clara was just sixteen, when her previous maid done ran off. If you want to know the details, find her.'"

How Clara kept from casting up her accounts right then

and there she didn't know. The maid in question, Flora, had stayed by Clara's side throughout the whole ordeal of going into hiding and living through the hellacious pregnancy and stillbirth that had followed. Clara had thought their bond was unbreakable.

Until Flora had gone and offered the scandal up to the first man who waved money under her nose. It had taken Clara's father everything in him, including a good chunk of the Dane fortune, to keep the whole thing quiet. No doubt if she could be found she would be more than willing to offer up that information again, especially if a duchess came to her door with the promise of more money.

In that moment she realized with devastating certainty that the fear would never end. Eventually the truth would out. And once it did, she would lose everything she held dear.

No, she reminded herself bitterly, she had already lost something that was infinitely precious to her. This would only complete the job.

Impotence washed over her. She was so damn tired of living this way. She clenched her hands in her lap, anger rearing up, replacing her helplessness. Well, no more. She'd lost enough to that one devastating mistake; she'd be damned if she lost anything else.

Anne finished then. With hardly a word to the startled maid, Clara bolted from the room. She was done being afraid.

Her sharp knock on the duchess's door was answered with alacrity by a pinch-faced maid. "Yes?" the woman queried, her insolent tone accompanied by a haughty stare down her nose.

"Is Her Grace within?"

"Yes, but—"

"Thank you," Clara said, pushing past the woman, leaving her sputtering behind her.

The duchess was sitting up in bed, a tray on her lap, a single steaming cup of chocolate clasped between her hands. Her eyes narrowed when she saw Clara. "Goodness," she drawled, taking a slow sip, eyeing Clara with disdain, "one would think no one in this household has any sense of privacy, the way people continue to barge into my room without permission."

"Enough," Clara bit out. "I came here to tell you to stop sending your lapdog to do your bidding."

"Pardon?"

"I know you've had your maid asking questions about me."

The maid in question gasped. "*Lapdog*? Why, I never—"

The duchess held up a beringed hand. The maid's jaw closed with a snap.

"Enough. Leave us."

The woman did as she was bid. And then Clara was alone with the duchess.

A slow, cold smile lifted the woman's lips as she considered Clara. "Frightened you with my inquiries, have I?"

"Not in the least," Clara responded, surprised to realize just how true that was. She was beyond fear. Having to push Quincy away had broken something in her. Now the only thing simmering in her breast was anger.

"Oh, come now," the duchess said. "You and I both know that's not true. Else why confront me once you learned of my attempts."

Clara shook her head in disbelief. "You won't even

deny what you've been doing? That you've been attempting to bring to light some past scandal you imagine I committed?"

One elegant shoulder lifted. "What is there to deny? I've stated before that I won't have you marrying Reigate. No one crosses me, my dear."

The confession that she and Quincy were not engaged in truth—and had never been—battered against Clara's lips, fighting to break free.

But she would not give the woman the satisfaction. Squeezing her hands into tight fists, she glared at the duchess. "You do not get to dictate my life," she said, voice trembling. "And you will not decree what Quincy does, either. He is a good man, who does not deserve a viper like you for a mother."

That seemed to finally light something in the other woman. She straightened, pinning Clara with a furious glare. "You have no idea what he deserves."

Clara gaped at her, stunned by the poison in the woman's words. There was pain, but also a deep disdain for Quincy. She gave the duchess a mournful look, that she could not see the treasure that her son was. "I do know what he deserves," she replied quietly. And like a bolt of lightning it hit her just how right she was: she truly did know. Quincy deserved the truth.

As much as she feared his reaction, he did not deserve her hastily patched excuses as to why she couldn't marry him. He was the best man she knew, so giving, so caring. He had lost his father young, had escaped the house of a woman who should have loved him unconditionally yet had only given him pain, had carved a life for himself. Then, upon returning home, he had learned of the deaths of his brothers, and that he was saddled with debts that could destroy his lifelong dreams.

Yet never in all that time had he lost his optimism for life. He had searched endlessly until he had found a solution, had shown her nothing but kindness in the process. Had taught her how to embrace a joy in life she had thought lost to her.

And what had she given him in return? Lies, and a refusal to allow him to speak his heart. Why? Because she feared that sharing her son with anyone would tarnish his memory? Because it might pain her to see Quincy's reaction to the truth of her ruination? She was a coward. Just as she was a coward to allow this woman to manipulate her and threaten her. And the duchess would never stop. She would keep at it until Clara was trampled to dust in the wake of her fury.

But instead of the expected despair at such a realization, Clara felt freed. She knew just what she had to do.

She smiled at the duchess. The woman blinked, seemingly not knowing how to take Clara's sudden change of mood.

Clara laughed, dipping into a deep, mocking curtsy. "Your Grace, I look forward to seeing you later."

And with that she turned and sailed from the room, her mind already racing ahead to what had to be done.

* * *

A morning's hard riding over Synne's hills did nothing to ease the ache in Quincy's chest. The wounds of Clara's refusal the night before were still fresh. But he wouldn't push his horse any farther. Nor could he escape seeing Clara again. And so, no better off than when he had fled at dawn, he turned his mount's head back to Danesford.

The one thing he did not expect to see when turning his horse into the stable yard, however, was Clara, seemingly waiting for him.

His hands must have tightened on the reins, for the horse gave an agitated whinny and stumbled to a halt, its shoulders quivering. Quincy patted its neck, murmuring comfortingly to it before dismounting and handing the reins over to a groom. The whole while he could not keep his eyes from Clara. She stood ramrod-straight, her face arranged in its typical calm lines. But there was a nervous energy about her, showing clearly in her tightly clasped hands and her white knuckles. She kept her gaze focused on him, ignoring the bustle around her, as he walked toward her.

For a moment he stood silent before her, fighting the overwhelming desire to take her in his arms. Only the memory of her face the night before kept him from doing so.

"What are you doing out here?" he asked, his voice gruff.

"I came to find you."

"Why?"

She flinched at his harsh tone but kept her gaze steady. "I've been unfair to you."

Well, he certainly hadn't expected that. Not knowing how to respond, he remained silent.

She dragged in a deep breath with seeming effort and raised her chin a fraction. "I've not been truthful with you, Quincy."

"So you lied when you told me you have no plans to ever marry?"

"Oh, no. That was the truth. But I have not given you the true reasons for it. I would tell you now."

A wild hope surged in his breast. He tamped it down as best he could. "I would very much like that," he said carefully.

She nodded, relief and fear flashing in the deep blue depths of her eyes. Then, with a blush, she started off for the house. He fell into step beside her, his hands in fists at his sides to keep from reaching for her. All the while his mind whirled. What did this mean? Was she going to finally trust him?

He quickly quieted the chorus of desperate questions. He could not bring himself to hope and then see it dashed to pieces again. So he kept his silence, giving her the space she seemed to need though it killed him.

He expected her to duck into any empty room to have this conversation over and done with. Instead she started up the stairs, making her way to the family quarters. Surely she wouldn't take him to her room. But no, they passed her door and kept on. He cast her a confused frown but she was focused on her destination.

When she finally stopped and turned to face him, he could only stare blankly at the door before them. It was Lenora's art studio. He had seen it upon arriving at Danesford, this place where Lenora created her magnificent paintings, whimsical watercolors that fairly breathed with a life of their own. Why Clara was bringing him here, however, was beyond him.

When he looked at her in question, she smiled. It was a small, sad thing that fairly broke his heart.

"You're not the only one I've kept the truth from, Quincy," she said, her voice quiet. "And I know now I can never be free until I lay out my past in front of everyone I love."

Love. The word swirled in the air between them. Did she love him then? Before he could ask her, he heard the muted sound of low, tense conversation within the confines of the room. Clara threw the door wide, and he stood stunned in the entry as he took in the tableau before him.

Peter and Lenora were there, seated together on a low settee, as well as Lady Tesh with Freya curled in her lap. Margery stood by the window, her troubled face illuminated by the early-afternoon sun streaming in through the floor-to-ceiling windows. Phoebe sat near Oswin, their hands clasped tight. And one other was there, who he could not comprehend being present for several long, confused seconds.

He frowned. "Mother?"

Her lips twisted. "Reigate."

Quincy cast a bewildered look to Clara, but she was already making her way across the room. Her back was a tense line beneath the delicate muslin of her gown, and she appeared as if she were ascending the gallows.

Feeling much the same, knowing that at the end of this he would either be raised to heaven or cast down to the pits of hell, Quincy set his jaw and followed her within, closing the door firmly behind him.

Chapter 21

*C*lara stopped when she reached the marble fireplace, closing her eyes for a moment and breathing deeply. She had been so sure of what had to be done when she'd left the duchess's room earlier that morning. And since then she'd fed the fire burning inside her to see this over and done with. It had kept her going as she'd written out notes to everyone she needed present; as she searched for Quincy, as she'd stood waiting for him in the stable yard while all around her the grooms and stable hands went about their busy day. For no mere note would do for Quincy.

Now that the moment of reckoning was before her, however, she didn't know how to begin.

Behind her she could hear faint shuffling, quiet whispers quickly hushed. They all knew something was wrong. She had seen it in their eyes when she'd entered the room with Quincy, a worried expectation.

All save for the duchess, who had sat apart from the others and considered her with narrowed eyes, suspicion clear on her cold face.

As if that woman heard Clara's thoughts, she suddenly spoke.

"Goodness, Lady Clara, you keep us in such suspense,"

she drawled. "I'm certain we would all like to leave this room this century. If you would be so kind as to tell us why you've dragged us in here when we should be with the rest of the guests belowstairs?"

Clara turned to face them as a low growl issued from Peter. "My cousin can take as long as she needs, Duchess," he said with a dark glare.

"Well, she's certainly doing that," the woman muttered.

Another growl from Peter, this one contained as Lenora spoke into the tense atmosphere. "I'm sure Clara is merely searching for the right words. And my husband is quite correct," she continued, her voice firm and brooking no argument, "Clara may take as long as she needs." She turned to her and gave her an encouraging nod that didn't hide the anxiety under the surface. "Whenever you're ready, dearest."

Clara took one final moment to drink in the faces of these people who loved her so well. The fear that had held her back for so many years rose up again, stronger than ever. She couldn't do this. It was a mistake; she would not be able to survive this if they all turned from her.

Her anxious gaze found Quincy's.

He sat poised at the edge of his chair, as if he feared what would be said and was ready to bolt from the room at the least provocation. Yet there was a steadiness to his gaze that grounded her. Just then he smiled. It was a small thing, barely even lifting the corners of his lips. But it gave her the encouragement she needed to do what had to be done. Didn't he deserve the truth? Didn't they all deserve the truth?

And, most important of all, didn't she deserve to be true to herself?

"I've brought you all here," she began, her voice a

weak thing but quickly gaining strength, "because there is something I need to say to you, something that I've been keeping from you these fifteen years. The reason I'm telling you now," she continued, "is because the duchess's recent actions have made me realize that I will never be fully free until the truth is out. And I would rather reveal it to you myself than have someone else do so."

Here she looked at the duchess full in the face. "I want to thank you, Your Grace," she said with a grim smile, "for making me realize that truthfulness with those I love is paramount to my happiness."

The woman merely stared back at her, the mutiny twisting her features not able to completely hide the undertone of fear there.

Dragging in a steadying breath, Clara turned to face her family. There would be no more cowering, no more hiding.

"When I was fifteen," she began, "there was a young man visiting the Isle who courted me in secret. He claimed he loved me, vowed to marry me. He told me he merely had to wait another few months, until he reached his majority, and we would be wed posthaste."

Phoebe, Oswin, Margery, and Lady Tesh sat in silence, their expressions confused. Peter and Lenora clasped hands, worry plain on their faces. They knew some of what was to come. The duchess looked angry enough to smite Clara on the spot.

And Quincy. His gaze was shuttered but unflinching. She looked away from him, knowing she wouldn't be able to continue if she witnessed his reaction, more frightened of it than of anyone else's.

"I took him at his word. It was foolish of me; I can see that now. But I was so eager to grow up and start a life of my own. I think I had become a bit resentful of how much I had missed out on after my mother's death, how much of my childhood I had left behind. I wanted to live for me. Which is no one's fault but my own," she hastily explained when Phoebe covered her mouth with a trembling hand. "I wanted you and our brother to have a mother-figure. And I will never regret helping to care for you both, will never regret the close relationship we've shared because of it.

"At the time, however, I was maturing into a woman and unsure of my place in the world. And that man exploited that fact. He made me believe I should live for nothing but myself, that my family had been selfish to take so much from me. Which, in my vanity, I allowed him to convince me of, though it was the farthest thing from the truth."

She paused, curling her hands into fists, her gaze dropping to the floor as she dug deep for strength. "He seduced me, and once he'd gotten what he wanted from me he left. I never heard from him again, though I wrote to him with increasing desperation. Especially after…" She swallowed hard, tried again. "Especially when I learned I was with child."

She did not raise her eyes to witness their reactions. She didn't need to. There were indrawn breaths, gasps, cries of disbelief. And then the duchess's strident voice above the others.

"I knew it!" she crowed. "Reigate, you cannot marry this woman. Think of the scandal. I will not see a loose strumpet as the next duchess—"

"Silence!" Quincy bellowed. He surged to his feet, glaring at his mother. Peter was at his side in an instant, his expression equally furious. Clara rather thought that if she were the duchess, she would keel over on the spot with two such massive, commanding men glowering at her. As it was, her heart beat out a pathetically hopeful rhythm that he did not hate her.

"If you say one thing further against Clara," Quincy said, his voice dropping to a deadly quiet that did not disguise the danger in it, "you will rue the day."

The woman stared at him in shock before, her lips pinching tight, she gave a sharp nod.

He turned back to Clara, nodding before he sat once more. Peter, too, nodded her way before taking his place at Lenora's side. Clara, for all she tried, could not discern a single emotion in their faces save for grim determination.

Her sister's agonized voice rose up, shattering the heavy silence. "Clara, is it true?"

At the sight of Phoebe, hand to her heart, eyes wide with shock, Clara nearly broke down.

But it was too late to stop now. Keeping her gaze steadily on her sister, she nodded. She expected Phoebe to sob, to break down in tears. Instead her sister lowered her hand to her lap and nodded once, as if to show she was well and Clara should continue.

And she did, letting the rest spill out in a rush, eager to have done with it. "When my father and I told everyone that I was traveling to visit with my old nurse up north, in reality she came here to stay with me, in a cottage close to Swallowhill. I hid away from the world, hid the truth from you all, to give birth to that child."

Not a one of them spoke, shock and grief and devastation all filling their faces, seeming to register them mute. The only face she refused to look at was Quincy's. She could not bear it if he were disgusted by her.

The seconds ticked by, the silence stretching. She bit her lip, her nerves beginning to fray.

Finally Aunt Olivia spoke—of course it would be Aunt Olivia. Though it was not with her usual brusqueness. No, her tone was gentler than Clara had ever heard it.

"What happened to the child, my dear?"

That one question did more to undermine the careful control she'd spent so long building up than anything thus far. "He did not make it," she managed through a throat tight with tears. "Not even long enough to take his first breath."

The last thing she saw before tears blurred her vision was Quincy's face, stark with shock.

* * *

Quincy had expected something painful in Clara's past, but he had never imagined something so devastating. To be a young, unmarried woman, seduced and abandoned, and then to find out she was with child…she must have been terrified. Worse, to have to hide away, to spend nine months growing a life inside you, only to lose that precious life in an instant. No wonder she had become so upset when he'd first suggested they marry. She must have thought him just like that coward who had used her, offering her false promises to get her to his bed.

Which brought him to the stark realization of just how much she wanted him, how much she must care for him, in order to ignore her fears and come to his bed.

At the sight of the tears welling up in Clara's eyes, however, at the sound of a sob quickly stifled, he forgot about everything else but comforting her.

Before he could so much as rise, however, Phoebe leapt to her feet, rushing to Clara and enveloping her in her arms. The rest of them hurried forward, until a veritable sea of Ashfords crowded her.

"My poor, dear sister," she crooned. "Why did you hide such a thing from us?"

Clara's voice rose up, muffled against her sister's neck. "Because I knew you would all despise me for it. I've threatened our family with a devastating scandal. It could ruin us all if it got out."

"Ruin us?" Lady Tesh scoffed. "My girl, none of us will speak a word of it, I assure you. And if a certain someone does"—she gave the duchess a furious warning glance—"they will regret it. Besides," she continued, turning a tender smile on her great-niece, "if you don't think we haven't weathered worse storms, you are a greater innocent than I thought. There are scandals aplenty in our history, and we've come through each one. Mayhap not unscathed, but stronger for it."

"She's right," Margery said with a soft smile, running a gentle hand over Clara's back. "And we could never despise you, dearest. You shall always be our darling Clara, who we all love so very much."

A sob broke free from Clara's lips. As she buried her face in her sister's neck and the rest of them consoled her, Quincy ached to go to her.

But now was not the time. Let her family show her that she was loved, that she had not lost their respect. There would be time for him to tell her his own feelings on the matter, and to renew his offer for her hand. There was no doubt in his mind that this was the reason she had refused him, some heroic attempt to protect him from this tragedy. When in reality it just proved to him that she was even stronger than he had believed her to be, and made him love her more.

To live with such a thing for so long would destroy anyone. Yet she had funneled that grief into a positive, throwing herself into loving her family in every way she could. He would be blessed indeed if she accepted him.

And then he would spend the rest of his life making her happy.

A sudden movement at the corner of his eye caught his attention. When he turned to find his mother slinking from the room, fury welled up in him. How this woman must have terrorized Clara into revealing this painful truth about herself.

He hurried after her. "Mother," he growled when he reached the hall.

"Not now, Reigate," she said over her shoulder, no doubt desperate to escape the unintended consequences of her actions.

"Yes, now, Mother," he spat. His long legs had him quickly overtaking her. He spun to face her, halting her in her tracks. "I told you to leave her alone. Yet you could not, could you?"

She threw her hands up in the air. "How could I? Does it surprise you that I would allow a woman such as that—"

"I warned you, madam," he snarled, "that I will not look kindly on any insult to Clara."

Her mouth closed with a snap. Though uncertainty flared in her eyes, she glared at him with a righteous fury. "I had a bride picked out for you. A young woman of good family who would provide us the means to recoup all we've lost."

"You mean you groomed a lonely girl, someone you

knew would be easily manipulated. You tried to fob her off on my brother. And when I arrived, you saw a way to control me, the one son you had no hold over, by transferring her to me. Though I wonder," he said with a curl of his lip, "that you had any control over your older sons. Didn't they utterly destroy the dukedom, after all?"

"I don't have to listen to this," she hissed.

"No, you're right in that," he replied. Sudden exhaustion dragged at him. He'd known all along that this woman, who should have loved him as unconditionally as Clara's family loved her, would never be capable of giving him what he'd needed from her. But as he was faced with the proof of her unswerving bitterness he realized that he didn't despise her for it. Rather, there was a deep grief for what they might have had. He felt the loss of it, of that thing she had stolen from not just him, but herself as well, down to his soul.

Had he returned to her house to truly say goodbye for good? Or had there been a part of himself that had hoped she might have changed? If that hope had ever been in him, however, it was dead now.

"After today I will not want anything further to do with you. But," he said when she made to go around him, "know one thing: you will not speak a word of Clara's past to anyone. If word gets out, I will know who caused it. And you will regret it."

Her eyes shot outraged fire at him. "You think to frighten me?"

"Yes," he said, the word blunt and hard. "And don't forget, I will not be alone in my revenge. The Duke of Dane will be behind me, as will Viscountess Tesh. I think it safe to say the punishment would be dire indeed."

Finally common sense seemed to make an appearance in the form of fear, quickly stifled under a blanket of pride. "Very well," she bit out. "I vow I shall not say a word."

With that she went to go around him again. This time he let her, painfully aware of just what she had stolen from him: a happy childhood, with wonderful memories that he should have been able to look back on with fondness as he grew older.

Impotent anger welled up in him, so unexpected he demanded, quite without thinking, "Why do you despise me? You're my mother; you should have loved me and supported me."

She froze, then turned slowly to face him. And he was stunned mute at the hatred twisting her beautiful features.

"If I act as if I despise you it is because I do. With everything in me I despise you."

He gaped at her. "You're a cruel woman."

"Cruel? Your father was the cruel one, foisting his bastard on me to raise as my own."

"It's a lie," he managed, shaking his head in desperate denial, his mind racing. His father had known how miserable Quincy had been, how horrible the duchess had made his life. Surely he would have told him if it was true.

"And what reason would I have to lie to you?" she demanded. "Revealing the truth now gives me no benefit. I cannot see you made illegitimate, for your father made sure everything was drawn up nice and tight. And I risk being kicked from my home and cut off."

Still he could not process what she had just revealed. Surely this was just some attempt to hurt him. The duchess had always gone out of her way to do that.

Yet he could not deny that, beyond that, there was no

benefit for her in this. And the woman never did anything without making certain she benefited from it.

He felt sick down to his soul. As he stood staring at her in shock, she smirked and started off down the hall.

But he could not leave it at this. "If you are not my mother," he demanded of her retreating form, "then who is?"

She didn't bother to even look over her shoulder. "Who do you think? That dubious honor belongs to Miss Willa Brandon, of course. Your father's whore."

Chapter 22

Quincy dismounted his horse and looked up at Swallowhill's weathered façade. Miss Willa Brandon. She had lived here, had died here. And all along she had been his mother?

He'd felt from the moment the duchess had spoken the words that she had not been lying. There had been a certainty in her voice, a fury at what she had been forced to endure, that had given an unmistakable ring of truth to her words.

How it must have pained her, to be confronted with proof of her husband's infidelity each day. And while he could pity her for it, he could not forgive her for what she had done to him. He had been an innocent, a child thrust into this world without a say in any of it. No, the fault in all of this lay with his father, and his father alone.

All this time, he'd thought his father above reproach. Which made the truth that much harder to stomach. The man he'd revered, the person he'd looked up to as what a good person should be, had been a mere figment of his imagination.

An ache started up in his chest, and he pressed a fist to it as if he could ease it by sheer will. But he knew nothing would take away this pain, the last gasping breath of that young boy who'd so idolized his father.

Had he visited that woman here, bedded down with her while his family remained in London? Or had he sent Miss Brandon here after getting her with child, to waste away her days in isolation from the world?

He thought of Clara, how she had been seduced, then sent away to birth her child. Had it been the same for Miss Brandon, sent away from everything she had no doubt loved? And why had she given Quincy up to be raised by another woman? Surely he would have been a damn sight better off with her, no matter the scandal that would have come with it, than he had been with the duchess.

He opened the door and stalked inside. The small hall was just as it had been on his last two visits. Yet he saw it with new eyes, knowing what that woman who'd lived here was to him. Taking the stairs two at a time, he quickly reached that same bedroom he'd found Clara in on their visit. The furniture was covered in their sheets, rising up like specters, his doubts and fears and regrets taking corporeal form around him. He passed them all by, instead striding to the out-of-place piece that had seemed to leave Clara so shaken, the one she had hastily covered up before exiting the room. With a flick of his wrist he pulled the fabric back to reveal a small cradle.

He sucked in his breath. His eyes traveled over the finely carved rosewood. Had he been birthed here, in this very room? Had he been laid in that cradle, perhaps rocked, sung to sleep?

The longing that flared up stunned him. For what? For a mother who might have loved him? No, he would not think of Miss Willa Brandon in such kind terms. She had never loved him. If she had, she would not have given him up.

Even so, he could not help reaching out and tracing the

delicate carvings on the headboard. Small flowers, vines intertwined—it was a thing of beauty. Care had been put into the creation of it.

But why was it here? From all accounts she had stayed at Swallowhill several years after he was born. Why not throw it out, or relegate it to the attic, or any one of a number of different options? Why keep it close by, where she could see it day in and day out? Perhaps she'd only given him up because she'd felt she had no choice. Perhaps she'd grieved for him, as Clara had grieved for her lost son.

He shook his head sharply, furious at himself for even considering such a charitable thought toward that woman. She was nothing like Clara.

Clara. Damn, but he ached for her. He'd left before he could tell her he still loved her, that he still wanted to marry her, no matter what was in her past. He gazed down at the cradle, weariness washing over him, his anger fading as quickly as it had come. There was no sense in wondering whether Miss Brandon had wanted to keep him or not; no matter how he tortured himself over it, he would never learn the truth.

Throwing the cover over the cradle, he determinedly turned his back on it and strode from the room and from the house. He would not return here. In a few days' time it would be Lord Fletcher's, and then he might never think of it again.

As if he had spirited him into being, he spied the man himself, pulling his horse up in the front drive. "Your Grace," he called cheerfully, dismounting and striding toward Quincy. "I didn't expect to see you here this afternoon, not with the festivities going on at Danesford."

Damnation, he'd had no idea the man was planning on

visiting the place. Burying his anger and grief as best he could, he nodded. "I was just leaving, actually. Are you here to take stock of what needs to be done?"

"That I am," the man said. "Though it may be more extensive than I first surmised."

"Don't think you shall get out of purchasing the place that easy," Quincy quipped, forcing a grin that felt stiff on his cheeks.

"I wouldn't dream of it. I'm quite eager to see it through. And," he said, with a wink, "I assume you're more than ready to get rid of the place and be on your way. All those fabulous destinations to see and all."

"That I am," Quincy agreed with feeling. In fact, his desire to see the place out of his hands had increased exponentially since learning of his true parentage.

Had it been just over an hour ago that he had learned the truth? It seemed an eternity. He was ready to leave this place, to return to Danesford.

To see Clara again and tell her, now that his mind was not reeling, how much he adored her.

"Splendid," Fletcher said. "And we are still set to meet the day after Lady Phoebe's wedding to sign the agreement?"

"That we are." He touched the brim of his hat, eager to be off. "I'll leave you to your survey, then."

"I thank you," Fletcher said. The man's chuckle followed Quincy as he turned away. "The sooner I can get to demolishing this place the happier I'll be."

Quincy stopped cold, his boots kicking up dirt. With a quick pivot he was back before Fletcher. "What do you mean, *demolishing*?"

"Oh, didn't I tell you? I had originally planned on making it my home. But after seeing the state of it, and the beautiful vistas, I've decided it makes more sense to raze the place to the ground. The Isle has become more popular over the past year, since the new Duke of Dane and his bride took up residence. No doubt it will only grow in popularity. I plan to capitalize on that."

"Capitalize," Quincy repeated blankly.

"Indeed. Though," the man said, chuckling, "I shouldn't be telling you my plans, as you'll no doubt increase the price. But I've a cunning idea for a small holiday village. This location is ideal, close to the beach, and yet far enough away from the center of town to be quite cozy and private. And there's enough room for me to build a new manor house for myself besides. One," he said with a grin, "that won't be in danger of falling down about my ears."

Quincy gaped at him. "You want to destroy the house, the gardens? The greenhouse?"

"Certainly. It would cost nearly as much to renovate it all, and this way I'll be set to make a tidy sum off it as well."

"Indeed," Quincy said, feeling nauseated. And not because of any fondness for the house. No, if it fell down in ruins this minute, he would not mind a bit. And he needed it sold, didn't he?

His disquiet, however, had everything to do with Clara. He had seen how much this place meant to her, the sorrow in her eyes when she had seen the ruin it was in, the love for what it had given her during that dark time in her life. He imagined her as she was then, her spirit broken, healing both physically and mentally from that devastating trauma, finding the peace within that greenhouse when she'd needed it most. If it was torn down, she would be destroyed.

If he searched for another buyer willing to pay as generous a price as Fletcher was, it might take years to unload the place. And the dukedom did not have years left. It would drain his savings dry before he was able to secure another buyer, the tenants requiring immediate help. No, it was Fletcher or nothing. Breaking Clara's heart or giving up his dreams.

As he took his leave, he searched his mind for a way, any way, to win in this scenario. But to his consternation, he couldn't think of a damn thing.

* * *

Clara had briefly considered retiring to her room for the remainder of the day. She was exhausted, after all, after the strain of the afternoon's revelations.

But she quickly discarded that idea. She was through with hiding away, through with shame and regret. The past was done; she would focus on the present and look toward the future. There was nothing she need worry about now that she knew she had her family's unconditional support and love.

Except for Quincy.

Clara's throat closed off as she thought of him. The young ladies surrounding her gave her curious looks. And no wonder, for hadn't she been in the midst of recounting some ball she'd attended in London? At least, she thought she had been. She breathed deeply, corralling her dangerously veering thoughts, and tried to remember just where she had been in the conversation. But she knew almost immediately it would be a battle lost.

With a forced smile she rose. "I am so sorry, but I just recalled something I need to see to. If you'll excuse me?"

The group smiled and nodded, but Clara was already hurrying across the crowded drawing room. The day had been filled with activities of every kind, from archery to croquet to footraces over the back lawn. Clara had kept herself at the busy center of it all, doing her best to lose herself in the festivities. Even so, she found herself looking for Quincy much more often than she liked.

She had expected him to react negatively to her past, of course. How could he not. She was that creature that all of society looked down on and shunned: a ruined woman. And worse, one who had born a child out of wedlock. At least he could now understand why she could not marry him.

But she had not expected him to run off without a word.

A sudden slender arm about her waist stopped her blind flight from the room. She turned to look at Phoebe, who smiled widely at her.

"Clara, dear, you look a bit tired. You should retire for the evening."

Clara blinked. Her sister looked positively mischievous, her eyes sparkling and an excited blush staining her cheeks. "I was just going to the ladies' retiring room," she said. "No need for concern; I'll be back in a thrice, as good as new."

"But I insist," Phoebe said, pushing Clara toward the door and out into the hall with surprising strength. "I'll need you ever so much in the next few days, and if you exhaust yourself tonight and grow ill, I'll be beside myself."

"Truly, Phoebe," Clara tried again, trying and failing to break her sister's hold on her waist, "I don't need to rest just yet. I'll be fine for another couple of hours until the rest of the party is ready to retire for the night." The last thing she wanted was to be alone. At least here, buried in the bustle of the evening, she could pretend all was well.

"Nonsense." Phoebe pushed her down the hall to the foot of the stairs. "Now, off to bed with you!"

Clara gaped at her. "Phoebe, what is wrong with you?"

To her confusion, Phoebe grinned. "Nothing at all. Everything is absolutely beautiful." With a little laugh, she hugged Clara. "You deserve every happiness in life, my dear sister," she murmured in her ear. Then, bestowing a quick kiss on Clara's cheek, she spun about and hurried back to the drawing room.

Overcome, Clara stared after her sister's retreating form and had the strangest desire to cry; she didn't know what had prompted those heartfelt words, but she felt them down to the depths of her soul.

But now that she was away from the commotion of the drawing room a sudden exhaustion came over her. Mayhap her sister was right, and a rest would be wise. It had been an uncommonly emotional, draining day. With a small sigh she started up the stairs. She did not expect sleep to come easily, however, no matter how tired she was. The moment she was alone and there was no longer any danger of prying eyes, she knew she would quickly find herself drowning under her thoughts of Quincy.

As she reached the privacy of the family quarters and the noise of the party faded behind her, she was proved right. Where had Quincy gone after her confession? One minute she had been enveloped in her family's loving arms, and the next both Quincy and his mother were absent. The duchess had quickly departed Danesford, Peter being more than happy to see her gone from the house with all haste. But there was no sign of Quincy. Clara had not dared to ask, and not one of her family mentioned him. Though that had not stopped their concerned glances from finding her. So she had doubled her efforts to remain cheerful, though inside she grew increasingly despondent. She had known there would be a risk in revealing her past. Her family's reaction had stunned her; she would always remain thankful for their unwavering love.

But that did not take away the sting of Quincy's abandonment.

Heaving a sigh, she let herself into the room, closing the door quietly behind her. A fire glowed in the hearth and she went to it, peeling off her gloves and holding out hands that seemed strangely chilled for the warmth of the summer night. It was silly, truly, to mourn his desertion. She had wanted him to understand why she had refused him. He had a right to know why she could not have a life with him.

Her heart broke at the thought that he could not even be in the same room—nay, the same house—with her.

Just then a beloved, familiar voice broke into her morose thoughts.

"I was beginning to think Phoebe wouldn't be able to convince you to retire. I shouldn't have doubted her."

Chapter 23

Clara gasped and spun around to face the dim room. Her imagination was playing tricks on her, surely; her great longing to have Quincy with her creating him out of thin air.

But no, there he was, seated in a chair in the deepest shadows. As she stared, stunned, he rose and came toward her.

He had removed his coat, waistcoat, and cravat, and had his sleeves rolled up to his elbows. A small smile played about his chiseled lips, his dark eyes fastened on her, more emotions than she could name filling their depths.

But there was a caution about him, too. As if he feared she would bolt at the slightest trigger. He stopped several feet from her. "Clara."

His voice was low and deep and utterly wonderful. She ached to close her eyes and let it rumble through her. But she wouldn't. There was still no hope for them, no chance for a future. Only now he must see it, too. Something that should not have brought her as much pain as it did.

She drew in an unsteady breath, fighting for composure though all she wanted to do was crumple to the floor and cry. "Where have you been?" she asked, her quiet voice nevertheless loud in the stillness of the room. She clasped her hands tightly before her to keep from reaching out for him.

"Swallowhill."

The single word startled her. "Swallowhill?" At his nod she asked, "All day?"

"No." A sad smile flitted about his lips, there and gone with the same swiftness as the birds the house had been named for. "I had... things to see to. In town."

She nodded, though she hadn't a clue what he was talking about. They stared at each other for a time, a horrible awkwardness between them. They had become so close over the past weeks, first as friends, then as partners. Then as lovers.

That magical time, however, seemed ages past. A great gulf separated them now, one she could never hope to bridge.

Even so, the whispered words spilled from her lips. "You were missed."

"Was I?" The question was so earnest, so full of longing, it finally snapped her carefully controlled emotions.

"I know what you must think of me," she rasped. "But I will not apologize for my past. I know I made horrible decisions that impacted not only my own life but those of the people I loved. And the repercussions will follow me all my days. I'm sure you see now why a marriage between us would have never worked. A woman with my background, with the threat of ruin hanging over my head, could never be a duchess—"

He stepped forward and pulled her into his arms. Though she knew better, much better, she went willingly, clinging to him, aware that this was where she had longed to be all along.

"You were dealt a devastating hand in life," he said,

his voice rumbling under her ear. "My heart breaks for what you've gone through. If I could call out the man who did it to you I would, and gladly. But know, here and now, that that time in your life does not define you. It has helped shape you, yes. But it is not who you are. You are not ruined, or broken, or a scandal. You are strong, and loving, and kind. I have never known a more wonderful woman in my life."

She did not realize she was crying until her tears began to soak the fine lawn of his shirt. She pressed her face into his chest, not wanting him to see how his words affected her—and how it was beginning to make her hope for something that could never be.

But he stepped back, crooking one finger to tilt her face up. And the love in his eyes stole her breath.

"You did not allow me to tell you before, but I will tell you now. I love you, Clara." He smiled tenderly as she sucked in a sharp breath, shock and wonder all coalescing in her breast. "I love you so much it was as if I had lost half of myself when I thought there was no chance of a future for us. I imagined sailing away from England, leaving you behind, and felt my heart would break in two, never to be mended no matter how far I sailed, how fast I ran. You are what makes me whole."

She blinked furiously to clear the tears clouding her vision, refusing to lose sight of his beloved face for a moment.

He took her hand in his, his thumb stroking over her knuckles. "I have not swerved from the desire to marry you, Clara. If anything, this last day has made me realize I could never find happiness with anyone but you. My life would be joyless without you in it."

She stared at him, stunned, hope beginning to rise up

though she refused to allow it to take purchase. "But my past," she said, wiping at her cheeks with her free hand. "You've been away from England too long; you don't know the scandal that could erupt. If it comes out, it would ruin you. You're a duke, Quincy."

"A title I never wanted, I assure you."

"That doesn't matter. It's not something you can escape. And because your status is so high, the fall will be that much greater. Everything you do will be scrutinized. The truth will come out eventually. And when it does, they'll scorn you behind your back, ruin your business dealings. They will be relentless."

"If you think I care about all that, you haven't been paying attention," he drawled.

"You say that now," she snapped, her patience beginning to unravel at his blind optimism. "But in a few years, when the glow of new love has faded, you will sing a different tune."

"Oh, well, as to that, my ability to hold a note is appalling, and so you may have no fears on that score."

The man was maddening; why could he not see reason? "Quincy—" she fairly growled.

But he held up his free hand. "But I'm not asking you to marry me."

"Er...good," she managed, painfully aware that as her frustration faded a yawning hopelessness was quickly taking its place. Finally, he saw reason. It was what she had been working toward. Yet she had not realized just how horrible this moment would be.

Once again, however, she had underestimated him.

"At least, not just yet." He grinned. "I have two very important things to take care of before I drop to my knee, you see. The first, of course, being my obvious lack of a ring. But when I visited the jewelers in town I looked at their wares—not a one of their pieces right—and I thought to myself, there is no way she will understand how much she means to me with a simple ring. Every man gives a woman a ring, after all. So I spent the better part of the day racking my brain, trying to come up with something that would show you the magnitude of my devotion."

He reached behind him and pulled something from the band of his breeches. When his hand reappeared, it was holding a legal-looking document.

She stared at the paper uncomprehendingly for a long moment. Yet he remained patient, the paper not so much as trembling in his steady grip.

Finally, she took it. And gasped when she read its contents.

Her eyes flew to his. The hope she'd been so furiously holding at bay broke through her defenses when she saw the certainty and love shining in his face. "Swallowhill is mine?"

"It is," he murmured.

"I don't understand."

"My love, surely you must see," he said tenderly, "you are worth more to me than anything in this world."

Her heart, which had been patiently waiting for her head to catch up to it, surged with a joyful beat. Even so, she shook her head, unable to make sense of it all. "But the sale...Lord Fletcher..."

"Was going to demolish it," he said quietly.

Her breath stalled, the idea of that beloved place being reduced to rubble a shock to her senses.

He nodded grimly. "And I could not see it torn down, knowing how much you loved it and what it was to you." He smiled again, not a trace of doubt in his eyes. "So it's yours, to do with as you wish. Even should you—" His voice faltered. And though he quickly brought it under control, the vulnerability was plain to see.

"Even should you refuse me when I finally ask you," he tried again, more subdued than before, "it will remain yours."

She gaped at him, stunned. "But your dreams to travel the world…" she whispered. "Selling Swallowhill was your one chance to save the dukedom and still have the funds for your journeys. I cannot ask you to give that up."

"You didn't ask me, my love. I do it, willingly and without even a moment's regret." He smiled, making no effort to hide the sheen of tears glistening in his eyes. "All I want is your happiness, Clara. And if that means I have to release you, giving you the means to be free the rest of your days, so be it."

As she continued to stare at him, unable to speak for the joy and fear battling within her, his expression fell. "Now for the second matter that must be dealt with before I can ask you to marry me. And it is by far the more painful of the two."

The sudden grim seriousness in his expression sent a chill through her. He released her hand and made his way to the hearth, looking down into the low fire. She could just make out the glow of the blaze highlighting the tic in his jaw and the tight lines at the corner of his eye.

Biting her lip, suddenly nervous, she held the deed tight and waited.

* * *

Quincy could barely hear the faint crackling of the fire for the pounding of his heartbeat in his ears. Why was he nervous? This was Clara. There was no one in this world he trusted more than her. She would never judge him for the circumstances of his birth.

Yet he couldn't shake this creeping fear in him that she might look at him differently. And in a flash he understood why she had been so reluctant to tell him of her own past. Though how much worse it must have been for her, how much strength it must have taken to lay her entire history at the feet of the people she loved.

Once again, he was struck by just how brave this woman was that he'd fallen in love with.

Drawing in a deep breath, he turned to face her. Her eyes were wide in her pale face, her teeth digging into her full bottom lip. He tried for a smile but couldn't quite manage one. "I've learned who Miss Willa Brandon was."

She blinked in surprise. No doubt she hadn't quite expected that. "And?" she prompted.

He drew in a deep breath before saying, in a rush, "She was my mother."

"Oh." The word escaped her on an exhale. Eyes wide with shock, she stumbled back to a chair and sank down in it. "Goodness. Then the cradle in the bedroom at Swallowhill...?"

"Was mine," he verified grimly, ignoring the pain in his chest as he recalled the beauty of the piece. As he watched the shifting emotions on her face, however, the question that had come to him at Swallowhill took shape again in his mind: Why had it still been in her bedroom?

Surely, she hadn't loved him.

"How did you find out?" Clara asked.

He shook his head, banishing his conflicting thoughts for Miss Brandon. He had no wish to think well of her.

"The duchess told me." His mouth twisted as he

approached her and sank to his haunches, taking up her hand in his. "She admitted that I was born out of wedlock, the product of my father's affair with Miss Brandon, and that he forced the duchess to raise me as her own."

Unshed tears shone in her eyes. "Oh, Quincy," she whispered, cupping his cheek in her palm.

The betrayal of a man he had revered still fresh and painful, he closed his eyes and cradled her hand to his face. "If you were to marry me, you would for all intents and purposes be marrying a bastard. I had to make certain before I asked you that I was as honest and open with you as you've been with me."

He expected all manner of reactions, from assurances to tears to denouncing him completely. What he did not expect was for her to scoff, "As if I would care about that."

His eyes flew open to find her looking at him with equal parts frustration and affection.

"You silly man," she continued. "I loved my son, who would have been a bastard had he lived, with everything in me. Do you honestly believe I could love you less for it?"

Love. Hope began to bloom in his chest. Before it could take hold, however, she frowned.

"But this makes no sense. From what you've told me of your father, it doesn't seem in character with him at all."

It was exactly what had been simmering in his gut throughout that horrible day, making the betrayal so much more potent. "There was no benefit to the duchess in lying to me. And that woman never did anything that wasn't of benefit to her."

"Your unhappiness would be reward enough," she

muttered acidly. "I swear, that woman is the devil incarnate."

He smiled, an unexpected lightness filling him as he pressed his lips to her palm.

"There must be something of your father's that tells the truth of the matter," she muttered, her outrage and frustration clear in her voice. "He loved you too well to leave you in the dark forever."

"I doubt it," he said, reaching out to tuck a stray curl behind her ear, anxious now to put this whole mess behind them and renew his offer of marriage. "My brothers either destroyed or sold off almost everything else. I was lucky they didn't know of the secret compartment in my father's desk, else I'd not even have my father's travel book. But I'm done with the past, Clara. I would focus on the possibility of a future together."

She hardly seemed to hear him, though her eyes went wide with dawning excitement. "The travel book. Of course. There was more in that compartment than the book. The bundle was there as well, with the deed, a dance card, a brooch. And—"

"The stack of letters," he breathed, finally catching up to her wonderfully agile mind.

"Please tell me you kept them."

He jumped to his feet, pulling her up with him. "I did," he said, grinning. "Not only that, but I had the wherewithal to bring the whole damn lot with me."

The smile she gave him was as bright as the sun. "Let's get them."

Excitement pumping through his veins, they slipped into the hall and hurried to his room. He wasted no time, lighting a fire in the hearth and heading for his trunk in the corner. The letters. How in hell had he never looked at the letters? He had given all the pieces in that bundle a cursory glance, of course—and it was only now he realized that the dance card and brooch with its lock of jet-black hair were quite possibly mementos of Miss Brandon. If that were the case, wasn't it possible the letters were, as well?

Of course, there was every chance they could have nothing to do with Miss Brandon—his father's correspondence with a friend or his parents, for instance. He shouldn't get his hopes up, not when it didn't matter a bit what the truth was.

But as he dropped to the floor and lifted the lid, he knew it did matter. The moment the duchess had revealed the truth it had destroyed something in him, that trust he'd had in his father. If there was even a chance he could understand why that man had kept something so important from him, he would take it.

They were easy to find, the neat bundle tied with ribbon sitting on the top with his father's book. He untied the packet, then lifted the letters out, surprised at how his fingers shook. As one he and Clara moved to the bed and sat down on its edge. Still he stared at the letters. What if they verified his worst fears, that his father had not been the man he'd loved and respected? What if they completely destroyed every good memory he'd ever had of him?

Clara's hand, gentle and calming, touched his back. He remembered that time at Dane House, when her touch had been the only thing tethering him to earth. How had he not known then and there that he loved her?

With her strength guiding him, he untied the ribbon and opened the first letter.

His father's familiar bold scrawl hit him like a runaway

carriage, knocking the breath from him. It didn't take long, however, to see the letter was not to him at all. No, it was to Miss Willa Brandon, and from before his marriage to the duchess. It was a long, rambling letter of flowery prose. But one line stood out from the rest.

I cannot wait to see you again, to hold you in my arms. Soon we shall be married; it seems I've waited for this day my whole life.

Quincy stared, stunned. His father had been engaged to Miss Brandon?

"Oh, Quincy," Clara said, reading over his shoulder. "He loved her very much."

He had. It was in every word, every line, nothing but the deepest regard. "Why didn't he marry her then?" he asked, his voice a hoarse thing. "Why marry the woman who would make his life such hell?"

She rubbed his back. "Mayhap the letters will explain why."

He nodded, then took a deep breath and reached for the next letter in the stack. When Clara made to rise, however, he grabbed her hand.

"And where do you think you're going?"

"To give you privacy." She gave him a sad smile. "I've a feeling the story won't be an easy one to learn."

"All the more reason to have you with me when I do," he murmured as he pulled her back down beside him. "Besides, I'll tell you everything anyway; you may as well save me a step by being here for the learning to begin with."

Smiling tenderly at him, she curled up against his side. Once he was certain she wasn't going anywhere, he took up the letter again. And together they began to read.

The story quickly took shape, a heartbreaking history in the carefully penned words: how they'd loved one another since childhood, had planned to marry. Then he was found in another woman's bed. Though he was certain he'd been drugged, Willa broke off their engagement.

There was a glaring lack of correspondence in the years that followed, but Quincy could piece together what occurred, his father's subsequent marriage to the duchess producing sons but no affection, where every day he grew more miserable.

Until the letters picked up again years later, when one night of passion forever altered their lives. And though she wanted that child with everything in her, though she loved it desperately, she made the duke promise to take it and raise it as his legitimate child, so it wouldn't have to live with the stigma of *bastard* and all the hardships that entailed for the rest of its life.

And all through the reading of that history Clara was beside him, reading over his shoulder, her presence like a balm to his soul. He didn't know that he would have been able to get through it without her, for the emotions coursing through him, from anger to hope to frustration to grief, were enough to destroy him, especially as such heartfelt anguish saturated every word.

Finally, after what felt hours, they reached the last letter, written just a few short months before the duke died. But it was written to Quincy.

He stared at his name on the missive, shock overriding his weariness, hands shaking. He felt battered both inside and out, as if who he was had been torn to shreds.

Thankfully Clara was there, her hand on his. And they opened the letter together.

My dear Quincy,

There was so much I wish I could have told you, my boy. I pray you'll forgive my cowardice. But my wife insisted on my silence on the matter in order for you to be claimed as my legitimate son. By the time you read this letter, and the other letters bundled with it, I will be dead and gone, and thus I consider our bargain at an end. So you see, I had always intended for you to know the truth one day. That I had to leave you so early, however, is one of my greatest heartaches.

I cannot begin to guess what might be going through your mind. To learn that one's parentage was a lie cannot be an easy thing. But know that you were conceived in love. If you take nothing else away from this, I will be content. The truth of the matter is, I loved Miss Willa Brandon. I had loved her since we were children. When she agreed to marry me, I was the happiest man in existence.

I think you have read enough to know why we never married. Please don't hate the duchess. I would not have that horrible emotion poisoning your heart. I have tried to teach you, as best I was able, to look for the good in life, to keep your gaze on the future, and leave behind the past. I pray you are happy, my boy. And know that your mother loved you.

Now I go to meet her in heaven, if God is forgiving. Enjoy your life, my son. And when you find love, don't let it go.

Your loving father

Quincy stared at the letter, aware of the realigning of those torn pieces of his old self into a new man. So much he'd thought was true had been a lie. Yet the most important thing had remained true: his father had loved him. Even more important, his mother—his *true* mother—had loved him just as deeply. She had loved him so well she'd made certain he would have a secure life, had given him up so he might live without the label *bastard*.

His throat burned with tears, of both grief and happiness. There had been so much unnecessary suffering, so much stolen. And yet he'd just been given a wonderful gift.

Clara's hand moved over his back again, returning him to the present. Speaking of gifts, he thought. His heart, already full, began to overflow with his happiness.

All it would take to make it complete was her accepting him.

Chapter 24

*C*lara stayed quiet as long as she was able, to give Quincy the time he needed to process what he'd just read. So much heartbreak, so many things conspiring against the duke and Willa. The tears that she'd fought during the reading of those letters threatened again, making her throat ache. And still he remained silent, merely staring at his father's last letter to him.

Hoping to bring him a modicum of comfort, she rubbed her hand over his broad back, soothing the bands of tense muscle. She felt him shift and relax under her palm. She laid her cheek on his shoulder, wishing she could mend whatever hurt he was feeling.

Not just in that moment. She wished she could be there for every hurt in the future, to help him heal, to bring him happiness.

To love him.

Hope bloomed that perhaps things between them could work. The duke's last sentence called to her: *And when you find love, don't let it go.*

Quincy was willing to marry her even with the tragedy in her past, even though it could rear up and ruin them at any time. And she saw so clearly that the heartbreak of trying to remain safe and secure wasn't worth losing his love.

As if she'd spoken aloud, he turned to her. And smiled.

The pain in his gaze was gone, and she could see clear to his soul. Her heart swelled at the sight.

"You're all right," she whispered.

"Yes." He smiled. "He loved me. And so did my mother."

She drank in the sight of his joy. "Of course they did. How could they not?"

He cupped her cheek, leaned in to kiss her.

There was nothing she wanted more in that moment than to melt in his arms, but there was still something that needed to be addressed. She planted her hands on his chest to keep him at bay.

He frowned, pulling back, hurt replacing his happiness. "I'm sorry. I shouldn't have done that."

"No, you shouldn't have. At least"—she smiled tenderly—"not until you've finished proposing to me."

The joy that filled him transformed him, the hopeful light that filled his features erasing any lingering lines of grief. It was as if the last piece of a puzzle had been snapped in place.

He dropped to his knees, taking her hands in his. She gripped his fingers tight, memorizing this moment, with this powerful man before her about to declare himself.

"Clara," he said, his voice thick, just as moved as she was if the shine in his dark eyes was proof, "will you marry me?"

"Yes." The one word spilled from her lips without hesitation, joy laced through it.

He rose to his feet and took her face between his hands, his gaze suffused with wonder. "You'll marry me?"

She grinned. "Yes, you wonderful man, I'll marry you. I love you, Quincy, so very much." She gave a small laugh. "I think I've loved you since that first time I saw you in Lady Tesh's drawing room."

"As have I," he murmured. He stroked a stray curl from her cheek, his gaze achingly tender. "Clara, you're my very heart and soul."

Tears sprang to her eyes. And then he was kissing her. Or she was kissing him. It didn't matter, really, she thought as she lost herself completely in his embrace. What mattered was they loved one another, and always would.

When last they'd come together her heart had been breaking, so certain had she been that they would soon part. She had made sure that every kiss, every caress, held an echo of her goodbye to him. To rise from his bed before dawn and leave him slumbering amid the rumpled sheets had nearly destroyed her.

This time, however, was a beginning. They went slowly, drawing their pleasure out, every kiss, every caress holding an echo of their declarations to one another, every sigh and whisper like a prayer in the dim room. He undressed her, worshipping each inch with infinite tenderness, hands and lips and tongue bringing her to heights she hadn't imagined possible. She did the same for him, taking her time, marveling at each bunch of muscle, the dusting of hair across his chest and flat stomach, the incredible beauty of him. She trailed her lips across his skin and tasted warm nights and dark skies and fresh winds blowing off the churning sea.

When their need for one another became too great to delay, he slid inside her with a hiss of satisfaction and began to move.

The pleasure built slowly, until she didn't know where one of them ended and the other began, until the frantic beat of his heart against her own could not be denied.

He paused, looking down on her. A fine sheen of sweat glistened on his brow, his eyes feverish with need. His manhood pulsed inside her, yet he held himself back.

She knew immediately why he did it, and her heart fairly burst with love for this man, who had shown her nothing but respect from the first and who would protect her even now if she needed it. Placing a hand on his cheek, she smiled into his eyes.

"You're my future now, Quincy," she whispered. "I want to feel you inside me."

He let loose a shuddering breath. "I love you," he rasped before taking her lips in a kiss. And then he was moving inside her again, and she moved with him, each stroke bringing them higher and higher until they came in a burst of stars. Together.

* * *

Quincy woke when the sky was still dark, only the faintest lighting of the pitch black outside the window to the deepest indigo proving that dawn would soon be here.

The dawn of his and Clara's future together.

She shifted in her sleep, her lithe body, warm and naked, settling more fully against his own. Joy filled him as he tightened his arm about her and kissed the mussed crown of her sable curls. His heart felt freer than it had ever been. There was no uncertainty, no fear, no anger. Only a deep, abiding conviction that he was where he was supposed to be.

He could feel the moment she woke; her body, which had been relaxed, stirred, her legs rubbing against his, her unbound hair rasping against his shoulder. She raised her head and smiled at him.

He pulled her down for a tender kiss. "Good morning," he murmured.

"Is it morning then?" she asked, her fingers stroking his hair back from his forehead.

"Not quite." He gathered her back into his arms.

She sighed, snuggling further into his embrace. "I wish I could stay here forever."

He felt the exact same. He would never grow tired of this, waking with the woman he loved. The idea of her leaving his bed to return to her room, all for propriety's sake, made him hold her all the tighter. He rather thought that a quick visit to London after Phoebe's wedding might not be remiss; a special license sounded like a wise course of action. He smiled into her hair, reveling in the way the delicate strands tickled his lips. And from the way she was rubbing her leg against his and trailing her fingers over his stomach, he had a feeling she would not argue.

He was looking out the window at a sky just beginning to show the faintest blush of sunrise, contemplating if he had time to make love to her once more before she left, when she raised her head again to look at him. Her eyes were sober in the predawn light. "Are you well?"

He knew what she was asking: was he still all right after the revelations of the night before, after learning the truth of his parentage. And he hadn't thought he could love her more. He smiled. "More than well, my love."

Relief blossomed in her gaze. "You're an amazing man."

He chuckled. "Just as well, as I'm marrying an amazing woman," he murmured, pulling her down for another kiss.

Some minutes later—happy, deliciously distracted minutes—she pulled back. "I'd best return to my room," she murmured.

He groaned, his arms tightening about her. "No."

"Yes," she said with a small laugh. "Besides, Phoebe's wedding is in just a few days. Once it's done I've a mind to start planning our own. After all, the quicker we marry the quicker we can head off to those places you've dreamed of sailing to."

He stilled, his stomach dropping. "But I thought you understood. Swallowhill will remain ours; we cannot sell it, doubly so now that I know what it was to my mother. I have enough funds to save the dukedom, but not enough to travel."

He expected sadness. What he did not expect, however, was laughter. She grinned, her eyes dancing, and laid a hand on his cheek.

"Do you think I come to you without a dowry?"

"Dowry," he repeated blankly.

She rolled her eyes. "Yes, dowry. My father was a generous man and made sure to provide for both my sister and me." The smile she gave him was full of love. "And so, do you think you could be content traveling the world with me by your side?"

His heart nearly burst with love for her. And yet he knew this was just the beginning; his love would grow each day, stretching to the horizon and beyond into forever.

"With you, my love, I'll go anywhere," he murmured before taking her lips in a kiss.

Epilogue

Quincy raised his head from the map he had spread out on his father's desk and looked out the window to the sea beyond. He took in the vast blue sky and the undulating waves with a happy sigh, contentment curling in his belly. They had been back for a month, but he was more than willing to stay just where he was for a good long while. There would be time to set sail again. After.

Just then a commotion could be heard from below. He smiled at the familiar, beloved sound, his gaze unerringly searching for and finding Clara. She was making her way back to the house through the lovingly restored gardens of Swallowhill, no doubt from an excursion to the greenhouse. She spent much of her time there, tending the plants they had brought back from their travels. It had been nearly a decade since they'd first set sail after their hasty wedding, and in that time she had accrued quite a collection. Most notably, the two imps at her side.

His gaze softened as he looked down on his children. Young Frederick, named for Clara's father, was tall for eight, nearly reaching his mother's shoulder. He walked at Lenora's side, his gaze steady on her as she related something or other to him. In his arms was a small gray bundle, a young rabbit he had found and was mending back to health, the latest in his growing menagerie. And then there was Willa.

At six she fairly ruled them all, with her black hair and mischievous smile. Clara was known to moan that she was so like Quincy she feared for her sanity once the girl reached adulthood, accompanied by a fond look for them both. Right now, Willa was dancing among the flowers, singing and bending to pick up a rock, a leaf, and whatever else might strike her fancy.

Clara looked up and spied him. She grinned and spoke to the children, and soon they were all waving their arms, their bright smiles in the early-afternoon sunlight making his heart expand in his chest. He remembered that long-ago day when he and Clara had stood poised at the beginning of their life together—how it felt as if he could not hold a bit more love in him.

Yet that had been proven wrong, for day in and day out he loved her and their children more and more.

She spoke to them again, and was soon leaving them to play in the fresh air while she walked toward the house. He heard the door opening and closing, and her step on the stairs. Anticipation raced through his veins. And then she was in the doorway.

"Quincy," she murmured.

In two long strides he reached her and she was in his arms. Her lips were sweet and eager, and he felt he could stand there forever kissing her and be utterly happy.

Until a nudge in his belly made him realize that was an impossibility.

He pulled back, grinning ruefully down at her stomach. "Madam, I do believe our daughter is going to be as precocious as her older sister when she arrives."

"Lord save me," Clara said with a happy laugh, her

hands lovingly drifting over her swollen belly. "But it could be a son, you know."

"Please, woman," he scoffed with mock outrage. "Have I ever been wrong?"

"No," she grumbled with obvious reluctance.

He laughed, and together they walked to the large window overlooking the garden. The children were on the ground, playing with the rabbit, Frederick as ever watchful over his sister. Clara smiled happily, then looked to the map on the desk. She ran her fingers over it, tracing the routes and notes they had made over the years, before giving his father's worn book, lying close by, a loving pat.

"And have you decided where you would like to go on our next adventure? The children are eager to visit Greece, but I've a mind to stay closer to home."

"I think closer to home is just the thing," Quincy said, laying a gentle hand over the swell of his wife's stomach. "What say you to an extended stay on the Isle?"

"I would like that very much," she murmured, covering his hand with her own. "Though are you certain you'll be happy staying still for so long? Life may get dull after a time."

"Ah, my love," he said, laughing, pulling her close, "our family is the best adventure I could have asked for."

Don't miss the next lush historical romance from Christina Britton!

Coming Summer 2021

About the Author

Christina Britton developed a passion for writing romance novels shortly after buying her first at the tender age of thirteen and spent much of her teenage years scribbling on whatever piece of paper she could find. Though for several years she put brush instead of pen to paper, she has returned to her first love and is now writing full-time. She spends her days dreaming of corsets and cravats and noblemen with tortured souls.

She lives with her husband and two children in the San Francisco Bay Area.

You can learn more at:
ChristinaBritton.com
Twitter @CBrittonAuthor
Facebook.com/ChristinaBrittonAuthor

Looking for more historical romances?
Get swept away by handsome rogues and clever
ladies from Forever!

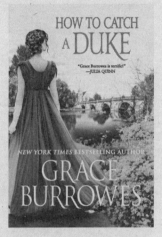

HOW TO CATCH A DUKE
by Grace Burrowes

Miss Abigail Abbott needs to disappear—permanently—and the only person she trusts to help is Lord Stephen Wentworth, heir to the Duke of Walden. Stephen is brilliant, charming, and absolutely ruthless. So ruthless that he proposes marriage to keep Abigail safe. But when she accepts his courtship of convenience, they discover intimate moments that they don't want to end. But can Stephen convince Abigail that their arrangement is more than a sham and that his love is real?

THE TRUTH ABOUT DUKES
by Grace Burrowes

Lady Constance Wentworth never has a daring thought (that she admits aloud) and never comes close to courting scandal . . . as far as anybody knows. Robert Rothmere is a scandal poised to explode. Unless he wants to end up locked away in a madhouse (again) by his enemies, he needs to marry a perfectly proper, deadly-dull duchess, immediately—but little does he know that the delightful lady he has in mind is hiding scandalous secrets of her own.

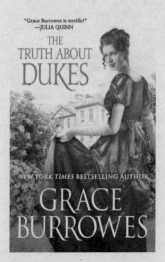

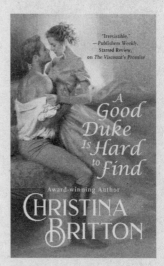

"Erica Ridley is a delight!"
—JULIA QUINN

The
DUKE
HEIST

NEW YORK TIMES BESTSELLING AUTHOR

ERICA
RIDLEY

THE DUKE HEIST
by Erica Ridley

When the only father Chloe Wynchester's ever known makes a dying wish for his adopted family to recover a missing painting, she's the one her siblings turn to for stealing it back. No one expects that in doing so, she'll also abduct a handsome duke. Lawrence Gosling, the Duke of Faircliffe, is shocked to find himself in a runaway carriage driven by a beautiful woman. But if handing over the painting means sacrificing his family's legacy, will he follow his plan—or true love?

A ROGUE TO REMEMBER
by Emily Sullivan

After five Seasons of turning down every marriage proposal, Lottie Carlisle's uncle has declared she must choose a husband, or he'll find one for her. Only Lottie has her own agenda—namely ruining herself and then posing as a widow in the countryside. But when Alec Gresham, the seasoned spy who broke Lottie's heart, appears at her doorstep to escort her home, it seems her best-laid plans appear to have been for naught…And it soon becomes clear that the feelings between them are far from buried.

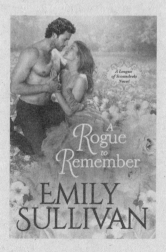

A League of Scoundrels Novel

A
Rogue
to
Remember

EMILY
SULLIVAN

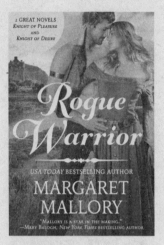

ROGUE WARRIOR (2-IN-1-EDITION)
by Margaret Mallory

Enjoy the first two books in the steamy medieval romance series All the King's Men! In *Knight of Desire*, warrior William FitzAlan and Lady Catherine Rayburn must learn to trust each other to save their lives and the love growing between them. In *Knight of Pleasure*, the charming Sir Stephen Carleton captures the heart of expert swordswoman Lady Isobel Hume, but he must prove his love when a threat leads Isobel into mortal danger.

ANY ROGUE WILL DO
by Bethany Bennett

For exactly one Season, Lady Charlotte Wentworth played the biddable female the *ton* expected—and all it got her was Society's mockery and derision. Now she's determined to take charge of her own future. So when an unwanted suitor tries to manipulate her into an engagement, she has a plan. He can't claim to be her fiancé if she's engaged to someone else. Even if it means asking for help from the last man she would ever marry.